# Sage Dreams, Eagle Visions

# Sage Dreams, Eagle Visions

Danielle M. Hornett

Michigan State University Press

*East Lansing*

Michigan State University Press is a member of the
Green Press Initiative and is committed to developing and encouraging ecologically
responsible publishing practices. For more information about the Green Press Initiative
and the use of recycled paper in book publishing, please visit
www.greenpressinitiative.org.


∞ The paper used in this publication meets the minimum requirements of
ANSI/NISO Z39.48-1992 (R 1997) (Permanence of Paper).

Michigan State University Press
East Lansing, Michigan 48823-5245
Printed and bound in the United States of America.

09 08 07 06 05 04 03 1 2 3 4 5 6 7 8 9 10

Library of Congress Cataloging-in-Publication Data

Hornett, Danielle M., 1942-
Sage dreams, eagle visions / Danielle M. Hornett.
p. cm. -- (Native American series)
ISBN 0-87013-660-7 (pbk. : alk. paper)
1. Ojibwa women--Fiction. 2. Depression, Mental--Fiction. 3. Indian
reservations--Fiction. 4. Racially mixed people--Fiction. 5. Spiritual
life--Fiction. 6. Ojibwa Indians--Fiction. 7. Wisconsin--Fiction.
8. Shamans--Fiction. I. Title. II. Native American series (East Lansing, Mich.)
PS3608.O765S24 2004
813'.6--dc22
2004000273

Cover design by Julia Herzog
Book design by Sean Harrington
Cover photograph by Cheryl Hornett

Visit Michigan State University Press on the World Wide Web at:
**www.msupress.msu.edu**

I lovingly dedicate this book to my parents, Dan and Eleanore (Plucinski) Hornett. Without them this story would not be: without them I would not be! Although they have walked on, their spirits guide my steps every day. My mother tried her hand at writing: thank you, Mom, for passing the love of reading and writing on to me.

# Acknowledgments

In the baker's dozen years it has taken to write this story, many friends and family members believed in me and encouraged my efforts: they were instrumental in my perseverance. Often, during the weeks or even months when I set this novel aside and felt that I did not have a story to tell, their expectations, and sometimes their not-so-subtle pushing, gave me what I needed to sit down in front of the computer again.

I gratefully acknowledge the following: Dr. Kimberly Blaeser (UW-Milwaukee), Dr. Ed Risden (St. Norbert College, DePere, Wisc.), Edward Micus (Mankato State University), Anne Ganey and Sheryl and Bruce Dowling from Mankato, Minnesota. These wonderful friends read/suggested, read/suggested, and read/suggested as this tale moved along. They will never know how important they were to the completion of this story. My husband, Bruce Pettibone (from the Ho-Chunk Nation of Wisconsin), shared, via storytelling, many of his experiences while he was traveling the country and then living in the Minneapolis area. Many of his experiences have been incorporated into *Sage Dreams, Eagle Visions*.

In addition, I must thank the Ojibwe Elders who lent me their personal stories: Vince and Mayta Bender from Bad River, Archie Mosay from the St. Croix area, and Porky White from Apple Valley. D. J. Jackson from Bad River helped with the Ojibwe language: *Chi miigwich*, D. J. Others along the way supported my efforts by laughing or crying in just the right places when they read some early excerpts: the beautiful Christina Hornett, my niece, for one.

# Prologue

The young girl squinted up at the old man walking beside her and watched his white ponytail, tied with a leather strip, flop around and hit against his back as he walked. She loved his toothless smile and his brown, prune-wrinkled face. *He sure is old*, she thought. *Probably even older than God.* Just then her great-uncle smiled down at her, his black eyes sparkling, like he was reading her thoughts. Gramma did that too, lots of times, so Amanda figured it was just something all old people could do.

This early morning, these two friends, each with a tin cup in hand, were looking for the new sweet strawberries that grew along the edges of the pond in the back of their cabin. Amanda loved these times, when she could be out and about helping with important tasks like this with either Gramma or Hobo, her gramma's brother. Anyone lucky enough to be at the cabin when they got back would share in their morning's bounty. There was nothing she liked better for breakfast than thick warm cream scraped off the morning's milk plopped on fresh berries.

Amanda suddenly let go of the old man's dry hand and skipped ahead. She had spotted something and wanted to investigate. Who knew? It might be important. "Uncle Hobo, look at what I found!" she squealed. "Feathers!"

Hobo jabbered excitedly in his unique mixture of English and Ojibwe. He had a hard time with just English. She'd found eagle feathers. "Aman-jii, you did good." He spoke quickly but quietly, trying to clarify his words with hand signs. He took *asema*, tobacco, from a pouch kept in his back pocket and poured some in his hands. He began singing in Ojibwe, and turned to face each of the four directions, offering his tobacco skyward as he did so. Amanda gazed skyward as the sun slipped behind a cloud. Surely this was a very good sign, she thought.

When he finished singing, Hobo sprinkled the tobacco on the ground, then he picked up the feathers and shook them slightly and smiled at her. The sun came back out from hiding. The warmth of the sun competed with the warmth of happiness she felt inside. Hobo was proud of her, she could tell.

They picked their empty tin cups up from where they had been dropped and headed back toward the cabin, fresh strawberries all but forgotten for today.

# Chapter 1

Amanda floated, as if on a current of air, between a distant dreamland and a long-forgotten memory.

*Buddy Day stood straight and proud in his army uniform on exactly the same spot where Amanda herself would stand in just three years. She would pretend not to be nervous, like Buddy did now. He might fool others, but he couldn't fool Amanda. Even were it not for the perspiration on his upper lip, she'd have sensed his uneasiness.*

*"I'm going to be an Okie," he said in what he thought was an Oklahoma drawl but sounded like John Wayne. Due to the lack of jobs on the reservation, and just a few weeks short of his nineteenth birthday, he was headed to Fort Sill to begin a military career. "I'll be making bucks while I'm training," he told her. "The best part is I'll get to go places, see the world. There's more out there than this rez," he told her wisely. Amanda punched his arm; he'd been too smug since returning from boot camp—his first time away from the reservation.*

*Even with Hobo's ceremony last night, calling on the spirit guardians for protection for her best friend, she was worried. She tried to shake the premonition—the feeling of loss—the fear that clung to her.*

*The Greyhound pulled into sight, rocking in the ruts of the poorly maintained road, and came to a noisy stop beside them. "This is it, Manda." Buddy tipped his hat. They laughed together as he rubbed the stubble on his head—the ponytail he'd had since grade school lost to clippers and left on some army barber's floor.*

*"I'll see you, ma'am," he said in his best Duke imitation. He picked up his satchel, then threw it down quickly and grabbed her, squashing her against his uniform. "I'll write you every week. I'll be okay, and I'll be back before you have time to miss me, I promise."*

Amanda shivered as the chill of the room brought her back to consciousness. The fire was almost out. She pulled the quilt from her legs, threw it around her shoulders, and moved to stack more logs in the fireplace. She walked to the door and looked out. The snow that started just after her arrival two days before had finally stopped. Dark green pine boughs bent under its weight; tiny white ridges sat atop telephone wires. By leaning the right side of her head against the window frame in the door and closing her left eye Amanda could barely make out the roof of the Day house. She longed to see a ribbon of smoke twist out of the chimney into the dark, sooty sky. There wasn't one. The house had been empty for many years.

Buddy had come home all right, much sooner than either of them expected. Completing the circle, he returned to the reservation in a casket, the victim of a bloody, senseless war in Southeast Asia. On a dark day in mid October, under a dark sky that threatened snow, Leonard "Buddy" Day was laid to rest, the first of four sons to join Goose and Katie Day in the peace of the next world. That was twenty years ago; Amanda still missed him.

The wind had switched direction and picked up in force, Amanda noticed. The tops of the trees began bending from a north wind, signaling three or four days of frigid air coming straight out of Canada. She shivered and hugged herself again. She hoped her car, used to a garage, and almost hidden by snow now, would still run.

"Most people take vacations in the northern part of Wisconsin during the summer," her boss teased as she prepared to leave. Ted, with his bad breath and obnoxious manner said, "Din't ya know, all In-juns love to run barefoot in the great outdoors—even in winter." Good old Ted, always ready with comments about anyone not like himself. Amanda hated the beaner jokes he'd tell Maria Helena de Jesus, their receptionist. Amanda figured that the fact he was a brilliant programmer and inventor of clever acronyms was the only thing that kept him with the company—it certainly wasn't his people skills. Maria Helena, on the other hand, loved people; she was the only one who worried about Amanda being by herself in the woods. Amanda tried more than once to assure her friend that Milwaukee scared her more than the reservation ever could.

The rumbling in her stomach reminded Amanda that she hadn't eaten since early morning. She was a little surprised when the light in the kitchen snapped on—the electricity hadn't been disrupted by the heavy snow. She'd been ready, just in case. Earlier she had cleaned four kerosene lamps, remembering when they were the only light for the cabin. Her first real memory of her grandparents was of them at the dining room table reading by the soft glow of the lanterns. Grandpa sat at one end, reading his Polish Bible, and Grandma at the other, with a well-worn Sears Roebuck catalog, wishing for things she'd never have. In turn, each catalog sat in a place of honor on the dresser in Grandma's room until a new one came; the old one was then retired to the outhouse for purposes, Amanda suspected, Mr. Sears and Mr. Roebuck hadn't intended.

Amanda smiled as she opened the white painted doors of the cupboard. Cans of vegetables, soup, tuna, peanut butter, and applesauce with white labels that read *Not to be sold or exchanged* were neatly stacked on the shelves. Uncle Dan had stocked the cabin with commodities, canned fruit he'd put up himself, and venison. Amanda grabbed the tuna and made a sandwich. That done, she tuned the radio to some soft rock music, sat down at the table, and dug a creased newspaper clipping out of her purse. "Three Killed on Icy Highway," it read.

*She'd waited for her friends until nine, then had gone to the office Christmas party by herself. She figured they'd show up sooner or later with some kind of crazy excuse. But they didn't. The driver of a van lost control on an icy Milwaukee freeway, and sideswiped David's compact, sending the small car careening across the median and into the path of an oncoming interstate transport truck.*

*When the three didn't show by 11:30, Amanda knew something was wrong. She ignored the "Hey, give the guy a break," shouts of Ken's buddies and began calling local hospitals. On the fourth try, she got the right one. The duty nurse fetched a doctor who told Amanda everything. His assurance that all three died on impact and didn't suffer did little to console her.*

*Through a fog, Amanda attended the closed-casket services, reminding herself that her friends were in those boxes and would not be coming back.*

*At Ken's funeral, she met his ex-wife and teenaged sons. They didn't know who she was. She wanted to tell them that Ken was special, but couldn't—she didn't really belong. She'd only dated Ken for six months; they'd known him much longer. "What a good man," she wanted to tell his children. "How kind and gentle," she tried to say to his parents. She ran from church immediately after Mass.*

*As if that wasn't enough, she attended Becca and David's double funer-*

al the next day; again she felt the outsider, an intruder into someone else's pain. As the day before, she couldn't share her loss, her fear, her anger. The family nodded to Amanda without speaking as they followed the caskets out of church.

She made it through the holidays by gritting her teeth and forcing herself to smile at people who greeted her with cheerful good wishes of the season. Worse yet, she was asked to train three replacement staff. She was already convinced they would be completely incompetent compared to their predecessors.

Insomnia visited nightly. Some days she wouldn't even go to work. She'd stay in bed, or make it to the sofa, and lay curled in a ball waiting for the pain to do its thing. When Amanda dragged herself to the office, her work showed the strain. She finally got scared enough to go to a doctor when, for two nights in a row, she forgot to exit off the freeway on to Locust to go home.

"Depression," Doc Bradley said. She started crying and couldn't stop. At his insistence she took four weeks vacation and sick leave, plus another four weeks, to rest—totally wiping out her savings.

In a daze Amanda paid two months rent in advance, notified the post office, farmed out her plants to Maria Helena, and had her phone disconnected. Panic attacked her as she headed her Escort north on Highway 43 out of Milwaukee: was this a mistake? Maybe she could just work harder—keep her mind off the bad things. She forced herself to keep going. A few more miles, she told herself, then I'll decide. A couple hours later, she was on the far side of Green Bay. By the time she got to Keshena, the trees got closer to the highway and brought with them peace, to replace the panic. For the first time in a long time she was going home.

The cabin, the only inheritance from her parents, was nestled in the northern section of the reservation and was referred to by locals as The Point. It was unique, with its two bedrooms on the bottom floor that stuck out like lopsided arms and an overhanging second story. At one time the large, open upstairs held ten beds, where first her grandparents' children, and later their grandchildren, slept. Downstairs, a long wide room made up both the living room and dining room—the dining area distinguishable by a long wooden table and eight chairs. There was a second table set—a heavy, blue Formica and chrome monstrosity—in the kitchen.

That was where she sat now, nibbling on her sandwich. Amanda wiped away a patch of frost from the window with the heel of her hand in order to see the pond tucked behind thick green pines and tall white birches that filled the backyard. The news clipping sat in front of her, forgotten also, as she stared out into the silent, white world disturbed only by the occasional thrum of eighteen-wheelers on the highway a quarter of a mile away.

*The old pump over the sink was running. Amanda and her mother were frantically trying to stop it, but no matter what they did, it kept running.*

*"Grab some plastic, Mandy," Mom yelled. "Whatever you can find . . . anything! Hurry . . . hurry, child!"*

*The girl pulled a loose piece of plastic from the screen on the back door and handed it to her mother.*

*"No, here, wrap it around the faucet while I hold it," Mom directed. Water was running down Mom's arms and dripping off her elbows as she tried to hold back the steady flow. Amanda's young hands clumsily wrapped the plastic over and around the heavy black faucet. She wrinkled her nose and held her breath, hating the wet metal smell. "There," she said and stepped back, pleased with herself.*

*A sizzling sound came from the plastic. Slowly it started to fill.*

*"Oh God," Mom yelled. "No . . . no!"*

*Amanda screamed, partly in horror, partly from delight, as the plastic grew like a balloon. It grew and grew. BANG!!!*

She woke, confused, as the sound of dripping continued. It took her a minute to realize the icicles were melting off the roof. Some things never changed, Amanda realized, like the fickle weather in this part of Wisconsin. One day it would be freezing, and the next day it would be summer warm. It hit her suddenly that for the first time in months she wanted to be part of the day. That thought propelled her out of bed and into snow boots.

Amanda knew where she wanted to go. Shin-high snow slowed her usual fast-paced walk as she followed the snow-hidden but familiar route to the pond behind the house. The path was all that was left of an old corduroy road that was built back when horse-drawn wagons loaded with felled trees used this road. Lumber companies had brought some prosperity to the reservation for a few years, but they eventually moved on. A few white families built homes back here after that, and the road was traveled for a short time by cars. But when the railroad pulled out, the white families left too, leaving a jobless reservation to the Indians. The road was used less and less until the tire tracks all but disappeared under a tangle of weeds and brush. It finally disintegrated into simple ruts kept open by an occasional hunter. She had always heard that one could (though she had never tried) walk all the way to the shores of Lake Superior, the great Gichi Gumii, on this old road. She whispered to herself as she trudged through the otherwise unblemished snow:

By the shores of Gichi Gumii, by the shining big sea water
Stood the wigwam of Nokomis, daughter of the moon, Nokomis,
Dark behind it rose the forest, rose the dark and gloomy pine trees,
Rose the firs with cones upon them . . .

*Sister Mary Angelica paced the floor, punctuating the last word of each line by jabbing the air with a long wooden pointer. Amanda knew Sister was trying to scare the Indian seventh graders at St. Ann's to get them to memorize the Longfellow poem. It was easy to know that Sister thought they were too lazy and too slow to appreciate poetry. Yeah, they hated the poetry, but they hated her as well. Truthfully, the kids couldn't have said which they hated more.*

*One day it suddenly hit Amanda that the Gichi Gumii in the poem was her Lake Superior and the "dark and gloomy pine trees" were her trees. After that she eagerly learned the poem, but didn't tell her classmates. Who wanted to be a brownnoser?*

She glanced up through the sparkling snow-covered pine branches and smiled at the sun. How could anyone think of the pines as dark and gloomy? They protected; they whispered to her at night, singing and sighing softly, as she drifted into sleep. Their voices changed—sometimes high and gentle like rippling laughter, sometimes low, like they were giving quiet orders. No matter how hard she tried, she could never quite make out the words. Amanda cocked her head back now and listened to their "welcome home" whisper as they swayed gracefully in the pre-spring breeze.

She arrived at the edge of the frozen pond and heard, through space and time, the laughter of her family as they splashed in the cool water on warm summer evenings. With no running water on the reservation, everyone—aunts, uncles, cousins—would descend on the pond, armed with soap and shampoo, to bathe the sweaty clay smell from their hair and bodies. Amanda wondered what today's ecologists would say about the suds left in the water after these evening rituals. As far as she could tell nothing they had done had harmed the frogs, snakes, and other creatures that would evacuate the pond each time the family invaded.

# Chapter 2

As the weather improved, so did Amanda's spirits. She decided it was time to visit old friends. After a morning walk to the pond, she baked a coffee cake. Reservation manners dictated that she couldn't visit Elders without taking gifts.

"Come on, sweetie, you can make it," she patted the Escort's dash. The little car swayed and lurched over uneven mounds of semi-melted snow in the unplowed driveway. Amanda didn't remember the highway being so far from the cabin. After sitting in the cold the Escort sputtered a bit at first, just enough to let her know it wasn't pleased with the recent lack of attention, but it ran smoothly once it caught. Finally the car shook and bumped onto the blacktop. Amanda breathed a sigh of relief, and turned left toward the village.

Her first stop was to see Ben and Yemmy Vincent—every reservation child's aunt, uncle, or grandparent. Even with the years creeping up on them, the Elders spent several hours a week teaching Ojibwe language, culture, and beadwork at the Tribal Community Center. Amanda turned slowly into their driveway, happy to see it'd been plowed. She rapped once on the weather-beaten door before letting herself in.

"Hello, hello," she called.

"In here," yelled Ben. He was sitting in a straight-backed chair pulled up to an old-fashioned wood stove, kept for sentimental reasons she supposed, or as a backup for the gas furnace, a "new-fangled thing." He probably didn't trust it. She grinned to herself, remembering her grandmother who had demanded that the outhouse stay up even after plumbing had come to the reservation and her uncles had built a bathroom in what used to be the kitchen pantry. More stubborn than any mule that ever lived, Gramma insisted on going outdoors for that summer and fall, ignoring the teasing, and giving in only when winter made it too miserable for the old lady to go outside. Still, months after she began to enjoy the new room, she grumbled constantly about "doing *that* in the house."

Ben was whittling a dance fan handle for his youngest grandchild, Nina Jo. "Me 'n' Yemmy sponsored her first Pow Wow dance last spring," he explained proudly as he held his work out for Amanda to see. "This is a gift for her one year Give-Away Feast. Gonna be in May." He held it up for her to admire, which she did. Then Amanda hugged the gruff-looking old man. "She's a lucky little girl." She glanced around. "Where's Yemmy?" she asked.

"Sleepin'. Life gets harder every winter. That arthritis is twistin' up her hands and legs something awful! Her medicine makes her sleep, and sleep helps the pain. But I'll go get her. You wait here."

"No, Ben, let her rest," Amanda protested. But he insisted. "That old woman would kill me if she missed you," he said.

While Yemmy was slowly making her way to the kitchen, Ben started fresh coffee. "You wouldn't like what I've been drinking all morning," he laughed. "In fact, I plan to use the leftovers to tar up the roof to keep the rain out this summer."

"You must be talking about your coffee," Yemmy grumbled. "Hello, child," she said in Amanda's direction. She hobbled down the hallway, wincing in pain, holding the wall for support. Ben hit the automatic switch on the coffee maker and moved across the room to help his wife into her chair. He made a show of wrapping blankets around her legs and shoulders. Yemmy slapped at his hands and insisted she could take care of herself. At seventy-five, despite the twisted hands and legs, Yemmy was still a dignified-looking lady. Her single silver braid fell over her shoulder and past her waist. Without realizing she did it, Amanda touched her own shoulder-length hair, permed city-style.

The old couple was at it as usual, grumbling at each other as they always did when others were around, though everyone knew they often held hands when no one was looking. *A relationship to be envied,* Amanda thought. Their love was based on a half century of struggle through good times and bad, and cemented by ten children. *The ties that bind,* Amanda smiled to herself.

Ben loved to tell old stories, and Amanda did her best to guide him that way with questions about family and reservation gossip. He finally got to her favorite story: about when he worked in a factory off the rez. "I'd walk seven miles, both ways, ever' day in ever' kind of weather." He said shaking his head at the memory. "Uphill both ways!" he laughed. "Got up at 5:00 ever' morning, left home at 6:00, got there 'bout 8:00, worked all day and left at

5:00 at night—wouldn't get home for supper until 7:00, would I, Ma? But to feed ten kids?" he chuckled, "You do what you gotta do." Amanda knew the story by heart and could have mouthed the words along with him had she wanted to. Ben was easily coaxed into continuing his stories. His next story was about why Yemmy was called Yemmy. Amanda often wondered that she didn't know Yemmy's real name. Not that it mattered; most others on the reservation didn't know or couldn't remember her given name either. She was simply, Yemmy Vincent. That said it all!

The story was that their oldest grandson, "Named for his gramps" Ben proudly announced at this point, had a speech problem and wasn't able to say *Grammy* which is what Ben called his wife after young Ben was born. Whenever Ben told the story, he'd affectionately mimic how young Ben said the name, causing listeners to laugh. Yemmy smiled and nodded, breaking in now and then with lighthearted remarks. From Ben's well-timed pauses and the twinkle in his eyes, his audience understood these were part of the storytelling ritual. He was talkative today, and with little encouragement he launched into more familiar stories, lulling Amanda into the past. When Ben got up to fill their coffee cups for the fourth time, he turned on the lights.

"Oh my God . . ." Amanda pointed at the clock. More than four hours had slipped by. "With all the holes and ruts in my driveway, I better head out now," she said. "I don't want to get stuck out there in the dark. I've got other days to visit." She hugged the elder couple.

"Come back real soon, my girl," Yemmy insisted. She covered Amanda's hands with her own bent and swollen ones.

Amanda leaned down to kiss the old lady's warm, dry cheek. "You couldn't keep me away with a team of horses," she said, borrowing one of Ben's old phrases. "I'd almost forgotten how much I've missed you two."

"It's been too long, child," Yemmy said. "Are you home for good this time?"

Amanda shook her head as she fumbled with her coat buttons, refusing to look up.

Ben threw his jacket on and walked to the car with her. He glanced around at the growing dusk, and studied the stars popping out in the night sky. He cupped his bare hands over his mouth and blew on them. "Gonna be a cold one tonight," he said looking back at Amanda. "You're family; you come back real soon." His breath in the cold evening air fogged up in front of his face, almost hiding pursed lips that he pointed toward the house with a jut of his chin. "That old gal in there doesn't get out much anymore, and she needs company other than mine." He gave Amanda a quick hug. "It's *real* good to see you, my girl."

She hugged him back. "Thanks Ben. I'll be back soon."

Even as warm thoughts of the Vincents filled Amanda, a cold lump formed somewhere deep inside and worked its way up to her chest. They were getting on in years. Amanda already dreaded the loss when they would be gone. She pulled herself free of that thought and turned and waved to Ben who was still standing on the porch holding the screen door open. The lump grew. She swiped the tears that were beginning to form in her eyes, hearing her mother tell her they would freeze on her cheeks if she left them there. Amanda cranked the heater up full blast and canted the front vents in her direction. The heat slowly seeped into the chilly car warming her face and fingers.

"*Triste-feliz,*" she whispered. She liked this expression—one that Maria Helena often used. It fit exactly the mix of sadness and happiness she felt now, something was wasn't easy to express in English. She and the car bounced over the mounds of snow that seemed to have multiplied themselves while she was gone. She enjoyed this new, but familiar, slower pace of life. It was different than she knew in Milwaukee. There she felt the need to be busy. To sit for hours, laughing, drinking coffee, visiting, was unthinkable. Amanda suddenly realized she missed more about the reservation than the people.

The old man stood on the stoop for a moment longer, watching the small car move to the end of the driveway. The brake lights flashed as Amanda slowed before making the turn onto the blacktop. Ben felt, rather than saw, her wave. He raised his hand in return. He felt a sadness he couldn't explain. Something was troubling Amanda. She'd tried to hide it behind the laughter at his stories, but it was there. It would have been invisible to many—only the old ones like him and Yemmy would have been aware of it. He doubted that she even knew of it. He blew on his hands; time to go in. Yemmy was waiting; the crease that appeared between her eyes when she worried stood out clearly. She raised her eyebrows, and he shrugged as he slipped off his jacket. Longtime mates, they didn't need words. He rinsed his coffee cup in the sink and went to sit beside the best part of his life.

Yemmy's hand, knuckles red and twisted, reached for him. "Something's wrong with our girl," she said. "Do you think she's heard about Brownie?"

"Maybe, but I think it's something else. It goes pretty deep."

"She don't want to talk about whatever it is. Why ain't she home for good this time? She needs to come home, Ben. Don't ya think?"

Ben picked up his piece of balsam wood and ran his hand over the grain, feeling for flaws. "Reckon she does, Mother, but not just yet. Anyway, it's not up to us."

Yemmy's voice came from a great distance. "I wish we could help," she sighed.

The old man smiled at his pretty wife. "She'll come to us when she's ready."

The next morning Amanda set out to visit her old hangout. When she stepped into the cool darkness of the all-purpose reservation mail drop/mini mart/gas station she felt fifteen again—when Weleski's had become the hot spot for reservation teens to lounge around the pop cooler and eye each other up. The younger kids secretly read the comic books they couldn't afford to buy, ignoring the hand-scribbled PAY BEFORE YOU READ! sign. She noticed the changes immediately. The old banged-up red pop cooler, filled with green-tinted bottles of pop sitting in ice-cold water, with aluminum sliding doors on top and Coca-Cola written in large, fancy white script on its side, was gone. The new upright looked like a refrigerator.

New additions included disposable diapers (there were always lots of babies on the reservation) and an open cooler with precut, plastic-wrapped meat instead of the fresh meat counter. Other things were missing: the penny-candy jars on the counter filled with peppermint sticks, licorice drops, and berry-flavored jawbreakers, as well as the rack of Dell and Marvel comic books that lined the east wall.

One thing hadn't changed though: "Winky" Weleski, nicknamed for the tic in his left eye, was still behind the worn linoleum-topped counter. *Will he ever change?* Amanda wondered. Winky looked the same as he did when she was fifteen: *old*—the exact same age of old, in fact. He still wore his infamous striped Oshkosh B'Gosh bib overalls. The kids used to wonder how *all* of Winky's overalls managed to stay the same degree of worn. As far as Amanda knew, no one on the reservation had ever seen Winky in new overalls or completely worn-out ones. A popular story in her day was that there was a betting pool you could buy into for a buck. They said whoever could name the date on which Winky would show up in new overalls would win. She smiled and wondered if the story was still whispered behind cupped hands. In spite of the life the story had, no one seemed to know who was taking the bets. Come to think of it, she'd never spoken to anyone who had laid down a dollar.

Winky smiled a crooked, nicotine smile as she walked over to the counter. "Yer Uncle Dan sed you was home." He didn't wait for her to speak. "Yer lookin' peeked girl, ain't ya takin' care a yerseff?" he asked.

"That's why I'm here, Winky," Amanda replied. "To rest up. I'm *trying* to take care of myself."

He tilted his head and squinted at her, checking for a lie. "Yep, I s'pect yer no different from the others. They all come home 'ventually," he said. "Sometimes even after they're old." He glanced at Amanda. "Cities ain't for Indians. The *gover*-ment never shoulda sent our people there in the first place. Relocation!" he huffed and shook his head. Amanda settled back for a 'Winky Sermon' as the kids used to call them. "Course they *said* it was for our own good, sames always, but they knew cities kilt Indians," he continued. "It was a *jest* a plan! Nothing but concrete streets with a bar on every corner. No way to live, no sir! We Chips need trees, good smellin' black earth under our feet, and fresh air. But the BIA knew that. You know the BIA use to be part of that there *War* Department—their *job* was to kill us off!"

He stopped and lit a cigarette. "Sure nuff . . . they knew the city kilt the spirit. Once it kilt the spirit, it kilt the Indian. An' that factory air, hanging thick over ever' city, *hell,* ain't no good for nobody's lungs. But they knew that too." He blew smoke rings into the air. Young Amanda's dream had been to catch the old man spouting off about pollution while dirtying her air. But she bit her tongue and found she couldn't say a thing—even now. She eyed the cigarette in his brown-stained fingers, smiled, and nodded as she used to do years ago. Winky loved to preach to the kids—on just about any subject. No one dared to talk back. They listened and nodded—small price to pay for such a cool hangout place, they figured.

Always the self-appointed town crier, Winky knew everybody and everybody's business—he didn't disappoint her today. "Don't know if you heard, but your ole boyfriend, Brownie, he got hisself tanked up one night and ran into the slough bridge . . . kilt hisself," Winky said. "Happened, um, two, three months ago, 'bout Christmas I guess. Now, ain't that a hellava time to leave a pretty wife and four young-uns?"

Amanda's breath stopped. Tears stung behind her lids; she blinked hard to keep them back.

Brownie was the only boyfriend she'd had on the reservation; a sweet, shy boy, one of the few full-bloods left.

*A couple of times a week, he'd ride his bicycle five miles over gravel roads to visit her, then stand quietly on the front porch until someone noticed him. Amanda would go out then, and they'd sit together quietly, hardly speaking, sometimes holding hands, until it was time for him to ride the five miles back to his own home. She expected him today.*

*When he'd speak to her she could hardly hear him, even when he was sitting right beside her. It made Dad's day to tease Amanda about Brownie.*

*"I worry about Mandy, Mother, she's on the porch talking to herself again." He'd made sure he was loud enough for them to hear. Too embarrassed to look at Brownie, Amanda blushed. She heard him shuffling, as if getting ready to run. Half-expecting him to bolt, she glanced at him out of the corner of her eye. His feet moved restlessly, but he stayed put. She reached over and took his hand.*

*Brownie lived with his father and two older brothers. Amanda always had to work to resist asking him about the gossip—that his ma had run off with the parish priest right after he was born. As far as Amanda had ever heard, no one on the reservation knew what happened to her; she just left and never came back. If Brownie's father knew anything, he never let on. Amanda's folks wouldn't discuss it. She asked once but Mom shushed her. "You mustn't say anything about Mrs. Brown," she scolded Amanda. In all the time Amanda had known Brownie, he mentioned his ma once, one Mother's Day, only to wonder if she was still alive.*

"And Annie?" she asked to get Winky on another subject. Annie was her cousin and childhood best friend—the sister she never had. They were always together.

*The girls sat on the cement bridge on Highway 2, swinging their blue-jeaned legs over the edge, enjoying the hot sun on their hair and faces, and making plans about what they'd be when they grew up. As they often did, they counted two-tone* cars. *Reservation cars didn't count, not that there were many. And there was only one two-tone Chevy that Amanda knew of, and that one was so rusty they called it a "three-tone" anyway.*

*"You get the cars that come from the left," Annie told her. It was an unwritten rule that whoever spoke up first would get to pick her direction. For some reason cars came most often from the right. "How do you figure?" Amanda asked Dad once. "Those cars have to be going someplace, and wouldn't you think that they'd have to travel in the other direction sometime?" The only public route through the rez was Highway 2. Dad shrugged, "Guess the folks who live in the east don't like to travel west," he grinned. "At least not on two-tone car-counting days," Amanda conceded.*

*Bored with the counting game, Annie pulled a badly creased fashion magazine from her back pocket. She loved to brag about the clothes she'd buy when she became a famous model. When it wasn't a magazine, she'd be thumbing through the Sears-Roebuck catalog. Annie and Grandma were two of a kind. They treated the catalog with the same reverence others had for their Sunday Missal.*

*Annie's dream to become rich and famous died the day she told Amanda she was pregnant—at fourteen. They both cried. "I'll never be a model now. I'll be fat and ugly," Annie said. "I'd rather die than stay here!"*

But she stayed, marrying Neil two years later, after their second baby. Three more kids, including a set of twins, followed quickly. With little in common anymore, Amanda stopped visiting Annie on her infrequent trips back to the reservation. What irony! Amanda decided. I loved the reservation and wanted to stay; Annie, who so desperately wanted to leave, stayed.

"Annie's oldest got herself a rich *white* boy," Winky was saying. "Heard she met him at school. Ya know, she went to that university in Mini-apples. She got her a *M.R.S.* degree," he chuckled. "Always wanted to leave the rez, like her ma. Neither thought they could be happy here. Mighta been a fact too. I never seen your friend smile much after she married." Winky paused and lit another smelly cigarette. "Guess she blamed Neil for keeping her down. But hell, he weren't so bad . . . she mighta done worse. Well, he drank some; most of 'em do 'round here." Winky stared at Amanda. "I heard he used to beat her up sometime. Musta been hard for her. She put up with it though. Hear she'd kick him out when she was fed up, but he'd come back, tail 'tween his legs and she'd take him in. Probably still would, come to think of it. Thought back then it cuz of the kids, but they're growed up now; jest got to be a habit I guess."

Winky blew lazy smoke rings into the air. "Pretty young-un too—guess if she wanted, she coulda been in those mag'zines she was forever buyin'," he said shaking his head.

This was too much bad news for one day. "I'm off to visit Uncle Dan," Amanda said and pushed herself away from the sticky counter. She wiped her hands on her pant legs.

"Yer uncle," Winky said, "comes in ever' day for our cribbage games." The games had begun after Aunt Molly's death from a cancer that ate her stomach and liver. Amanda's aunt and uncle had been childless and enjoyed each other's company more than anyone she knew. Uncle Dan was lost without his partner. The games with Winky started as a way for him to kill time but soon became a ritual, and they formed the basis of a friendship between two lonely old men. "He comes in 'bout three ever' afternoon, if ya wanna stay and see him," Winky offered.

"Thanks Winky, but I think I'll run by his house. Maybe I can drop him off later and save him the walk."

"Don't know about that . . . does him good to walk," Winky told her. "The di-bee-tees bothers his legs ya see, gives him *real* bad trouble sometimes. He needs to walk, girl . . . keeps the circulation up, don't ya see."

"Well Amanda," she scolded herself as she climbed into the Escort, "*That visit* certainly did wonders for your depression now, didn't it?"

Dan's house, like many on the reservation, badly needed repair. The once-bright yellow paint hung in uneven strips off the side of the cottage, leaving large brown bare spots. She rapped once on the door and let herself in.

"Hello, hello. . . ." she called.

Her uncle was standing just inside the door. He hugged her. "Hey there, I'm just starting lunch, grilled commodity cheese *sang-witches* and '*mato* soup. Sit down," he ordered cheerfully. "Been waiting on you. How's things at the cabin?"

"Great, thanks. What a nice surprise. I didn't expect you to do all that," she said and hugged him a second time. "But I have to admit, it felt good, especially with all the snow. At least I knew I wasn't going to starve." She laughed, and looked down at herself, "Not that it was a worry." For the past six months she'd soothed her anxiety with food—her "drug of choice," Doc Bradley had called it.

"Anything for you, my girl. Sit, sit. Tell me what's new with you." Dan beamed at her. He pulled out a chair and motioned to it with his chin. He hung her coat on a hook behind the kitchen door and sat down.

Before she knew it Amanda was telling Uncle Dan everything—things she'd told only her doctor until now. She felt like a snowball rolling downhill: once she started she couldn't stop. She told him about the nightmares she'd had for months after her parents' deaths; her disastrous marriage—his jealousies; and, finally, the accident that took her three best friends from her. With the words came the pain. Tears ran down her cheeks. Dan continued working at the stove, listening, glancing at her, but not interrupting except to hand her a box of Kleenex from a shelf above the sink. He poured the thick tomato mixture into cracked orange and yellow ceramic mugs with *Soup* written on the side. He cut the sandwiches into fourths and pointed at the table with his lips. Amanda blew her nose and dried her eyes before she pulled her chair closer to the table.

Sniffling, she picked up her sandwich, surprised she was hungry. She knew her uncle well enough not to push, but she couldn't help wishing he'd say something. They dunked grilled cheese quarters into the soup; the silence broken only by the raspy sound of Uncle Dan's whiskers on a paper napkin as he wiped soup from his chin. It wasn't until they were clearing the table that he spoke.

"I don't know what to say, Sis. Alls I know is that as much as I'd like, there ain't no magic words to make you feel better. That kinda pain is too deep. But I can say this: you should use it," he said. "Don't let it use you. It took me a long time to learn that. I reckon there's reasons for our losses, even if we don't think so. Maybe we're never to understand. We got to trust the Creator. But it's hard, no lyin' 'bout that." He leaned against the sink and folded his arms. "When I lost your Aunt Molly, I wanted to die too. Even prayed I would." He glanced at his niece. "Lotsa people would think that's awful, but I reckon you understand." She nodded. Dan paused and looked at Amanda from under his bushy eyebrows. "I made it through only cuz of what Molly said to me before she died. She had enough faith for both of us, ya see." He shook his head and gazed out the window before going on. His voice was almost a whisper. "She reminded me that life is a gift; the Earthmaker made us for a reason. She accepted that her purpose for being on earth was over

. . . much better than I accepted it." He swallowed noisily. "I know she's pain-free an' waiting . . . just like she promised."

Hot tears again poured down Amanda's cheeks and rolled down her chin; tears for herself and her uncle. Uncle Dan put his big bear arms around her, gently pushed back her bangs and kissed her forehead. "I won't try to cheer you up, Sis. Go ahead and cry. If you don't, it'll eat away at you as surely as the cancer ate my Molly."

Amanda loved this old man, her father's youngest brother. She leaned into him. He held her and rocked back and forth feeling as good as the old blanket Amanda carried around with her until she was almost five. Not wanting to be alone, she stayed into the afternoon. At 2:30 Dan began staring at the clock; it was getting close to his cribbage time. To her surprise, he accepted the offer of a ride. Her heart ached as she watched him shuffle into Winky's. He had aged so ungracefully. It saddened her to see that the light that left his eyes when Aunt Molly died still hadn't returned after all these years.

She put the car in gear and pulled away from the only place to one-stop-shop on the rez. She left the village behind and exited the highway onto a muddy road about three miles from the Point. As always, at the final turn, she gasped. The lake looked like it was suspended above the road. She remembered the first time she'd come here with her folks; she'd clung to their hands, afraid the water would come crashing down and pull them into itself. The lake was endless, the curve of the horizon clearly visible. Even in winter it was wonderful! Nowhere was her belief in God, the Earthmaker, Gichi Manidoo, the Creator stronger than when she was here.

She stepped out of the car, and her neck scarf unwound in the frigid gusts coming off the lake. In a few minutes her cheeks burned from the cold. Amanda sought refuge in the Escort. Her mind slid back to her earlier life on the reservation.

*She climbed on the tired-looking Greyhound, carrying a small, battered, olive green suitcase that held about everything she owned. Brownie stood with her parents outside the tiny depot and waved his goodbye. All three were crying. Amanda waved back, trying to hide her guilt; she was scared, but excited too. Something was waiting for her outside this reservation. An unsatisfying year of odd jobs following high school graduation had prompted this decision. Her parents encouraged her to try college, never anticipating she would educate herself out of a home. But four years later, when she walked across a stage with a diploma in computer science in hand, she suddenly realized the reservation didn't have a place for her anymore if she wanted to stay in her field. She moved to Milwaukee, where she lived and worked with strangers. Amanda often daydreamed about going home but couldn't disappoint her parents. Every time Mom called she'd tell Amanda how proud they were of her, so she didn't tell her how lonely she was. It was hard to make friends in a city where everyone was too busy to be friendly; she didn't even know any people in her building. Once in a while she'd see them picking up mail after work or on the weekends, or she'd run into them in the laundry room where they'd nod cautious hellos. Seeing little encouragement in their eyes, Amanda kept to herself.*

*Then the first call came. She was working alone in her apartment, as she often did in the evening, when the phone rang. Amanda jumped, and she cursed softly when she hit her knee on the leg of the computer table. "Honey, your dad's having surgery tomorrow morning," Mom said. "But don't come home," she added quickly. "It's nothing serious, we just thought you should know." They chatted a little longer—kept it light.*

*Her parents would live forever, at least that's what she'd have thought had she given it any thought. She ignored the anxiousness in Mom's voice, and disregarded the fear chewing at her insides. She didn't go home. Everyone knew Mom was the classic worrier, and Dad had a good doctor: "the best," Mom said. But somehow he died the next afternoon of complications. Amanda hadn't even said good-bye.*

*A few short months later she was all alone in the world. She'd been concerned about Mom after Dad's funeral and tried to convince herself she meant to call— but she was so busy, always something new coming up at work. And Mom was naturally a little lost; Dad had always taken care of her. How was Amanda supposed to know a broken heart could kill? She asked herself this over and over again. This time it was Uncle Dan who called. At first the words wouldn't come. Only repeated swallowing sounded hollowly through the phone line. Amanda waited, refusing to help him, as if refusing to accept what she knew was coming would forever postpone the news. He cleared his throat several times. Finally he croaked, "Come home, Mandy, it's your ma."*

*Amanda didn't return to the reservation for several years after Mom's*

*funeral—it wasn't home anymore. She missed her mother's weekly phone calls—
even the pesty ones. Eventually, loneliness drew her into marriage with a jealous, abusive, non-Indian. She met him after working late one night. She dropped
by the corner bar on her way home so she didn't have to face the small empty
apartment and eat a sandwich over the kitchen sink again. It didn't matter that
she wouldn't know anyone there. She would still enjoy conversation and music,
even if she wasn't part of it.*

*He was sitting alone, nursing a beer; he smiled when she walked in. On a
whim, she sat down at the bar next to him, instead of at a table alone. He was
friendly, charming, and witty. He made her laugh. When she got up to go home,
he grabbed her left hand, "No ring. Not married?" She saw him several times
over the next few months. He called, sent cards and flowers, teased like Dad did.*
Why not? *she thought.*

*Amanda didn't like his jealousy or his temper, but she was sure they would
end when they married. They didn't. She put up with pain and fear for two years.
Her Catholic upbringing excluded divorce. Finally, unable to bear the humili-
ation any longer, she asked her dead parents for forgiveness, and filed. He ha-
rassed her for the he next six months. It was a long time before she stopped being
afraid to answer the door or the phone.*

*Amanda threw herself all the harder into her work. For the first time since
sixth grade, she wished she'd taken Sr. Mary Estelle's advice and become a
nun. She rejected all attention, male and female, except from Becca, a coworker
who refused to believe that anyone could refuse her offer of friendship. Amanda
thanked the Creator many times that Becca didn't give up easily. She listened,
counseled, argued, teased, and supported Amanda in a way nobody had since
Mom died. To get Becca to back off, Amanda gave in and saw a counselor. She
found herself sitting across from a middle-aged black woman whose eyes looked
like she had suffered too. Amanda saw Gloria for several months before she was
ready to trust a man again. But fate inserted itself, and just six short months after she began dating Ken an inexperienced driver lost control on an icy Milwaukee freeway, changing the direction of Amanda's life.*

Amanda smiled as memories of Annie washed over her. Annie's dream of
fame and fortune had been replaced by five children and a husband who used
his fistsagainst her. How unfair that Annie should experience the same kind

of abuse at the hands of a husband that she had at the hands of her alcoholic
father.

*Fear and disgust filled Amanda. Uncle Lem was drunk again. Payday, she thought.*
*He was cussing and hollering at everyone. The dog, Aunt Caren, and his kids all*
*tried to stay out of his way. Amanda ran for the back door and the safety of her*
*own home. She dragged Annie with her; tears streamed down their faces. "Why*
*does he do that?" Annie sobbed. "Mama is so good to him. Sometimes I wish he*
*was dead!"*

*Amanda stared at her cousin, "That's an awful way to talk about your dad."*
*But she knew why Annie dreamed of escape. Sometimes Amanda tried to talk to*
*Mom about it. "That's not our problem, Mandy," Mom would say. Dad turned*
*sad eyes away and shook his head. Lem was his oldest brother.*

*While they were hiding in the attic bedroom, Amanda saw Annie's green eyes*
*sparkle with a mixture of excitement and tears. "You'll be my manager," she said*
*hugging Amanda. "All topnotch models have one." Her voice took on her idea*
*of a British accent. "We'll travel all over the world, and counts and earls will*
*beg for our hands in marriage. But we'll be fussy, of course, we won't take just*
*anyone. He'll have to be handsome as well as rich!" Amanda, caught up in the*
*fantasy, smiled at her beautiful cousin and wondered if she'd know a count or*
*earl if she saw one.*

Amanda rolled down the window of the Escort and sucked cold air into her lungs.
Somehow, she decided, she must have used up her share of happiness. It seemed as
elusive to her now as the shimmering water images that lay across the highway on
hot summer days and taunted two young Indian girls into chasing them.

*"There's another one!" Amanda squealed. Bored waiting for two-toned cars,*
*she and Annie tried to catch the mirages that wavered across the blacktop.*
*Whoever could sneak up on one and capture it with her feet would be declared*
*the supreme winner. When that didn't work, the girls teamed up to double their*
*chances. Giggling, they tried to figure out where the mirages would appear next,*
*believing that determination would win out. But each time the girls got close, the*
*mirages disappeared, only to pop up farther down the road.*

Exhausted by tears and wanting nothing more than to sleep, Amanda stretched and rolled up the window. As she turned the key in the ignition, a shadow moved over the front of the car. She stretched her neck to look out the front windshield. A large eagle swooped in over the lake and began four circles, passing over the car and the lake. On its fourth pass over the lake, the Grandfather's messenger caught an updraft and floated out of sight, disappearing into the high, thin clouds slowly, like a fade out in a movie.

"Quite the imagination you have, Sis," Amanda chided herself. She smiled at the old familiar name her uncle had used earlier today. She swore every female in her family was tagged "Sis" sometime during her life. Amanda never knew if it was a term of endearment or if, because of so many kids in the family, it was simply easier to address all the girls that way instead of trying to remember all their names—which is what she suspected. At least once at every family get-together, someone yelled "Sis!" and a dozen young and not-so-young females of all shapes and sizes would answer. Her dad had suggested that they all take numbers: Sis #1, Sis #2 . . . !

Amanda went to bed early that night. She slid easily into sleep and dreamt of wonderful, soaring eagles, strangely colored in shades of turquoise, yellow, brown, and white. They alternately swooped close to her head one minute, then faded into ghosts the next.

# Chapter 3

The third week at the Point was so warm that Amanda was comfortable outdoors with only a heavy sweater. These days she was taking afternoon, as well as morning, walks. The warm days had melted most of the snow and fooled the trees into sprouting prematurely. Amanda began to believe that spring wasn't just flirting with winter-tired residents. For the first time in years she found herself worrying about late frosts that could kill tender young buds. Small patches of brown earth were visible through the disappearing snow. Unable to be absorbed into the still-frozen ground, water sat in puddles along the path. On days like this, Amanda thought she could smell Arbutus in bloom, even though it was still too early. That unforgettable odor was her favorite memory of spring on the reservation. Today she started walking down the highway on another familiar path.

*Buddy held the aromatic flowers in his chubby hand while Amanda tied the short woody stems together with colored yarn swiped from Gram's sewing box. His fingers kept getting in the way. "How many you think we'll sell today, Mandy?" The sweat on his forehead plastered his dark bangs against his broad face. He pushed them back with his forearm, trying not to let go of a second, already-tied bundle of flowers clenched tightly in his left hand. His hair, clotted with sweat, stood in spikes.*

*"None, if you keep looking like a Martian," she said. "Now, hold still!" He grinned his lopsided grin and patted his hair down with the backside of his full hand. It was a warm spring Saturday and they had high hopes of lots of tourists passing through the rez today.*

*"I don't know. Maybe two dollars," she continued. They had high hopes. Dad was going into town this afternoon and promised they could ride along. It had been a long time since either of them had been there.*

*"With the money we saved from last weekend, we should have enough to go to*

*a matinee, plus get one comic book each,* plus," *he emphasized, "a double, maybe even a* triple-*dip ice cream cone." Buddy was the youngest of four boys. He was chubby and inactive and was treated harshly by his older, athletic brothers. Although he was three years older than Amanda, an only child, the two fell into an easy friendship. Besides selling flowers on the roadside, they liked to read and were constantly exchanging comic books. Most of the time they couldn't remember who had whose book. But the bond that really cemented their friendship was their mutual love of fishing. When he was in a good mood, Buddy's father, Goose, took the kids with him to the nearby state forest for a day. When they were forced to stay home, they put hooks on homemade poles and, even knowing they would be unsuccessful, tried for the catfish that swam lazily along the muddy bottom of the pond in back of Grandma and Grandpa's house.*

*"What are you doing, Buddy?" Amanda asked one day while they were relaxing at the pond.*

*Buddy was jerking his head right and left, snapping at the air so hard, his teeth clicked. "I'm trying to catch some flies in case we run out of worms."*

*"Oh, Buddy," she shook her head.*

*"Damn!" he said, "I had one, but I swallowed it."*

*"Buddy Day, you're disgusting!" She swore he did things like this deliberately to get her goat.*

*The fight of a lifetime, their only fight ever, happened on the day Buddy caught a beautiful rainbow trout.*

*"What a beauty," Buddy said proudly. "Look Manda. It's a damn winner if I ever seen one." At the house, he placed his prize-winning fish on the back porch on old newspaper. He centered it carefully, fussed to get it just right, and re-centered it. He grinned foolishly. "Those assholes won't tease me no more," Buddy said.*

*"Don't swear," Amanda scolded.*

*But before his brothers returned home, the family tomcat found himself face to face with a temptation he couldn't resist. Unaware of the cat, and with Amanda walking proudly at his side, Buddy led his unbelieving brothers around to the back of the house. "You'll just see," Buddy was saying for the fourth or fifth time.*

*"What's this?" Bernard laughed. He poked at what was left of the once beautiful trout with the toe of his shoe. Joe and Ambrose joined in the laughter, and punched each other on their arms and chests.*

"Man! Oh man!" Buddy cried. He spotted the contented cat sitting on the edge of the porch, carefully washing the last of the feast from his face with his front paws. In two steps Buddy reached the old tom.

"God damn you, you scroungy no-good bastard! Damn cat anyway!" The confused animal ducked the kick and jumped off the porch, scrambling for shelter under the lilac trees.

Amanda couldn't help herself. She joined Buddy's brothers in uncontrolled laughter until tears ran down her face and she doubled over with cramps. She caught her breath, meaning to tell Buddy she was sorry, but all that came out was a squeaky, "Just like a Tom and Jerry cartoon," and the laughter began again.

Buddy couldn't take it any more. His face turned a strange ashen color; tears of frustration rolled down his fat cheeks. He looked at Amanda with accusing eyes. Amanda felt his pain and tried to stop laughing, but couldn't. The harder she tried, the harder she laughed. Her cheek muscles hurt, but she still couldn't stop. Each time she thought she'd laughed herself out, one of the boys snickered, and she began again. Without another word Buddy shuffled off into the woods, shoulders stooped. She found out later that he hadn't returned home until dark. Amanda knew then how hurt he was—he'd missed supper, something he never did. She tried for the umpteenth time to apologize, but Buddy would have none of it. "You're a traitor, Amanda," he accused. "I wouldn't have done that to you."

She knew it was true; she hated the tone of his voice. She suffered through a whole month of his sulking before he finally permitted her to speak to him without turning his back. She crossed her heart and hoped to die, "I will never turn against you again . . . even with your brothers."

"Especially with my brothers," he snarled. They hooked pinky fingers, but Amanda still wasn't sure she was really forgiven.

Amanda left the blacktop and turned into a driveway, overgrown with weeds that led to the Days' house. A badly decayed For Sale sign was partially hidden by a pile of dirty snow and red willow. Old age and neglect were visible; boarded windows and doors belied the earlier occupation of a once happy family.

The Day boys' hearty laughter rang from the house, and the smell of cooking drifted out from the kitchen. Mrs. Day was always cooking or baking. Her choc-

*olate chip cookies were even better than Mom's, Amanda thought, feeling a lit-tle guilty, though she rationalized her guilt by deciding it was because Mrs. Day had to feed four boys and a husband and Mom only had a husband and one daughter.*

*Katie Day was a short, slight, dark woman who always seemed to be in motion—she reminded Amanda of the hummingbirds that flittered around the tall purple flowers next to Gram's front porch. Mrs. Day wasn't exactly unfriend-ly, more like distracted. The constant teasing and joking of the men in the family didn't penetrate Katie Day's private world either. Some reservation folks whis-pered about Buddy's mother behind their hands. She was rarely seen in town, and when she went she seldom spoke to people. "Real odd," some said about her. "Full-blood," the older folks nodded knowingly.*

*Amanda wasn't quite afraid of Mrs. Day, but she shied from contact with Buddy's mother just the same, maybe because she seemed to look through Aman-da instead of at her. Amanda didn't put Buddy's mother into the category of a witch—not exactly—but something similar, but a little less scary.*

*One day she was forced to submit to Mrs. Day's touch. Barefoot as usual, Amanda and Buddy were running in his backyard when she stepped on a rusty needle. She was sure it was buried too deep to be taken out; certainly the foot would have to be cut off. Goose dropped the ax he was sharpening and carried Amanda to the house, all the while trying to soothe her sobs. At first Amanda screamed with pain, then when she realized where Goose was taking her, she screamed with fear. Buddy's mother brooked no nonsense from her own kids, and she would have none from Amanda. She took the foot firmly in her hand and insisted the needle would come out—and she'd do it—right now!*

*As Mrs. Day removed the needle from Amanda's heel, she spoke softly in Ojibwe, sounding an awful lot like Hobo. She blew gently on the foot the whole time. Amanda, finally deciding there was nothing else to do but sit quietly, stared at the straight part in Mrs. Day's long black hair that fell forward, covering her face. She was mesmerized by the soft, singsong voice. Needle out, Mrs. Day placed a cold hunk of salt pork on the wound before bandaging the aching foot. Amanda's tears dried on her cheeks. Then the most wonderful thing happened: Katie Day pushed back her hair and smiled up into Amanda's face, "There you are, my girl," she said patting Amanda's leg. "You'll be as good as new tomorrow."*

*Whenever she went to Buddy's house after that, Amanda ran straight for the kitchen with wildflowers or ladybugs for Mrs. Day. With a soft "Thank you," Mrs. Day would take the flowers and put them in a glass canning jar on the windowsill. She'd cup her hands around the ladybugs, whisper to them, and let them fly out the back door with a shake of her hand. "They will bring good luck to us, Amanda." Amanda liked the* us *and the happiness she saw in Katie Day's eyes then, but as long as she waited for it, she never again saw the beautiful smile.*

Amanda stared at the broken slats under the front porch remembering another hot day summers ago.

*Buddy came running to meet her as she trudged slowly up the driveway to the Day house, loving the intense heat of the August midday. His round face was smeared with sweat and dust, his T-shirt and pants were covered with red clay.*

*"Hurry, Mandy, hurry!" he yelled before he turned and ran back to the porch. He fell to his hands and knees and scooted from one side of the porch to the other, like some dizzy crab, still motioning for Amanda over his shoulder. Amanda, worried he might have had heat stroke, hurried to his side.*

*"Look," he whispered in a squeaky voice, motioning for her to crouch beside him. As she did she heard the high-pitched mewing of newborn kittens in the darkness beneath the porch. She eagerly joined Buddy as he crawled around, first squinting between one pair of slats, then another, trying to spot them. "You can have first pick, Mandy," he said, "any one you want. You pick first."*

Amanda never did get one of those kittens, for either the old tom killed them (as her uncle's stories said male cats did), or the mother moved them to another spot. That was what Amanda wanted to believe. Buddy, on the other hand, convinced himself that his brothers had destroyed the kittens to hurt him.

Now the broken slats of the porch hung in disarray; many were missing, giving the house the appearance of a jack-o-lantern. Storms of past years had ripped shingles off the roof. Some were completely gone, others clung desperately by a nail or two. Sadness seized Amanda. She missed her friend now more than ever. Buddy's parents were gone, too. They'd been killed in a head-on crash with a drunk driver when he was only sixteen.

She turned away from the house to cut through Mr. Day's apple orchard—at least Mr. Day's idea of an orchard: approximately forty trees, his pride and joy. His apple cider was well-known across the rez, and he cared for his trees in a way that he never had for anything else, including his wife and sons. The trees were dead, joining the house in years of sad neglect.

Amanda cleared the woods farther from the cabin than she had expected. She had forgotten familiar landmarks, or they had changed. She was tired and cold. The wind had picked up and changed direction again, coming directly off the lake. It tugged at her jacket and rearranged her hair. Amanda shivered and hugged herself. Spending the rest of the afternoon by the fireplace with her unfinished book and a mug of hot apple cider sounded good to her. She turned up her jacket collar and headed directly into the wind and toward the warmth of the cabin.

# Chapter 4

A few days later, Amanda woke with a nagging sense that something was about to happen, or maybe that she'd forgotten something she should have done. A quick mental check for any unfinished business to explain the disquiet brought nothing. She shook her head to rid herself of the heavy sleep that clung to her. Even with a conscious effort to ignore the premonition, restlessness drove her out of the cabin by mid morning. The air was chilly with early spring. Amanda turned toward the pond, which had quickly become her favorite spot—again.

Uncle Hobo, Grandma's brother who lived with the family at the cabin off and on for most of his adult life, walked with her as her feet moved over the path. She smiled as she felt him now, accompanying her as surely as he had some thirty years ago. Hobo, as he was known on the reservation, had been one of Amanda's favorite people. He seemed to enjoy her young company as well. Early on summer mornings the two of them would grab tin measuring cups from the pantry and head for the pond to collect the sweet wild strawberries that grew there. Anyone fortunate enough to be at the cabin when they returned would be invited to enjoy the berries with thick, sweet, still-warm cream scooped off the top of that morning's milk.

*Slipping her free hand easily into her great uncle's crinkled, dry one, Amanda squinted up at Gram's brother. He was the oldest person Amanda knew—probably even as old as God, she thought. Hobo was very thin and stood ramrod straight. He never seemed to be in a hurry, but always walked like he was on his way to someplace special. Amanda tried to walk like him, stretching her little legs as far as she could. He kept his long white hair tied at the back of his neck in a ponytail and held by a brown, leather strip. As he walked, Amanda watched his ponytail bounce on his back with a life of its own. She tossed her head from side to side, feeling her braids hit against the sides of her shoulders. Sometimes she could talk mom into a ponytail, but not too often. Her hair liked to slip out of the tail and look "lazy" as Mom called it—better to have it in braids so it would behave.*

*Amanda fought scarves and hats, just like Uncle Hobo did. Any time Amanda got the sniffles, Mom would say, "See, that's what you get for not listening to me and going without your scarf." Although most of the men on the reservation wore caps of some kind, even in summer, Hobo remained hatless in all kinds of weather, and he never ever got the sniffles.*

*Whenever Grandma expected Hobo at the cabin Amanda would sit on an old wooden stool and watch for him from the kitchen window. She felt a thrill when he'd finally appear, an apparition forming out of the dusk itself. In winter, with red nose and cheeks and twinkling black eyes, he teased his sister in Ojibwe when she scolded him for being out in the cold without what she considered proper winter attire: a hat. Amanda never tired of watching them play out this game.*

Amanda never knew her great uncle by any name other than Hobo, although she was sure it was a nickname. Nor did she ever find out where he went when he disappeared for short periods of time. She did think it strange that grandmother never seemed concerned about or surprised by Hobo's comings and goings.

The ancient one spoke mostly old Ojibwe, with a smattering of English mixed in. This strange language confused young Amanda. When he talked to her, she would gaze intensely into his brown, wrinkled face that looked a lot like the prunes grandma ate, searching for clues. She knew that what he was saying was important, but she was baffled by the code. He was always patient, repeating his words and using exaggerated hand-signs in an attempt to communicate with her. Maybe that's why she loved him so much. She never felt like she was a bother to him. As she got older, Amanda came to realize that her great-uncle was considered a spiritual man on the reservation, and that his disappearances from Gram's house had to do with him going where he was needed. She understood that when someone requested him he had to go. One thing always puzzled her: how did he know he was needed? He couldn't read or write, not that he ever received any mail anyway, nor did he have access to a phone—there were none on the reservation. Not quite sure if it was possible, Amanda suspected that he just *knew*.

She finally reached the pond and stood watching the ripples that formed at the edge where the ice had started to melt. Trees near the pond were reflected in the choppy water, and they undulated in a weird dance as the water worked its way to the shore. A sudden movement off to her right pulled Amanda's attention from the hypnotic display. Amazed, she watched an eagle settle herself on a branch of the nearest pine.

She was huge. Amanda had never been this close to an eagle before, except at the Milwaukee zoo. Her heart pounded against her ribs as she watched her spread her wings to their full width, showing off spotted feathers on their undersides. The hair on her arms raised. She realized the eagle, her head jutting forward, her great curved beak opening and closing as if in mute conversation, was watching her.

"Do eagles attack people?" Amanda whispered, half hoping the sound would frighten off the great bird and half afraid it would cause her to come at her. She tried unsuccessfully to rein in her heart as it raced. Had she heard stories about eagles and humans? Amanda couldn't decide if she should run or stand still. Before she could do either, the eagle pushed herself off the branch and swooped, with a noisy rush of wings towards her. Unable to duck or even blink, Amanda held her breath. The eagle flew directly overhead, touching her only with the air disturbed by her swift passage. Before she could turn to follow the eagle's flight, Amanda heard the high-pitched scream of a dying rabbit and felt its pain as it fell victim to sharp claws. By the time she fully turned, the eagle had returned to the sky, with the rabbit clutched talons. Relief for herself, mixed with sadness for the defenseless rabbit, rushed through her. The eagle circled overhead showing off her prize before disappearing beyond the tall pines.

Amanda's gaze left the now empty sky and dropped to the blood-spotted snow where the eagle had just captured its meal. A spotted, dark brown and white tail feather lost by the eagle lay on the snow. Amanda reached for the feather. Her hand stopped just inches from it as, from a memory, Hobo whispered to her. He reminded her of a time long ago while they were gathering berries, and she had made a similar, wonderful discovery.

*Amanda was watching her great-uncle's face as he spoke to her in his Ojibwe-English singsong voice. They were walking to the pond to pick the small, sweet strawberries that grew there. On an impulse, she pulled her hand from his and skipped ahead to the edge of the water. "Uncle Hobo," she squealed and pointed to something that lay on the ground. "Look at what I found! Feathers!"*

*He moved as quickly as his seventy-five-year-old body would allow. Several eagle feathers lay in a small pile half covered by the tall grass. Amanda watched as the Elder put his cup down and took some tobacco from the leather pouch he kept in his pocket. "Asema," he told her. She nodded; she already knew that. He began singing in Ojibwe and offered the tobacco to the four directions, to the sky, and to the ground before sprinkling it around the feathers. The sun slipped behind a cloud. Amanda thought that had to be a good sign, and she smiled at her great-uncle. Singing a thank-you song, he picked up the feathers and again turned in a clockwise direction, stopping at each of the four direction points. When this was done, he offered them to the sky and to the ground, turning left to right, showing the sky what he was holding. Amanda stood by quietly, knowing, without being told, that was what Hobo expected her to do.*

*When his song was finished, Hobo turned to her and used hand motions to explain what happened. She watched him carefully and listened as hard as she could trying to make sense of the Ojibwe and English mix. Even without knowing all the words, she understood that a trade had just taken place, and she felt the glow of pride; she'd been the one to find the feathers—Uncle Hobo was proud too, she could tell.*

Amanda knew what she had to do; she raced back to the cabin. Gasping for breath, she pulled out drawers, opened the doors to cabinets and closets, and peeked behind furniture in a search for tobacco of any kind. She finally located a crushed pack with four cigarettes behind the refrigerator—stale to the point of being dust, but they would do. With the blood pounding in her ears like mini-drums, she ran back to the pond, hoping the feather would still be there, but also afraid that it would be. She realized this discovery was what she had waited for all morning.

Amanda stabbed at the dry cigarette papers with her thumbnails. Her hands were suddenly clumsy; her fingers didn't want to work. "Come on," she breathed. The cigarettes broke open. She sprinkled the tobacco on the ground around the feather, whispering thanks to the eagle. She prayed its spirit understood English and would forgive her ignorance of her ancestors' language. She picked up the feather and lifted it skyward, turning slowly in a clockwise direction. She followed Hobo's example as closely as she could remember it. She felt him here now, helping her do things in the right way. She turned slowly left to right, not surprised at the warmth that began in her hands and flowed downward through her body. Her heart filled with gratitude for this unearned gift; she was unaware of the tears that slid down her face.

Amanda kept the feather near her all day, glancing at it occasionally, expecting it to disappear as if it hadn't really existed. Several times that afternoon she tried to read, but she finally gave up, admitting that her eyes were just skimming over words that didn't have a chance of holding her interest today. She picked up the feather again and examined it. It was almost, but not quite, symmetrical. A slightly larger portion of it lay to the left side of the quill. Amanda shaped her hands into an imaginary fan and decided that the feather had come from the left side of the eagle's tail. "Hmmm, does that have any significance?" she asked the feather, holding it toward the light of the window. "I'll ask Ben and Yemmy tomorrow. They'll tell me what to do with you."

That night, Amanda placed the feather on a small table at the foot of her bed and stood looking at it before crawling under the quilts. Feeling comfort in its closeness, she fell asleep quickly. Sometime near dawn she jerked awake, feeling, rather than hearing, someone or something in her room. Moving quietly, Amanda rolled onto her side and reached for the lamp on the nightstand. Her hand froze in mid air. She held her breath, listening, trying to make sense of a faint rustling sound coming from somewhere inside the room. Confused more than scared, she turned toward the nightstand and gasped. An eagle sat there, clearly visible in the still-dark of the early morning. She shimmered with a light coming from inside her like the old TV lamps that sat atop the first televisions on the rez.

The eagle stood exactly where she had placed the feather, and Amanda wondered if she was there to claim what she had lost. She held the same posture she had that morning in the pine tree: wings outspread, head jutting forward. Her beak was moving in mock conversation, except this time, incredibly, she *was* speaking.

Amanda clutched the quilts and pulled them up to her neck, hitting her chin with her knuckles. Even as she pulled them close, she realized what little protection they offered. She hadn't felt this kind of fear since she'd been a child listening to Gram's *jiibik* stories and she saw shadows moving in the corners of her bedroom. She willed herself not to faint, tried to steady her short, choppy breathing. Somewhere in the night—or maybe in her mind—she heard the cry of a dying rabbit, and she realized there was no escape for her either.

How had she gotten into the room? Amanda was afraid to take her eyes off her to see if the window was open. Stunned, Amanda continued to stare at the eagle until her eyes hurt—they were so dry, she was afraid to blink, even if she could. The eagle continued speaking—not in "Eagle" (if there was such a thing) or Ojibwe, but in English.

"*Nishiime,* Little Sister," she repeated, her soft feminine voice belying her fearsome posture, "I am Migizi; the spirit of Migizi sent by the Creator who lets me be visible. I have been with you for a long time, and I will always be with you. Do not be afraid of me. I have a message for you. Our Creator is pleased with your life. You represent him well. But he asks you to do more. He wants you to move outside of yourself and respond to your people. There is much you can do; many ways you can help. Look around. See what He sees. With His help, you have survived tests and grown stronger. He wants you to know there will be more. Each time you succeed, you move a step closer to becoming what He wants you to be. Every day you become stronger. The Grandfather wants you to understand that He is pleased that you are living up to his plan. Your needs will be met by meeting the needs of others."

Amanda swallowed past a lump that had lodged itself in her throat, "What does that mean? Why me?"

"*Nishiime,*" the eagle said again, "Do not be afraid." She flapped her wings as if she was about to take off, then settled them close to her body and pulled her head in. She seemed to be trying to look less threatening. "You must listen to me now. And listen carefully."

Amanda couldn't move. Panic began in her lower body and worked its way to her voice. "I'm dreaming, I must be dreaming," she squeaked. "This can't be!" she shouted, not sure if she had actually spoken or if the words hadn't moved beyond her thought of them.

"You are awake, *Nishiime.* Now, listen carefully while I speak. I will not be allowed to come to you like this again for a while," the eagle said. Through a haze, Amanda heard the eagle continue to speak of tests, past and present. She assured Amanda of the Grandfather's favor with her life. "Gifts and honors will come," she told her. "You need only to trust the direction of your life." After while, the eagle sat without further movement, even her beak was still. Yet it seemed to Amanda that she continued to speak, repeating herself often, as if speaking to a child.

Amanda did her best to concentrate on what she was hearing. She ignored the thought that inserted itself continually into her mind: that eagles can*not* speak. She felt a familiar frustration from long ago when she had stuggled to understand uncle Hobo's communication. She understood the importance of what was being said; it was the delivery that was incomprehensible. In spite of the terror she felt, and without any awareness of how or when it happened, Amanda fell asleep.

# Chapter 5

Amanda groaned and squeezed her eyes tight to keep out the sun that was forcing its way through the east window. Giving up, she threw back her covers and stumbled to the end of her bed. She carefully picked up the feather and caressed it, remembering the wildest dream she'd ever had. No way could an eagle have actually appeared in her room in the middle of the night and spoken to her. Maybe the medicine for depression that she was still taking was too strong or, worse, maybe the isolation was getting to her. The dream clung to her all morning. Several times Amanda felt something hover near, heard the fluttering of invisible wings. Every noise made her jump. From the corner of her eye, she would glimpse shadows ducking quickly behind her. Every nerve was raw. Even the kitchen clock teased her, moving in slow motion. By 9:30 she had waited long enough. The Vincents would be up; Elders always got up early.

She had barely lifted her arm to knock when the door opened. "Come in, come in," Ben said cheerfully. "We've been expecting you. Knew you'd be by today, didn't we, Yemmy?"

"Gosh, yes. Before we went to bed last night Ben insisted on making sweet rolls. Said we'd have company today. He used to be able to do that all the time. Lately started thinking he'd lost his knack for intuitin' guests . . . along with his *manly* figure." Yemmy had a wicked cackle when she wanted.

Ben growled and patted his rounded belly. "You don't mind cuddlin' up to this on cold nights, old girl."

Yemmy blew through her pursed lips and waved her hand in his direction. She moved slowly to her chair. "I don't need your help, dirty ole man. Keep your hands to yourself."

"You must be feeling pretty good today, Yemmy. You're walking better," Amanda said.

"She is, ain't she? Must be this warm weather," Ben agreed. "I noticed she ain't been so ornery!" He snuck a glance at his wife.

"Old man!" Yemmy scolded. "You! You're the ornery one around here." Ben snickered as he placed his sweet rolls and tub of Land O'Lakes on the table. He poured three cups full of strong-smelling coffee.

Amanda sipped the steaming liquid and nibbled half-heartedly on a hot roll while deciding how to bring the conversation around to her dream. With the sunshine this morning, she felt more than a little foolish. But knowing she needed the advice of those who understood the old ways, she took a deep breath and plunged in. The Elders watched her as she told them the dream as she remembered it. She again felt like the little girl who, years ago, would sit in her parents' bright kitchen and tell them about a nightmare she'd had. The telling dissolved the leftover fear. *"Like a dream-catcher,"* Gram whispered in her mind. Her parents never laughed at her; neither did Ben and Yemmy.

Yemmy patted Amanda's hand. "What a wonderful gift, my girl." She looked at Ben for confirmation.

"Yes, indeed." He spoke quietly to Yemmy in Ojibwe and she nodded. "We think you should visit Noah," he said to Amanda in English. "He'll know what it means. I'll call him right now. Any luck, he'll see us today."

Yemmy smiled proudly at Amanda. "Ben will help you," she said. "So will Noah."

Ben used the telephone in the living room. Amanda heard snatches of him speaking Ojibwe. Waiting for the verdict, she chewed her thumbnail, a habit she thought she'd broken.

"Why me?" she asked Yemmy.

The old lady shrugged. "It ain't up to us to question the Creator's ways," she said. "I reckon it happened for a reason." She shrugged again and adjusted her glasses to look more closely at her young companion.

"I'm not sure," Amanda grimaced. "Yeah, I guess." She sipped her coffee, which was getting cold. She jumped when Ben spoke. "Noah's leaving this afternoon, but he can see us if we go right now." Ben's eyes sparkled. "He says to bring the feather with you."

"It's in the car," Amanda said. "Who is this Noah, anyhow?" she asked.

"He was one of your Uncle Hobo's students. I'm guessin' he'll be good as Hobo one day."

"Maybe even better!" Yemmy jumped in. Her smiled showed she was pretty fond of this Noah.

"What will he do for us?" Amanda looked from one elder to the other. "Will you two stay there with me?"

"That depends, my girl. We'll see what Noah tells us. Finish up your coffee, and let's go," Ben said. He began wrapping the sweet rolls in tinfoil. "Better if you follow us out there, Mandy. That way if Noah wants you to stay awhile, we'll all have our own ways back home." Ben was urging Yemmy into her coat.

"It will be good to see that young man again," Yemmy said. "Ben, grab up some meat from the freezer, will you? No tellin' when he last ate a decent meal."

"Oh, but she's a fusser," Ben told Amanda shaking his head. "Can't stop motherin', even with all the kids gone. She mothers me 'most to death some days. I believe she'd care for ever' stray that came by if she had her way." By now Ben was holding the kitchen door open.

"Well, why not? And I'm fixin' to tell Noah you said he was a stray." Yemmy said.

"Hey!" Ben scolded. "You do that and you'll walk home, old lady." He winked at Amanda.

Amanda followed the elder couple west, several miles past Winky's. They finally turned off the highway onto a bumpy clay road that narrowed with each twist and turn. They turned again onto a red clay driveway. For all she could tell, they'd traveled in a big circle. "If a person didn't know where she was going, she wouldn't find this place," Amanda told her Escort. She was grateful for the elder couple; with all the twists and turns and the unmarked roads, who knows where she would have ended up? She hoped that if they left her here she could find her way back. "Maybe I should have dropped cookie crumbs," she mumbled to herself.

Just as she began to wonder if they were lost, she spotted a small cabin. A medium-sized, shaggy dog of questionable ancestry lay on the small, slanted porch. He lifted his head and barked once and watched until the cars stopped. When he recognized the Vincents, he wagged his tail and moved to allow the two-leggeds to enter the house. Before Ben could knock, the inside door opened and the screen was pushed outward by a dark, well-muscled arm covered by a red flannel shirtsleeve rolled to the elbow. A deep laugh accompanied, "*Aaniin. Aaniin ezhi ayaayeg?*"

Ben stepped back to allow Yemmy to enter the cabin first. "*Nimino ayaamin,*" he answered.

The flannel-covered arm went around Yemmy's shoulders, and a long black braid swung into view as the still shadowed man bent down to hug the elder woman.

"*Giin dash?*" Yemmy grumbled and hugged back.

"*Geget!*"

Ben motioned Amanda to step in front of him. A large hand grasped Amanda's in a warm handshake.

"Hello! *Boozhoo. Aaniin, ezhi ayaayan?*"

"*Boozhoo,*" she responded with the Ojibwe greeting word. She liked his handshake, felt a strength and confidence that made her feel safe even without knowing the man. Amanda sensed a solidness as she slipped by him into his living room. She glanced around, feeling the comfort in the spartan, tidy home. It lacked any feminine touch, she decided.

Noah ushered them into his kitchen, which was tiny in comparison to Amanda's. Ben made introductions in English, then addressed Noah in Ojibwe. Amanda saw him slip Noah a box of tobacco and felt Noah glance at her. Ben talked a while longer, gesturing more than once with his lips toward Amanda. Then Noah smiled at her and nodded to a chair with his chin. "*Namadabig.* Please sit. *Miigwich* for coming." Then the inevitable, "Coffee?"

Yemmy handed Noah a frozen white package and then began unwrapping the sweet rolls. Ben grabbed butter from the fridge and a knife from the counter and put them down in front of Amanda. He then excused himself, explaining that what he needed to tell Noah was more respectfully done in the native tongue. He spoke quietly in Ojibwe, fingering the edge of the table, not looking at anyone. Amanda wished again that she had learned the language. She studied the room, pretending the exclusion didn't bother her. She nibbled her thumbnail, knowing she wouldn't have anything left if the discussion went on much longer. Several times she felt Noah look at her. Between his glances, she watched him; she had the impression that she should know this man. With little effort she'd catch the hint of a younger, thinner face framed by shoulder-length hair passing gauze-like over his. It appeared and disappeared when she'd blink.

Feeling her confusion, Noah smiled in her direction. She felt heat rise on her face.

She'd done some pretty good damage to her nail by the time Ben and Yemmy got up to leave. They assured her that she was in good hands and that Noah was more than happy to listen and help.

"Well, Amanda," Noah said as he refilled their coffee cups. "You've had quite an experience. Want to tell me about it?" He settled himself into a chair directly across from her.

"Didn't Ben tell you?" She didn't mean to sound so abrupt.

"Sure, but I'd rather hear it from you," he ignored her tone. "I want to understand how you felt when it happened. Ben wasn't there and you were. I want to hear it everything—sounds, feelings. . . ."

Without knowing she was going to ask she blurted, "Why do I feel like I should know you?"

The corners of his eyes had permanent crinkles that deepened when he smiled. Quietly he said, "You do know me, Manda, but I'm not surprised you don't remember. I was a couple years behind you in school, and I quit when they wanted me to repeat the ninth grade for the second time."

"School was like jail for me," he said. "So it didn't do much good to be there, and the good Sisters kept telling me I was a dummy, so pretty soon I started to believe them, I guess." He paused and took a long drink of coffee. "Besides," he chuckled, "You were too interested in my cousin to notice any other guy."

"Brownie's your cousin?" She struggled to fit this information with the gauzy face that lit over Noah's again. She felt something slip into place. "A singer!" she said. "You sang at the school drum, right?"

His smile broadened. "Uh-huh. Funny isn't it, that I could remember all those songs but not my prayers or the times table?" he laughed. "Remember Sister Mary Joseph? She would yell at me: 'How can you remember so many songs but have zero (he made a large circle with his hands) in your head when it comes to other things?'" He spoke in Sister Mary Jo's high, quavery voice. Amanda laughed with him.

"I guess I tried her patience more than once," he continued. He got up and poured them each another cup of coffee. "I'd sit at my desk with my eyes closed and imagine myself at the drum, so when she called on me I didn't have the foggiest notion of what she was talking about. Cracked me a good many times with that ruler of hers," he rubbed his knuckles chuckling. "Guess she thought a rap with that stick would help my attention span. Never did though." His laugh was infectious.

Amanda enjoyed the Sister School memories. "Junior Brown!" she squealed. "I remember you now. You should have gotten an A+ in imitations. I loved your Ed Sullivan's 'Really big *shew*,' and especially your Father Heenan's 'That will be three Hail Marys, and don't do it again.' You were *really* good!"

"Yeah, but not very nice," he said. "Clowning made it easier to be at school. Only went cuz of my ma."

Amanda laughed. "I remember one Christmas when you were one of the Wise Men in the program, and you used Father's voice when you put your gift in the manger. Man, we all cracked up, and so did the audience. I was one of the angels, and we could see Father off-stage, and his face got red and puffy like his collar was on too tight. Remember that?"

Noah shifted in his chair, lifted and rubbed his right buttock. "How could I forget? Father didn't have much of a sense of humor. Kept me out of any more school plays though."

He topped off their coffee. "Well, back to business. I hate to rush you, but I gotta take off soon." He saw the disappointment on her face. "I'll be back the beginning of next week. Tell me about Migizi, and we'll talk when you come see me again on Tuesday."

Amanda kneaded her left fingers with her right hand as she retold what she had shared with the Vincents earlier. She couldn't help feeling foolish, like she was telling a dream she believed in.

"Migizi called you 'Sister'? Ben said you were special."

Amanda blushed. "What does it all mean? The eagle kept saying things about tests, and honors. . . . I can't really believe I'm sitting here telling you an eagle talked to me!"

"Migizi," he interrupted. "Call it by its name."

"Migizi," she corrected herself, "talked about past and future tests. I'm sorry I don't remember the exact words. I *heard* the words, you know, but they didn't register—I mean, it didn't make sense."

He nodded. "Yeah, I see that, but you shoulda known Migizi wasn't going to hurt you."

"I know that *now*, but in the middle of the night?" she shrugged. "Anyway, who'd expect to find an eagle sitting in her room *talking? I* sure didn't. I was scared and trying to figure out if I was dreaming or not. It felt real, but it didn't. I just don't know." She shrugged and looked out the window.

"That's okay. The message is more important than the words," Noah said. "It sounds to me like you've been tested already. We're all sent tests, everyday. And most of the time we pass them, but there's always more." He squinted his eyes and stared at her and tapped the edge of his bottom lip with his index finger, a habit she now remembered.

"What do you think it means?" she asked.

"I don't know," he shrugged. "Only the Grandfather knows for sure. Maybe you're being tested now, maybe rewarded, or it could any number of things. Do you have Miigwan with you?" he asked.

"The feather? Yes, in the car. Should I get it?" Anticipation had already moved Amanda from her chair. She retrieved the feather from under the sun visor of the Escort and held it upright by the quill when she handed it to Noah. He took it from her and stroked it gently before placing it beside a large half-shell, a braid of sweet grass, a spray of cedar, and a bundle of sage tied with red twine that had replaced their coffee cups on the table. "It's good to bless a feather within four days," Noah said. "Take off your glasses and jewelry," he said.

She removed her watch and earrings but hesitated at her glasses—a habit; she hated the way people had always stared. Then she realized Noah already knew about her mismatched eyes—she hadn't worn glasses in grade school. It had never seemed to matter to anyone on the reservation. She slipped her glasses into the pocket of her jacket slung across the back of her chair.

The blessing was simple and fast. First Noah smudged himself, then Amanda, with sage. He prayed in Ojibwe, and repeated the prayers in English so she could understand. "It's a beautiful feather, Manda. You're definitely recognized in the spirit world," he told her while he carefully placed the ceremonial materials, except for the shell, in a soft-sided, brown leather bag. He put the shell on the windowsill to cool.

"And that means?" she asked, wondering how many times she'd asked that already.

"Don't know. Maybe it means you're now being called on to share with others what you've learned, or it could mean you need to get ready to learn something yourself." He shrugged. "I can't really say. But one thing's for sure: you're on your way to becoming fully human." His eyes crinkled when he smiled. "What do *you* think it means?" he asked. "That's more important than what I think."

She stared at him a full minute, unable to answer. "I don't know. That's why I came to you."

"Manda," he said, his voice softening, "you were sent to me for a purpose, same as Migizi was sent to you, but only you will be able to figure that out. I can work with you, give suggestions, pray with you, but I can't tell you what you need to do or how to do it. Only the Grandfather can lead you to that understanding."

Again disappointment clouded her face. Noah reached across the table and laid his strong hand over hers. "Come back Tuesday. Meantime, pray! Grandfather didn't bring you this far to abandon you. Be patient, and don't rush to find answers; they'll be wrong if you force it. But don't fight it, either. Give yourself a chance. You're loved in spirit world; I can tell." At her questioning look he added, "Migizi wouldn't have come to visit you otherwise. That doesn't happen to just anybody, you know. I only know of two others who have been given such a gift." He stood and smiled. "Cheer up, and don't worry. The answers will come when the time is right."

She got up and reached for her jacket. Noah came around the table and held it for her. "I'm honored that Ben and Yemmy brought you to me. Here, wait a sec!" He left the room and returned with a red cotton scarf. He wrapped it around the feather. "The red will protect it," he said handing it to her. "Take good care of it, and it will take good care of you. Bead the quill if you want. Hang it on the east wall when you're home, and take it with you when you travel. You know about putting it away when you're on your moon cycle?" Amanda nodded. She remembered that both her mother and grandmother removed or covered any eagle feathers during each month.

Noah and his four-legged friend walked Amanda to her Escort. He held the door open and leaned down and gave her directions back to the main road. His braids fell into the car. She could smell wood smoke and sage. It reminded her of Gramma and Hobo. His willingness to help touched her deeply, and she wondered how to thank him even though she was leaving with more questions than she had come with.

"Think you can find your way back to the highway?" Noah asked as he shut the door.

She nodded and started the car. All she wanted was for Tuesday to hurry up and get there!

# Chapter 6

Noah had recognized Amanda as soon as he spotted her standing on his small front porch waiting to enter his cabin. She was older, but she was recognizable. Imagine that, after all these years! When Ben had called to ask if he could bring someone by, he hadn't given a name, and Noah hadn't asked. Ben had only said a young woman needed some spiritual advice, more spiritual than Ben felt he could give. Even as Noah was getting ready to ask if their visit could wait until he got back next week, he felt a familiar gentle push from a stronger force. "Okay, if you can come right away," came out instead. A faint, somewhat electrical sensation began sizzling somewhere above his head. Seconds later it spread into his chest and out to his arms and legs. The skin on his arms rose in gooseflesh; the hair on his neck rose as if danger was close. This was no danger, of course. He'd learned early on that it meant "pay attention." This sensation had been part of his life since he'd been a teenager, and it directed his behavior then, as it did now. It compelled him to tell Ben that he'd see them if they'd come without delay.

The Bronco was already packed, he rationalized, and their visit would delay him for just a short time. No problem, really. Had Noah not had the gentle shove from his guardian spirit, it would still have been hard to say no to Ben and Yemmy. They'd become his family after Hobo died. For the past fifteen years or so, Yemmy had seen to it that he had something sweet to eat. His fondness for chocolate was Yemmy's favorite temptation whenever they invited him to eat with them.

Twenty minutes after the call, the three of them stood on his porch, ready to enter the space he shared with Niijii, his only companion. His best friend was black and shaggy, and smelled like dog. Noah deliberately ignored the signs of age that had recently started creeping up on his four-legged housemate. He figured that by refusing to recognize the inevitable he could delay it a while longer.

Amanda's story had moved him. He'd known two others who had been visited by Migizi. One was his teacher, Hobo, and the other a young woman on the Flambeau reserve who'd gained great spiritual direction and had clearly been chosen by the Grandfather as a liaison between him and the earth people. Kate was strong, physically and spiritually. She was well chosen and would serve the Creator in a good way. Noah was proud to be able to work with her on occasion. Amanda was different. She wasn't ready to take up the path, although it seemed clear to Noah that was Migizi's message. Her gifts—her promise—scared her, he thought.

Brownie's old girlfriend! Amanda was the only female Brownie had ever shown real affection for, except Paula, the woman he eventually married. When they were kids, Noah ("Junior"), and his cousin Donald ("Brownie") were closer than most brothers. Brownie spent more time at Noah's house than his own—he'd even called Noah's mother "Mom" from the time he was about three years old. Brownie's dad and brothers never seemed to care if he was home or not, so neither did Brownie. When Brownie was old enough to notice girls, Amanda *almost* replaced Noah in his life. That was okay with Noah. Around that same time Hobo had asked Noah's parents for permission to teach their son traditional spiritual ways. They agreed. Noah had special gifts, Hobo had told his folks, but to use them he needed direction and guidance. So when Brownie started hanging around with Amanda, Noah spent more and more time with his new teacher. Noah's mom had always told him that he was different, but it took him a while to realize that he knew things that other kids didn't, that he could *feel* houses, situations, even people. The invisible friends that other kids had were not invisible to Noah. When he was little, this scared him, but with Hobo's help Noah learned to appreciate his special gift. Even after new interests kept them apart, the two cousins remained best friends.

Brownie was fourteen when he first noticed Amanda was a girl, but because he was so shy, it was a year before he ever spoke to her about anything other than school. When all the kids went to Weleski's to hang out, Brownie would sit alone in back of the long rectangular room on the Coca-Cola machine, staring at his shoes like he was trying to figure out what they were and how they came to be attached to the end of his legs. He'd never join in the joking. He listened to the others tease and watched as they experimented touching the opposite sex by pushing and shoving. Blushing, Brownie would only smile at the antics. But when the two boys were alone, he'd share his heart with Noah, the only person he trusted.

Noah usually resisted teasing his sensitive cousin, but one day he asked Brownie if he and Mandy ever actually spoke to each other or if they just looked at each other when they were alone together. Brownie punched him in the arm, grinned, but didn't answer. Noah liked the way Brownie's eyes sparkled when he talked about Amanda.

One day Brownie asked Noah to help him find a special birthday gift for Amanda's fifteenth birthday. After careful consideration, they selected a small cross that was different than anything they'd seen before—it had tiny white and green gems (*genuine* fake, they teased) that sparkled along each arm. In the center, where the arms came together, was a hole. They discovered that when they'd put their eye to it, they could read the entire Lord's Prayer. How could the prayer be written so small? they wondered. Brownie carried the cross in his pocket for almost two months past Amanda's birthday before he was brave enough to give it to her—fearing, Noah guessed, that she might not like it. She loved it, of course. Noah often saw it around her neck. Even back then he felt warmth for the girl who showed signs of caring for his cousin as much as he did.

When Amanda and Brownie got together, others didn't exist. Their friends teased them that, even in a crowd, the two could communicate without speaking. Everyone knew they would marry someday and have a bunch of little Mandys and Brownies running barefoot around the rez. But shortly after their high school graduation Mandy left the reservation for college and returned only to visit her folks. Curiously the bond they had wasn't able to stretch that far. Brownie never let on that he suspected she wouldn't come back. Until the news hit the rez that she'd married, he waited. Word of her marriage finally convinced Brownie that he was waiting for nothing.

*"That half-breed married a white man," Brownie spat at Noah. He turned on his heel and stomped away. Noah couldn't believe his ears. "Half-breed" was about the worst thing that Brownie could say about anybody. Noah wanted to go after him, but he knew his cousin had to work this out by himself. An hour later it became too much for him, and he gave up worrying at home and began searching the reservation from one end to the other with no luck. Three days later he came across Brownie's rusty Rambler sitting empty in the ditch on the slough road. It tilted at a serious angle; the driver's door hung open. The inside of the car reeked of the aftermath of too much booze. Brownie stayed drunk for two weeks.*

*He never mentioned Amanda's name to Noah again until he insisted that his
first daughter be named Amanda Ashley. They called the girl Ashley, at Paula's
insistence.*

Paula Newman was sixteen and already had a child when she and Brownie
became a couple. Despite a fourteen-year age difference, they married and had
three children of their own almost immediately. Paula doted on Brownie, but that
didn't make him happy. Brownie had at least two affairs that everyone on the
reservation knew about during his short marriage. Noah had tried to counsel his
cousin about responsibility, but he was rebuffed with a cold stare and a hard curse.
Brownie's death a couple of months ago left Paula alone again—this time with four
young children.

While he and Ben had been talking that afternoon, Noah had noticed Amanda
looking at him. Inwardly he grinned, enjoying that she was trying to figure out
who he was. Gone was the skinny boy from catechism class, and he wore his long
hair in two braids now. His Prince Valiant hair of grade school days—the nuns
insisted their boys have short hair—he left behind when he left school. He was
surprised that she remembered him anyway. His name was different too: everyone called him Junior at school; even the Sisters called him that. Hobo was the one
who started calling him Noah. The old man laughed and said that *Junior* might
not give too much confidence to those who came to him for ceremonies. Noah
wanted to, but didn't dare, ask if Hobo was a confidence-building name. But because people respected Hobo, Noah's name change stuck, something that didn't
happen often on the rez. Many adults still bore the horror of names that had been
given to them in childhood due to some long-forgotten circumstance. Names like
Duck-Eye, Goose, Johnny Cake, and John-Pork were common around the rez.

The circle works, Noah thought, as he threw a small sack of sandwiches on
the back seat and climbed into his Bronco, patting the seat beside him. Panting
hard, Niijii partially jumped, partially lumbered onto the seat and looked at Noah
expectantly.

"It's amazing, Niijii. Amanda's great uncle was my teacher, and now here she
is, looking to me for the same kind of direction I got from Hobo. Things always
come full circle if we wait long enough."

Niijii whimpered agreement and settled down for the ride to Paula's.

# Chapter 7

Amanda wandered around the cabin, in and out of every room, searching a way to make the evening pass more quickly. She'd pick up something, puzzle as to why it was in her hand, put it down, and move to something new. She made a peanut butter sandwich and left it, having eaten only one bite, somewhere in the house. Around midnight she wrote a list of things to do to keep busy over the next few days. Visiting Annie was first. A quick glance at the phone book proved fruitless; either Annie didn't have a phone or she had an unlisted number. "Never mind," she mumbled as she put the directory away. Winky would have the information. She grinned knowing he could not only give her the directions to Annie's house but her minute-by-minute schedule if asked for it.

Uncle Dan made the list too. Maybe he'd tell her something about Noah, Amanda thought. Even if he couldn't, she was eager to see him again. *Note to office* was written below Dan's name. It wouldn't do for her office colleagues to think she had frozen to death in the past month. She stayed up past her normal bedtime to be as sleepy as possible when she finally crawled into bed and wrapped her grandmother's quilts around her. It didn't work. As tired as she was, her mind replayed the day. She practiced the relaxation technique she had learned from Gloria, but that didn't help either. Thoughts of Ben and Yemmy, Noah, the eagle, the feather blessing, fears of tests, honor, and responsibilities whirled through her head. When she finally drifted off, colored eagles flew in and out of her room. A turquoise and yellow Migizi sat on the night table and spoke to her in a mixture of Ojibwe and English in a voice that sounded first like Hobo, then like Noah, telling her things she couldn't understand.

Saturday was bright and cheery, unlike Amanda. She never did function well after too little sleep. She sighed deeply. "The sun is shining; today is a good day for visiting old friends," she tried to convince herself. What she really wanted to do was crawl back under the covers, but she knew that wasn't the way to get healthy. A young Amanda had enjoyed helping Mom in the kitchen, but she hadn't done much cooking since moving to Milwaukee. She would tackle it today. She decided to make gingersnap cookies, Annie's favorite when they were kids. Amanda hoped they still were.

She warily eyed the sagging steps as she climbed to Annie's porch, hoping the creaking was from the cold. She knocked on the weather-beaten door and stepped back. She stuffed her empty hand into her pocket to control the urge to pick at the blue paint pulling away from the door in brittle chips. She waited, then rapped again, harder this time. Amanda was turning to leave when she heard footsteps.

The smile on her face failed when Annie opened the door. She'd obviously woken her cousin from a nap: puffy bags under her eyes dominated Annie's thin face. Her once-shiny ebony hair was dull and stringy. She still wore it pulled back, held by two barrettes. The style that once showed off her green doe-eyes and wonderful cheekbones now made her look skeletal. She wore a faded pink chenille bathrobe with large red and blue flowers that was held together by a leather belt, cinched at her waist, and blue plastic flip-flops. "Classic tacky" is how they would have described this look years ago.

"Heard you was around," Annie said, putting her thin arms around Amanda. "Thought maybe you decided not to come see me." Even her smiled looked tired. "Come on in."

"Not in a million years, Annie. Things got crazy in my former life, and I needed some quiet time to myself. I'm getting a handle on things now, though," she added in response to Annie's raised eyebrows.

"Your *former* life? Does that mean you're not going back to Milwaukee?"

"No, huh-uh. That's just an expression. I've got to go back. I still have a job there. But how are *you* doing?" Amanda handed over the coffee can filled with gingersnaps.

"Fair-to-middlin'," Annie said in her best Winky imitation. "Come in; sit down." She opened the can.

"Oh! My favorites! You remembered. Thanks!" Annie piled the cookies on a plate and set in it the middle of the table. "Coffee to go with these?"

"If you don't mind, what else you got? All I've done since I've been here is drink coffee. Talk about a caffeine high! My hair could curl naturally, no mousse needed!"

"Yeah," Annie laughed, "Life on the rez. Everyone keeps a pot going. Okay then, how about some apple cider instead—hot?"

"Great! I think I can deal with gingersnaps and cider," Amanda answered. "Sounds like Grandma's house."

Annie nodded as she shuffled over to the stove and poured cider into a pan. She dug in the cupboard and came up with a half-dozen cinnamon sticks. "So what have you been up to, Manda?"

Amanda skimmed over the last fifteen years barely mentioning her marriage and leaving out anything about the accident that sent her back here. Annie didn't look like she needed to hear about "last straws."

"Uh-huh, we was all surprised to hear you married a white guy. Wondered why you never brought him around the rez. What—he didn't like Indians?" Annie threw Amanda a sideways glance like she used to when she pretended she was teasing, but she really wasn't. She placed a steaming mug of cider in front of Amanda.

"No, I don't think he did. He treated me like—I don't know—like a bastard child, I guess. He mostly let me know I wasn't good enough for him. I don't know if he wanted a slave or if he was embarrassed by me. He sure didn't want a wife." She shook her head. "He wouldn't take me anyplace with him, expected me to stay home and take care of his castle while he did whatever he wanted, which was to visit bars, whenever he wanted. When I didn't . . ." she pursed her lips and dropped the subject, remembering Winky saying that Neil used to beat Annie.

"No kids, huh?" Annie asked. She dunked a gingersnap into her cider and sucked on it.

"Huh-uh. No time. I'm a career woman," Amanda teased in their old British accent, but Annie didn't laugh.

An awkward silence sat between them while the two women sipped cider and munched gingersnaps.

"How 'bout you?" Amanda asked finally. "Your kids are all grown by now. That must feel good." Annie hauled herself heavily from the kitchen chair and went into the living room. The backs of her flip-flops scraped the tired linoleum, making it sound like she was barely moving. She returned with a handful of pictures. She passed each photo in turn to Amanda.

"Here's Larry, my baby. Big baby, huh? He's nineteen and finally in his last year in high school. We was never sure he would really graduate, but looks like he's gonna make it. Wants to *hang out* this summer, he says, and go into the service in the fall. He's decided Navy, like his Uncle Melvin. Maggie, the twin, lives with me—off and on, mostly off these days," Annie chuckled. "You know how that goes. She's twenty now, pretty, and she knows it. Works part-time at the Ironwood newspaper and part-time at the rectory. We only got a part-time priest anyway nowdays. He's got a Indian parish up in Watersmeet too—that's where he stays mostly. Mark, the other twin, is at the Tech school up by Rhinelander studying auto body. He says there's always rez-rods in need of a good body man, so he'll never be outta work." The women laughed.

"He's got that right," Amanda said, remembering how her dad used a clothes hanger to keep the trunk of their old Plymouth shut, and how the front bumper hung inches lower on one side than the other.

"Neil Jr. lives on the reservation," Annie continued. "He and his woman have one of those new HUD houses down on East River Road. Ella, that's my oldest girl, married herself an accountant and lives in Duluth." Her voice trailed off wearily. "She got herself a good life." Annie sighed and took back the pictures Amanda handed her.

"What a nice family! Sooo, what do you do with yourself now, Annie? Your days must be pretty quiet."

"Yep, that they are. Ella's expecting late summer, you know. My first grandchild. Can you imagine, me a *granny?*" Amanda shook her head. "Me neither," Annie laughed. "Granny Annie! Ellie wants me to go stay with her for a while after the baby comes," she said.

"And then?" Amanda prompted.

"Who knows?" Annie shrugged. "Scrub floors, sell crafts, work for Winky," she laughed. "What can I do? I'm not trained for nothing. Never did a damn thing except be a mother. When the kids was little I was happy just being home with 'em. Guess I was always meant to be a homebody." Amanda watched Annie twist a narrow gold wedding ring on her left hand with the thumb and forefinger of her right.

Amanda was embarrassed. This was none of her business, she realized. Maybe if she had been around more, she'd have a right to show this kind of interest in her cousin's private life.

Another stretch of silence followed. Amanda was just beginning to wonder why she had come after all this time when Annie said, "Remember when we used to walk down to Winky's on the railroad tracks, singing at the top of our lungs to scare away the bears?"

"Yeah, well, our singing would have done it! That's the reason that I gave the Sisters about why I couldn't be a nun. I said I couldn't sing." Amanda laughed, "Actually, *they* told *me*."

"Hey, remember the time we pooled our money and bought a half-gallon of strawberry ice cream and ate the whole thing before we got home? Did we get sick or what? I thought I'd *never* eat strawberry ice cream again!"

"*I* never did!" Annie's giggle delighted Amanda. "Okay, how about the time we each put a dozen pieces of Bazooka bubble gum in our mouths when we went to bed, and you had that big gob stuck in your hair when we got up the next morning? Damn, but you were a mess!"

"Yeah, and I was in a worse mess after I got home and Ma chopped off all my hair," Annie whined, as if it had been yesterday.

"And you wore those ugly babushkas for two months!" Annie wiped tears from her eyes.

"God! That was so awful," Amanda remembered with a shudder. "And just to be mean, Sister Mary Francis made me take them off in school because they *aren't part of the uniform*," she mimicked her old teacher. "Then she had the nerve to tell me I looked cute!" Amanda pulled her hair back and tucked it behind her ears. "Cute?" She twisted her head left and right to model the severe hairstyle, "I looked like a baby elephant. Cute? And I thought nuns weren't supposed to lie," she giggled.

"Bet you never slept with ten pieces of Bazooka in your mouth again," Annie teased.

"Slept with it? I never even put another piece of Bazooka in my mouth, period!"

Amanda met Annie's laughing eyes across the table and the decades disappeared.

*"Hey, let's go over to Old Man Jasper's and pick on those dumb white kids. Why'd he bring them around to the rez anyway? If he wants to sleep with an ugly old white woman, he should do it in town," Annie spat.*

*"You mean Yellow Hair and Dog Eyes?" Amanda asked, trying to hide her guilt. She liked being part of the teasing, but felt bad talking about someone's eyes.*

*Who was she to talk?*

*"Yeah,"* Annie answered. *"Did you see the look on that stupid ole girl's face when Punky Jakes told her she musta been related to Custer, and we'd do to her what the Sioux did to him? All she ever does is cry. What a baby. I guess* white *kids is like that. Ain't tough like us Indians!"*

"Oh, we were mean!" Amanda said. "Why'd we call that boy Dog Eyes anyway?"

"Cuz he had blue eyes, remember?" Annie was still laughing. "Darned if I know why. I don't think I'd ever seen a dog with blue eyes—at least not up to that point in my life."

"Me neither, come to think of it. They didn't stay here long, huh? S'pose we had anything to do with that?"

"Nah! Course not," Annie said. Then, looking at Amanda, she added, "Well, maybe!" They laughed again.

"Speaking of blue eyes, remember when Pete was killed in that hunting accident and Heenan came to class to tell us and said if Pete had been in school like he was supposed to be it wouldn't of happened? He said he hoped it would be a lesson for us. I remember thinking it was strange the way his blue eyes sparkled when he said that."

"I never forgave him, ya know?" Annie said quietly, remembering her brother fondly. "Even if he was a priest. And I've hated blue eyes ever since. Did I tell you I told him that in confession?"

Amanda shook her head. "No! What did he say?"

"I don't remember, something about forgiving being next to Godliness, or some shit like that."

Both women sighed. Amanda said, "Hey, Annie, speaking of confession, remember the time we cut through the Thomas' yard, and Mr. T. was beating up his wife? I was scared."

*Mrs. Thomas was crying. "Please, don't hit me again! I'm sorry, I'm sorry!" she sobbed.*

*"Shut yer damn trap, woman. I should just kill you and be done with it, you miserable creepin' whore!"*

*"Don't, don't say that, Ike. Stop, please stop." The woman's voice trailed off, but the crying continued.*

*The sound of glass shattering cut through the evening air, and the girls jumped, looking at each other with wide eyes.*

*More crying, half muffled, half screeching.*

*"I'm scared, Manda. What if he kills her, and we don't get help. What'll happen then?" Annie whimpered.*

*"Well, if he doesn't kill her, and we tell someone, we're gonna get killed. We're supposed to be at the 4-H meeting, remember?"*

*"Well, I don't know about you, but I'm going to confession tomorrow night. If he kills her, we'll be guilty, too," Annie said. She tugged nervously at her cousin's sleeve.*

*"Don't be ridiculous, Annie, he ain't gonna kill her," But Amanda wondered if that was true.*

The two friends quietly sat looking at each other while childhood memories slid across their minds, most of them happy, but a few too painful to speak aloud.

This time Amanda broke the silence. "Remember the birthstone ring that I got from my folks for eighth grade graduation, and Donny Connor stole it and told everybody we were going steady? I think that was the first time I ever really hated anyone."

"Besides those white kids, you mean!" Annie continued, "Ah, you just thought Brownie would hear about it and cause trouble. He was quiet, but he never took shit from no one. He'd of beat Donny half to death, and he'd of deserved it too," she laughed. "I never did like that guy and, believe it or not, he's gotten worse with age, like sour milk, not good wine." Annie held her hand out to Amanda across the table. "I s'pose you've heard about Brownie?"

Amanda nodded as thoughts of her first boyfriend swept over her. She took Annie's hand and squeezed. "Okay, here's one," she said after a minute. "Remember when you stole your dad's cigarettes and we snuck off to the pines behind your house to smoke?"

"Smoking ain't the right word, Manda. If I remember right, we just kinda lit them and let them burn themselves out in our fingers."

"Yeah, well, we thought we were pretty grown-up anyway," Amanda chuckled. "Man, Uncle Lem sure was mad when he caught you sneaking them back into his jacket pocket, wasn't he?"

"That's cuz I tried to tell him that I was just taking them out, but he could smell the smoke on my hands. I went to bed without supper that night, for lying more than for smoking. Was he pissed!"

"Bet you even wished you had some strawberry ice cream that night!" Amanda laughed.

"Ain't that the truth!" Annie puckered her face. "How about the time Old Man Jakes put his racing boat on the river and a bunch of us decided to take it for a trial run? We got almost to the middle before it sank."

"God, yes. Punky Jakes got a whipping, but he didn't tell on us. Boy, I loved him for that. Then we hid out under the bridge figuring out a story to tell our folks about how we got soaked on a sunny day, and all the while Punky was taking his licks and screaming bloody murder," Amanda remembered. "We didn't even feel guilty, just worried about ourselves. I don't know if I could have been so loyal! Old Man Jakes hit hard, I bet."

The women tossed memories back and forth like a basketball, drank more cider, and shared more laughter. The hours passed quickly. Way too soon it was time for Amanda to leave. They walked to the door with their arms around each other. Amanda could feel Annie's ribs and her fragile frame trembling.

"Let's go shopping or catch a movie or have lunch next week," Amanda suggested. The words were out of her mouth before she could stop them. She already knew what Annie's reaction would be.

Annie pulled back. "Sure, I'll call you," she lied.

Amanda started the car and turned to wave. Annie was wiping tears from eyes with the corner of her terrycloth robe. Amanda fought the urge to run back and hold her. Tears stung her own eyes. She put the Escort in gear and edged on to the muddy road, saying a silent prayer for her unhappy cousin.

# Chapter 8

Amanda drove straight to Uncle Dan's. He was at the kitchen table, concentrating on a basket in front of him. He spotted Amanda through the window and motioned her into the house with a wave of his arm.

"Hi, what you up to?" she asked slipping off her parka. She kissed the top of his bent head, slung her jacket over the back of a wooden straight-backed chair, and opened the refrigerator door—all in one motion.

Dan laughed. "Good to see you making yourself at home. Feeling more like your old self?" he asked.

"Yeah, guess I am. Can I help you here?"

"Nope. Almost done. Just cleaning some manomin for supper. I'm fixin' Dan's Delicious Delicacy. Want to stay and eat with me?"

"Gee, I don't know. Before I commit to it, just what *is* Dan's Delicious Whatzit?"

"Wild rice and hot dogs!" he announced proudly. "The best this side of town. Looks like you could use someone to cook for you. Been losin' some weight, Sis?"

"Maybe a little," she answered. "But not much. I've been eating better that I usually do—healthier anyway. No McDonald's here. Most likely it's the walking I'm doing: tightened up all the flabby muscles." Amanda patted her thighs and backside with both hands.

She sat at the corner of the table with a bowl of fruit Jell-O she'd confiscated from Dan's refrigerator. "Got any Cool Whip to go with this?"

Dan looked over his glasses at her. "Huh-uh. I can't eat that stuff, so I don't even keep it around. It would be too tempting, and I'm a weak man." He smiled and went back to his work. "Heard you been to see Noah. What ya think of him?"

"How'd you know that?" Her spoon froze halfway to her mouth.

"You know there's no secrets on the rez. You ain't been gone that long," he answered.

"Oh, yeah, I forgot," Amanda said. She realized that the minute she pulled in front of Annie's the news was already on its way to the far reaches of the reservation. "That's one thing that makes the rez so different from the city. A person can stay pretty well unknown in a place like Milwaukee if she wants to. Not like this place," Amanda said.

Uncle Dan glanced at her again without a word.

"I liked him," she answered her uncle's question. "I was surprised to find out who he is. Funny, isn't it? How things work out, I mean. He was such a clown back when I knew him, doing imitations and stuff. And look at him now: he's in a serious type of business. Is that all he does?" she added as an afterthought.

"What do you mean, all he does? You mean like for a business or a job? Yeah. But that's enough, 'm guessin'. That kind of a life can keep ya pretty busy, wouldn't ya think? Someone always askin' for help or ceremonies." Dan, looking for agreement, raised his bushy eyebrows.

"How did he get hooked up with Hobo?" Amanda asked. "I didn't know Hobo had students."

"Hobo kinda rescued him, you might say. Noah wasn't much for school. Smart boy, though—good head on his shoulders. But even as a young-un he was more interested in plants and medicines and being out in the woods—not much interested in book-learnin' from what I remember." Dan continued picking at the wild rice as he spoke. "Hobo recognized Noah's gifts and took him on as a student, after he went and asked Noah's folks. His pa couldn't have cared less, but his ma wanted the best for all her young-uns, so she turned him over to Hobo. Hobo took care of Noah when he was young, and Noah took care of Hobo as he got older. Worked out well for both, I reckon."

"How old was Noah when he started working with Hobo?"

"Oh, I don't rightly know: fourteen or fifteen, maybe sixteen. Old enough to quit school anyhow."

"Spiritual gifts appear in one that young?" she asked.

"Hobo had a special knack for recognizing the good ones, even at a real young age," Dan answered. He pushed the basket away from him. "There, that's done!" He rubbed his eyes. "I don't know, Sis. Seems it's getting harder to see that little stuff anymore." He got up and moved over to the sink. "Hobo seen somethin' in you, too. Bet ya didn't know that, did you? He even asked your folks if he could work with you."

She shook her head, mouth open, Jell-O forgotten.

"They said no." He continued, "Your ma was strict Catholic, ya know. She thought Indian religion was some sort of superstition. Seems to me the same thing could be said 'bout Christian teachings. Ain't superstition when ya believe in what you can't see or touch?"

Amanda didn't want to get caught up in this debate with her uncle, at least not right now, so she didn't answer.

Dan removed his glasses and made short thrusts toward her with them as he continued. "Those priests that came here years ago tried to wipe out Indian *heathen* religions. That's what they called them. But I always thought that was wrong. We all pray to the same Creator, regardless of what we call Him, at least I think so. We're all the same to our Creator—none better and none worse, at least to start out with. Our own personal choices, well now, that's a different story. But all in all, we're all family in the eyes of the Great Spirit. Never did understand how those missionaries could think we Indians was going to hell."

Amanda leaned forward in her chair, barely hearing his words. "Are you saying Hobo wanted to teach me, too, and my folks just said no? How could they? Why *would* they, for heaven's sake?"

"Well now, don't be upset. It's a little late for that, don't ya think? Hobo wasn't happy when they said no, either, but he respected your folks' right to say it. When you was little, you could *feel* things. Do you 'member that?"

"Feel things? Like what? What kind of things?" Amanda asked.

Dan finished rinsing the rice and put it on the stove. "Oh, let's see. One time you two was walkin' down by the pond, and you said there was a baby rabbit there and it was *real* scared. He said ya looked around a bit before you found it hidden in some bushes. Claimed ya could feel houses and people, too—knew good ones from bad ones."

"What else?" Her arms raised in goose flesh. She wanted to tell him she could *still* feel things.

"Oh, let's see." He thought a minute then continued. "One night you was playin' in the house when ya jumped up and told him a bird was callin' ya. Your folks thought their Mandy was being silly, but Hobo believed in ya. He bundled ya both up and ya went outside and poked around until you found an owl out there that had hurt its wing. Seems like you two patched it up and took care of it until it was able to fend for itself. Do you remember that?"

"Kind of. I have a faint memory of a big bird," she said. A worry crease formed on her forehead as she thought about it. "It almost seems like a story I'd heard. I must have pretty young."

"Around five, I'd say."

"And Hobo really wanted to teach me?" she asked again. "How could my folks say no? I can't believe it. What an honor!"

"Don't be too hard on them, Sis. They just wanted what was best. Your ma thought Indian stuff was pretty hocus-pocus, you know. That always surprised me cause of her pa. He was traditional, *real* traditional. He was from up around Bayfield somewhere. He knew a lot. Your ma didn't want you learnin' the language either. Guess she thought it would keep you back. She wanted you to grow up *white,* I reckon," he teased. "They wanted you to move off the rez and get yourself a good life. At least that's what your ma wanted."

"Seems to me there can be a pretty good life here," Amanda said defensively.

"Depends. Depends," Dan repeated. "What we make of our life is up to us. But it works out best if it matches what the Grandfather has in mind for us."

"Tell me more about Hobo and his powers," she begged. She rinsed her bowl out at the sink to get rid of the Jell-O for which she'd lost her appetite.

"Well, first off, Hobo never claimed to have *powers.* Whatever he did, he gave credit to the Creator. He claimed he was only the Grandfather's helper. He said any power that people saw only came *through* him. You know, he did what people call Healing Ceremonies. He claimed he never *healed* anyone. Said he simply asked the Grandfather to help the sick person."

Uncle Dan added bacon drippings to the rice and stirred it. "Like with your Aunt Molly," he continued, "he says to us that he couldn't change the Grandfather's plans just cuz we'd like things to be different. He said his job was to make changes easier for the Creator's children. He told me and Molly that he'd pray for the sickness to pass on, but if it wasn't to be, he'd help us prepare for her journey."

Dan sighed deeply and cleared his throat. "He did, too," he continued. "Me and Hobo was both with her when she passed over. I was holdin' one hand and Hobo was holdin' the other. Right in that room back there." He pointed with his lips toward his bedroom. I'd asked if she wanted to go the hospital, you know?

The pain was getting *real* bad at the end. But she said she didn't want to be shot up with drugs. Said she wanted a clear head when she met her maker. She did, too. She was a stubborn lady! She smiled and thanked Hobo, then she told me then she loved me and she'd be waiting for me." Dan's voice broke. He sniffled and turned back to the stove to stir the rice that was starting to boil.

"I saw spirit lights circlin' her when she died." He cleared his throat and turned back to Amanda. "Hobo said the spirits loved her and had come to take her home. Then she was gone." He snapped his fingers. "Just her shell laying on the bed: that poor old body that'd been filled with pain for so long. She was finally at peace." He turned his sad eyes toward his niece. "So much pain, and for what?" Dan paused and took several deep breaths. He moved to his chair and sat down. He looked around the room before he finally turned back to Amanda. "Her pain was gone, but mine was just startin'. Hobo helped *me* then." He paused. "I was angry at first. Ya know? Real angry at the Grandfather. But Hobo said death is naturally part of life, and the world wasn't made for any of us alone. We all got a place in it." Dan frowned at Amanda and nodded as if to himself. "We follow the Creator's plan for us, like it or not. Instead of being angry, Hobo said I should be happy that I had Molly for so long—maybe longer than I deserved. She was a very good lady, you know," he said.

Amanda nodded, "Yeah, she was a *very* special lady. I always loved her."

Dan continued, "Hobo told me to be thankful for the time I had with her. Grandfather could have given her to someone else. If he had, my life would have been pitiful without her. You know, His creations are selfish.

"We say, 'Grandfather, I want this,' or 'I need that,' like we got a right! We need be sayin', 'Grandfather, *thank* you for all you have given me,' don't ya think?" Dan lapsed into silence.

They sat quietly for a long time, neither wanting to voice their thoughts.

Finally Amanda whispered, "Do you think Noah is very much like Hobo?"

"I'd be surprised if he wasn't," Dan answered. "He was with Hobo for quite a few years."

Dan got up and limped to the refrigerator. He pulled out a salad and a package of hot dogs.

Amanda watched her uncle, remembering what Winky said about the circulation in Dan's legs.

"How many hot dogs can you eat?" he asked over his shoulder. "Two or three?"

"Two," Amanda answered, "unless they're the real skinny ones."

"Three then. Set the table?" he asked.

While she put familiar chipped Melmac on the table, she thought about Hobo and Noah: so different, yet so much alike. "Hobo never married, did he? What about Noah?" Amanda asked her uncle.

Dan raised his eyebrows at her. "Why? You interested?" he teased.

The blush started at Amanda's neck and worked its way up. "No, course not. I was just thinking how demanding a life like that is and thought how hard it would be for a family to be a part of it or not part of it. I remember how often Hobo was gone. He almost seemed a little sad sometimes when he'd come back."

"You're right there," Dan said. "Don't think I ever heard of either one of them having a woman in his life, at least not for long. Does seem like Noah had a lady friend once," he frowned. "Guess those guys are kinda like priests. You know, givin' 100 percent to their parishes, no split energies or havin' to make family choices. Sure must be tough. Molly made my life easy just by being here. I think priests should have helpmates. If'n I was Pope, I'd decree they all have wives, make it a *requirement*. Why should they have to go it alone? I know there were many times I never would've made it without my Molly."

Amanda giggled trying to picture rough, crusty old Uncle Dan as the Pope. She thought about Hobo's comings and goings, the pleasures he seemed to take from little things that happened in the family. "No wonder Hobo liked it at Grandma's. We were the only family he had. That was probably the only place for him to get any comfort and love like the rest of us had. Gram waited on him hand 'n' foot, you know."

"Yep, he was your grandma's favorite brother. Real proud of him, she was."

Amanda and Dan chatted as they ate. Together they cleaned the kitchen after their meal. Dan washed while Amanda wiped. Then he insisted they light a fire in the fireplace. "Nothing's better on a chilly night," he said. "Molly and I used to sit here at the end of every day, even when we didn't need a fire. And I surely would take pleasure from your company tonight, Sis," he said quietly.

Amanda hugged him, also happy not to spend another evening alone. She embraced the thought that she was looking forward to passing time with another person rather than seeking solitude, a hopeful sign she was on the mend. She thought quickly about calling Gloria, then decided not to.

They passed the evening in front of the crackling fire, Dan sharing unremembered stories about her early life and stories about her parents. Amanda laughed often. "When I was a kid, my folks were just my folks, not real people with lives or dreams of their own," she laughed when Dan told her about their scrimping and planning for a house of their own that never happened.

"Your pa was one of those rare ones who could mesh Native Spiritual stuff and Catholic stuff. Not everyone can do that. That was special, I think. Your ma, now, she didn't exactly agree." Dan said. "Your dad, he was real proud when Hobo showed an interest in you, but he gave in to your ma. She didn't want that at all. And your dad, he spoiled his bride," Dan told her. "Morris treated her like she was a princess or something. They sat good together, like me and Molly, not needing anyone else. And when you came along, my oh my, you was like a double layer of whipped chocolate frostin' on a wedding cake. Your ma protected you like crazy. Until Hobo wanted to teach ya, he was about the only person that your ma trusted you with exceptin' your pa and grandma. She got a little nervous if you was with Hobo after that. Maybe she worried he'd try to teach you anyways. But that weren't necessary. Hobo, he was a man of his word. Real honorable he was."

Dan chuckled. "After you started off to school she'd sometimes let you come here. My, but my Molly loved you like you was her very own. Used to 'bout tickle her to death the way you'd prance about the kitchen trying to help her cook or clean. You'd put on one of her big aprons, and it would hang from way up here— he pointed under his arms—clean to the floor. You used to have a real sweet tooth. Ever grow out of it?"

"No! I wish I had. I could still live on chocolate candy, pie, cake, ice cream, or really any kind of dessert," she laughed. "Know what I finally figured out? The more calories something has, the better it tastes."

"I know what ya mean. You best be careful though, Sis. I ate too much sugar when I was a kid and now I'm paying for it with this here *sugar diabetes*. I never wanted sweets so much as after the doctor told me I couldn't have 'em," Dan chuckled again. "Molly even stopped bakin' so's not to tempt me. She knew me good!"

Several times during the evening, Amanda tried to bring the conversation back to Noah. She couldn't decide if Dan was avoiding the subject or if he really didn't know much about him—which she found difficult to believe: everybody knew everything about everyone on the reservation. Whichever it was, Noah would remain a mystery, at least for tonight.

Her uncle stoked the fire twice before beginning to show signs of becoming tired. Reluctantly, she decided it was time to go. But when she rose to leave, Dan asked her to stay the night. "I'll make up the sofa," he offered. "And I can have company when I go to Mass in the mornin'. 'Sides, in case ya haven't noticed, it's warmed up a bit, meanin' bears will be coming out of hibernatin'. They'll be *plenty* hungry and patrolling for food. You don't want to be some bear's supper now, do you?"

"If you think you've scared me into staying, you're right," Amanda lied. She knew bears are as afraid of people as people are afraid of bears, but her uncle's attempt to keep her there touched her.

He pulled several quilts out of an old beat-up trunk set against the north wall. "These are some that your Aunt Molly made," he said proudly. "She'd be real pleased to know they was keeping you warm tonight."

# Chapter 9

Amanda wrinkled her nose as she pulled on yesterday's clothes. She hoped people on the reservation still went to church in jeans and sweatshirts. "Hey Uncle," she yelled. "Got some deodorant?"

She parked in front of the church where she'd made her First Communion and Confirmation. She had made her first friends, other than cousins, that is, here. As far back as she could remember, church had always been the center for community activities.

*Another second Sunday of the month: that meant that after Mass they'd go down to the basement for the rummage sale. Amanda's parents gave her the usual nickel for the grab bag bins. She couldn't wait. Through the entire service she squirmed and wiggled until Mom got mad. The nickel felt warm in her hand. Maybe that meant she'd find an extra special surprise today. She tossed it from hand to hand until she dropped it again. Ma shushed her for the third time. "Once more and it's mine," her mother whispered fiercely, just as Mass ended.*

*Finally! Amanda ran down the concrete steps so she could be first at the bins.*

*"Hello, Amanda," Sr. Mary David said. "What are you going to buy today?"*

*Amanda threw the old nun a smile and ran to the bins against the back wall without answering. She was already feeling, shaking, even smelling packages when her parents got there. As he always did, Dad teased her about her shopping style. She didn't care. Her wonderful discoveries made it easy to ignore him.*

*The grab bag bins were actually old apple crates brimming over with all sorts of wonderful packages. Each package was wrapped in newspaper and tied with twine. Her fingers touched a magical one—she could tell. It didn't rattle and it didn't smell, but it had an interesting shape. She gave her nickel to Sr. Mary*

*David and signaled her folks. Oh no! They were visiting with Andy and Vicki Connors. She rolled her eyes. This could go on forever! She danced from foot to foot, anxious to be off so she could open her package. Her palms were sweating. Newsprint stained her fingers. She wiped her hands on her skirt. Why didn't they hurry?*

*By the time they all got to the car Amanda was almost sick with anticipation. She waited until Dad started the car before she carefully opened the package. She couldn't believe her eyes. Someone must have made a mistake, she decided. Probably one of the new Sisters accidentally got this package mixed in with the other rummage stuff! She held a small wooden cross. It was painted antique gold. Most surely this was a sign that she was special in God's eyes. She knew exactly where it would go when she got it home.*

*"No, Daddy, put it right there!" Mandy pointed above the door in her bedroom.*

*Dad was teasing again. "How 'bout here?" he asked, holding the crude cross up against the side window.*

*"Daddy!" She changed tactics. "Ma, come help me. Make Daddy put it up over the door." It had to be over the door, Amanda figured. How else could she see it easily when she went to sleep at night?*

*"All right, all right!" Dad held the cross up beside the doorway, "Here?"*

*"Daddy! Ma!"*

*Dad laughed and finally gave in. He nailed the homemade (and ugly to his mind) cross over her bedroom door. Amanda knew it was wrong, but she secretly savored the Sin of Pride at owning this wonderful thing. Surely it was an omen that she alone found this particular grab bag. Every night she'd stare at it until she could no longer keep her eyes open.*

The church filled slowly. Community people greeted each other warmly and visited in the foyer as they had every Sunday for years. Even as a child Amanda thought that was peculiar. The reservation was so small that probably everybody had seen each other just the day before. But they still had their Sunday morning visits.

Uncle Dan and Aunt Molly had been long-time members of St. Mary's, so Dan and Amanda were stopped often as they made their way to a center pew. Dan introduced Amanda to some that she recognized, at least by name.

Others were new. How strange, she thought, to be in a familiar place with so many strangers.

Just as Mass was about to begin, Uncle Dan nudged her with his elbow and pointed back over his shoulder with his chin at a beautiful, slender young woman whose straight black hair fell to her knees. In her arms she carried a baby. Two boys, about five and six, followed closely behind, each clasping the hand of a little girl toddling awkwardly between them. "Brownie's widow and kids," he whispered.

Amanda watched the young family settle themselves in the pew directly in front of her and her uncle. The younger boy turned and stared at her for several seconds until his mother put an arm around his shoulder, gently directing his attention to the front of the church. Without being told, Amanda would have known whose child he was. She recognized Brownie's almond-shaped eyes and that peculiar shade of chocolate. The eyes were ringed with long black eyelashes, the envy of any girl.

Unable to keep her eyes off her, Amanda stared at the back of the woman's head, watching her shiny hair ripple every time she moved. She knew Brownie had remained a bachelor for years, but she hadn't realized that, when he had finally married, he had married someone so young. The woman's youthfulness bothered Amanda. She tried to concentrate on the Mass, but her thoughts and eyes kept returning to the young mother and four children sitting in front of her. Brownie's dad had refused to step foot in church after his wife had left with the priest; he didn't allow his children to come, either, even though they went to Catholic school. Amanda thought it curious that Brownie would have returned to the church. But he must have; otherwise, why would his wife and children be here?

Even though she fought it, Amanda spent the remainder of Mass remembering what happened to her and Brownie. They'd been a couple from the time either of them was old enough to notice the opposite sex until she left for college: a *storybook* couple, everyone teased. Amanda had believed it too. To her regret, their relationship fell apart as the time between their seeing each other grew longer and their time together grew shorter. Sometimes she hated that she was a serious student whose studies kept her away from the rez more and more often. Her heart hurt for a long time after she finally realized there was nothing left for them, although she shouldn't have been surprised; Brownie let her know early on that he wasn't interested in leaving the rez, and she realized she wouldn't stay. Seeing this woman who filled the role in Brownie's life that should have been hers left Amanda with feelings that she didn't care to identify.

Dan sensed Amanda's interest in Brownie's widow, and as the congregation gathered on the church steps to greet their part-time priest, he asked if she'd like to meet Mrs. Brown. Amanda shook her head, unable to speak. She didn't want to talk to Brownie's wife, at least not just yet, though she couldn't have said why.

"Mandy!" a voice called, saving her from trying to explain this feeling to her uncle. "Hey, Mandy! Wait!" A heavy-set man with a long ponytail half-ran, half-jogged, up to them. "I thought that was you. Man! It's been a *coon's* age! Are you still in Milwaukee? Whatcha doin' here?"

She struggled for recognition. "Punky Jakes," she laughed and held out her hand. "Annie and I were just talking about you yesterday. Yes, I'm still in Milwaukee. How are you?"

"Too bad—about Milwaukee I mean. I thought you'd tell me we was gonna have you back. I'm still on the rez, divorced like most everyone else 'round here. My kid lives with her ma in Chicago. Man, you're lookin' good, Mandy! What about you: you still married? Hey, heard you married a white guy. Got any kids?" His high voice was a mismatch for his enormous size.

Not sure if she should be flattered, or even if she wanted to be, Amanda said she was divorced. The light in Punky's small, obsidian eyes brightened. "Hey, I got a idea. Want to do something today?" he asked excitedly.

Amanda didn't want to hurt her old buddy, but she didn't want to do anything to encourage this overblown boy-man either. Uncle Dan jumped to her rescue. "I'm sorry, Punky: I'm afraid I got dibs on Amanda today."

She threw her uncle a look of appreciation. "I'm sorry Punky, but I'm sure we'll run into each other again before I go back." She offered a hand that Punky took without enthusiasm.

"Yeah, okay." He looked crestfallen enough to make her feel sorry for him, but she knew she wasn't up to taking care of strays right now.

"He certainly has put on a lot of weight," she said to her uncle as they watched Punky waddle away from them. "Some people sure change, don't they? He used to be so skinny! I remember Mom saying he had a tapeworm for sure. He was *always* eating; remember? But he never seemed to get any fatter, just taller. Guess it finally caught up to him."

"That, and the booze, will get ya ever time," Dan said.

She watched her uncle climb slowly into the car; his legs seemed to be bothering him quite a bit today. "You really don't have to spend the day with me," Dan said as he buckled up. "Just wanted to save you from lyin' to your new admirer, just coming out of church and all," he laughed.

"You know what? I'd like to go out to the cemetery," she said suddenly. "Would you go with me?"

"That's not a bad idea," Dan answered. "It's been a spell since I been there, too."

They made the two-mile trip in silence. The road to the small reservation cemetery had been plowed since the storm a few weeks ago, but it showed little evidence of recent use. Amanda had only traveled this way twice since the funerals of her parents years ago. She excused this sin of omission by telling herself that she couldn't find solace in a place of death. She'd avoided pain of their passing by diving into her work; if she kept busy enough, she figured, she wouldn't have to think about unpleasant things. Dr. Bradley had asked her to think about how unhealthy that was.

Amanda held her uncle's arm and leaned against him as they made their way toward the family plot. Their feet left the only visible tracks in snow that was crusty from the constant melting and freezing in late winter. Blue jays screeched protest at the human disruption. "I was a regular visitor here when Molly first died," her uncle said. "Then one day I realized she wasn't here; this hole only had the remains of the body that carried her spirit around. Not that it wasn't a good body," he chuckled awkwardly, "but I just couldn't feel her here anymore, you know?"

Looking around, Amanda nodded. "For such a full place, it sure feels empty." They stood by her parents' graves. Amanda refused to look at the headstone. She chose to remember the laughter of her parents' house, not the funerals. "I hate it that I didn't tell them how much I loved them," she said. "You think they knew?"

"Course they did, Sis. They loved ya a whole lot, and they knew you loved them. It was hard for them to say it, so I reckon you didn't learn neither. I think them boarding schools are to blame. When you only got one or two supervisors for sixty, seventy kids, no way is there near enough attention to go around. We never learned how to give or accept love, not that there was any, at least not much, let alone talk about it. But we knew when we loved or were loved, you bet, even if we didn't know how to say it."

"I've thought about that a lot," Amanda said. "Those boarding schools left my generation fumbling around trying to get past an older generation's experiences. Sad, isn't it?"

Dan grunted. "Mandy, whether we could talk about it or not, me an' you are lucky we had so much love in our lives. Lots, don't you know. Now, *that's* what's sad!"

She nodded and looked at the graves of other lost relatives. Besides her father, Dan had three other brothers buried here, along with two sisters. Dan and his sister Eileen, who lived in a nursing home in Minneapolis, were all who were left of a family of eight siblings. "It must be hard to have lost so much family," she said, taking her uncle's hand. "When I was little, I always told my mom that I wanted brothers and sisters. She'd laugh and say she'd see what she could do about it. Now more than ever, I wish I had them—even *one* would do. I feel so alone sometimes."

Dan hugged her. "What say we get outta here and go join the living," he said. "Speaking of lucky, you get to buy breakfast! What do ya think of that?"

"It's a deal!" she said, hugging back.


Amanda stayed with her uncle until mid-afternoon. He seemed as grateful for the company as she was herself, and he shared amusing stories of the good ole days when he and her dad raised ruckus on the rez—like the time they sewed up one of Grandpa's pigs who got sliced up on a barbed wire fence with Gram's needle and thread, or the time they stole old man Plucinski's chickens and sold them back to him. Dan's eyes twinkled and sometimes teared as he shared the antics of himself and his brothers. "The girls now, they was pretty sweet. Didn't get into trouble like us boys did."

Amanda's own eyes blurred with tears. "I'm sorry I let so much time go by without seeing you, Uncle Dan."

He smiled and rubbed his eyes. Amanda saw a loneliness in them that reflected her own. Dan's love of life had dimmed when his partner passed on.


Late in the afternoon Amanda found the energy to leave. She kissed her uncle goodbye, promising to call soon.

Back at the cabin, she drew a warm bath with six inches of bubbles and she soaked until her fingertips wrinkled. The shower at Uncle Dan's had left much to be desired, what with the need to twist and turn in order to rinse off the soap. He'd always been frugal: a characteristic that brought on much teasing by reservation folk, including Aunt Molly. Amanda thought that now he was concerned about putting money into a home that he wouldn't need for too many more years.

She spent the evening trying to read, content to be alone. After two days, she felt like she'd O.D.'d on people, and she worried briefly that she might not be recovering, as she wanted to believe. Most of the evening the newest John Sandford paperback sat open on her lap while she gazed into the fire, thinking about Brownie, his family, and his cousin Noah.

Dark, low-hanging clouds that let loose with occasional flurries greeted Amanda on Monday. She studied the sky on her morning walk, deciding the threat was worse than anything they really had to offer. This was the kind of day that made her want to dig out an apron and be domestic. Back at the cabin, as she worked on a chocolate fudge cake, her favorite, Amanda wondered why people say they are going to whip up a cake—it's work if you do it right. She complemented herself as she applied the frosting artistically, occasionally stepping back, closing one eye and squinting at her masterpiece over her thumb. No doubt about it, she hadn't lost her touch!

That done, Amanda piled her hair on top of her head, dug out the jeans that would let her scrunch easily, and pulled on a gray sweatshirt that had lost its sleeves to scissors long ago. She began dusting, waxing, and scrubbing. She hummed as she worked.

# Chapter 10

Noah craned his neck and looked out of the side window of his beat-up Bronco to squint at the sky. The worst of the storm would stay in northern Minnesota, but he figured he'd have to put up with flurries all the way home. He hoped the Aikens weren't insulted by his early morning exit. They'd been good to him all weekend—as always. The storm was just the excuse he needed to be on his way back home. He didn't want to be trapped by a Minnesota blizzard, and, truthfully, he was anxious to see Amanda again. She needed his help—whatever it was to be. His prayers over the weekend had brought nothing from the Grandfather. He'd just have to trust that the Creator would let him know what he needed to do when the time came.

As he headed the Bronco south and east Noah thought about Amanda's unusual eyes: pretty, but full of pain. As soon as he saw her on his porch he knew she was special: a pale, barely visible light surrounded her head like a mantilla. He would have helped her even without the light, because of Brownie. Noah missed his cousin; he'd lost a lot when Brownie hit the slough bridge. He'd also gained the responsibility for a family that should have passed to one of Brownie's brothers. But, as he lay dying, Brownie asked Noah to take care of his wife and kids, so Noah inherited the task. There was no way he could refuse it. To make things worse, Paula never made any effort to hide the fact that Noah held her interest now that Brownie was gone. She knew the responsibility passed on by her husband gave her a chance to get a father for her kids. Others noticed her attention toward Noah and whispered about the young widow. But Paula was no fool. As much as she'd loved Brownie, she knew he never really loved her. She probably knew about his affairs too, Noah thought. Brownie hadn't been very discreet—especially when he'd been drinking.

Noah's ideas varied greatly from Paula's. His duties in the community were a full-time job. He couldn't see how *any* woman, let alone one with four kids, could be a part of his life, but he was well aware that Paula chose to interpret his responsibility to her as an opportunity. He'd be an uncle to the kids, but not a father. Under different circumstances he might have been interested. Paula was extremely beautiful, with good nesting tendencies: wife material, if one was looking.

She was extremely insightful, with an unusual background that allowed for long, interesting conversations between them. She was contemporary in her beliefs, but had been raised in a Catholic home by traditional Indian parents. Paula was always questioning and challenging and keeping him on his toes.

But, like Hobo, Noah had long absences away from home and no financial security. Many times those he helped gave him money, but usually only enough to cover gas for travel. More often than not he was paid in leather or other goods. He thanked the Grandfather often for the Vincents, who wouldn't let him go hungry. The old phrase, for better or worse, would mean worse for any woman in his life, unless she thrived on hunger and loneliness. Not that he hadn't been tempted: he was a man, after all. Two losses made him decide to follow his teacher's ways and avoid temptation.

The first woman he'd been serious about was the granddaughter of a spiritual leader from north of the Twin Cities. Jessie was his love for almost a year, until she started to compete. Instead of the helpmate he hoped for, he found himself constantly questioned or second-guessed. Not that it was her fault: she couldn't help her path any more than he could shape his own. They parted as friends, more or less.

The second, a much younger woman from Mole Lake, entered his life shortly after he and Jessie had gone their separate ways. His position in the community excited her, but that excitement dimmed quickly when she was left on her own too often with little if any notice. She took it as a personal rejection. She pouted; they fought. When it became too difficult, the relationship ended, and not on good terms by any stretch of the imagination. One evening when he came home from a weekend away Noah found all his clothes strewn about the yard. He grinned now as he thought about that night. As he was picking up his clothes, he swore he could hear Hobo chuckling in the breeze. He decided then and there to walk his path alone.

After that he kept all females at arm's length, which wasn't easy. He smiled as he thought about how the families he helped would parade nieces, daughters, sisters, even aunts, in front of him. He didn't know there were that many single women around.

Noah finally reached the Wisconsin border and pulled into an Amoco station just outside of Superior. He stretched as he got out. The dark sky was teasing with flurries again. While stretching a second time, his bones cracked, protesting the many hours in one position. His stomach growled and demanded food. With only an hour to home, he'd forego food, he decided, but another coffee sounded good. He could use the caffeine.

The ceremonies always took a lot out of him. As usual, when folks heard he was coming, the one ceremony he was called to do became at least three. Hobo had taught him to, tired or not, do his best when asked.

"That will be $21.60, sir," the young attendant repeated.

Noah had been staring into space. "Sorry, guess I was asleep on my feet."

"Better be careful driving then. Looks like the roads might get nasty. Going far?"

"Just an hour or so up the road," he pointed east with his chin. He collected his change from the boy, who was now dancing from one foot to the other in an attempt to keep warm. Noah clapped the boy's shoulder and, as an afterthought, handed back three dollars. "Have yourself a good day, bro. Keep warm."

"Thanks, dude, you too." The boy put the money in his pocket and rubbed his ungloved hands together. "Well, see ya," he waved a reddened hand at Noah and started for the warmth of the station.

Noah stood beside the Bronco a moment longer, staring up at the sky before brushing the snow off his bare head and climbing in. He glanced back at the station. The boy, standing just inside the door, waved again.

Back on familiar roads Noah felt the excitement of being close to home. Only an hour to go. He thought of Niijii and hoped he'd fared well. He missed the days when his shaggy four-legged friend had been able to travel with him. Age made the long hours in a confined space too hard for Niijii, and he also needed more duty stops.

Noah's thoughts turned again to Amanda. "She's lost," he nodded to himself. On the second night of the ceremonies, as he was preparing his flags, he closed his eyes for a second to rest. A field of tall grass, as far as he could see, colored several shades of green and yellow, rushed in his direction and flowed under him from behind his eyelids. The swiftly moving ground made him dizzy, and he felt himself sway. Suddenly, about a foot off the ground, a fiery greenish-gold fireball whirled towards him. Four feet in front of his face, as he was getting ready to duck, it blew apart, sending pieces flying in all directions like fireworks. He opened his eyes. No one seemed to have noticed anything. Only a minute had passed in this world's time. All during the ceremony Noah waited for an explanation of this vision from the Grandfather. None came. He didn't know why, but he suspected it had something to do with Amanda.

Finally his headlights caught the sign announcing that he'd reached the reservation. He knew he should pick up his shaggy partner from Paula's. Her kids loved Niijii, while he tolerated them. But at the last minute he drove five miles past her driveway and turned into Amanda's instead. He sat in his vehicle a full fifteen minutes, staring at the cabin, wondering if he should go in.

By mid-afternoon the cabin sparkled and Amanda's face shone with perspiration. She leaned on the mop handle and admired her bedroom floor, amazed that physical labor could make her feel so good. She couldn't remember when she'd worked so hard. A sharp knock on the front door startled her. "Someone got lost," she said aloud. She frowned, realizing she was talking to herself more often these days. In the month she'd been at the cabin, no one had visited, not even the bears Dan had warned her about. Amanda tucked a few loose hairs behind barrettes and wiped her face on the bottom of her sweatshirt. She shrugged—too late to do anything about her appearance now. She opened the door, holding the mop over her shoulder like a saber.

Noah stood there, the collar of his denim jacket turned up to protect his neck, his long braids tucked inside. His hands were jammed into his pockets, and his head was bare except for a sprinkling of snow. He grinned as he looked at her and raised his eyebrows.

"Oh my God!" Surprise was in her voice. "Noah, what . . . ?"

"Looks like I came at a bad time," he said. He made a show of looking her up and down. "Shame on the man who comes between a woman and her housework." No smile.

Amanda's hands flew to her hair. She fought the urge to slam the door shut; she felt like a first-class household drudge. She blushed. "Oh my God!" She said again.

"You already said that," Noah teased. "You want I should come back later?" he asked.

"Oh, no! Come in. I wasn't expecting company; no one ever comes out this way.

I thought you were going to be gone until tomorrow." Amanda fought to keep her hands from covering the sweat stains on the front of her shirt. "Can I offer you some cake or coffee? Have you eaten? I could fix you a sandwich, or there's some apple cider I could heat or—can I take your coat?" she stopped, suddenly aware she was babbling. *Get a grip, Amanda,* she chided herself, *or he'll think you're ready for the nuthouse.*

Noah took off his jacket and handed it to her. She led the way into the kitchen, jacket in one hand, mop still in the other. "I've been on the road since five this morning and haven't eaten. I wanted to get back before the snow got too bad. Looks like I made it," he said. He looked around the room. "I'll take you up on your offer of a sandwich, if it ain't too much trouble, and maybe some of that great-looking chocolate cake." He pointed his lips at the counter. "How'd you know it was my favorite?" he asked. He ran his finger around the edge of the plate picking off some frosting and sticking it in his mouth.

"Don't flatter yourself; it's mine too. I could live on chocolate: my childhood passion that forgot to stay in my childhood," Amanda responded.

"Then we have something in common," he said as he helped himself to coffee.

Amanda washed her hands in the kitchen sink and struggled for something to say. Curiosity finally got the best of her. "Where did you come from today," she asked. "Or shouldn't I be so nosy?"

"No, you can ask," Noah said. "I was up north, in Minnesota. It's beautiful in the northern part. Ever been?"

"No, but I'd like to go sometime." She pulled a two-day-old venison roast out of the fridge and started cutting thin slices.

Noah leaned back against the counter, sipped his coffee, and watched her. Every once in a while he'd reach in quickly to pick off a small chunk of venison. "What next?" he asked in mock surprise. "Chocolate cake *and* venison!"

Amanda had a sudden impulse to slap his hand like she'd seen her mother do when her father helped himself to whatever she was preparing. Instead, she ignored his stealing and concentrated on slicing the meat. "You could grab the mustard and cheese or whatever else you'd like out of the fridge," she told him.

He studied the refrigerator. "Did you know you can tell a lot about a people just by looking in their fridges and cupboards?" he asked.

"Really? Where'd you learn that?"

"I saw it on *Oprah,* so it must be true," he laughed.

"You watch *Oprah?*" she asked. "You don't look the type!" When he didn't say anything, she continued, "Well, what does my fridge say about me?"

"It tells me you're very organized," he said as he shuffled things around noisily. "Um, you don't like lots of frills or nonsense," he continued, moving things and clanking jars together. "You like commodity cheese and pickles, hot peppers, and Diet Coke!" He put a half empty jar of dill pickles on the counter, along with the mustard and mayonnaise.

"Both?" she asked.

"Yeah, I like mixed flavors. Don't you?"

"Nope, 'fraid I like my flavors straight-up."

Noah leaned against the counter again, arms folded loosely across his chest as he watched her make sandwiches. He reminded her of her dad. She laid the sandwiches on the table and excused herself. "I need to freshen up a bit," she said.

"You look fine to me," he teased. "Don't do it on my account."

Amanda grinned at him and ducked into the bathroom. She splashed water on her face and pulled on a clean sweatshirt. She hated the way her hair clung to her when it was dirty. She ran a comb through it and shook her head, but it didn't help. She put on her tinted glasses. "This is as good as it gets today, girl," she whispered to her reflection.

When she returned to the kitchen, Noah was helping himself to another sandwich. "Hope it's okay. I am hungry, and this is great. My place never has good stuff like this."

"I'm glad you're making yourself at home."

"You got a nice place here. It feels good," he said. "So what have you been up to the last couple of days?" He wiped the counter off with his hand and turned to offer her half of his sandwich.

She took it from him, suddenly aware that she hadn't eaten all day either. Between bites she told him about her visit to Annie's and Uncle Dan's, but left out St. Mary's Church and seeing Brownie's family.

Noah emptied the coffee into his cup and started a new pot. He ran the water and scooped grounds into the pot while she cut the cake. When she put a piece in front of him, he frowned. He examined it closely as he turned the plate solemnly, with the air of a ritual. Amanda watched, waiting for him to say something. The worry line between her eyes deepened as he turned the plate around a second time bending lower over the cake. She opened her mouth to speak but didn't know what to say.

"Are you putting me on a diet?" he asked. "Is this all I get?" He looked up into her worried face and broke into laughter. "I told you it was my favorite!"

Ignoring his laughter, Amanda picked up his dessert plate and placed it on the counter. She picked up the entire cake and put it down in front of him. "Please don't think I'm selfish. I just thought you might like to eat your cake one piece at a time," she said. With one motion she grabbed the fork from his hand and replaced it with a large stirring spoon. Remembering her gramma's words, said: *"Ahaw! Wiisinin!"*

This time they laughed together. Noah retrieved his plate and fork. He grinned at her between bites. As the afternoon moved into evening, their conversation stayed light and friendly. Noah offered to make a fire in exchange for more cake and coffee. They spoke mostly about Hobo. He'd loved her great-uncle as she had, Amanda realized. He called Hobo his grandfather. She shared her memories of her childhood on the reservation. At midnight Noah stood up and asked for his coat. "I should have been in bed hours ago," he laughed. "I need my beauty rest. *Miigwich* for the great food. It hit the spot," he said and rubbed his stomach.

"Thanks for the company," she answered.

"Amanda," he said, using her formal name for the first time today, "have you thought more about the gift of the feather and why you're here?" When she shook her head, he continued: "I'd like to help you discover what you're being called to do. You have gifts. I see it, and Hobo saw it. And more important, Migizi said so. Are you willing to learn? It's never too late, you know."

"Of course I've thought about it, but I don't know what to do," she said.

"Find out why Migizi was sent to you. My humble opinion is that it's worth checking into."

She noticed he was watching her carefully. "How? What can I do? Should I still come see you tomorrow?"

"Yeah. Think you can find my place again?" he asked. "It's pretty far out in the boonies."

"I've got it down," she replied. "If I get lost, I'll send up smoke signals, and you can come find me."

His handshake was strong and warm. "Good, I'll see you then." He was gone.

# Chapter 11

When Noah had left the night before, some of the warmth of the room had departed with him, leaving an emptiness in which Amanda was strangely content. She was wondering about this as she pulled up at his place just as the clock in the dash turned to eleven. His shaggy friend occupied the same spot on the little porch. The dog lifted his head and, when he recognized Amanda, gruffed once in greeting.

Noah was waiting, dressed in his denim coat and walking boots. "*Bimosedaa,*" he said, pointing with his chin towards the woods behind his house. "Let's walk." The sun shone brightly in the trees, inviting them. The dog looked at Noah as if to ask, "Should I stay and watch the house, or should I come with you?"

"Is he always so expressive?" Amanda asked.

"Yeah, he sure is. He talks to me a lot, don't you big guy?" Noah patted the dog's head. "He adopted me about twelve years ago. Just showed up one night, fully growed and fully miserable," he laughed. "What a sorry sight! Talk about skinny and hungry! His hair was matted; he even had some bald spots. I almost put him out of his misery right then and there, but I decided to give him a week. Best thing I ever did." The dog looked at Noah with love in his eyes, looking like he understood every word spoken by the man. "I really needed a friend then too," he continued. "That wasn't too long after Hobo passed on to the spirit world."

"How do you think Uncle Hobo would feel at being replaced by a dog?" she asked.

"Ah, he'd love it," Noah answered grinning.

"Come, Niijii, my friend," Noah said to the shaggy creature. "You can use the exercise." Tail in motion, Niijii jumped off the porch with more energy than he looked like he should have. As they walked, Noah touched the new buds sprouting early on the branches that hung in their path. "See them come to life again. Ain't it something? Spring is the time for celebrating new life. Nature's time for rest is over. *Omakakii,* the frog, and *agongo,* the chipmunk, will come out of hibernation." He glanced at Amanda and smiled. "Even *zagime* will be back."

"Who's that?" Amanda asked.

"Mr. Mosquito!" he laughed. "We need him, too."

Amanda smiled, sure she was being teased.

"We lowly humans need to recognize the lessons nature gives us." Noah became serious again. "We should be using winter as quiet time given by the Grandfather to rest up and think about our lives: where we've been, where we're going. You know, correct any mistakes we made last year and figure how to get back on the right track. We should be getting ready for Grandfather's world. That's what it's all about you know: preparing."

His voice was hardly above a whisper. "Spring is the Indian New Year." He looked at the sky. "The old ones never followed the white man's calendar for any-thing—like the seasons: they decided for themselves when they'll come. We've lost that. But there are some traditional folks who follow the old calendar. They say the paper calendar is too damn demanding."

"Isn't that what's called *progress?*" Amanda asked.

He shrugged. "Is it really progress? Look at how the world is. We're kill-ing it, killing our animal relatives, ourselves, and somehow say it's okay cuz it's *progress!*"

Amanda took a deep breath through her nose and exhaled loudly through her mouth. "I know the air is polluted in other places, but it sure smells good and clean around here."

They walked along in silence. Niijii took short romps into the woods but came back to the rutted road every few minutes to check up on the two humans who trusted him to keep watch.

"We're all connected: plants, animals, humans. We're all supposed to be responsible for each other. Animals seem to remember that better than most peo-ple. See how Niijii is taking care of us?" Noah asked.

"That's because he loves you so much," Amanda said. "I think if it was just me walking out here with him today he wouldn't act that way."

"You don't know that. He can tell you're a friend, can't you Big Boy?"

Niijii woofed once in answer without looking back.

"We two-leggeds are the most selfish creatures on earth, you know," Noah continued.

The words of her uncle, spoken at the cemetery, echoed in Amanda's ears.

"You're lucky, Amanda. You've got the chance here to reflect on your life. You can make changes if you want to." His fingers tenderly pinched a young pea-green bud without breaking it.

"I'm not sure I would consider it *lucky*," she said. "I wouldn't have planned this. Three of my best friends died! Why should they die in order to get me to look at *my* life?" She glared at him without realizing it. "I can't believe that's part of the Creator's great plan for me. That sure as hell doesn't make sense!" Her voice shook.

"I'm sorry," he said quietly. "I didn't know where your pain came from." He studied the sky again as though he might find the answer there. "We two-leggeds think we know what's fair or unfair, but we don't. We'll never know why things happen. That's not our job. That's why we are called by the Creator to have *faith*."

Amanda's thoughts tumbled crazily. She was glad she was back here but she certainly would have picked a different reason given a choice. Yet in a strange way she *was* thankful. Without the accident that pushed her to the breaking point, she wouldn't have come at all. She wouldn't have Migizi's gift. She wouldn't have met Noah and now have the opportunity to seek the path she had been turned from long ago by her parents. Nor would she have become reacquainted with Dan and Annie. "But my friends were innocent. How could Grandfather take lives to help me?" She hated the whimper in her voice.

"We don't know that's why they died. They each had their own destiny, just as you have yours and I have mine. But think about it for a minute: when we stand back and out of the way, things seem to be fit together, like a puzzle. Sometimes it takes a long time to see it, most times we never do. It's best not to analyze everything. Instead we should just accept that things happen for reasons that are the Grandfather's, not ours. I think we need to do that to be happy in this life."

They walked quietly side-by-side, enjoying the warmth of the sun and the soft whisper of the wind playing in the pines. From his self-appointed post, Niijii occasionally glanced over his shoulder, silently asserting that he was part of the trio.

"What are you feeling, Manda?" Noah asked finally breaking the silence.

"Confused," she answered. "I don't know whether to be happy or sad right now." *Triste-feliz* came to her mind, and she explained the expression to Noah.

"I like that," he said. "It's so . . . exact!" She shared his laughter.

"The truth be told," she continued. "I do believe we are part of a greater plan. I just don't know where I fit in. I'm thirty-seven; isn't that late to make major changes?" She was silent for a moment in case he wanted to respond, but he didn't say anything. "Uncle Dan said Hobo wanted to work with me when I was young, but my folks wouldn't let him," she continued. "What am I to learn now? Here you are, maybe able to teach me what Hobo should have," Amanda said as she looked at Noah sideways gauging any reaction, "so I'm confused."

"Why does that confuse you?" Noah looked directly at her for the first time since they left the cabin.

"Well first of all, it seems pretty late to start questioning what I'm doing and where I'm going, don't you think? Maybe I should just get into my car and go back to Milwaukee. It's lonely there, people aren't very friendly, but at least I knew what I was going to do from one day to the next and why." She finished lamely, "And because of an accidental walk by a pond and finding the feather, I'm feeling misplaced." She swiped angrily at the tears that suddenly appeared on her cheeks.

Noah looked everywhere but at her. "I know 'tis easier said than done," he said, "but why don't you relax and let the Grandfather take care of you? That walk wasn't accidental, just remember that."

"Let go and let God? Isn't that a Christian motto?"

"Christians know about the Grandfather too. He hasn't exactly kept himself a secret," Noah smiled.

She grinned. "What about the gifts Migizi told me I have?"

"What about them?"

"Am I expected to do something about them? What can I do? How do I even know what they are? Besides," she squinted at him against the sun, "I've always heard women are supposed to keep to the background and not get involved with men things."

"Manda," he laughed, "You've seen too many cowboy-and-Indian movies. They always show Indian women walking three feet behind their men. You've seen it a hundred times," he said. "John Wayne rides into camp and spots a beautiful Indian princess dressed in white beaded buckskin—never mind that we never had royalty! She's standing by the fire, dutifully chewing on deer hide and glancing up seductively behind her long lashes. Maybe that's what the white guys want for their women, but Indian men don't, and we never did."

Amanda smiled, picturing a darkly painted Debra Paget secretly casting adoring eyes at the white hero.

"Traditionals hold Indian women in high esteem," he continued. "After all, they're the life-givers, the first teachers of our young, the guardians of our future. They were always involved in making important tribal and family decisions. Did you know they even got to pick the chiefs, and if the chiefs didn't behave, those grandmothers axed 'em," he snapped his fingers. "Man, John Wayne would have sung soprano if he'd treated real Indian women like he did in the movies. Our women were free long before white women." He looked at Amanda with laughter in his eyes. "How do you feel about being held in such a position?"

"Scared," she answered, "and proud!"

"Good," he nodded. "I like that. It's important to remember that the Grandfather is the only one who can show us who has the gift of teaching or healing, then each person has to decide if he *or she*," he emphasized, "wants to do something with it." His voice took on its teasing tone, "But late thirties," he teased, "I don't know. That does seem pretty *old*."

Amanda grinned, but refused to satisfy his remark with one of her own.

"If we pay attention, we see the signs," he was serious again. "Then we can learn. Nobody's forced by the Creator to do anything. He loves us and gives us a choice. You're the only one who can decide what to do about Migizi's visit." He took her shoulders and turned her to face him. She grew uncomfortable under his steady gaze and blushed. She turned toward the woods.

Noah knew when not to push. He indicated with his chin that he wanted to continue to walk. "Your uncle touched many lives in a good way," he said. "Our people are richer because of his knowledge and caring. He was always ready to help anyone, any time, day, night, winter, summer, rain, snow—it didn't matter . . . kinda like the mailman," he chuckled. Without a response from Amanda, he continued, "If he couldn't find a ride, he'd walk. He loved to help." They walked in silence. "That's what I want folks to say about me: 'he loved to help.' Do you think that's egotistical of me?" he asked.

"Of course it is!" she teased. "But it's also a good reason for living. Besides, would you want people going around saying, 'I'm sure sorry Noah lived. He spread such misery and pain,'" she laughed. "But if you'd like me to say that about you after you're gone, I will!"

"And why do you think I'm going first?" he teased back. He laughed when she shrugged. Without a spoken decision, they turned and began walking back toward Noah's cabin. "I don't have any chocolate cake, but I got coffee and some store-bought donuts—powdered-sugar coated," he tempted.

"Powered sugar? You're on!" Amanda said. Her step was a bit lighter now.

Back at the cabin, while Noah put on a fresh pot of coffee, Niijii made himself comfortable in front of the wood stove. Amanda snuggled into an old chair that was already formed to fit the human body. She laughed when the dog stretched and groaned in obvious pleasure.

Noah heard him from the kitchen. "Got to warm up those old bones," he said affectionately. "I figure Niijii must be fourteen, fifteen in human years; that would make him pretty old in dog years."

Niijii half-woofed in response, too tired to open his eyes. He knew he was the topic of conversation between these two humans. Amanda smiled. She enjoyed the comfortable relationship Noah shared with this shaggy four-legged.

"*Niijii* means friend, doesn't it?" she asked as Noah entered the room. He was carrying two coffee cups in one hand and an open box of doughnuts in the other. He settled himself into a chair across from Amanda and balanced the donuts on one knee. The box tipped, threatening to topple when he leaned forward to offer Amanda her cup.

"Yep, and that's exactly what he is. The best friend I ever had." He laughed when Niijii opened one eye and looked at him, ears twitching. Noah sipped his coffee. "When you going back to Milwaukee? How much longer will you live there?"

"Why?" Amanda's heart dropped. "Will that make a difference? Do I have to live on the rez to learn more about tradition?" She thought he hesitated a moment too long.

"It would be easier if you were here. Long distance learning," he shrugged, "too many starts and stops, but I guess we could get together when you come back for a weekend unless I'm on one of my trips."

She wrapped her hands around the coffee cup. Up til now, she hadn't really thought about going back to Milwaukee, nor had she thought about *not* going back. That would be crazy, she thought. "I have a job," she finally said. "They depend on me, and I like my work. Besides, what could I do here?"

Noah didn't answer. He reached down to pet Niijii, who opened both eyes this time and looked at the man.

Amanda could have sworn the dog smiled.

Silence bounced off the walls. Amanda's insides began to knot; she didn't know what else to say. Making a show of leaving, she brushed nonexistent sugar from her face and hands and waited. Noah watched her passively. Sudden anger or frustration, she didn't know which, passed through her. Fighting to keep the quaver from her voice, she asked if she could come back in two days.

"Friday would be better," Noah said. "Same time?"

She nodded, not trusting her voice.

Noah walked her to the door and shook her hand in a strangely distracted way. She turned to face him and was surprised to notice that he wasn't any taller than she. He always looked so much bigger. She shifted her weight from one foot to the other, waiting for something to be said. But not knowing what it was or who was supposed to say it, she turned to the screen door and pushed it open. It screeched with a protest that made her teeth hurt.

He finally spoke. "Pray with your feather, Amanda, and trust. Your prayers will be answered. Migizi and I will both be here to help you." His voice came from a distance; neither his eyes nor his words were directed at her, reminding her of a priest dismissing the last repentant after a long day. *Go and sin no more, my child.*

As the Escort took her from Noah's cabin, she was filled with a sense of time flying by at top speed, taking any control she'd had over her life with it. In little more than three weeks she'd be back in Milwaukee. How could she even consider not returning to her job? For a brief second Amanda wondered what kind of work she might find in the small city just off the reservation. She shook her head to throw off the thought.

Amanda glanced at her watch, then turned the car around. She wanted to see her uncle and knew she'd find him at Winky's.

Winky's mini mart was dark. Removing her glasses didn't help much. How on earth can he work in here? she wondered. Her uncle's chuckle came from the back of the long, rectangular room. The two men were playing cribbage on a card table that looked like it could be the same one that was set up at the back of the store when she was a kid.

"Winky, I declare! Look what the wind blew in!" her uncle said. "Isn't she a pretty sight?"

"Sunshine for these tired old eyes, fer sure!" Winky answered. "Suppose she's gonna hustle you on home, or ya think she heard we was the two best *ket-ches* on the rez and came to check us out?"

"Well I'm blood-related, so she can't be after me, but could be she's after you. Everyone knows you stashed away a fortune over the years. She's single, and you know them single girls like money even if an old *geezer* has to come with it."

"Ya think she could really be after my money?" Amanda couldn't tell if Winky was laughing or wheezing.

"Buddy, as your best friend, I gotta warn you 'bout your competition. Old Punky Jake's squinty-ginters sure brightened up when he saw this little lady at church on Sunday. Like a puppy dog he was, panting away with his mouth watering and his tongue hangin' out to next Tuesday."

"A St. Bernard puppy dog, you mean," Winky laughed wickedly.

"A *slobbering* St. Bernard puppy," her uncle added.

"All right, guys! You can stop anytime! I came by because I wanted some company. Thought you two would be better than nothing, but now I'm not so sure," Amanda said.

The two old men slapped each other's knees and laughed. Amanda walked over to the pop machine and dug some coins out of her jean pockets. "I liked the old cooler better, Winky," she said. "I think the pop tasted better from those green bottles. It tasted colder somehow. Maybe it was that ice cold water it sat in."

"That's not why you liked it. You an' every other kid learned how to pull those bottles out without payin', that's why you liked it. Don't think I din't know!"

Amanda's face got hot remembering a time when she'd done just that. She was glad it was it was dark so the men couldn't see her blush. She grabbed a can of Diet Coke and walked back to the table. "Who's winning?"

"This skinny old Indian skunked me twice today. Musta ate Lucky Charms for breakfast," Dan chuckled.

Winky snorted and winked at her—or was it just his tic? "I don't need luck to beat this here tired old man."

"Gonna stay an' eat with me this evening, Sis?" her uncle asked. He concentrated on the cards.

"You planning to fix your world-famous delicacy again? What was it, hot dogs?"

"She's got ya there Dan," Winky wheezed.

"What? Girl, you think that's all I eat?" He looked at her and grinned. "As a matter of fact, I haven't quite decided *what* I'm gonna fix tonight, so, do you want to stay or not?"

"Why don't you let me fix supper?" Amanda offered, grabbing an excuse not to be alone. "I have mom's fry bread recipe," she tempted them.

"Fry bread!" Winky said. "Dan, take the young-un up on her offer. I haven't had decent fry bread in *years!*"

"Winky, you old fart, you're lyin'! I seen you eat plenty of fry bread at our last Pow Wow, right over there in the Community Center. You're just trying to make us feel sorry for you, but it ain't gonna work."

"Aw, you can't count Pow Wow fry bread. I mean *special-made* stuff, like this girl here is talkin' 'bout."

"Why don't I go on up to the house and start it? I'll come back and pick you up later, Uncle."

"Got a better idea. Why don't you run along an' fix supper, an' Winky here can drive me up hisself. I bet you could make enough so's we can feed this skinny old man. That way, I won't have to listen to his grumblin' about being neglected for the next say, four, five months."

"Began to think you'd never ask," Winky laughed. "I was runnin' outta hints." Turning, he pointed toward the shelves.

"Go ahead, grab up what you need, girl. If'n you're willing to fix supper, least I kin contribute."

Figuring Dan had a cupboard full of commodity flour, honey, and canned milk, she took yeast and eggs.

"Grab up some bacon, too, girl. You do know how to fix gravy from the drippin's, don't ya'?"

"Christ a'mighty, Winky!" her uncle said. "Ya just begged supper off the girl, and now you're tellin' her what ya want to eat on top of it? Ain't never seen anything like you, old man!"

"I finally figured out why you two are such good friends: you're just alike," Amanda laughed and grabbed a bag from under the counter. "I think I have everything I need, Winky, thanks. See you two at the house."

"We'll be there 'bout 6:30, Sis." Uncle Dan said. He added quietly, "Feels real family with you here."

She heard the catch in his voice. She blinked back tears and waved at the two men without answering as she went out the door.

Dan's house was unlocked as usual; people on the rez still trusted one another. She liked being back in the familiar kitchen. Not much had changed since Aunt Molly lived here except that it wasn't as clean. She attacked the sink full of dishes first. The smell of the sudsy water brought back memories of busy but fun times getting ready for family feasts. Not only did Aunt Molly love to cook, but she just happened to be a great chef. She always had something going for the family, the sick, or the elderly of the community. Amanda hummed to herself as she kneaded the fry bread dough. The sandwiches she had made for Noah earlier this week were the first food she had fixed for anyone but herself since the last time she made dinner for Ken, just before the accident.

She stopped kneading and gazed out the window. She knew in her heart that she missed Ken, but, strangely, she had to struggle now even to remember what he looked like. Even his smile, his best feature, was difficult to bring to mind. Piece by piece he wasn't all that handsome, she remembered, but he fit together well. Could it really have been only weeks ago that she arrived from Milwaukee and sat in the cabin watching a snowstorm? The city, her job, and Ken felt like they belonged to a different lifetime, to a different Amanda. She wondered again if she could make a life here. No, she didn't see that as a possibility. She sprinkled more flour on the counter and went back to working the bread. Once she returned to the city, she'd feel the same about the time spent here, she imagined.

Dan and Winky arrived exactly at 6:30. Amanda had already set the table with the mismatched dishes. Bacon, gravy, boiled potatoes, and wild rice were already in bowls on the table. Amanda was just taking the last two pieces of bread out of the grease and laying them on paper towels when the men walked in the door. The golden-brown bread looked great, she thought to herself, just right. To the men she said, "I hope I haven't lost my touch, guys."

"My gawd, girl! What's that wonderful smell? Maybe I will let you marry me after all," Winky said.

Dan hung his coat over the back of a chair and gave her a big hug. "Mandy, I can't tell ya how good it feels to have ya here. You *sure* you got to go back to that city? I'd love for ya to stay on."

"You two would just keep me in a kitchen. I didn't get a college degree to be a maid, you know, not even yours, Uncle."

"Heck, girl, a woman's place is *in* the kitchen. Din't they teach you nothin' in that fancy school of yers?" Winky asked. He dipped a finger into the gravy.

"Winky, don't be gross! Sit down, both of you. Everything's ready. Fry bread isn't good when it's cold."

Noises of appreciation came from the two old men as she set the bread in front of them. Amanda giggled as, between mouthfuls, they nodded and mumbled how good everything was.

After supper the two men insisted that she go into the living room while they did dishes. She glanced through the *TV Guide,* listened to the noise—*lots* of noise—that came from the other room, and resisted the urge to check on them. They finally joined her in front of the fireplace.

This was the first time Amanda had been in Winky's company outside of the store. She decided he was as much fun as her uncle. The two men brought back the reservation of yesterday with their stories—old friends returned to life. Stories about her father made her laugh. The antics of that young boy hardly fit the man she knew as Dad.

Winky started every story after story with, "Dan, remember when . . ."

Finally Dan had his chance. "Winky, can you remember back when your name was Walter?"

"Ya know," Winky frowned, "seems like I do remember *somethin'* like that, by golly." His eye seemed to tic faster just to prove his point.

Winky continued his visit to the past by telling Amanda about his family. She was surprised to learn that he had been married and he had a daughter. Amanda and her young friends had nicknamed Winky "The Hermit" because he never seemed to have any friends, let alone women friends. *Gay* wasn't a word used back then—at least not on the reservation. If it had been, that's what they would have called him. His wife, Theresa, had died in a sanitarium a few years after their marriage. "A lot of TB on the rez then," he explained. "Bad water, mostly." Two-year-old Angela died a year later, during a measles epidemic. "All those kid sicknesses kilt a lot of Indian babies in them days. Now they got all them there shots." His voice filled with tenderness; tears filled his eyes, and he wiped them with dark, paper-thin hands. Amanda tried to imagine this hoary old man as a young husband and loving father.

By 10:30 both men were yawning. Dan invited Amanda to spend another night. She turned him down, then spent five minutes trying to convince Winky that she didn't need to be escorted home.

"We don't want ya getting stuck somewhere out in this cold, do we Dan? I live out near the Point, anyways," he assured her. "Won't be any bother at all to follow you out there to make sure you're safe."

Knowing this was an argument she was going to lose, she gave in. "That'd be great, Winky, thanks."

"I'll jest stick close so's I'll make sure nothing happens, okay?"

The door to his hand-painted blue pickup screeched and clunked like it was losing parts when he pulled it open. It sounded almost as bad when he pulled it shut. "Typical rez truck," she told her Escort as it purred to life. On the ride home Amanda wondered what life would have been like if she'd stayed on the reservation and married Brownie. This time tonight, with these two old men, made her wish she had done things differently.

Out on the highway Winky stuck about two car lengths behind her. Amanda kept her speed at fifty. Winky's truck didn't look like it could keep up if she went faster. Glancing in her rearview mirror, she half expected to see bits and pieces of his truck go every which way each time he hit a bump in the road. One of his headlights was out, and the other was pretty dim. She turned into her long driveway and was surprised when Winky stayed with her. She thought he'd turn around by the highway—he really did want to make sure she was safe! Amanda pulled into her spot next to the house and turned off the engine. Winky stopped, and then waited in his still running truck. The engine was sputtering badly and showing signs of smoke, but still running. Amanda unlocked the front door of the cabin, reached in and switched on the light. She turned and waved.

Winky tapped the truck's horn, which sounded like a cross between a foghorn and a hoarse bullfrog, and struggled to shift. The sound made Amanda's teeth ache. After protesting loudly, the truck finally slipped into gear. Winky then made himself a road around the oak tree. Amanda grinned as she noticed that his truck had a taillight out too.

# Chapter 12

Amanda woke around midnight, gasping for breath, struggling to throw off the remains of a nightmare. The sheets were wet with sweat. A loud crack ripped through the cabin. The room went in and out of focus with the strobe effect of lightning, making the dream all the harder to shake off. She glanced at the nightstand where she kept Miigwan when she slept, half expecting to see Migizi. The stand was empty except for the feather. She ran her fingers through her damp hair as snatches of the dream—something to do with her father or possibly Hobo—tugged at her.

Not really wanting to leave her bed, but needing water, she slipped on her moccasins and shuffled out to the kitchen without turning on a light. Rain tapped noisily on all the windows. Over the edge of the plastic cup Amanda watched huge drops splat against the panes and race each other down the glass. Strange to have a thunderstorm now: unless someone was playing a trick on her and had changed the calendar, technically, it was still winter.

*In the moonlit kitchen her grandmother went from window to window, locking each in turn and pulling the curtains together. She moved quickly, her white nightgown billowing out behind her, afraid of getting caught in the window when lightning flashed again, making the outdoors as bright as midday. "Mandy, stay back," she whispered. "The lightning is dangerous. Go back to bed. Hurry now, hurry."*

*Amanda wasn't afraid of storms, so she sure didn't understand her grandmother's concern. She loved to watch the long shards of electricity flash from the sky and hear the rumble of thunder roll across the heavens. "But Gram—" she started to complain.*

*"Manda! Go to bed and cover up. Now!" Grammy turned and glared at the child. "Move, and don't give me no more sass, girl!" There was no arguing with Grandma when she used that tone of voice.*

Amanda watched Grandma fade away with the locking of the last window. She rinsed her glass and turned it upside down in the sink. Hobo's curious Ojibwe and English whisper came out of the dark—something about the first thunder of the year. Amanda couldn't make out the words. They were lost in a deep rumble of thunder. Long ago it might have been important, but it didn't seem to matter much at this moment. Back in bed, Amanda snuggled down between the heavy flannel sheets and listened to the storm move off to the east as she drifted into sleep again.

Her first thought upon waking Wednesday morning was that Friday was still two days away—two *long* days away. She prayed with Miigwan, as she did every morning now, thanking the Creator for each new day and asking guidance in making decisions about her life. The brave nineteen-year-old who left the reservation almost twenty years before had disappeared, and left in her place was a woman with a fear of change. She complained to Miigwan during her prayers, "How am I supposed to know what to do? Where do I belong now?"

At mid-morning she took her daily walk to the pond. False spring had become the real thing. Last night's storm was the finishing touch. Except in areas where snow had piled up in mounds or lay in the shade of trees, the earth's winter-white blanket was gone. She took a deep breath. The air was fresh and clean. She thought of Noah's words about spring and new life. Amanda touched the tiny green buds that had begun to decorate each winter-bare branch and whispered a silent prayer of thanks. She'd let too much time pass since appreciating the gifts of nature. The years in the city had, as Winky said, dulled her senses; she'd become a victim of the city.

*"Is this it, Gamma?" Amanda asked as she picked a piece of sage. She wrinkled her nose and studied the woolly, greenish-blue leaves before handing the branch to the old lady in the long dress and faded blue shawl.*

*Her grandmother took the sage with one hand and reclaimed the hand of the five-year-old Amanda with the other. They continued to walk down the path behind the cabin. "Yes, Manda, that's it. Isn't it beautiful?"*

*"It don't smell so boo-tiful," The little girl said knowingly. She loved these times, when Grandmother would bring her out into the woods, often with Uncle Hobo; she felt safe. The two old people always had a burnt sage smell to their hair and clothes. Burnt sage smelled okay, better than the just-picked stuff.*

*Amanda knew the sage was used for medicine. Often her grandmother would tie it in small bundles wrapped with red string and put them on the windowsills in different rooms of the house, "for protection, Mandy," Gram would say. New sage was picked every year. It was an important chore, and Amanda was proud to be a part of it—like today.*

*When Hobo was with them, the two Elders spoke only Ojibwe. That was okay with Amanda; she knew it was hard for Hobo to speak English. He'd try, but his English words got mixed with Indian words. She'd try hard to understand him, but when she couldn't, he'd smile his toothless smile and make hand gestures that sometimes helped.*

*Sometimes just she and Gramma came to pick the sage, then Gram would tell stories of the old days as they walked slowly over the dirt road that led from the pond to the place where the sage grew. Amanda tried to imagine this old lady as a young girl and Uncle Hobo as a young boy riding horses through these woods. But as hard as she tried, it was beyond her five-year-old imagination, so what she saw were childish bodies topped by the heads of her Gram and Great-uncle as she knew them now. Even at her age she recognized this as silly and, although she wanted to giggle, she struggled to act grown-up, knowing that's what Gramma would want. At times like this, Gramma would look down at her and smile like she was reading her mind. Hobo did it too. Amanda thought this was probably something all old people could do. Today Gramma's voice soothed the little girl as she drew pictures with her words. Amanda looked up at Gram, enthralled by the retelling of events that had happened over sixty years ago.*

The shrill screech of an eagle passing overhead jerked Amanda back to the present. "Migizi," she whispered. The great bird circled twice before it disappeared into the clouds. Amanda stared after it. Was Migizi's sudden appearance a sign or a coincidence? "Trust your prayers, Amanda," a voice whispered in the breeze.

"Thank you, Grandfather, for sharing your messenger with me." Amanda had lost her self-consciousness over praying at odd times during the day. She'd lost her sense of prayer in Milwaukee, even on Sundays. Here it felt right to give thanks at any time.

That evening Amanda made two pudding pies and put one of them in the freezer to take to Noah on Friday. It was chocolate, and it had to be better that the stale doughnuts that he'd fed her, she told herself. The second pie she'd take to Ben and Yemmy the next day.

She had already put the car in park position at the Vincents' when she noticed Noah's Bronco in the back—too late to retreat without drawing attention to herself. She didn't want Noah thinking she was following him. Just then Ben and Noah came around the corner of the house. They were laughing; Noah was patting Ben on the back. Amanda liked the laughter and teasing that constantly happened whenever Indian people got together. In hard times humor made life bearable, especially when Indians could make fun of themselves. She thought it was a gift from the Creator that Indians could see something funny in anything. Amanda had, at times, been the brunt of the humor, but she wasn't alone; everyone on the rez had a turn sooner or later. The old-timers had used humor to teach manners, correct mistakes, or show disappointment—or as often as not, just for fun at the expense of others.

The men waited for her on the steps. "Amanda! Good to see you. Enter, enter," Ben hugged her. Noah held the door for them both and grinned at her as she passed.

Yemmy was at the sink. "Well, look here! Two of my favorite young folks. What a nice surprise! Ben, pull that other chair from the porch, will you?" She wiped her soapy hands on a towel before hugging Amanda.

"I'll get it, Nokomis," Noah said. He touched Amanda's shoulder as he passed. "What a nice surprise."

Ben made coffee, while Amanda helped Yemmy make sandwiches. Noah set the table. He helped himself to the cupboards like a member of the family. Amanda envied the way he could be comfortable anywhere.

It wasn't long before the conversation turned to food. Noah praised Amanda's cooking, making the simple venison sandwiches from the other day sound like a gift from the gods. His description of her chocolate cake embarrassed her. Now he fussed about her pie.

"This woman knows the way to a man's heart," he said helping himself to a second piece.

"Speaking of heart, you need a good woman in your life, Noah," Yemmy told him. "Land sakes, boy, you always eat like its been a week from Tuesday when you last seen food. You need someone to cook for you . . . on a daily basis. For company, too. An' I mean company other than that smelly ole dog that follows you everywhere." Yemmy beamed at Amanda. Amanda blushed and studied the half-eaten sandwich in her hand.

"Oh, I don't know," Noah said. "I don't expect I'll have Niijii too many more years. I'm gonna miss him. But he's all the company I need right now."

"I'm not talking about *that* kind of company, and you know it! Besides, Niijii can't cook for you."

"Maybe not," Ben laughed, "but I seen him wash Noah's plates—one dish at a time . . . on the floor."

"Oh, Ben, don't be disgusting!" Yemmy scolded and slapped at his arm with a crippled hand.

"We're planning to collect some red willow," Noah told Amanda still laughing. "Want to come with us?"

That was it! Amanda suddenly remembered that Hobo wouldn't collect red willow in the spring until after the first thunder. That's what he was telling her last night. It is time to collect willow!

Yemmy jumped at the chance to continue matchmaking. "Yeah, go, Amanda. This old man shouldn't be out trampin' in the woods. He'll keel over with a heart attack one of these days. He can stay put and help me here. You two young-uns go and bring some back to us." Amanda saw Yemmy tap Ben on the leg with her knife as she spoke although she was looking straight at Noah.

"Yeah, I was figgerin' on fixin' a flower garden this year. Can't never start too early," Ben said and looked out the window. Even Yemmy laughed at the obvious; snow patches still dotted the yard.

"Sounds like the bear story Uncle Dan told me the other night," Amanda said.

"Sure, come along Manda. I can use the help," Noah insisted. "Have you collected willow before?"

"I didn't collect it myself, but I used to go with Hobo when I was little," she said. "It would be wonderful to go with you, thanks. Let me help Yemmy with dishes first."

While Yemmy cleared the table and Amanda started washing, the men went outside. Amanda recognized the familiar ritual. Her father, uncles, boy cousins, and her grandfather always had always gone outside after a meal for as long as she could remember, and in any kind of weather. Curiosity had always tugged at her—she wanted to sneak out to find out just where they went and what they did. But as hard as she tried, she never got past the sentinels: the women of the family.

# Chapter 13

As they drove along the slough road, a battered black pickup passed them, swerving recklessly and throwing mud and gravel into the side of Noah's Bronco. Three teenaged boys whooped and waved from the open windows of the truck. The boy on the passenger side of the truck took off a red beaded cap and saluted. Freed, his long dark hair blew wildly in the wind. Once the truck cleared the Bronco by a car length, it sped up and moved back into the right lane, throwing more mud and gravel back at them.

"I wonder if their mothers know they're skipping school," Noah said gruffly.

"Do you know them?" she asked.

"'Fraid so. The driver's a Buckley kid. The one with the cap is my nephew, Luke. He's been giving his ma a rough time lately, hanging with some pretty tough kids."

Amanda waited.

"I've been meaning to have a talk with the boy, but can't seem to catch up with him. His pa's in lock-up again, and my sister, Sherry, just got a new job, so she's not home much anymore. Basically, he's a good kid," he said looking at Amanda. "He just needs a little direction once in a while."

"Like, from his uncle?" she asked.

Noah grinned at her. "Yeah, like from his uncle," he said through his smile.

Just ahead of them Amanda saw the slough bridge. One side showed signs of recent scarring, the scars beginning to rust. She looked at Noah, then back at the bridge, unable to ask. He nodded. "This is where it happened. Wasn't any reason for him to be out here 'cept he was drinking. Lucky some kids came along and we was able to get him to the hospital. At least he didn't die out here alone. No one knows for sure how long he'd been here before those kids showed up. Punky said Brownie was at work a few days before and was sober then." Noah paused and cleared his throat. "He was unconscious quite a while, but came around just at the end. Both me and Paula was at the hospital when he died."

"Did he know you were there?" she asked.

"Yeah, and he knew he was dying. Said he'd seen his ma. Said she was coming for him. He said he was ready to go with her." He paused. He kinda beamed when he said she looked just like her pictures."

Amanda turned her head away from Noah and forced back the tears burning behind her lids.

"Then he asked me to take care of Paula and the kids."

Amanda thought about the young family that sat in front of her and Dan in church. Through her jacket, she rubbed the goose bumps that rose on her arms. "How's his family doing?" she asked.

"Okay. Yeah, they're okay. Paula thinks she needs a man around all the time. She's really stronger than that, but she doesn't want to be. I guess she's one of those women who likes taking care of a man." He paused then added, almost to himself, "She'll be fine."

Amanda wondered at the tone of his voice. "She must have her hands full with those little ones. What about her folks? Do they help out?"

"When they can. They're from over by Balsam Lake and get this way a couple times a month. They stay for a few days, then go back. They got their own lives. Paula says they been trying to get her to go back to the Lake with them, but for some reason Paula says she wants to stay on here."

Amanda turned to look at the bridge that was lost behind a bend in the road. She shivered, imagining she felt Brownie beside her.

Noah found a wide spot beside the road and pulled the Bronco over. Amanda looked at the field of red willow. "Do you know how many times I've passed by here and never noticed the willow?"

"No. How many?"

She threw him a look.

Noah grinned at her and reached under the seat and pulled out two knives and a small leather pouch. He opened the pouch and shook some tobacco into her palm before walking to the side of the road. Noah prayed, first in Ojibwe, then in English. He nodded to her, and she repeated the English words before laying her tobacco on the ground beside his. "Don't cut yourself," he laughed as he handed her the smaller of the knives.

"Not to worry," she assured him. "I hate to see blood, especially mine." Silently they worked in different directions. At first Amanda watched Noah and selected the same size willow he did. She learned quickly. She began humming an old Simon and Garfunkel tune "Scarborough Fair."

"That's nice," Noah teased. "It means you're enjoying your work."

She smiled and didn't respond, but she quit humming.

"Tell me," he continued, "Were you humming the other day when you were scrubbing your house down?"

Amanda blushed remembering how she looked when he showed up at her door and didn't answer. She refused to get into that discussion.

An hour later Noah said, "I think we have enough to keep us busy, let's go to the house and get something hot to drink. Ain't ya gettin' cold?"

In truth, Amanda hadn't felt a chill, but with his question she became aware that her feet were wet. And freezing. At the Bronco she handed Noah the red willow, but she held back the few stems of barely budding pussy willow she'd gathered. "When I was a kid, I read a Golden Book story about pussy willows with little furry kitty heads that meowed," she told him. "It was a great story. I loved it. Ever since then, I half-expect to see little furry faces staring at me whenever I pick them. It would weird me out if it happened! Strange, the kind of things we remember, huh?"

Noah laughed, "Someday I'll tell you some of the fantasies that hooked me as a kid."

"Oh, I can't wait," she teased.

Back at Noah's cabin Amanda took off her shoes and put her wet stocking feet against the side of the stove. Niijii settled down beside her in a way that suggested she was no longer a guest, but a friend. Noah brought coffee in and sat on the floor beside them. "I'm glad you came along today, Amanda," he said.

Amanda waited. In the short time they'd been together, she recognized that he used her formal name when he was about to talk about important things.

He fooled her. "Tell me about your job."

"Not much to tell. I work hard, make good money, and buy things. That's the American way, huh? Most of the time I like my job, and the people in the office are nice." Then remembering of Ted-the-Obnoxious, she added, "Well, most of them anyway. And I'm good at what I do—no genius, but I can function pretty well at most any computer, thank you." She blew on her coffee and waited.

He squinted as he looked at her and tapped his lower lip with his finger. "That doesn't tell me much. Tell me about you. How do you feel *inside* about your job?"

"Well, at first it was really awful. Besides missing home, Milwaukee wasn't ready for an Indian woman to do computer work. So of course I wanted to prove that I could do even better work than any white man or woman there. I liked doing that." She smiled. "Then just when things started going right, bad things began to happen. My parents passed on just a few months apart from each other." Her voice broke.

"Uh-huh, I remember. It must have been hard for you." He looked at Niijii instead of at her.

She nodded. "I can't tell you how alone I felt. They were all I had in the whole world. I guess I always thought they'd be here for me, you know?" She drew a deep breath. "Then I got into a nasty marriage. Don't ask me why. Maybe I just needed someone. But it turned out he was worse than no one at all." She laughed and cleared her throat. "Made me a little leery of men for a while. Finally I started dating a man I worked with, Ken, and then just before Christmas that accident . . ." She sipped her coffee while she fought for control.

Noah continued to stroke Niijii's head and to look out the window. The old dog stretched and closed his eyes. "I thought about getting married once," he said abruptly. "Came close, but it wasn't to be."

"What happened?" She was interested.

"She's the granddaughter of one of our spiritual leaders in Minneapolis, so I figured she'd understand what my life's about. I'd hoped she'd be a support in my work, but she took up the path herself and decided she could do better. Maybe she can. So instead of being partners, it felt like we were competing. That's how it felt to me anyway. Not even so much in our work as in our words. Strange, ain't it? Nice girl though—sometimes I miss her—but she couldn't cook," he laughed. "She never made me a chocolate cake!"

Amanda frowned at him. "You're weird, you know it? You tease at the most unusual times."

He ignored that comment and continued, "Maybe the moral of both our stories is that it's not up to us to plan what part others will play in our lives." He stared at her, his expression unreadable.

"Ever see her?" Amanda asked. She'd tried not to ask the question, but curiosity had the best of her.

"Sometimes. Last time was about a year ago. She's making her own way. Doing a good job too—she's got the gift all right. And she's got a good family to help her."

"You chose a lonely profession," Amanda said. "I remember how lonesome Hobo seemed at times."

"I didn't choose it; it chose me."

"If you'd had the opportunity to choose, knowing what you know now, with all the good, the bad, and the loneliness, would you still be doing it?"

"Absolutely!" He answered so abruptly that Niijii jumped and opened his eyes. He studied the man for a minute before deciding all was well, then he looked at Amanda as if to say: "Just put up with him. This crazy two-legged can't help himself," and he closed his eyes again.

Never a dog person, Amanda was really beginning to enjoy this shaggy animal. She grinned and stroked his head. Niijii moaned with pleasure.

Noah suggested it was time for him to take Amanda back to pick up her car. "We don't want to stay away too long," he said. "Yemmy will have a field day. She's been trying to fix me up for as long as I can remember."

"They're really good people, and they like you, you know. Especially Yemmy."

"She's a born mother. She takes care of anyone who needs it, like me," he laughed. Amanda loved his laugh: it started deep inside and rumbled through his chest before it tumbled out of his mouth.

She stayed only a short time with the Vincents. To keep from hurting their feelings, she begged the need of a hot shower to chase the chills away. Noah left at the same time. When they reached the end of the driveway he waved as he turned his Bronco in the opposite direction.

Amanda took her time getting ready the next morning. She put on mascara for the first time since she'd arrived on the rez. Most of the curl was gone from her last perm. Her hair hung loosely past her shoulders—the longest she'd worn it in a while. The recent time out in the sun on her daily walks had put a reddish tint into her normally dark-brown hair. More than once Amanda wished she had inherited her dad's blue-black hair. She squinted her eyes and studied herself for a minute before putting on the heavily tinted glasses she'd worn since she left for college. The first time he'd seen them, Dad had teased her about trying to look "like a bookworm" to impress her professors, but he suspected her mismatched eyes attracted staring and rude questions in Milwaukee. Even though the people here weren't taken aback, the glasses had become such a part of her everyday dress she felt naked without them.

She grabbed the pie she'd taken from the freezer as she went out the door and headed for Noah's. She rode with her window down, breathing in the crisp air as it rushed in and kissed her face and blew wisps of hair across her forehead and into her eyes. Her spirits soared, and she laughed out loud thinking about how in Milwaukee she would carefully comb every hair in place and use half a bottle of spray to keep it from doing exactly what it was doing now.

She was surprised to see a car in Noah's driveway. It was an old one, the big heavy kind that looked and handled like a houseboat. There was so much rust on the back wheel panels that Amanda wondered what held the bumper on. Instead of Niijii, a woman's laughter greeted her as she stepped onto the porch.

Noah opened the door on her second knock. He was wearing a faded denim shirt with Indian designs embroidered on the pockets in teal, red, and purple. A black T-shirt showed underneath. "Amanda, enter." He touched her shoulder as she stepped past him.

"Am I interrupting? I thought I was supposed to come today?"

"No, I mean, yeah. No, you're not interrupting, and yeah, I was expecting you today. I have company, but she'll leave soon. Come in and join us."

To Amanda's surprise, the woman holding a baby and sitting in Noah's kitchen was Brownie's widow. Next to her a little girl knelt on a chair, bent over a project on the table. Paula's long hair was in two braids. She looked like a sweet, innocent teenager until she saw Amanda. A new, fleeting expression passed over her face before she arranged it in a non-expression.

"Amanda, meet Paula Brown. And these two are Ashley," he pointed to the oldest one with his lips, "and Zowie," he nodded at the baby in Paula's arms. "Brownie liked to say he had kids from A to Z," he laughed. "And Paula, this is Amanda Aaron."

Ashley was struggling with a large crayon and concentrating on a giant coloring book on the table in front of her. She was frowning. Her tongue stuck out between her teeth.

She glanced sideways at Amanda when she heard her name, but quickly turned her attention back to her chore.

"What beautiful children," Amanda said. She held her hand out to Paula. "I'm happy to meet you."

Paula took her hand, but dropped it quickly and spoke in Ojibwe. Amanda turned to Noah for help.

"She wants to know if you speak Ojibwe," he said in obvious discomfort.

"No, I'm sorry, I don't, Paula," she said. "Do you speak English?" As she said it, she blushed and wanted to take it back, afraid Paula would think she was baiting her, even though she knew she herself had just been baited. Everybody on the reservation could speak English, even the elders. Paula threw her a look that suggested they had begun a battle of some kind.

Noah ignored them both. "That pie looks great," he said. "Is it for now?"

"Of course," she breathed a sigh of relief and handed him the pie.

"More chocolate. You're going to spoil me. Would you like some, Paula?"

Paula shook her head and said something quietly in Ojibwe. Amanda suspected she'd just been insulted.

Spitefully, she wished Paula would take her kids and go home. Instead, Paula opened her blouse and began to nurse Zowie. She crooned softly in Ojibwe, her large milk-filled breast bared, Amanda suspected, for Noah's benefit, especially since Zowie hadn't fussed and there was a pink bay blanket lying on her lap (which she ignored). Amanda wondered if Noah knew what was going on. Zowie sucked on her mother halfheartedly, more interested in sleeping than eating. Amanda felt a challenge in the glance that Paula threw in her direction.

Noah was clearing off the table in front of Ashley. "Want some chocolate num-num?" he asked.

Ashley looked at the pie and nodded solemnly. "Numm, numm," she said, handing her crayon to Noah.

"Okay then. Let's fix you a bib, and you'll be all set, my girl." Amanda held back laughter as she watched Noah's thick fingers working a knot into the towel behind Ashley's back while trying not to get the dark curls caught in it.

After making sure Ashley was settled with a piece of pie, Noah set coffee and a piece of pie in front of Amanda. "Sit, sit," he said, after he suddenly realized she was still standing. He dragged a chair out from behind the table and set it between him and Paula. Amanda felt that she'd just been placed in the middle in more ways than one. She worked to keep her hand from shaking as she lifted a forkful of pie from the plate to her mouth; she couldn't even taste it.

To ignore being ignored by Paula, Amanda talked to Ashley. The little girl was delighted to be the center of attention. She held up each spoonful of pie to show Amanda before she *almost* got most of it in her mouth. Amanda and Noah laughed as blobs of chocolate landed on the towel or stuck to her face. Brownie lived in the child's eyes. The shape was the same; the coloring was different. "She looks like Brownie," Amanda said to Paula. Paula nodded, her expression unreadable. Hostility radiated from Paula. It had to do either with Brownie or with Noah, she suspected. Maybe both.

Amanda sensed Noah's discomfort. He didn't seem to know how to react to the hostility. The pie tasted like paste suddenly, and the knot in Amanda's stomach grew and her face got warm. She had just made up her mind to leave when Paula announced she had to go. She left her blouse unbuttoned, her dark nipple hard and wet, while she wrapped baby Zowie in the pink blanket.

Noah wiped the chocolate off Ashley's face and helped with her jacket. "I'll be right back," he told Amanda. "I'll carry this little fuzzy," he tickled Ashley, "critter out to the car for Paula." Ashley giggled and put her arms around his neck, snuggling tight against him. A hurried glance at Paula told Amanda the move hadn't been wasted on her. A stab of something like jealousy hit Amanda.

"Nice to meet you, Paula," Amanda said determined not show her relief at their leaving.

Paula nodded and said with a lack of enthusiasm, "I'm sure we'll meet again."

Amanda could hear Paula thinking, "Unless I can help it, that is."

She was pouring herself another cup of coffee when Noah returned. She wanted to ask about Paula's attitude, but didn't know how. "Nice family," she said instead. "Where were the boys today?"

"With their grandpa, Walt. He takes them out to the woods whenever he can to teach 'em the old ways."

"Paula's very pretty." She wanted to add, *too bad she's such a shit.*

"She's a good mother," Noah said. He wouldn't meet Amanda's eyes.

Amanda wanted to go out and come in again . . . to start over.

"Would you like to get out and get some fresh air?" Noah asked.

"Yeah, I'd like that." Amanda rinsed their dishes in the sink before putting on her jacket.

Noah was at a distance today, detached. She wondered if he was moody or troubled, or if Paula had said something at the car. He seemed out of focus—definitely out of sorts. For a second she wished she could talk things over with Niijii. It seemed to her that the dog was probably the only one who knew this man well. She giggled at the picture of her sitting on the porch having a serious discussion with the shaggy four-legged.

Noah raised his eyebrows and pushed opened the front door.

"I'll tell you someday," she said putting her head down so he couldn't see her blush.

Today they headed opposite the direction they had three days ago. A path ran in back of Noah's place, past two small log cabins that sat side-by-side and obviously had been empty for a long time. Small triangular windows set in each door had been broken, and pointed shards of glass jutted out in all directions, like transparent teeth. The cabins looked haunted.

"Spirits live there," Noah said as though reading her mind.

*Just like Hobo,* she thought. "Do you believe in ghosts?" Amanda asked.

"I said 'spirits,' not ghosts."

"Oh, is there a difference?" Was he kidding her?

It was his turn to wonder if she was pulling his leg. He looked at her and decided she wasn't.

"Sure! Ghosts are considered to be something that remains of dead humans: unhappy souls that hang around for some reason. People think they're dangerous. You know, Halloween, hauntings, headless horsemen, that kind of stuff." He paused to see if she was going to question him. She didn't. "Spirits, on the other hand, are the Grandfather's helpers. They come to guide our paths because either we call them or the Creator sends them. But, they can also be the spirit of someone who lived before too."

"Have you ever seen spirits?" she asked.

He frowned at her. "All the time," he said when he finally realized she expected an answer. "I saw some at your cabin the other evening. I wondered if you saw them."

"I wouldn't even know what to look for," she said.

"They come in all sorts of different colors and shapes," he continued. "They can be fat, skinny, red, blue, mostly white. Sometimes they float, sometimes they zoom." He waved his arm over his head and ducked like he was afraid of being hit by a flying object.

She laughed. "I feel like I've been missing something."

"Oh, you've probably seen them, you just didn't know it. But once you recognize them, you'll see them a lot. The important thing is they've recognized you." They walked a few minutes without speaking. "You have to believe in them to see them," he added.

They continued in silence until, unable to be patient any longer, she blurted, "Why doesn't Paula like me?"

"How do you know she doesn't?"

Amanda glared at him. "Come on! You felt it. You must have. I just don't like it. If she has a reason, okay. I just hate to be disliked for no reason."

"Maybe Paula thinks she has a reason."

"Does she? Like what?"

"Ask her."

"I'm asking you. Won't you tell me?"

He looked over her shoulder, a small vertical crease formed between his eyes. "I can tell you what I think. Maybe it's the reason, maybe not. You might not like it."

She nodded and waited, unwilling to beg.

"She knows about you and Brownie." He looked at Amanda. "Even though she's never met you, she's always been jealous." He waited. "Did you know Ashley's first name is Amanda? Ashley's her middle name."

Amanda's mouth dropped open.

"Paula probably feels you are a threat."

"But that was so long ago," Amanda began, "and Brownie's dead. How can I be a threat now?"

"She heard Brownie ask me to care for his family. I think she wants to be part of my life," he paused. "She likes to have a man around, and for now, I'm it. And then you come and bring me food. She might think you're taking part of my life from her." He shrugged. "But that might not be it at all. What do I know? I'm just a man. None of us know how women think."

She was only half listening. She was stuck on the thought of Brownie naming his daughter *Amanda* Ashley.

"Jeffy was a baby, just starting to walk, when Brownie and Paula married. Brownie treated the boy like his own, and Jeff loved him. Brownie's the only dad the kid ever knew," Noah continued. "He might not have been the best husband, but he was a good dad. Paula is alone now, with three more kids, and she wants a father for them."

"Now I know why she doesn't want to go back to Balsam Lake. Are you up to having a wife and four kids?" Amanda asked half-teasing, hoping she had already guessed the answer.

Noah scowled, glanced at her, then looked away quickly. They walked in silence again. "Amanda," he finally said, "I'm going to a ceremony in Minneapolis on Sunday. Would you like to go?"

"Can I? What would I need to do?" Both excitement and fear were evident in her voice, even to her.

"Keep me company. I think it would be good for you. I won't be running the ceremony," he paused. "A friend's grandfather, a *real* spiritual man, will do that. He's in his nineties, a Lakota who's got more gifts than I'll ever have. He's doing a ceremony for his grandchildren. I think you'd like it." His raised eyebrows asked the question.

Amanda exhaled, unaware she'd been holding her breath. "Wow. I don't know what to say. Can I call you and let you know tomorrow?"

Noah grunted and abruptly turned on his heel and began walking toward the cabin. With no other choice, Amanda followed. She tried to hide her disappointment when he went directly to her car and opened the door.

"I've been dismissed?" The words were out before she could stop them.

"I've got to prepare for the trip," he said, all business. He glanced into the car. "Where's your feather? It should be with you."

Defensive words rushed to her lips, but she bit them back—first the dismissal, now a reprimand for not having the feather with her. She slid behind the wheel of the Escort and buckled her seat belt before looking up at him.

Noah was grinning. He bent and knocked on the window. The odor of sage hit her when the window was halfway down. He squeezed her chin between the thumb and forefinger of his right hand. "I'll check in with you tomorrow," he said. He slapped the car top with his open palm and walked away.

"Bye," Amanda tossed out the window, feeling like she was talking to herself.

"Bye," he answered without turning.

*Well, so much for . . . what?* Amanda couldn't decide. But she knew she didn't like this feeling.

# Chapter 14

Noah closed the door behind him and looked out the window. Amanda's car was already out of sight. He'd surprised himself when he'd asked her to go to Minneapolis for the ceremonies on Sunday. In some ways she exhausted him. She was a test and a challenge presented by the Grandfather, of that he was sure. She didn't realize that she had gifts and that they were waiting to be claimed and nurtured. In last night's dream, Hobo told him she needed help. Hobo hadn't spoken a name, but Noah was certain he meant Amanda. It stood to reason that Hobo would be watching out for his great-niece. Noah wasn't sure he could give her what she needed—she needed so much. He saw the disappointment each time she couldn't have all the time or the answers she wanted. She was a sponge, ready to absorb anything he would tell her. She was perceptive, too, but didn't recognize that either. He shook his head and reached down to pet Niijii, who stood beside him, giving his full support to this needy two-legged.

"Fretting won't help me," he told Niijii. "Grandfather will tell me what to do in his own good time. I got to trust that. But I'm worried about what's gonna happen when she goes back to Milwaukee. If she goes, I don't think she'll be back. What do you think, my friend?" he asked a puzzled Niijii.

Niijii whimpered and shifted his weight.

"You're right," Noah told him. "Time to sit down." Noah sank into his old chair, and Niijii lay beside the stove. With a deep sigh, the dog drifted quickly off to sleep.

Noah's thoughts leapt to Paula. She acted like a spoiled brat today; she was becoming a problem. Somehow she had the idea that Brownie wanted Noah to be her mate, so that's what she expected to happen. Noah liked Paula okay—but four kids! He'd have to be out of his mind to take on that kind of responsibility, even if what he felt for her was love. No, he'd be like his teacher and give everything he had to serve his community. If he were better with words, it would be easy to tell Paula that all they could ever be was friends; he'd always be a big brother to her and an uncle to her kids. He got up to get himself some coffee. Niijii opened his eyes and watched until Noah reached the kitchen door, then he scrambled to his feet and followed.

"Funny," Noah said. Niijii sat down by his water dish and waited. "I can talk to spirits and even shaggy black dogs, but talking to humans makes me tongue-tied." Niijii tilted his head to one side and waited.

Noah never had a gift for conversation, which was probably one reason he didn't do well in school. The kids were expected to do book reports: stand in front of the whole class and talk! He'd never been a good reader, either, and spelling—man, what was that about? Why couldn't English be easier? *Spell it like it sounds,* he thought, *what's the big deal?* And those *blackbirds* were always making students *explain* themselves. He couldn't do that. He would get frustrated and walk away . . . only to be punished. He thought of Amanda's suggestion that he had "dismissed" her.

Amanda! He needed to be patient. The Grandfather had never let him down before. This was just another test. He reached down for Niijii's dish, and then he filled it in the sink. "Here you go, big guy," Noah told the dog. Niijii waited to see if the human was through talking. When no more words seemed to be coming, he bent his shaggy head to the bowl and quenched his thirst.

After quickly gulping another cup of coffee at the sink, Noah, with Niijii close on his heels, made his way back to the living room. Noah slid into his old chair, and Niijii once again lay by the fire. Within minutes, both were snoring softly.

Amanda drove directly to Winky's. He was busy today. She waved, and he pointed his chin in greeting.

Even with several customers hovering around, he moved at a snail's pace, visiting with each person as he took their money and packed up their groceries. Amanda grinned. This slow-moving old man would never have survived the city. She dug change out of her jacket pocket and moved to the pop machine. As she reached out to stick the quarters into the slot, an arm, covered in tired black leather, shot out, hitting her hand and sending the quarters careening across the worn black and white tiles.

A flash of red caught her eye as she stepped back and turned to defend herself. She recognized one of the boys from the racing pickup truck on the slough road.

"Sorry," he said in an unsorry voice. Then, "Hey, ain't you the new lady in town?" He threw back his head, lifted his sunglasses, and squinted at her.

"Is this the way you treat new ladies in town?" She didn't try to hide the anger in her voice.

"Hey, I said I was sorry; gimme a break, bitch!" The boy grabbed a Mountain Dew from the slot, adjusted his red beaded cap, and sauntered to the door, slamming it shut behind him.

"Never mind him; he can be a real jerk," Winky yelled to her.

Flushed, Amanda nodded. She located her scattered coins and got a diet pop from the machine. She waited at the cribbage table in the back until the last customer closed the door and Winky joined her.

"So, m'lady, what ya been up to?" His chair creaked in protest as he leaned back and lit a cigarette.

"Mmmm," she said swallowing a mouthful of Coke. "Went out to Noah's and met Brownie's widow. Didn't get a friendly reception there either. Suddenly I feel like an outsider around here. Well, I guess I am."

Winky chuckled and patted her hand in an unusual gesture. "Feelin' a little down, are ya?"

"Oh, just a little, I guess. Most of the time I feel like I'm getting better, then . . ." tears choked her.

Winky, fumbling uncomfortably with his cigarette, was visibly relieved when the door opened. A pregnant, giggling young woman with a dirty smock peeking out from under an equally dirty sweater, and an older, heavier Neil Butler staggered in. A sobbing two-year-old, with tear-streaked face, clung tightly to his neck.

"Well, whada ya know? If it ain't *Miss Manda*. I heard you was here," he slurred. Neil's younger, handsome face was hidden under the bloat that comes from years of heavy drinking. He bent toward Amanda as if to kiss her cheek. She drew back, choking on smells older and stronger than the liquor on his breath.

"Well, Miz Uppity, ain't it? I s'pose yer too good for us now that yer a *edjua-cated* Indian." The last word came out like a bad taste. He turned to the woman. "Bicky, this is my Old Lady's best friend, Amanda *A*-Ron!" Spittle formed on his bottom lip. "Guess she's too good for the rez now."

The smile on Bicky's face turned into a sneer. "Then why doesn't she go back where she came from?"

Amanda grabbed her jacket. "Winky, I'm going to Uncle Dan's. I'll talk to you later."

"Bitch!" Neil yelled as the door closed behind her.

Tears burned behind Amanda's lids. She wheeled the Escort out of the parking lot, throwing chunks of loose mud from the back tires towards the store.

Without thinking, she turned down the muddy, rutted street to Annie's. A large young woman with heavy lidded eyes answered the door on the third knock. "Hi, I'm Amanda; is Annie here?"

"Amanda!" Annie yelled from another room. "Winnie, it's Mandy, let her in."

The smile on Winnie's face did little to relieve the sullen bored look and the tired eyes. She nodded, then led the way to the kitchen. Surprisingly, Winnie moved with that strange swaying grace that many heavy people have. *That's good*, Amanda thought in a nasty mood, *that seems to be her best feature*.

"Mandy, I'm glad you're here." Annie was wearing the same ugly housecoat she had on during Amanda's earlier visit. "Sit down, have some coffee. This here's Winnie, my daughter-in-law."

Even with Winnie ignoring the introduction, this was the best welcome Amanda had had all day. She sat. Winnie put an empty cup in front of Amanda then went back to the ironing board. A stack of freshly ironed clothes rested on one end of the wooden table, and an overflowing plastic laundry basket sat on a chair beside her.

"What you been up to?" Annie's shaking hand brought a lighter to the cigarette in her mouth.

"I was just at Winky's. Guess who I saw?" Annie shrugged. "Neil came in while I was there."

Annie looked at her, an unasked question in her eyes.

"I didn't know the girl," Amanda said softly already sorry she'd brought it up.

No tears, no anger. Annie just looked tired. "Her name's Jenny Bicknell," Annie said. "She moved here with her ma and brother 'bout ten years ago. They lived with Old Man Jankowski til he got hit by a car one night walking home from work—back three, four years ago now. The girl lives with her ma in a trailer behind Meritt's bait shop in Saxon. Her brother's doing time over in Green Bay. They say he robbed Ron's Liquor Store last year with a *water gun* for God's sake. *Good* family, as we used to say." She and Winnie laughed. Without so much as a pause in her conversation, Annie struggled to her feet and poured each of them a cup of the strongest coffee Amanda had ever tasted. Annie grunted as she lowered herself back into the chair.

"Neil took up with the girl a few years back. Got one kid by her. I hear she's carrying again. She's just a kid herself—can't be much more than twenty. The stuff we called jailbait when we was kids, remember?"

Annie stopped talking and took a sip of the strong black medicine water. She didn't wait for an answer. "Hope he takes better care of them kids than he did ours." She picked up her smoke from the edge of the table. From the looks of it, Annie often left cigarettes burning along the edge.

Winnie snorted and glanced at her mother-in-law.

Annie smiled. "Winnie's seen it all. She's been part of the family for, what, seven, eight years now?"

"Officially only three," Winnie mumbled. "But you've known me lot longer than that."

"Where does the time go?" Annie sighed deeply.

Winnie chuckled, "Ma, you quit keeping track of time years ago."

Suddenly Amanda liked Winnie, flat face, bored eyes, and all. Love filled the younger woman's eyes when she looked at Annie.

Annie changed the subject. "You been out to see Noah?"

Choking on her coffee, Amanda said, "No secrets on the rez are there? Some things never change."

"You got that right. Well, what ya think of him?" Annie pushed.

"He's different than I remember." Without knowing she was going to do it, Amanda suddenly found herself telling them about the way Paula made her feel.

"Paula's a good kid," Annie said. "I hear she's got eyes for Noah. She's pretty enough to have any guy on the reservation, but I guess she figures she'll keep the Brown family name and get a sweetie at the same time."

"Noah might have somethin' to say about that," Winnie surprised them both. She hung up the blue shirt she'd finished ironing and grabbed a faded red striped blouse and laid it across the ironing board. "Paula can be real pushy, but I got a feelin' that Noah has his own mind. He don't need no woman with four kids already neither; he needs himself a *helpin'* woman."

"My, my," Annie chuckled. "When did you become such a expert on Noah?"

Winnie smiled but didn't answer.

"Don't think I told you this, Amanda, but Winnie here is my laundry girl, dishwasher, and house maid all rolled into one. I don't know how I made it before she came along."

Winnie bent her head to hide her face behind her hair. "Aw, Ma, I don't do that much."

"Of course you do, my girl, and I'm not too proud to say so."

Amanda spent the rest of the afternoon with Annie and her daughter-in-law. Despite her sullen looks, Winnie had a flair for distortion and exaggeration. She entertained her mother-in-law and Amanda with stories and reservation gossip. More than once the three women had to stop and wipe laughter tears from their cheeks.

When Amanda finally left, it was too late to go to Dan's, so she drove straight to the Point. Amanda would see her uncle tomorrow. She had plenty to keep her mind busy tonight.

# Chapter 15

After her morning prayers and two cups of coffee, Amanda headed for the pond. Isolated flakes of snow drifted from heavy clouds that hid the sun. Remembering last night's dream, she searched the sky for Migizi.

*She gasped for breath as she ran through a tunnel that seemed to go nowhere. She didn't know how she'd gotten here or what she was running from. Darkness filled the tunnel except for a soft overhead glow coming from an invisible source somewhere near the ceiling. Amanda doubled over in pain and clasped her side. She took several deep breaths to calm herself and ease the pain. The noise came again, from behind her: the rustling of hundreds of wings. She forced herself to move on without any sense of direction or any idea where she was going.*

*Suddenly the floor of the tunnel tilted upward. Inspired, she ran faster. Finally she spotted a light in the distance. As she neared the opening, the sound of rustling wings deafened her. She put her hands over her ears to muffle the noise. A dozen eagles flew single file a few feet above her head, stirring up the air and heading for the mouth of the tunnel. She watched, still frightened, but amazed. Never had she seen such colors! The first three were dark brown, the next three bright turquoise, the three that followed were gold, and the final three were a dazzling white. They swooped low over her; she ducked. They flew out of the tunnel and into the night without a sound. By the time Amanda reached the opening, they were out of sight. She heard a screech and looked back over her shoulder.*

A sound drew Amanda's eyes skyward, but if Migizi was there, she was hidden behind the clouds. The dream clung stubbornly. She'd ask Noah what the colors she'd dreamed about, twice now, meant. She reached the pond. The unfrozen water at the edge was choppy and dark, reflecting the sky. Within minutes, the snow began in earnest. She started back to the cabin and more hot coffee.

She decided to surprise her uncle by making him lunch. She turned the Escort toward town, planning to buy groceries. On a whim, she pulled into the parking lot of the newly built Wal-Mart at the edge of town. She pushed the cart around the store, aimlessly browsing, first through the Pharmacy section, then Health and Beauty Aids. She bought hand lotion and shampoo. As she passed the Intimate Apparel, she thought of Annie. A glance at her checkbook confirmed what she knew: she'd hardly spent any money since she'd been here. Amanda carefully selected a pale gold bathrobe with matching slippers. Then she made her way to the magazine and book section. Maybe the latest Stephen King novel was out in paperback.

"Mandy?" a voice behind her inquired. "Is that you?"

Amanda turned. A short lady, with wide streaks of silver in her bangs and at the temples of her otherwise obsidian hair, smiled broadly. "I knew I'd see you sooner or later. Course I seen tire tracks goin' up the driveway, so I knew you was home. How are you, sweetheart?"

"Miz Goshen?" Her mother's best friend, a little grayer and a lot heavier, but with the same pixie smile Amanda remembered, beamed at her.

The woman nodded and put her arms around Amanda. "Lord, girl," Rose Goshen continued. "I haven't seen you since your ma's funeral. How have you *been?*"

Guilt washed over Amanda. Mrs. Goshen lived in the small house on the highway next to the cabin road. When Amanda's mother was alive, the women saw each other practically every day. Mom wouldn't be happy if she knew Amanda hadn't made an effort to see her old friend. "I've been meaning to come see you," Amanda lied. "But I've been busy trying to catch up to everyone and rest up at the same time, you know? But you were next on my list."

"Wonderful! Oh how wonderful! Well, as I said, I seen your tracks but didn't want to impose. Knew you'd come by soon's you could. How does it seem to be home?"

"Just great. In fact, I'm thinking about moving back." *Why'd I say that?* she asked herself.

"Your folks would like that. I don't know how many times I heard Peggy say she wished she'd never let you leave. But she wanted what was best for you. Didn't want you *stagnatin'* on the rez." She laughed. "It'd sure be nice to see flowers growing in her garden again. I walk back there 'bout everyday during the good months you know, just to keep an eye on the place. I miss seeing your ma out there on her knees planting bulbs or pulling weeds. Keep expecting to see those green shutters on the windows that Morris was painting just before he took sick. I s'pose you'll be putting them up if you move back. He'd like that."

More guilt. Amanda hadn't known about the shutters and couldn't remember if Mom had ever mentioned them. They were probably rotting in the shed out back. She smiled remembering how Mom loved her flowers and how she'd start spending time in her garden as soon as the weather allowed her to be outside each spring.

"What are you doing tonight?" Rose Goshen asked suddenly. "How'd you like to come with me to the Bingo? It's just over in the Community Center. I never win, but it's a great excuse to get out to visit, and it's cheap entertainment. And of course," she whispered in conspiracy. "It's the only time I treat myself to pie. You know the ladies make homemade pies and sell slices at intermission as a fundraiser. I never bake for myself anymore, so it's a real treat for me. Why don't you come?"

"Oh thanks, but I can't," Amanda tried to sound contrite. "I'm going away for the weekend and I gotta pack, wash my hair, you know, all the usual stuff. Maybe I can join you some other time?"

"Of course, sweetheart," Rose patted her hand. "Well, I got to run now. I do all my errands on Saturday morning, don't you know." Rose Goshen laughed. "Got to be a habit I guess. Since Elmer died, I don't have no excuse not to go anytime I feel like it, but you know, after running errands every Saturday for who knows how many years, it just somehow feels *obscene* to do it any other time," she paused for breath. "But please, come see me soon, okay?"

"I promise." Amanda returned the woman's hug and watched her hustle off to the express checkout line. It seemed Rose and her mother had been best friends forever. Funny that she'd forgotten to stop by.

After a few more minutes Amanda checked out and put the package in the car. In spite of the snow, which had gotten heavier, she walked to Spiels Suds and Supermarket down the block. She phoned Noah from one of the public phones in the store's lobby to tell him that she'd be going with him. No answer.

She picked up chicken breasts, brown rice, whole-wheat dinner rolls, fruit, and lettuce. She debated over the tomatoes—she hated winter tomatoes: they crunched like apples and tasted like cardboard. In the end, she put them back. She really wanted to treat Dan, so she bought almond slivers for the rice and mushrooms for the chicken. She tossed a few more items into the cart, then made her way to the front of the store, keeping an eye out for strangers from her past.

Dan was in the living room: a cartoon show blasted from the TV.

"Surprise!" she yelled from the kitchen doorway. "I brought lunch. Hope you're in the mood for chicken, hot dogs, and rice. Just kidding about the hot dogs!" She laughed.

Her uncle limped into the kitchen with a paperback in one hand. "Here, let me help," he said grabbing a bag with his free hand. "I was just sitting in there thinking it was 'bout time to eat. I'm glad you came. It's kinda lonely here all by myself on such a gloomy day."

"Guess who I ran into at Wal-Mart! Rose Goshen. Remember her? She's looking pretty spry, and lonely too. Have you ever thought about getting together with her for anything?"

"Land sakes, girl. I wouldn't know how to do that anymore."

"Well," Amanda did her best to sound disgusted, "I wasn't suggesting you do anything but keep each other company once in a while. But if I had been suggesting something more intimate," she teased, "I hear it's like riding a bike: it's something you don't forget how to do. It's suppose to all come back with a little practice."

She pulled the head of lettuce from bag and handed it to him.

Dan hooted! "You need balance for that. I haven't had any balance for years. I'd kill myself for sure."

They laughed together. Amanda abruptly hugged her uncle.

"Besides," he continued. "I'd feel like I was cheating on your Aunt Molly."

"Ummm, I don't think Aunt Molly would want you to be lonely all the time. Anyway, I do feel bad about not going to see Rose. She and my mom were such good friends. They were always at each others' houses"

"But she was your ma's friend, not yours," he countered. "Don't feel bad. You got to make friends your own age. By the way, I hear you might be going away with Noah for the weekend. Is that why you're so eager to get me some company?"

"No! Good God! Can't anyone keep a secret around here?"

"Nope!" he grinned at her. "And don't change the subject. You're goin', ain't ya?"

"Yes, if he hasn't already left. In fact, I'll call him right now if it's okay with you."

"My house is your house, Sis." He pointed his chin at the phone. "Help yourself."

Amanda counted seven rings and hung up. "Nope, not home. I hope he didn't leave without me."

"Oh, I don't think he's the type that would leave after he invited someone to go with. He's probably prowling the woods somewhere. Now, how you need help?"

"I don't. You just go back to your book and let me spoil you. What ya reading anyway?"

"Oh, some ole shoot-em-up by Louie L'Amour. You know, I'm getting so forgetful, that sometimes I get almost all the way through one of these things before I realize I read it already," he laughed at himself. "Are ya sure there's no help wanted?"

"No, I insist! You go back to the other room and get comfortable. Let me make you a *spectacular* lunch."

"Okay, okay. You win." Dan scratched his day-old beard. "You know, you sounded just like your Aunt Molly right then."

"I'll take that as a compliment." Amanda hummed as she began cutting up the chicken.

While fixing the meal and without any luck, she tried twice more to reach Noah. Even with Dan's assurance he wouldn't have left her, she was starting to worry. Without much enthusiasm, she gave her uncle a ride to Winky's later that afternoon.

"Wanna come in and watch two old coots try to beat each other's brains out at cribbage?" he asked.

"No thanks, Uncle Dan. I want to pack for the weekend, if I'm still going."

"Oh he's around, don't worry." Dan waved as he shut the door, then he quickly grabbed the handle and reopened it. "Call me when you get back. I'll be wanting to hear all about it."

"I will," Amanda promised and waved.

She was surprised to find a note stuck in the cabin door. "I'll pick you up at 7:30 tomorrow. Dress Warm, Noah." She stuck the note in her jacket pocket, satisfied that he hadn't gone off without her.

The night dragged. Amanda picked through her clothes three times trying to find just the right thing. *What does one wear to a ceremony, anyway?* she wondered. She'd brought three pairs of jeans, a few sweatshirts, and a couple of sweaters. She had one denim skirt that she'd stuck in at the last minute; she'd take that.

She prayed with her feather before going to sleep that night, asking for an open mind and a good heart to get the most from this special opportunity.

# Chapter 16

*The two girls frantically climbed the rocks, ignoring the pain of skin scraping off their hands and knees. They could hear it behind them, growling, claws clicking like castanets as they tried for purchase.*

*"Hurry, Annie!" Amanda urged breathlessly.*

*"I can't go faster, look at my hands—they hurt—they're bleeding."*

*"More than that will bleed if you don't hurry! He's gaining on us," Amanda screamed. She reached behind her, grabbed her cousin's arm, and pulled. "Move!"*

*Annie began to cry. "I gotta give up, Mandy. I'm too tired. I can't make it. Go on, don't wait for me."*

*Amanda refused to let go of Annie's arm. "You can't stay here," she grit her teeth as she pulled harder.*

*Annie's arm was slick with sweat. Amanda's hand slipped.*

*"Annie, damn it! You've got to try. I won't let you give up! You can't. Come on, help me Annie," Amanda screamed. "Move your feet! Come on!"*

*The bear was close now. They could smell its foul breath. It closed its eyes and shook its massive head; saliva flew from its mouth. To their horror, wet foaming flecks landed on the girls' bare legs. Suddenly the beast stopped growling and looked over its left shoulder.*

*The girls looked too. A large, green whirling ball of light was zooming towards them. The three stood mesmerized by the spiraling, growing fireworks.*

*"What the hell is that, Amanda?" Annie whispered. She used the back of her arm to wipe the tears off her face. "Amanda?"*

*"I don't know. Jesus, Annie, would you look at that thing?"*

*The twirling ball traveled toward them with unbelievable speed. It came to within six feet, five feet, four feet, in a few heartbeats. Amanda opened her mouth to scream. Before a sound came out, the green fireball exploded; sizzling pieces of light went flying in every direction. The girls reached for each other. The bear screamed, hideously sounding too human, and disappeared over the edge.*

Amanda struggled to open her eyes. She was sweating. What a dream! Annie, the bear, the fireball—how were they all connected? She glanced over at the clock. The red digital numbers told her it was only 5:30. She knew she wouldn't get back to sleep. She pushed her legs over the side of the bed and wrapped her robe around herself, pulling the belt tight. The book she'd put down on the end table in the living room last week was still waiting for her. She grabbed it and took it to the kitchen table where it lay while she made coffee.

After twenty minutes of not understanding what she was reading, she closed the book. The dream kept interfering, confusing her thoughts. The words muddied on the pages. What should have been easy reading had become a mind exercise, too difficult to do when she was so tired and so distracted.

Amanda studied the calendar from Winky's mini mart that Uncle Dan had tacked to the wall next to the refrigerator. A typical winter scene graced this month—a snow-covered red barn with a partially fallen wooden fence in the foreground. Towards the back sat a two-story farmhouse with smoke rising softly from its chimney, suggesting safety. Safety! In two weeks she would close the cabin and go back to Milwaukee. Where was the safety?

The clock told her it was almost 6:00, still too dark to go for her morning walk. She made sandwiches and threw a few cookies and two apples into a brown paper sack for the trip. 6:15. Amanda changed into jeans and a heavy black sweater. She pulled on knee-high brown boots and threw a windbreaker over her sweater. In an unusual move, she wrapped a scarf around her neck, sure Gramma would approve.

The sun was just coming up. Amanda held her breath while she watched it change the horizon to a dark red. From a great distance, she heard Hobo's broken English telling her it was the best time of the day—the time when the space between the spirit world and the world of the humans was the thinnest. This was the time to talk to the spirits, to petition for favors, to make promises and to give thanks. Amanda wished she had been able to understand more of what the old man told her.

The path to the pond, invisible just six weeks ago, had become a muddy rut. She smiled, happy that she'd left her mark on nature after such a short time here. Overhead, geese honked their good-byes as they prepared to head back to Canada. Squirrels were waking up and chattered at Amanda as she made her way to the water.

The sun was struggling to get past clouds that held a hint of rain. It felt more like a fall day than spring. A good day for traveling, she supposed.

Amanda was out front when Noah pulled into the yard. She hefted the strap of her overnight bag onto her shoulder, and he grabbed the paper bag.

"Here, let me take the lightest one," he laughed. "What's this anyway?" he asked, shaking the bag.

"Oh, just a snack. I can't eat breakfast when I first get up, so I fixed a sandwich and threw in some fruit for later. Sound okay?"

"Yeah, I don't eat breakfast neither. Seems like you're always wanting to feed me. Do you think I'm undernourished?"

"No, course not. I guess I'm like my mom. She always fed everyone, including Punky Jakes."

"And look what happened to him," Noah said. He threw the sandwiches on the backseat of the Bronco.

"Got your feather?" he asked her.

"Right here," she said pointing to the overnight bag she was storing behind her seat. "It's wrapped in the red scarf with two cardboard pieces around it to keep it from breaking."

"Good. You're a fast learner," he smiled. "Soon you'll be teaching me."

Climbing into the passenger's side she asked, "Where's Niijii? I thought he might be coming with us."

"Nowadays he stays with Paula or the Vincents. It's too hard for him to travel distances anymore. I sure do hate that. He used to be such good company."

"So, am I his substitute?" Amanda teased.

Noah laughed, "I said you were a fast learner." He slipped off his jacket and rolled up his flannel shirtsleeves before climbing into the driver's seat.

"Well, let's do it, Mandy. Get comfortable—we've got a good four hours on the road."

Amanda couldn't decide if it was the upcoming ceremonies, her early morning walk, or the thought of going back to Milwaukee soon, but she found it difficult to sit still even in the confines of the seat belt. She stared out the window, trying to enjoy the morning, trying to calm herself.

She watched as the trees receded from the road as they left the reservation. Pictures of Hobo flashed through her mind. She missed his funny mixture of English and Ojibwe, his ramrod-straight back, his long strides, his ponytail with a life of its own, his toothless smile, and his incredible snappy black eyes.

Suddenly she remembered she wanted to ask Noah about the dawn.

"Noah, can I ask you something?"

"Sure, if it ain't personal."

"What if it is?"

"Then I probably won't answer," he laughed at her.

"Well, it isn't," she said. "Tell me about dawn."

"Dawn who? I don't know any Dawn. I thought you said it wasn't going to be personal."

"Not Dawn who," she laughed, "Dawn *what!* I mean 'the dawn,' as in the break of day."

"Oh," he laughed with her. "What do you want to know—if you're gonna ask why it comes up everyday, I don't know. That's one of the Grandfather's mysteries."

"No, not that. But my question does have to do with another mystery. I remember Hobo telling me something about the special time that happens at dawn when the spirits are closest to us. I want to know more."

Noah was quiet for several minutes. Then he cleared his throat. "All things, birds, animals, the wind, trees, insects, Mother Earth, the stars, sun, and moon—everything—they all speak one language. The exact time that the sun comes up, that's the time when it all happens." He was quiet again. "And if a person has a good heart, mind, body, and spirit, as a human being, during that exact period, he or she can join in and listen to that language, and hear what they have to say. It's when the universe speaks." He paused before he continued "It's at that exact time when the space between the spirit world and our world is open and we can communicate with all of the Grandfather's world."

He glanced at her before continuing. "A lot of people don't know the story. They get too busy with jobs and money, or their own worries. They don't take the time to live the old ways—to notice the opportunities they've been given. I'm glad you asked. It means you're opening your mind again."

"Again?"

"Sure. When we're kids, our minds are always open. We believe. We trust. We learn. Don't you remember? But when we grow up we forget what it means to trust in something bigger than ourselves. We become too . . ." he seemed to be struggling for the right word.

"Smug?" she suggested. "Sophisticated? Lazy?"

"Smug! Yeah, that's a good word. We begin to think we can control everything and everyone. We forget we're mere humans, who can be wiped away with just a blink of the Grandfather's eye."

Noah pulled to the left to pass a slow moving car. The elder couple waved as he pulled up alongside. Amanda smiled at them. The old man could barely see over the steering wheel. No wonder he was driving so slow. Noah honked and pulled back into his lane before continuing.

"You know the Old Ones say a good Ojibwe won't let the sun come up on him while he's still in bed. He'd lose favor with the Grandfather if he was too lazy to get up to greet the gift of a new day."

"Yipes," was all Amanda could manage. But she was thinking about his words.

Ninety minutes later they stopped at a small town just on the other side of the Mississippi. Noah got gas and filled his coffee mug. Amanda bought juice to wash down her sandwich.

As they were getting into the Bronco, an eagle cry made them look up. Overhead, Migizi circled slowly.

"Your helper is traveling with us, protecting you," Noah smiled at her. "That's a good sign."

Amanda returned his smile. "I feel very lucky today." They watched as Migizi moved to the south.

"Time to go. Looks like she's gonna lead the way," Noah said.

Amanda laughed and waved at the retreating eagle. "Thanks, Sister Eagle. We're coming!"

Noah squeezed her shoulder. "You've come a long way in such a short time, do you know that?"

Amanda felt the pride shine in her smile. She slammed the door and buckled her seat belt. "That reminds me," she said. "I had the strangest dream last night. I was alone in a tunnel, running toward the entrance when I heard wings flapping. I looked up and saw a dozen eagles overhead."

"Ummmm," Noah said. "What a nice dream. No wonder you feel lucky today."

"The eagle part isn't the strange part. It was their colors," she continued. "I've never seen anything like it. The first three were a deep brown, the second three were brilliant turquoise, the next three were gold, and the last three were bright white. I've dreamt about those colors before. Any idea what they could mean?"

"It could mean you have a great colorizing dream system," he teased. "Or maybe you're going to start dancing and those will be the colors of your outfit. Have you ever thought about dancing?"

"Not since I was a kid. I used to go to Pow Wows with my dad and my grandma. She always wanted me to dance. Sometimes she'd lend me one of her shawls and we'd go into the arena together. I always loved that."

"Any reason why you didn't start?"

"Mom, I guess. Dad wouldn't argue with her. She always got her way, and she never wanted me to get into dancing—or ceremonies either I'm guessing. I can't understand why Dad never stood up for what he wanted."

"You sound angry," he glanced at her. "Are you mad at him for that?"

"Not really. At least I don't think so. I know I don't understand it." Amanda fell silent. She leaned back into her seat and closed her eyes. She didn't wake up until they were passing the White Bear Avenue exit.

"Welcome back, sleepyhead," Noah laughed. "Good thing my radio works, otherwise I would have had to sing to keep myself awake. Here I thought I was going to have conversation to keep me alert and on the road. A lot of good you did me!"

"Ummm, geez, I'm sorry. I didn't realize I was so tired. Must have been all the running I did last night in that tunnel." She stretched and laughed. "What time is it?"

Noah glanced at the Bronco's clock. "Almost noon. Are you up for some strong coffee and a lot of BS?"

"Sure, where do we go for that?"

"I got a friend who's got a 'skin craft and gift store down on the Ave. I can't come to town without stopping by. She'd kill me if I did. You don't mind, do ya?"

"Course not, it's your trip. I'm just along for the ride."

They rode the miles between the twin cities in silence. Amanda ran her fingers through her hair and shook her head. She liked the feeling of her hair hitting her shoulders. It had been a while since she'd worn it this long—since college anyway. Her bangs were well past her eyes now, and she held them back with a bobby pin.

Noah pulled the Bronco up in front of a store. In its large window several star quilts, in rainbow colors, were displayed.

"Did your friend make these? They're gorgeous," Amanda said.

"She makes them. I don't know if she made these or not. Let's go ask her." Noah jumped out of his vehicle, and he was walking into the store before Amanda got her car door opened. By the time she stepped inside, Noah was laughing and hugging a small Indian woman in a wheelchair.

"Amanda, come meet my sister, Teri."

"Amanda, come in," the woman said holding out her hand. "Any friend of this *'Shinab* is a friend of mine."

Amanda took the offered hand. It was strong and firm.

"Help yourself to some coffee," Teri said. "I just made it this morning, so it can't be tooooo bad yet. Well, how the hell ya been?" she asked Noah. "And what brings you this way?"

"Ceremonies tonight! Frank Walking Good Heart is in town. *HoWa,* Ter! Don't you keep up with the news any more?" This was the first time Amanda had heard the name of the Sioux spiritual man.

"I heard he was coming. I s'pose Jessie brought him in?"

"Yeah. He don't do much anymore. I guess if I live to be ninety, I'd slow down too. I figure he'd do anything for Jessie." Noah had moved behind the counter and filled his travel mug with coffee. He held the pot out to Amanda with eyebrows raised, then set it back down when she shook her head. Noah took several swallows and refilled the mug before joining Amanda. "Looks like you've been busy, Sis. You've really got the place filled up."

"Keeps me out of trouble," Teri laughed.

Amanda admired the earrings and barrettes in the case. "Did you do these all yourself?" she asked Teri.

"Not all, but probably most. Got a couple of friends who bead, and a sister, and two of my kids. Helps us all out, if you know what I mean," she laughed again.

"Uh. That's a really unusual one. Nice colors. Who did that one?"

"This one?" Teri pointed to a gold, brown, and turquoise one.

"Yeah. I've never seen those colors together . . . or that design either. It's really pretty."

Teri took the barrette out of the case and held it up against Amanda's hair. "Looks good there, don't you think?" she asked Noah. He smiled.

"It's yours," Teri said holding it out toward Amanda.

"Oh no! I can't take it," Amanda protested.

"Sure you can. Don't hurt my feelings, girl. I said, take it! Its mine to give."

Amanda took the barrette and replaced the bobby pin that held back her bangs.

"Like it?" she asked Noah and preened, turning her head. She smiled when he nodded.

"I know I should give you something back," Amanda started to say.

"You already have. You brought this here man to see me, that's enough," Teri laughed. "He stays away too long. I suppose he's gonna tell me he's been busy," she said to Noah.

"I can't take credit for that. He brought me."

"Let's not argue semantics," Teri answered.

Noah and Teri teased back and forth between a steady line of customers that came and went. Finally, at 1:30 Noah called the pizza joint next door, and the three of them ate lunch and continued to visit.

At mid-afternoon Noah announced it was time to go. "We gotta split, Ter. I need to stop over at the Indian museum. I promised Paula and the Vincents I'd pick up some beads for them. They can't get fancy cut-glass up at home." He bent to kiss Teri on the head. "Coming tonight?"

"I can't. I been teaching beading at the Indian Center. Got a class for some white folks that married Indians. They pay pretty good, ya know. Kinda makes up for what I don't do on a good day here. Wish I could join you two. But you go and enjoy yourselves. Say hi to Jessie for me." She held her hand out to Amanda. "Don't be a stranger now. Come back any time you can. And bring this big lug with you," she squeezed Noah's hand with her other.

"I will. And thanks for the barrette. I'll take care of it."

Teri smiled. "Good, I like to hear that. I like knowing it's gone to someone who appreciates it."

Outside, Amanda waited for Noah to unlock her door. "She's nice. But I don't remember you having a sister who lived in the city," Amanda said.

"She's not my birth sister. Just a good friend who always has been like family to me. You know, puts up with me when I'm in town, scolds me when she thinks I need it, things like that."

"Well, she thinks the world of you, that's for sure. It was sweet of her to give me the barrette. Do you think she made it herself? She never did tell me exactly."

"Sure. She liked that you admired it. You made her happy, so she wanted to make you happy."

Two blocks away, they pulled up in front of the museum bead store. Amanda looked around and frowned. "Why didn't we walk?"

"What? Walk around in a city filled with Indians? Hey, it's a jungle out there. Why would we want to walk?"

Amanda couldn't tell if he was joking.

"Coming?" he asked.

"Of course, you're not gonna leave me out here all alone in this jungle, are you?"

Amanda had never seen the like. Beads hung from every conceivable space, on all four walls; they overflowed trays in display cases, and sat in small glass cylinders in three round turnstiles sitting on the corner of the main counter. They came in every color imaginable, and then some.

"How do you know what Paula and the Vincents want?" she asked.

"ESP," Noah said. "And this." He pulled a folded slip of paper from his back pocket.

It took almost forty-five minutes to select enough beads to satisfy him. The young woman helping them waited patiently as Noah held up hank after hank of beads to the light and fingered the small cylinders. A baby with fat cheeks and a head chock-full of bushy black hair swung in a new blue wind-up swing behind the counter and watched with liquid black eyes as his mother walked back and forth, bringing beads to the counter for Noah's inspection.

When the beads were paid for, Noah looked at Amanda. "I think we'll go by Pete's place first and see what kind of sleeping arrangements we can make, then we'll go over to Jessie's and check on the plans for tonight. How does that sound?"

"Like I said before, I go where you go."

From the Bronco's window, Amanda watched Indians, Blacks, and Asians on the city sidewalks. Most walked in pairs, but many solitary figures stood on the street corners, watching back.

Noah checked a hand-drawn map several times before pulling up in front of an apartment complex. Four cedar buildings sat around a horseshoe drive.

"This doesn't look like any housing project I've ever seen before," Amanda said.

"This is called 'Wind Spirit Circle,'" Noah said. "Only Indian people live here. It's a special project between the city's Indian community and the city council. The city's fathers finally decided they could accept input from the Indian community. It's supposed to be a model for other cities where there are lots of Indian folks."

"Isn't that discriminatory?" she asked.

"Guess not. Besides, once Indian families started to move in here, you don't think others would be breaking down doors to get into the neighborhood, do you?"

Amanda shrugged.

"Come on, let's go see if we can find my man Pete."

Amanda followed Noah to the second building on the right side of the drive. Each building had eight apartments. Noah read the mailboxes, then pushed the black button under #3: Greengrass.

"Who is it?" came an Indian male voice.

"Nanook from the North," Noah yelled into the speaker. "I got a lady with me so watch your mouth."

"Hey, *Dok-sha,* come in. I been expecting you."

"Get ready," Noah told Amanda. "You're gonna meet a good one!" He grabbed the door and pulled when the buzzer sounded. They walked down the hall. The door to #3 opened as they got there.

A big man, well over six feet tall, and pushing 350 pounds from the topside, greeted them. He wrapped his arms around Noah, almost completely covering him. The man's long hair hung loose, covering his face. "How the hell are you, Bro?" he roared. He reminded Amanda of Philbert from the *Pow Wow Highway* movie.

Noah stepped back and slapped the human mountain on his back. "Pete, I want you to meet Amanda."

Amanda held her ground, willing herself not to move as Pete took a giant step toward her; she was ready for anything. He held out his hand; Amanda's own disappeared inside his huge paw.

"She's a pretty one," he said, then added something in Ojibwe. Amanda could have sworn Noah blushed.

"Let's not take up space in the hall," Pete roared. "Come in, you two. Take a load off." He beamed at them and led the way into his apartment. "Let me make some room here," Pete said. He moved around his kitchen and small living room, pulling towels off the backs of chairs, a shirt and pants off the sofa, and another shirt and some socks off the living room floor. "It's kinda messy since Harriet left. She kept the place clean. Me? I'm your basic slob," he laughed.

"She left you again?" Noah asked. "Man, when you two gonna stop fighting and live right? You know you guys were meant for each other."

"I try to tell her that," Pete moaned. "But, hell, she don't listen. You ever known an Ojib woman who wasn't stubborn? Ain't nothing like them when they get mad. Lord, help me! Harriet's just like my ma that way!"

Noah winked at Amanda. Pete opened a door off the living room and threw the clothes in, not watching where they landed. The arm of one of his shirts kept the door from shutting tightly. "Let's have some good *mukade-mashkiki-waboo,*" Pete suggested. He grabbed three cups from a doorless cupboard, gave them a quick run-by under the faucet, then filled them with strong-smelling coffee. Amanda, who normally would have passed on milk and sugar, didn't.

While Noah and Pete talked about ceremonies, Amanda walked to the living room and studied pictures that stood in a tall bookcase. Several showed Pete with a tall, slender Indian woman. In most she was looking at him with adoring eyes. In one she was standing next to him, turned sideways, with her arms wrapped around his nonexistent waist; she was smiling happily into the camera. *Hello, Harriet,* Amanda thought. The woman had very dark skin and striking blue eyes. Only one picture showed anyone else posing with the couple: Pete was sitting in a chair with a newborn cradled in his arms. Harriet was standing behind him, her chin resting on his head, her hair falling down either side of his face to mid-chest. A gentle, satisfied smile graced her face.

Amanda studied the picture. The couple looked very young—she wondered that no other picture even hinted at a child.

"How does that sound, Amanda?" Noah was asking.

"What? I'm sorry, I was looking at the photos. Hope you don't mind, Pete," she said.

"Heck no . . . make yourself at home, Niijiikwe."

"Pete says I can come back with him tonight whenever we finish. I'll bunk on the floor, and you can have the couch. But his sister or Jessie will have room. That might be more comfortable. You wouldn't mind, would you?"

"Course not. But I don't want to be a pest either. I can go to a motel," she suggested.

"Nonsense," Pete roared. "If'n Jessie don't have room, Teena does. Teena's home folk. She'll make you comfortable at her place. Might talk your ear off, but you'll like her."

"Okay. Sure," Amanda conceded.

"We're going over to Jessie's now," Noah said. "Pete says the ceremonies start about nine. We'll have to stop and find something to take to the feast with us, but Jessie can tell us what we need."

Noah stood by the door next to Pete, dwarfed by the big man. "We'll see you later then," Pete was saying.

# Chapter 17

The woman who answered the door was beautiful. She was a little shorter than Amanda, slightly stockier. Huge dimples in each cheek of her round moon face accompanied sparkling white teeth when she smiled. Thick black hair hung below her waist in the kind of waves usually seen only in commercials. Her coffee-and-cream skin was flawless. Her black, almond eyes were ringed with miles of lashes that looked free of mascara. When she saw Noah she squealed and threw her arms around him. Noah broke away.

"Amanda, this is Jessie. Jess, this is Amanda."

Both of Jessie's warm hands wrapped around Amanda's outstretched one. "Come in, please. I'm so glad you're here. Let me take your coats."

The apartment where Amanda found herself now was a complete contrast to the one they just left. It was open, and spotless, with all-white walls and white carpeting. Two spotted black-and-white eagle feathers with quills wrapped with red twine, and tied together, hung in the hallway. A beige, white, and turquoise Indian rug almost completely covered one wall in the living room. The kitchen walls boasted wallpaper in a pastel pink, tan, and turquoise Southwest design. Jessie herself wore an ankle-length black skirt with a dark red silk blouse. Her red-and-white beaded earrings swung hypnotically each time she moved her head.

"I'm so pleased that you could come, Noah," she said. "Grandpa Frank will be glad to see you again too. He doesn't do much of these anymore. In fact, I'm not sure he really wanted to do this one, but I begged," Jessie laughed. "He never could say no to me. I'm spoiled and I know it!"

Amanda was willing to bet not many men could say no to Jessie.

"Amanda, *miigwich* for coming too. I'm sure you can imagine how proud I am of my grandpa. He's the one who's really been responsible for my life and learning. Besides, even if he wasn't my grandpa, I'd think he was a very special man." Her dimples sunk back into her cheeks as she flashed a charming smile at Amanda.

"Come," she linked one arm in Noah's, and one in Amanda's, and led them to the kitchen. She gave them each a glass and a bottle of raspberry flavored water.

"Tell me what you've been up to," she asked Noah. "Are you studying with this guy?" she asked Amanda in the same breath.

Before Amanda could respond, Noah answered. "I'm always busy, and yes, Amanda's a student. She's also an old friend. Believe it or not, we knew each other in grade school. The great circle doesn't disappoint. I don't see her for years, and one day, there she was, standing on my porch. She's Hobo's great-niece."

Jessie smiled at Amanda again. "No kidding? That's wonderful! Hobo was a real special man. Good heart, and really gifted. I'm glad you came. I'm sure you will enjoy tonight. My grandfather and I are both honored."

At first Jessie and Noah tried to include Amanda in their discussion, but that didn't last. They talked about old friends and a shared past that she wasn't part of. Amanda's only contribution was when her stomach growled after her second glass of water. She looked at the ceiling, pretending she hadn't heard it and hoping the others hadn't.

"Once you get to the ceremony, you won't notice the hunger," Jessie laughed dashing her hopes. "And we'll have a wonderful feast after that."

"That reminds me, what can we pick up to take with us?" Noah asked.

"Nothing. You're my guests, and I made more than enough."

"Jessie, when did you learn to cook?" Noah sounded surprised.

Amanda looked at Jessie with renewed interest. *"But she couldn't cook,"* Noah had said about the lady from his past—the one he almost married.

Noah caught Amanda's eye and smiled, realizing that she'd just figured it out.

A rap at the door saved him from speaking. Jessie jumped up and fairly ran to the door, her long hair flowing behind her like a train. For a quick second, Amanda wanted to hate the woman, but she had to admit she wasn't anything if she wasn't nice.

"Hurry up, Jessie," a man's deep voice boomed out from the hallway.

"Hold your horses," she shouted back, "I'm coming!"

She swung the door open. A man stepped through and grabbed Jessie in a playful hug.

"Move over Daddy, I want in too," a girl said from the hallway.

The man stepped aside and a fairer, smaller version of Jessie walked in. She appeared to be about twelve. Her hair waved like Jessie's. It hung to her waist, but the sides were cut short and combed back from her face. The top was styled in spikes. She had three earrings in each ear.

"Hi, Aunt Jess," the girl said. She was about to hug Jessie when she spotted Noah. She squealed and sprang across the kitchen floor. She met Noah just as he stood up, and hit him so hard that they both fell backwards into his chair.

"Noah! I'm sooooo glad you're here," she cooed. "I've missed you!" She planted a noisy kiss on his cheek.

Noah pushed her off. "Yeah, me too." He rubbed his nose and blinked watering eyes. But I didn't think you'd break my nose to prove it." Then he laughed and hugged her back.

The girl spotted Amanda. "Who's that?" she asked.

"This is Amanda. Amanda, I'd like you to meet Angela . . . she looks like a girl, but she's really a truck in disguise. In fact her Indian name is Mack-kwe, like the *bull*dog truck." He was still rubbing his nose.

Angela swatted his arm without looking—she was scowling at Amanda. Finally remembering her manners, she held out her hand. "I'm happy to meet you, Amanda."

Amanda took the hand that had at least one ring on every finger, including the thumb. "Hello, Angela. I'm happy to meet you too."

They smiled at each other. Angela's dimples dug deep into her cheeks. She turned back to Noah. "Is she your new girlfriend?"

"What if she is?" Noah teased.

Amanda blushed; Angela scowled again.

Jessie and the man were standing by the table. "Amanda, this is my brother, Roger."

Roger was slightly taller than Jessie. His face showed scars of teenage acne. He wore his hair in braids, parted on the side. His ears hosted round shell earrings. He nodded at Amanda, and held his hand out to Noah.

"Good to see you, brother," he said in a deep bass voice. "How was the trip? How long can you stay?"

"The trip wasn't bad. Hardly any traffic. The only bad thing was that I had to sing to myself the whole time to stay awake. And here that's why I brought Mandy along, but she went to sleep on me." Noah grinned at Amanda, then he turned back to Roger, "We gotta head back tomorrow."

"I wish you'd come when you could stay a while," Jessie said.

"Me too," Angela added. She was playing with Noah's left braid. "You promised you'd come for a visit."

"Leave Noah alone," Roger said gruffly. "You know he's busy." He ignored Angela's wrinkled nose. "I hate to rush off," he said, "but we came on a mission. We're here to get Jessie. Grandpa Frank wants a family blessing before the ceremony, so we all have to be there." He turned to Jessie. "Are you ready?"

"Sure am. You'll need to help me with this food though." Jessie knelt down in front of the refrigerator and pulled out a large meat loaf. She laid it on top of the stove and handed Roger two gallon-sized ice cream pails filled with potato salad. She held out two bags of cut up veggies to Angela. "Here you go, Sis. You help too."

Angela pushed herself away from Noah's chair reluctantly. "You're coming to the ceremony, aren't you?" she asked him, and she smiled when he nodded.

Jessie held the meat loaf up for Noah's inspection. "See, I really did learn how to cook," she told him.

"Yeah, but not very well," her niece said as she sprinted past her aunt. She waved at Noah with her free hand. "See ya," she squealed.

"Later, brother," Roger said to Noah. He nodded to Amanda again.

"Make yourselves at home," Jessie said at the door. "Just pull this bugger tight behind you. Sometimes it don't latch too good. Give it a little tug, like this, and it'll click. See ya both later." Jessie stepped into the hall.

Just before the door shut, she pushed it open again.

"Please try to be there by 8:30. Grandpa Frank tires easily, so we want to finish at a decent time."

"We'll be on time. Don't worry," Noah answered. He waved her away.

She shut the door for the last time. Amanda looked at Noah.

"What now, coach?" Amanda asked. She looked at her watch. It was just past six o'clock.

"I don't know about you, but I'm tired. I didn't get much sleep last night. Mrs. Eldon had another bout with her heart, and her son wanted me to pray with him. We went from early afternoon til 1:30 this morning." He yawned. "On my way to their place, I stopped to tell you what time I'd pick you up today, but you weren't home, so I stuck that note in the door." He yawned again . . . loudly this time. "I'll flip you for the bedroom," he laughed.

"No, you go ahead. I'm too excited to sleep. I think I'll read a bit. What time do you want me to wake you?"

"About an hour from now. But no need to wake me; I'll set the clock in my head. Please, no comments from the peanut gallery," Noah laughed. He stopped by the bathroom, then went into the bedroom and shut the door.

After Amanda walked the perimeter of the room admiring Jessie's art, and secretly looking for leftover evidence of Noah in the apartment, she wandered over to the sofa and flipped through the magazines she picked up off an end table. Jessica read *People, Newsweek,* and *Midwest Living.* Amanda decided on *People.*

# Chapter 18

Noah shook her shoulder lightly. "Come on, Amanda. Wake up. I overslept."

"Oh God. I was more tired than I thought," Amanda groaned, trying to shake off heavy sleep. "What a weird dream I had. I dreamt about a spinning green fireball." She groaned again when Noah flipped on the overhead light.

He continued walking toward the kitchen. "A green fireball?" he asked over his shoulder.

"Yeah. It seemed like it was full of electricity, or some other kind of light. Maybe lightning. I don't know what it was. It looked like a giant sparkler. It whirled toward me, then exploded about four or five feet in front of me. It's scary but not really, you know?" Amanda pushed herself off the sofa and stretched. "Are we going to be late?"

"No, we'll make it if we leave in ten minutes, it's a good half-hour drive out there."

"Out where?"

"The ceremonies are held at a county park outside of town. It's quiet, safe, and private."

Amanda splashed cold water on her face and ran a comb through her hair. The dream haze dissolved quickly; she was anxious for the ceremony. Noah was too. When she left the bathroom he was standing by the kitchen door with his coat already on; hers was thrown over his arm. He held it out to her.

"Think you're ready for tonight?" he asked.

"As ready as I'll ever be, I guess." She grinned with foolish excitement.

On the way to the park, Amanda gazed at the lights that spread out in both directions from the freeway.

"Must be a million lights out there, huh?" Noah was reading her mind again.

"So much happening out there and we don't even know it. Amazing, isn't it?"

"Yeah, I guess. But I'd still rather be in the woods where the only lights come from amazing fireflies." He glanced at her. "So, have you become completely *citified,* or do fireflies sound like a nice option?"

Without answering, Amanda continued to watch the lights. "Just think about all the people out there. Every light represents life and death, joy and grief, love and hate."

It was his turn not to answer. He stared straight ahead at the road, moving easily in and out of traffic.

About twenty minutes later they pulled into the parking lot in front of a small converted school in the county park. The lot was packed. Amanda wondered where everyone was. The building appeared to be dark, but on closer inspection she saw tiny slits of light sneaking out from small cracks along the windows at both the upper and basement levels.

"Frank always draws a crowd," Noah said. "He's got a good reputation." He grinned. "Well, let's go in."

Angela ran over to Amanda and Noah when they stepped into the large room. She dragged a girl of about ten in her wake. She smiled shyly at Noah.

"This is Kimberly Wapoose," Angela told them. Turning to the girl she said, "This is Noah. He's the guy I told you about. The one that almost married my Aunt Jessie."

"Hi Kim," Amanda said ignoring the remark.

"Kimberly," the girl said. "I don't like to be called Kim."

"Kimberly," Amanda corrected herself. "I am happy to meet you." *Good going, Amanda,* she told herself.

"*Posoh* Kimberly," Noah took the girl's limp hand.

The coatroom promised a temporary refuge. "Let me take your jacket, Noah," Amanda suggested.

"You must be Amanda," a woman's voice boomed from the other end of the closet-sized room as Amanda walked in. A woman at least a head taller and fifty pounds heavier than Amanda was coming toward her. She reminded Amanda of Alice in Wonderland after eating those growing mushrooms.

"*Boozhoo!* I'm Teena Greengrass. Pete's sister. He said you'd be here. It's great you'll be staying with me tonight. I don't never get much company, but I love it! I'm really happy to meet you." Teena pumped Amanda's hand up and down quickly. Amanda couldn't help but laugh.

Teena pulled two Ziplock bags from her long, pleated, blue skirt and held one out to Amanda. "Here, put your jewelry in these, so you don't lose it. You got to take your glasses off, too, but you can wait until the ceremony starts. I don't want you falling down the stairs cuz you can't see." Teena shook when she laughed.

Having met Pete, Amanda would have known Teena without an introduction. Except for being female, she looked and sounded exactly like her brother. Her dark brown hair hung free to her waist, and her black eyes danced with friendliness. Amanda guessed no one would remain a stranger for long with either Greengrass.

"Come on, Mandy. Can I call you Mandy? Everyone should be downstairs now. It'll be starting any minute now. Do you need to pee? Once we're down there, the doors will be locked, so no one goes in or out. Can't interrupt the ceremony, so best get comfortable now." She paused for breath before continuing. "Noah's downstairs already. Pete says this is your first ceremony. Ain't it great? Grandfather Frank is just *wonderful!* I've been to his ceremonies before of course. I hope you and Noah sit with me. I'm no expert, but I've been to plenty, so if you have any questions, just ask me. You're not scared, are you?" Teena was breathless.

"No," Amanda hesitated. "Should I be? What do I need to know?"

"Ain't Noah told you nothin'?"

"Well yeah, a few things, but I'm still not sure what to expect. I am a little nervous," she admitted.

"Ahhh, no worry. Ya don't need to know nothin' special. Just when to pray or pass. I passed the first time, but that's just me. I used to be shy, can you believe it? Wanted to do things the right way, ya know? I'm sitting at the far end so you'll have plenty of time to see what to do before it's your turn."

Teena opened the basement door. She motioned Amanda through. Amanda held her breath to squeeze by the big woman. Twenty or thirty people sat around the room, leaning against the walls with their eyes closed or talking quietly with their neighbors. Some sat on blankets, rugs, or cushions, while others sat on the cool tile floor itself. All had their shoes off.

An old man sat in a straight-back chair in the middle of a blanket in the center of the room. He was facing away from the door Amanda and Teena had just come through. Noah was squatting beside the Elder, talking quietly, one hand resting on the Elder's thin, flannel-covered shoulder. He turned when the door opened and beckoned Amanda over with his head. Amanda looked at Teena, who motioned with her chin.

"Go," she whispered. "Meet Grandfather Frank."

Amanda drew near the blanket. Noah reached for her hand and pulled her towards them. "Amanda, meet a very special man, Frank Walking Good Heart. Grandfather, this is Amanda, the Ojibwe woman I mentioned."

Frank Walking Good Heart raised his eyes to Amanda and smiled a toothless but beautiful smile. In that moment Amanda saw Hobo. Instead of having snapping black eyes like her great-uncle's, Grandfather Frank's eyes were the softest, kindest brown eyes she'd ever seen. They were almost sad. His face was radiant and peaceful, but cracked and lined like dried mud. He said something to Noah that Amanda couldn't understand. Noah smiled.

"He says you're pretty," Noah said. "And he wants you to take off your glasses so he can see your heart."

Amanda took her glasses off with one hand and took the old man's offered hand with the other. "I'm honored, Grandfather," she said. Noah smiled his approval. So did Grandfather Frank.

The Elder spoke again to Noah. "He asks if you have any special requests or prayers this evening," Noah interpreted.

"Not really," Amanda stammered. In her head she had questions and requests but didn't know how to explain them.

Noah stood up. "It's almost time to start, and he has more people to greet." They nodded to the man waiting patiently behind them for his turn with Frank. Teena had put two Minnesota Timberwolves stadium cushions on the floor against the south wall. She patted them. "Here . . . sit down."

Amanda sat and looked around at the gathering. Jessie was talking to a group of women on the other side of the room, and she smiled when she caught Amanda's eye. Wearing a black silk top that highlighted her skin, Jessie radiated the same tranquility as her grandfather. Amanda felt a tug of envy.

After speaking a few minutes with the man who had been standing behind Noah and Amanda, Grandfather Frank nodded to Jessie. She crossed to the front of the room and stood quietly while a young boy took the chair from the Elder and put it to the side of the room. Then he helped the old man kneel at the front of the blanket. While Grandfather Frank opened a small satchel that had seen many years of use and took from it the articles needed to build his altar, Noah got up and locked the basement door. Jessie stood quietly until the altar was set before she spoke, "I will interpret for my grandfather tonight." Someone turned the lights off.

With lengthy prayers, first by the Elder and then by the twenty or more others sitting around the room, the ceremony should have felt long. Each person first thanked the Creator for earthly blessings received, then petitioned for favors, but before Amanda realized it, the ceremony ended.

Feeling like she was coming out of a deep dream, Amanda blinked as her eyes adjusted to the lights that were suddenly turned on. She had felt the air tighten when the spirits had entered the room, and it had grown even heavier as the Elder recited his litany that called on the Creator and His helpers to come and listen to their prayers. It had changed again as the spirits left with the "going-home" song. The room was totally silent now: the people, the air, everything. Amanda felt like she was in a vacuum. She sighed deeply and looked at the others in the room, searching for signs that they felt different after this experience.

She looked at the spiritual man, hoping to see how he had been changed because of communication with other world beings. All she saw was a tired old man putting his things back into an equally tired old bag in the reverse order that he'd taken them out. His pipe and sage bundle went in last. Once that was finished, people went up one by one or in pairs to retrieve feathers or other items they'd laid on the blanket to be blessed.

Something inside Amanda stirred and demanded recognition and acceptance. Those beings, at work earlier in the darkened room, would not be denied. She struggled to make sense of it all.

"Well . . . what did you think?" Noah asked. "Amanda?" He nudged her when she didn't answer.

She blinked and looked at him. "What?"

"I don't know what to say," she said when he repeated his question. She looked at him again, then at Teena. "They were here, weren't they? I mean spirits? Were they spirits? They're real, aren't they?"

Noah laughed. Teena's bear hug crushed her from the other side.

"Of course they are, girl," she said. "I told you Grandfather Frank has many spirit helpers; they all come when he calls. He's a powerful man." Amanda decided to ask Teena more questions later. "Let's go upstairs and eat," Teena said.

"Aren't you hungry?" In the excitement Amanda had forgotten how her stomach growled with hunger.

Upstairs the noise level contrasted with the calm and quiet of the basement. People ate and visited and took turns stopping to say a few words to Jessie and her grandfather. Some gave Grandfather Frank gifts; others slipped money or tobacco into the Elder's hand. The old man was tired, but he greeted each well-wisher in a way that said he or she was the most important person in the world to him. Noah waited until the others were finished before he nodded to Amanda and Teena. They moved forward together.

Grandfather Frank acknowledged Teena by name. She beamed at the recognition and lowered her eyes without speaking. The old man spoke to Noah at length, then turned and looked at Amanda.

When Noah didn't move or speak, Jessie smiled and took both Amanda's cold hands in her own warm ones. She nodded when Grandfather Frank stopped speaking.

"My grandfather welcomes his new granddaughter. He says he will pray for you. He knows you are working hard to make difficult choices. He says the spirits told him we must all respect your decision, whatever it is. He says it is hard for you, so we must not push." The old man interrupted, then Jessie translated. "The spirits say they are here for you—to guide you—and help you if you call on them. She stopped and waited while he spoke again. She nodded at him, then continued, "Our grandfather says you should wait for them to instruct you." He spoke again, and again the translation came from Jessie, "He says your spirit helpers are strong, and you should not be afraid of them. You must trust in your prayers. Let them help you. In the end, you will make the right decision."

Jessie and Grandfather Frank stopped speaking.

Amanda smiled at the Elder, fighting tears. He reached out to touch her cheek, and spoke one word.

"*Ogichidaakwe.*" He smiled his toothless Hobo smile and blessed her.

# Chapter 19

At 3:30 in the morning Teena and Amanda were still in their nightgowns, sitting at a tiny table in Teena's apartment on the near north side of Minneapolis. Teena poured hot milk into mugs. "This will help you relax. It's an old trick Granny Greengrass used to pull on me 'n' Pete. I always thought she slipped something else in it, cuz it worked like a wonder drug." She laughed and handed Amanda a cup.

A single bed that pulled out of the wall was ready for Teena; a fluffy blue-and-white star quilt was spread over the bed. The sofa had been made up for Amanda. A purple down comforter lay invitingly on the end of the sofa. Amanda looked at it longingly, hoping Teena was winding down.

Teena continued, "It was hard on us kids, being with Pops in the Dells for six months, and the next six months with Ma at St. Croix. Seems our folks couldn't spend ten minutes together without fighting. I can't begin to imagine how they stopped spattin' long enough to make me 'n' Pete."

Amanda nodded—her usual response to Teena. She hadn't said more than a dozen words the whole evening. Teena enjoyed a good listener and didn't need a response to keep on talking. She told and retold her story for another hour with shorter and shorter pauses before starting in again.

Finally, exhausted, the women crawled into their beds at 4:30. Within minutes Teena was snoring softly. Amanda rolled from one side to another, trying to get comfortable. Each time she closed her eyes she saw spirits zooming overhead or lazily zigzagging around the basement room, as they had during the ceremony. During the ceremony, one had zoomed past her, then returned to stop directly in front of her, as if checking her out. She'd been surprised and delighted and had to force herself not to laugh. Teena had squeezed her arm then; she'd seen it too.

The sun was just beginning to peek through the blinds when a dreamless sleep caught up with Amanda.

Noah knocked on Teena's door promptly at eleven. His face was drawn, and his eyes were bloodshot.

"Didn't you get any sleep last night?" Teena asked. "Black medicine, strong, good, coming right up."

"I got about an hour," Noah said. "Pete and I went to a sweat, started at daybreak."

"Was it a good one? How many folks? Who ran it?" Teena placed a mug of steaming black coffee in front of him and poured herself another cup.

"Yeah it was good. Roger ran it. We were six." He sipped the hot brew. "Ummm . . . this is good."

"Hi." Amanda came in from the bathroom and sat across from Noah at the table. She picked up her own cup of coffee. She smiled at Teena, then looked at Noah. "You look terrible!"

"Thanks a lot," he laughed. "Are you about ready to hit the road?"

"Sure am!"

"Let me fix you something to eat real quick," Teena offered.

"That's okay. We'll stop after a couple of hours so I don't fall asleep at the wheel." He stood and stretched.

Amanda swallowed the last of her coffee. She grabbed her jacket from the closet next to the door. Teena hugged her. "You're always welcome here, honey. Come back real soon, okay? And keep an eye on this ole Chip so he don't run you guys off the road." She threw her arms around Noah. "Take care of yourself, Brother, and don't stay away so long next time. It was great to see ya. You got lots of friends here ya know."

Noah put his arms around Teena and squeezed. "I know, Niijiikwe. Take care of yourself too, hear?"

Despite her intentions to keep Noah company Amanda was asleep before they left St. Paul's city limits.

She woke when Noah pulled into a truck stop on the Wisconsin side of the Mississippi. They ate a trucker's-sized breakfast in silence and were standing beside the Bronco within thirty minutes.

Noah rubbed his eyes. "Would you mind driving for an hour? I don't think I can take any more. If I can just rest a bit I'll be fine for the final stretch."

Amanda caught the keys he tossed to her. She'd never driven anything as big as the Bronco before. It sure didn't handle like the Escort, but after a few minutes she knew she would manage. Noah was asleep immediately, and he slept until they pulled into her driveway.

He blinked, yawned loudly, then smiled at her. "Thanks, I needed that."

"Are you okay to drive home?" Amanda asked. "Want to come in? I'll make coffee," she offered.

"Not this time. I need to continue my beauty rest," he laughed. "I'll talk to you tomorrow. I'll give a call. Thanks for going with me." He gave her a quick hug as they crossed in front of the Bronco. A surprised Amanda said, "Thanks for taking me, Noah. I have so much to talk to you about, I'll probably have to make a list."

"I know," he said. He slid into the driver's seat and waved. "Tomorrow," he yelled through the glass.

Noah yawned again and blinked his eyes rapidly to clear them. The two-hour rest while Mandy drove did little to revitalize him. "Please Mrs. Eldon," he whispered to himself, "Stay well tonight." Twenty-four hours of sleep sounded good right now. Thoughts of the sweat ceremony kept pushing forward in his mind, despite his attempt to hold them back. His mind wasn't clear enough to think through and understand all that he had heard. His thoughts wandered: "*Some of us will be back together in four years for a special ceremony,*" Roger was saying. "*I will invite you here to join me as we celebrate a special event.*"

*Noah breathed in the steamy air through his nose. An upcoming ceremony four years from now barely penetrated his prayers, hardly seemed worth mentioning.*

*Roger roared with laughter. "I see a pipe, a wedding pipe. Someone here will be getting married."*

*The men chuckled.*

*Pete said, "I got me a wife that I can't keep around now; it ain't gonna be me."*

*"Me either," chimed in Joe, a friend of Pete's. "I don't need two wives."*

*"You're too ugly to get another woman to fall in love with you. Course you ain't gonna have two wives," someone said.*

*Grandfather Frank surprised them all. "My age," he said in a quiet voice, "a wife would kill me."* He paused before continuing, *"But what a good way to die!"*

*Another round of hearty laughter.*

*The young man who had helped Frank during the ceremony last night spoke next.* *"I'm too young. I'll only be eighteen in four years. A wife would probably kill me, too, if my mother didn't first."* *More laughter.*

*Noah wiped sweat from his eyes.* *"Guess that leaves me and Jason,"* he said. *"Hobo said it was best to go it alone. 'Women get in a man's way,' were his exact words. Beside, I don't even have a woman in my life."*

*"He said four years from now, buddy. A lot can happen in four years,"* Pete chuckled.

*Noah snickered. It wouldn't happen.*

*"I got me a good woman,"* Jason said. *"But she's got me on permanent hold."* He coughed. *"We'll all meet the Creator face-to-face before she says yes to marriage."*

*"She got you trained right, boy,"* Grandfather Frank teased. *"She don't need to marry you."*

*Jason Blackbull was new to the men's circle in the sweat. He was invited by Roger and introduced as Jessie's friend. Noah had noticed the tall Sioux who'd kept to himself at Frank's ceremony. Several of the young women did too, but he ignored their attempts for his attention. He was movie-star handsome. A classic face, long shiny braids, clear, honest eyes; a good mate for Jessie, Noah thought.*

*Roger poured more water on the sacred fire. The rocks hissed and steam rose. He sang a personal song before he spoke again.*

*"The pipe is on antlers in someone's home. Four family ribbons hang from it."* *The men were quiet now; teasing stopped. Roger was about to tell them something important.* *"Each ribbon is a different color. There are four colors. I see brown, turquoise, gold, and white. Whose colors are these?"*

*No one answered. Noah stared silently into the blackness of the lodge. He hadn't counted on anything like this. A partnership decided by the Grandfather and tied together by a pipe ceremony, is forever. There is no denying or refusing such a thing. What a responsibility! He'd been given four years to prepare himself . . . and her. The seasons came and went so quickly anymore. At least he knew she would be staying on the reservation instead of going back to Milwaukee. She didn't know it yet, and he'd have to be careful not to let her know what he knew—not push her. She'd have to think that that decision was hers or the Grandfather's. If only she'd relax and let the spirits guide her. He prayed in silence for strength and wisdom. A few hours ago, just after the ceremony, Grandfather Frank told Amanda through Jessie that she would make the right decision. And he warned all others to leave her alone while she made it.*

*"Aw haw," someone said. The lodge was quiet.*

*Frank Walking Good Heart laughed, breaking the silence. "My new granddaughter, with the pretty eyes, is a lucky woman."*

*The men in the lodge grunted assent.*

*Roger began the fourth and final round.*

Noah turned into the Vincent's yard. Paula's kids had been too much for Niijii last time, so he stayed with Ben and Yemmy this trip. He'd be more than ready to go home, Noah thought. Soon Noah would tell Ben what he had learned this weekend, but he wanted to get used to the idea himself first. Ben would keep the secret, but Noah wouldn't dare tell Yemmy. That old woman would be so excited she'd post a banner in front of the church by next Sunday.

Noah's obligatory cup of coffee turned into three, plus a meal with homemade bread bought at the church bake sale this morning. He ate while he gave the Elders news of the people they knew in Minnesota.

"Did you see Jessie?" Yemmy asked without looking at him.

"Of course," he said. "And she's more beautiful than ever. I don't know how I ever let her get away," he teased. Yemmy was more angry and hurt than Noah when he and Jessie broke up, and of course she blamed Jessie for it all. Noah always suspected Yemmy was afraid they would get back together.

"Now don't get this old woman riled up," Ben begged him with a scowl. "You can go home, but I gotta stay and live with her."

"You need a helpmate, Noah," Yemmy said ignoring her husband. "Not someone who's always gonna try to outdo you. No amount of *pretty* can make up for the lack of real love and respect."

Her tone and the look in her eyes indicated that was the end of the discussion.

Amanda headed for the bathroom and poured half a box of bubble bath into the tub filling with hot water. While it filled, she unwrapped the Miigwan and placed it on the nightstand at the foot of her bed. Tomorrow, she thought, she would ask Ben to bead the quill so she could hang it on the wall in her apartment in Milwaukee.

She soaked in the bubbles for twenty minutes, then climbed in between fresh sheets just as the sun slipped behind the pines. She couldn't remember when she'd been so tired. Spirits, colored eagles, whirling green fireballs of light, Hobo, Noah, and Jessie found their way into her dreams. She woke fifteen hours later when the phone intruded. It was Uncle Dan.

"Good morning, Sis. Curiosity got the best of me. How was the trip?"

Amanda croaked a reply.

Dan laughed, "Want to say that again, or do you want to call me when you're awake?"

"Yeah, could I? I haven't even had my coffee yet." Amanda's mouth felt ugly. "I need to brush my teeth. It tastes like a skunk crawled through my mouth and died in there."

Dan laughed. "Why don't you just come on over when you wake up? I'm anxious to see you. I bought some *ho-made* raisin-cinnamon bread at the church yesterday. Miz Lorenzo made it. She's a great cook. Do you remember her? She used to cook for the school years ago. Might have been after your time though. Am I tempting you?"

Amanda smiled in spite of her tiredness. Uncle Dan was manipulating again. He knew what he was doing when he bought the bread. Aunt Molly used to make it all the time, and she loved it when Amanda and her cousins stuffed themselves. Amanda hesitated. Noah was going to call, but that could be a daylong wait. Right now she wanted to see her uncle.

"I'll come only if you promise to toast it," she told him.

"It's a deal. I'll be waiting."

"Give me about an hour," Amanda said. "I'll be there." She hung up and stumbled toward the bathroom.

First things first: her kidneys were protesting fifteen hours without relief.

After two cups of coffee and a shower, Amanda wrapped the feather in its red scarf and grabbed a jar of apple butter. She was humming as she went out the door. It was nine-thirty. She felt human again.

The sun sparkled on the frost covering the still-bare trees. Geese honked overhead, traveling north in their usual V formation. What a beautiful day! Amanda thanked the Grandfather for his creations, for Uncle Dan, and for rediscovered friends. She put the wrapped feather above the passenger's-side visor and turned the key. Her Escort coughed a bit before catching. She patted the dash . . . glad to be alive.

Dan was peering out the kitchen window when Amanda pulled into the yard. He let the curtain fall back and pushed the bar down on the toaster. He was putting two coffee mugs on the table when she came in.

Amanda hugged him. "You're a lifesaver. Left to myself I probably would have slept the whole day away, or just dragged around the cabin. Um, what's this?"

Dan placed a cereal bowl filled with vanilla yogurt spooned over sliced bananas, green grapes, and apple chunks in front of her. He beamed. "I'm taking care of you. This is *health* food. I saw it on TV last week."

"Wow, this is great. I didn't know how hungry I was!" She picked up her spoon without waiting for him.

"Couldn't wait for you to get back so's I could spoil you." He laughed and hugged her again. "Now, tell me good 'n' true, could you get this kind of attention back in the Beer City?" He buttered her toast and laid it on a paper towel in front of her.

She hugged him as he leaned over. "Have I ever told you how much I love you, Uncle Dan?"

His chin quivering slightly, and fighting tears, he asked, "You sure you have to go back?"

"I think so." She let it drop and bit into her toast. "Let me tell you about the weekend."

"Tell me then," Dan said. He recovered his voice and looked at her over his glasses as he put a spoonful of health food into his mouth.

Between bites Amanda tried to explain the lighting and the spirit lights. Words didn't seem to be enough, so she swung her arms around trying to show the greatness of her experience.

Dan nodded. "Yeah, I remember. I didn't know how to tell Hobo I'd seen spirit lights around Molly. How do you say something like that without sounding crazy? Fact is, I thought I was crazy. You're privileged, my girl."

"Ummm. I know. I feel overwhelmed, confused, and most of the time now, just plain scared."

Dan reached out and patted her hand. "Your ma, she couldn't believe for nothin'! But your grandma was a believer! She had to be with a brother like Hobo.

She saw so many things firsthand, she never questioned *either* religion like your ma did. She knew the Indian's Creator and the white man's God was the same."

"But wasn't Ma's father kind of a spiritual man too? How could she not believe?"

Dan shook his head still confused. "Wondered that myself many a time."

"Grandma was lucky. I guess people long ago could believe like we can't. Maybe the Church's insistence that there is only one Christian God limits our ability to experience the Great Spirit. What do you think?"

"I think you had a good weekend! Sounds to me like you learnt somethin'," Dan said. He got up to get more coffee. He grimaced when he pushed himself away from the table. His limp was worse today. "I think you should ask Noah," he said over his shoulder. "I wish I could answer that, but I'm just a God-fearin' man who learnt his Catholic catechism, then reached out for more when my Molly got sick." He filled their cups and sat back down. "Hobo died not too long after Molly did. I never got the chance to talk to him about the spirit world he worked in. I know he'd helped me if'n I could have come out of my dark hole long enough to ask him, but I waited too long." He slurped his hot coffee. "Guess maybe that's why I'm excited about what you've been learning. It's almost like a second chance for me, through you."

Amanda sipped her own coffee and watched her uncle. He looked tired today. For the first time she felt scared of losing him. She reached across the table and squeezed his hand gently.

# Chapter 20

Amanda pulled in to Ben and Yemmy's driveway. Although it was only 4:30, the lights were on in the Vincents' kitchen. Despite the sun smiling on the earth longer these days, dusk already surrounded the little house in the woods.

Amanda had stayed with Dan until he went to Winky's. As they pulled up in front of the rez one-stop, Punky waddled over to the car. Dan climbed out and walked around the front of the Escort where he waited, grinning at Amanda from behind Punky's broad back.

*"Hi, Manda! Good to see you," Punky talked around the giant Snickers Bar he was chewing. "Whatcha up to ta'day?" He swallowed noisily.*

*Amanda stared at the chocolate smudge on his cheek. Dan called to her. "Hey girl, ya coming in or not?"*

*She smiled her best apologetic smile, "Sorry, Punky. Looks like I'm being paged." She shut off the car's engine and rolled the window up. Punky stepped back when she opened the door and slid out.*

*He saluted her with the remains of his candy bar. "Hey, I'll see you soon, okay?"*

*"Sure," she said and stepped around him. She hooked her elbow in Uncle Dan's. "Thanks, that's the second time you've saved me from that old friend."*

*Dan patted her hand and opened the door, motioning her through in front of him. She'd only stopped to say hi, forgetting that no one just says hi to Winky. He'd been waiting to give her a hard time about running away for the weekend with Noah.*

*"You shoulda seen the scowl on the pretty face of young Missus Brown," Winky teased her. "HoWa! Was she upset when she learnt you left town with Junior!" He laughed until he coughed.*

*Amanda walked over to the Coke machine so he wouldn't see her face.*

*"Yep," he continued. "Dan, your niece started a mighty stir when she climbed into Noah's Bronc and lit out for those Twin Cities! Jest the two of 'em too. Tsk, tsk, tsk!" He shook his head.*

*"I don't think you're funny," Amanda told him over her shoulder. "Not only are you not funny, you're just plain disgusting!" She walked to the counter and stared at him as solemnly as she could to no effect.*

*Winky continued, "I tole her, I said, 'Miz Brown, that young-un has a right to go where she wants to go and with who she wants.' Don't think Paula agreed with me though." He slapped the counter and laughed until he wheezed.*

Getting ready to go to the door, she laughed and made a face. Gossip spread quickly on the rez. She hoped Winky's version was the worst she'd hear.

"Come in," Ben yelled when she knocked on the door. "We been waitin' on you!"

"Hello child," Yemmy said. "Come sit down. Ben bought some brownies at the bake sale yesterday. I think that's the only time he goes to church any more: when he can buy some sweets. I don't bake like I used to. My old hands are too bad most of the time. Jeannie, Flora too, bake a lot though and bring us stuff."

Yemmy settled herself in her rocker by the wood stove. Ben helped her wrap the quilt around her legs.

"How's the arthritis today, Yemmy?" Amanda asked.

"It gets better day by day as spring comes on, but when the sun goes down, my joints flare up. So, how was the trip?" Yemmy asked. "I went to a Walking Good Heart ceremony myself years ago. Remember Ben, right after Miz Streeter's two young-uns went through the ice and drowned. Is he still good?" she asked Amanda.

"I should say so!" Amanda said. "But before we get to that, Ben, I have a great favor to ask."

"Go ahead, my girl. What can I do for you?"

"I wanted to ask you if you could bead the quill of the feather Noah blessed. I don't know how. The thing is tough," she wrinkled her nose, "I'll be leaving for Milwaukee in less than two weeks. Do you think you can have it done in time?"

"Heck, yes! I can have it done by next Thursday or Friday. Depends on what this old girl here has me doing around the house," he winked at Yemmy. "What colors do you want? We got some good-uns that Noah brought back from the city."

"Well, the night before I went to Minneapolis I dreamed about different colored eagles. When I asked Noah about the colors, he thought they might be my dance colors if I ever decide to dance."

"Ben, go get those new beads for this girl's feather," Yemmy urged.

"I'll go get the feather. But first . . ." She handed Ben tobacco. *"Miigwich."*

Amanda was headed for the door when Ben called, "On your way back, grab that there box off the top of the fridge and look inside."

She did as he asked. She opened the box at the table. Nina Jo's fan was inside, wrapped in white tissue. It was made of four red tail hawk feathers. The handle that Amanda saw Ben carving weeks before was wrapped in white leather with three rows of royal blue, burgundy, and yellow beads around the top edge. A small hole was drilled in the bottom of the handle, and a burgundy leather strap ran through it. Amanda was fingering the strap when Ben came back into the room.

"That's so's it won't fall, in case she lets go for some reason. What do you think?" He beamed.

"It's wonderful, Ben. You do beautiful work! She's going to be *so* proud to carry it!"

Ben smiled. Yemmy chimed in. "Yep, my old man does good work. He'll do your feather proud."

"I know he will. I can't think of anyone I'd rather have do it than you, Ben."

He blushed. "Sure would be nice if you could be here to see Nina Jo get her fan," Ben suggested slyly. "It will only be a few more weeks—on Mother's Day. You can stay on that long, can't ya?"

"I don't think so," Amanda stammered. She began examining the beads Ben placed in front of her. She selected a deep, dark brown, a brilliant satin turquoise, a golden yellow, and white satin.

"These will go good together," Ben said. "Leave Miigwan with me, and she'll be ready in a couple days." Before he sat down, Ben put a plate of brownies and a cup of coffee in front of Amanda.

She reached for a brownie. Between bites she told the same story of her weekend that she'd told her uncle earlier. Yemmy rocked slowly and nodded her head from time to time. Ben smiled often. "I'm glad you had a good time," he said at one point. "I like the part when Grandfather Frank blessed you. That was a real special kind of thing."

By the time Amanda reached home that night, she was exhausted. After two tellings, the ceremony, the spirits were more dream-like and far away than ever.

Something was missing when she finally climbed into bed that night—perhaps her feather.

After her walk the next morning, Amanda carried her cup of coffee up the steep stairs to the long, dorm-like room. Several trunks sat against the walls, and cardboard boxes were stacked on top of each other in the corners. Three quilts, not good for much other than dust rags now, were piled on a bare bedspring on a twin frame. Amanda pulled out the trunks one-by-one and went through their contents. Clothes, outdated and smelling of mothballs, filled most of them. Old shoes, kept by her mother for who knows what, filled the smallest trunk. Shoes with bulky, square Cuban heels, thin stiletto heels, no heels . . . Mom believed in saving everything—maybe she hoped they would come back in style.

Amanda held up a shoe next to her foot and shook her head. She had always had big feet. She grinned when she remembered how her uncles teased her and Grandpa would grin and say: "Mandy's got good understanding." That had always made her feel better until she was old enough to realize what he was really saying: *under-standing* indeed! She pushed that trunk up against the wall again, and pulled out the last one.

She found what she was looking for: a square Christmas tin that once held fruitcake, or cookies, or some of Gram's homemade candy. It was badly scratched and dented. She struggled with the cover. Inside were odd pieces of jewelry—none in much better shape than the box. She dumped the contents onto her lap in order to sort through the mess. She found Grandma's pin: a small blue medal of the Blessed Virgin surrounded by tiny blue stones in a sunray design. Grandma wore it on her good winter coat: her going-to-church coat.

Her hand picked out a tiny cross with several green and white stones missing. She squinted into the hole in the center, still amazed by the wonder of it. The Lord's Prayer was still visible—just barely. How she marveled at it when she wore it years ago: how could anything like that be written so small?

*It was July, three weeks after her birthday. She knew Brownie would be up today; she felt it. She waited on the front porch pretending to read* Little Women, *but she mostly kept her eyes on the long driveway instead of the book in her hands. Finally, she saw him peddling up the drive in the hot sun. Jimbo, Grandma's old dog, taking refuge from the heat under the porch, spotted him at the same time. He lifted his head for two quick barks to let everyone know he was still on duty. Then he closed his eyes and went back to sleep.*

*Brownie smiled all the way up the drive, "showing all his teeth," as dad would say. Amanda smiled back. When Brownie reached the porch he swung his leg over the seat of his bike and let it fall in the grass. He took his wet T-shirt off and wiped the sweat from his face. He ran the shirt over his thin chest, and tied it to the handlebars of his bike. All this before he said, "Hi, Manda."*

*Amanda handed him her lemonade. Drops of water ran down the sides of the brightly colored metal tumbler where her fingers touched the tin. Much of the ice had already melted, but it was still cold. He liked that.*

*"I'll get some more," she said.*

*When she came back with two more tumblers, he was sitting on the step where she had been.*

*"Whatcha readin'?" he inquired.*

*She held the book up for his inspection. "Little Women. It's pretty good. I read it before."*

*"Then why ya readin' it again?"*

*"Cuz I like it," she grinned at him. They listened to the muffled voices coming from the house.*

*He looked off toward the pond. "Wanna go for a walk?"*

*They sauntered away from the house walking so close together, their arms touched. They hooked pinky fingers without looking at each other. At the pond Amanda pulled the back of her full cotton skirt through her legs and wrapped it into the front of her waistband before wading in. Brownie walked in without rolling up his jeans. Amanda watched the water seep up his pant legs, darkening the faded denim.*

*"Are you going to the dance on Friday?" Brownie asked. The youth group, under the direction of Fr. Heenan, had dances for community teens once a month. She always went; so did Brownie.*

*"I s'pose so. Aren't you?"*

*He nodded and shuffled uncomfortably in the water. "Well," he said finally, "I have something for you to wear." He reached into his jeans pocket and pulled out a wadded hanky. "I know your birthday was last month, and I knew you'd get presents from your family, so I waited to give you this. . . . Happy Birthday." He carefully unwrapped the hanky and held up a tiny cross, with green and white stones, on a dainty chain. "If you put your eye to that hole, and look into the sun, you can read the Lord's Prayer," Brownie told her.*

*Amanda squealed. "You're right. Just look at that!" She tried to hand it back to him but he shook his head.*

*"I already seen it. It's yours to look at."*

*"Thank you, Brownie. That's very sweet. I'll keep it forever." She held up her long braid and he fastened the delicate chain around her neck. She twisted her shoulders showing it off. It glistened in the sun.*

*"It's beautiful! I'll wear it always," Amanda whispered.*

*Brownie blushed and looked off over his shoulder toward the woods.*

*When they got back to the house, dad was loading Brownie's bike into the trunk of the Buick.*

*"Hey Dad! You ain't stealing Brownie's bike, are you?" Amanda yelled.*

*"Ahh, you caught me. I figure to get a couple bucks at Harold's pawn shop," Dad laughed. "I got to run to Winky's and pick up some stuff for your ma. Thought it was hot enough, Brownie might like a ride back to town."*

*Brownie nodded his thanks. He never spoke around adults if he didn't have to. Dad noticed the cross sparkling on Amanda's neck. He caught her eye and smiled, but kept silent. "Want to ride with us, Sis?"*

*"Sure." She climbed into the big car between her dad and Brownie. No one spoke. Amanda fingered her treasure. She'd never felt so lucky, at least not since the time she found the painted wooden cross at the church rummage sale, the one she made Dad put above her door so she could look at it every night. Each time they hit a pothole in the road, and there were plenty, Brownie would bump up against her side. They would both blush without looking at each other.*

Amanda clenched the cross tightly in her fist. So long ago; a lifetime ago. Brownie was dead. She missed him; she missed the past. She suddenly wanted her childhood, and her parents, and her friends back.

Amanda put everything away except the cross and two photo albums that were wrapped in old newspaper and tied with twine, probably from the incredible roll that Grandma always had going. Gram saved everything, including twine. *"You never know when you're gonna need it,"* she would say as she wound it over and around the already good-sized roll. Once when one of her famous rolls of twine reached the size of a basketball, Dad had threatened to play with it. Amanda smiled at the memory. What a pack rat Grandma had been, and Mom too!

She put the albums under her left arm and held her empty coffee cup in the little finger of her left hand. The cross was still clenched in her right fist when she went downstairs. The clock over the fireplace announced that four hours had slipped away since she went to the dorm room. Her stomach told her it was time for food.

As she passed the front door a sharp rap made her jump. She opened the door with the thumb and forefinger of her right hand. Noah and Niijii stood there. "I was about to leave; thought you weren't gonna answer the door. I knew you was home cuz your car is here." He looked at her. "How come I always get here when you're cleaning?"

Amanda looked down at herself. Her sweatshirt, her knees, and hands were dusty. She laughed. "Just lucky, I guess. I decided to dig around upstairs to see what hidden treasures lurked in all the old trunks and boxes up there." She stepped back so he could enter.

"Looks like you were successful. Whatcha find? Anything worth big bucks?"

"As a matter of fact, I did. Look." She opened her hand. The tiny cross lay in her palm.

"I'll be darned," Noah said. He picked it up gently and held it to his eye. "You can still see it. I'll be darned," he said again. "Man, what a long time ago that was." He handed it back to her.

Niijii pushed past Noah and began to explore the cabin. Noah and Amanda walked to the kitchen.

"Here, let me take those," he offered. She handed him the cup, and he took the albums out from under her arm and laid them on the counter.

"I'm about to find something to eat. You hungry?" she asked.

"Déjà vu again," he laughed. "I'm always hungry." He opened the refrigerator. "What you got today?"

They made tuna sandwiches. Noah watched her as they ate. Finally he said, "Well, was it what you expected?"

"And more!" Even she heard the awe in her voice. "We're talking about the ceremony, right?" When he nodded, she continued. "You couldn't have prepared me for it. It was wonderful—it was scary! It was . . ." she'd reached the limits of language for her experience, and threw open her arms.

Noah nodded. "That's good. Yep, that's good." He fidgeted with his plate, turning it this way and that. He seemed to be struggling for words. She waited, but he didn't speak.

Amanda finally broke the silence. "The other day when we came back, I thought I had so much to talk to you about, but now I can't think of anything. Isn't that crazy? Not that I know more than I did then, but I'm at a loss," she shrugged.

"You'll find the answers in yourself anyways. That's why I didn't call yesterday. You gotta have time to think about what you saw. When I first realized I saw and heard things that other people didn't, believe me, I worried." He grinned at her. "Remember when Evie Rooder's ma went to the County Institution? They said it was cuz she heard voices. I sure didn't want that to happen to me. So I kept my mouth shut." He paused. "It's a good sign that you're working it out yourself and not wanting me to give you the answers."

"Tell me," she suddenly asked, "do you ever feel like Hobo is still around? I mean, *here* at the cabin."

"Uh-huh, right from the first time I visited you here. But that's no surprise. I'd expect he'd be keeping an eye on things. This here's his home." Noah paused to sip his coffee. "Had any more interesting dreams?"

"I dream every night. The dreams are usually pretty jumbled up. Course, they always make sense when I'm dreaming them. You know, like being able to fly down stairs when you're being chased?"

"Lot of folks get jumbled up during the day and find peace when they're dreaming. You're the opposite."

"Is that good?" she asked.

"It can't be bad." He grinned at her.

Niijii came in from the other room, where he had fallen asleep on one of the braided rugs in front of the sofa. Now he sat in front of Noah and looked at him as if to say he was ready to hit the road.

"Quit nagging me," Noah told him. Niijii laid his head on Noah's knee, cocked his crooked ears, and raised one eyebrow. "Okay, guess it's time to go. Niijii's had enough of being away from home. I brought him with me today so he wouldn't think I was desertin' him again. He's stuck pretty close since I been back." Noah rubbed the old dog's head. "What's on your agenda for the next couple of days?" he asked.

"Are you asking me or Niijii?" Amanda teased.

"You." He pursed his lips and pointed them at his shaggy black friend. "I know what he's going to do."

"I'm going to go see Annie tomorrow. I worry about her. She's always been thin but she's downright skinny now. I don't think she's very healthy."

"Yeah, she's had it pretty rough now and then. In a way she's lucky though. She's got one great daughter-in-law who takes good care of her. Have you met the solemn Ms. Winnie yet?" Amanda smiled and nodded. He continued. "Your company will do her good," he said. "Until Brownie came along, you and her were like a pair of Siamese twins, weren't you?"

"Uh-huh. She was the best friend I've ever had—really more like a sister. I never had one, you know."

"Well," he drawled softly. "If I'd known you wanted a sister, for two cents, I'd have given you mine." Noah laughed. "We're friends now, but when we was kids, man, it was a matter of who was gonna kill who first." He laughed again. "I guess we stopped fightin' when she got big enough to knock the shit outta me!"

Niijii barked impatiently. "Okay, okay." Noah stood, and Niijii bounced excitedly. "Manda, I'll talk to you soon." The trio made their way to the front door. "Tell Annie hello for me," Noah held out his hand.

After Noah and Niijii left, Amanda cleaned up the kitchen, then spent an hour going through her jewelry to see if could find a chain that would go with the cross. She didn't.

# Chapter 21

The days were getting warmer. "Up north" folks had decided spring was here to stay, and they were welcoming it in their favorite ways: working in their yards, gossiping with neighbors, or just sitting on their stoops enjoying the warming sun. Annie was in a wooden rocker, head back against the chair, eyes closed, pushing herself back and forth slowly, listening to the hypnotic squeak of dried pine wood.

When Amanda pulled up in front of the house Winnie stopped sweeping up the red clay that was clinging to the sidewalk and waved. Iron-rich soil stuck to everything since the thaw. Amanda had noticed this morning when she climbed into the Escort that it needed a good washing, as did her shoes. Annie lifted her head when she heard the car door slam, and she smiled at Amanda.

"Since when do you need to sit in the sun for color?" Amanda called to her cousin. "You're dark enough!"

"I used to be," Annie said. "But I got pale like you *city* Indians this past winter. I'm working on my reservation tan." She was dressed in a heavy blue sweater, and she had a quilt wrapped around her legs. A pot of hot tea sat on the white table beside her. "Sit down, Cousin. Winnie, would you be a dear and bring Manda a cup?"

"Winnie, never mind. I'll get it myself." Amanda slipped off her shoes and let herself into the kitchen. She grabbed a cup with a *News from the Sloughs* logo off a wobbly wooden cup rack and returned to the porch. "Tea time! Remember how we used to pretend we were *royalty* or something and drink Kool-Aid from those little pink-and-white plastic cups?" she asked as she filled her cup with green tea.

"Yeah, and ever' one of them had chips on the rim that scratched our lips, even when they was new. I remember that," Annie said. "Sure didn't take much to make us happy back then, did it Sis?"

Amanda stuck out her little finger in exaggeration as she drank. "You gonna join us, Winnie?"

"You wouldn't catch me dead drinking that wimpy stuff," Winnie grumbled. "In fact, it would probably kill me. I'll get me some coffee just as soon as I finish here."

"Winnie won't drink tea. She won't even drink decaf coffee," Annie said.

"Nope, I gotta have high octane all the way or none at all," Winnie stated. "Same's my men."

Amanda stopped in the middle of a sip and stared at the big woman: she was full of surprises! Winnie's head was down, concentrating on her work, so her hair slid across her cheeks and hid her smile.

The women visited for the next hour. It got chilly fast as the sun sank behind the pines across the road. "Ma, we best get you inside," Winnie said. "Don't want you catching your death of cold."

"Oh, you worry too much, my girl," Annie grumbled, but she let Winnie help her from the chair. "Why don't you stay and eat with us, Mandy? What we having for supper anyway?" she asked Winnie.

"I seen you got a quart of venison up in the cupboard, and I'll fry up those leftover spuds. I might even spoil you and cream up some green beans how ya like them."

Annie squeezed Winnie's arm. "Ah, what a treat. Hey, call J.R. and tell him join us. He hasn't seen his Auntie Mandy for years."

Amanda felt a twinge of guilt in mid-step. She hadn't seen J.R. since he was four or five.

"I'm gonna lay down for an hour," Annie said. "Please stay, Cousin. I'm a little tired right now. All's I need is a bit of rest and I'll be ready to eat."

Amanda agreed. She watched Annie make her way slowly down the hall. "Winnie," she said quietly when Annie disappeared into her room. "What's going on with her?"

Winnie lowered her eyes. "She made me promise not to say nothin' cuz she don't want for you to know. She don't want ya worryin' 'bout her: she said so. She'd kill me if I told ya."

"Told me what, Winnie?"

"Well, see," Winnie paused, "she had a cancer operation 'bout six-seven months back. The doc, he said he got it all, but she ain't comin' round like she should. We all can see that." Winnie looked at Amanda, black eyes swimming in tears. "I don't know what I'm gonna do if we lose her. She's been a better ma to me than my own ever was."

Amanda crossed the room and put her arms around Winnie. To her surprise, Winnie hugged back. "Today is the first day I got her to dress up and go outside," she sobbed. "That's a good sign, don't ya think?"

"I think it's a wonderful sign." Amanda held Winnie for a few minutes before the big woman pulled away and blew her nose. "Winnie, I wish I had known," Amanda continued. "Not that I could have changed anything, but maybe . . ."

"I got to call J.R.," Winnie said wiping her eyes. She left the kitchen and went into the living room. Amanda heard her talking softly on the phone. "J.R.'ll be here in a couple of hours," Winnie announced when she came back into the kitchen. "He's gonna bring a apple pie. I did some up and put them in the freezer. He's gonna bake one and bring it so's it will be warm for us."

While Amanda washed the dishes and Winnie worked at the stove, Winnie filled her in on practically everything that her nephew had done in the last fifteen years. Every ten minutes or so Amanda saw Winnie glance at the clock hanging over the sink. Winnie actually squealed when J.R. walked in the door.

J.R. was a handsome man. Amanda would have recognized him on the street even after not seeing him for years. Other than a handlebar mustache and about six inches in height, he looked like his dad at the same age—slender, thin dark face, smiling light gray eyes, and dimpled chin. He was balancing a pie on what remained of his right arm. Amanda stared the end of his right shirt-sleeve that was sewn shut.

"Lost it to a nasty factory machine in Duluth; ain't that the shits?" J.R. laughed and put his left arm around Amanda. Winnie took the apple pie off his right and put in on the counter. "Hello Auntie. Long time, no see," he said. "You're lookin' pretty good. Are ya behavin'?"

Annie came into the kitchen before Amanda could respond. J.R. went to his mother and kissed her on the forehead. "How ya doin' today, good-lookin'?" He tried to hide the concern in his gray eyes behind a grin. Annie let him help her into a chair.

"Ain't he somethin'?" Annie asked Amanda. Amanda nodded agreement.

Winnie hugged her husband. "Dinner's ready," she said. She laughed and ducked away as he tried to grab a handful of her bountiful behind when she walked past him.

"Ready when you are!" he said in a suggestive tone.

The evening passed slowly. Amanda saw Annie look at Winnie, and she could tell that she knew that Winnie had spilled the beans, but no one talked about it. J.R. waited on his mother, hovering over her like a mother hen with her chick.

Finally, trying to keep the relief from her voice, Amanda said, "I better hit the road." It was only 8:30.

Thursday broke dark with heavy rain pounding the roof of the cabin. Amanda woke tired, glad for the excuse to stay indoors and away from people. She fixed toast and coffee for herself and carried it into the living room to sit in front of the fireplace. An hour later she curled up on the sofa, pulled an afghan over her, and took a two-hour nap. She woke again just before noon and wandered around the cabin looking for something to do and hoping she wouldn't find anything. On her third trip through, she spotted the albums that Noah had put on the kitchen counter. She laid them out in front of the fireplace and stoked the coals.

The photos were old black-and-white pictures of her parents, other family that she'd seen before, and some she hadn't: Mom and Dad, a young couple in their teens, smiling into the camera; Mom with her hair pulled up from each side of her face and pinned on top in two large rolls curled towards the center part; Dad, young and slender, astride a horse; a side view of Mom, very pregnant, must have been taken close to Amanda's birthday; Dad in his uniform—unsmiling, but proud. Amanda knew he'd been in the service, but he never talked about it. There was a crinkled photo of Gram standing on the front porch in her apron, waving at the person holding the camera. Jimbo sat beside her, tongue lolling out the side of his mouth, looking off toward the woods. There was another of Mom and Dad standing beside an old car, with a baby Amanda sitting on the fender between them; one of a two-year-old Amanda holding an Easter basket, with something, chocolate probably, smeared all over her face. She smiled at a photo of Uncle Dan and Aunt Molly in front of their house, stiff, afraid to move. Off to the side, a small black dog was walking around the corner of the house, apparently not wanting his picture taken. The rest were photos of people and places that Amanda didn't recognize.

The phone rang. It was Uncle Dan.

"Hey, Sis. Just checking to see if you were all snuggled in today and not out running around in the rain."

"I'm fine," she answered. "In fact, I'm sitting in front of a nice fire with a bunch of old pictures that I found in the attic. Just saw one of you and Aunt Molly when you two were just kids. You look about twenty or so!"

"They must be old," Dan chuckled. "I don't remember them havin' cameras back then. I'd like to see 'em. Why don't you come over and spend Sunday with me. Bring 'em along." He paused, "In fact, come early and go to Mass with me first. I'll even buy us a downtown breakfast brunch afterward."

"Can't pass that up! Thanks Uncle, I can almost smell the bacon now," she laughed. "I'll see you then."

Amanda was eager to get off the phone. Dan's voice held a peculiar edge; Amanda felt her own tighten. Time was going by too fast, and they both recognized it. She hung up and stared at the black plastic box. She was going to miss him. She wiped at the surprising tears that suddenly formed on her cheeks. She went back to the photos, but they didn't hold her interest now.

The day had been so dark it was hard to tell if dusk had arrived. Amanda started turning on lights at about three o'clock. It felt like bedtime. When she made her way to the kitchen and snapped the light on, a loud snort from the other side of rear door made her jump. She thought of her uncle's warning about bears coming out of hibernation and being hungry. Old Indians in the community used to tell stories about bears eating people in order to scare the kids, but as far as she could remember only an occasional hunter who happened to get between a mother and her cub had actually been attacked by a bear—no one had been assaulted by one that broke down a door first. Folks in this part of this country knew why, and how, to leave the big creatures alone. They learned young.

*Gramma screamed and dropped a pan. Dad and Amanda ran for the kitchen. By the time they arrived, Gram was laughing and pointing at the kitchen window. A young black bear was looking in at them, wondering what the fuss was all about. He must have been attracted by the smell of the pies Gram was baking.*

*It was summer, and the windows were wide open in the steamy kitchen. Screens weren't popular on the reservation. Bees, flies, and other winged insects had free and regular access to human habitats. The bear's nose was twitching as he sniffed the wonderful spicy smells. His groan was a groan of anticipated pleasure.*

*A three-year-old Amanda squealed with delight and ran towards the window.*

*"No!" Gram and Dad yelled at the same time. Amanda stopped short and burst into tears, not from fear of the bear, but from the raised voices of those who loved her.*

*"Shoo! Shoo!" Gram, standing in the middle of the room, flapped her apron at the bear. The bear took one long last sniff at the air and dropped to the ground with a disgusted grunt. Within minutes they heard him shuffling off into the woods. His groan now one of pain and remorse.*

After that day Dad teased Gram unmercifully by telling stories about the effect her baking had on area wildlife to anyone who would listen.

Apparently the bear outside the cabin now decided there wasn't anything to be gained here. Amanda heard him moving off.

Despite her morning nap, Amanda was tired and went to bed early. The rain continued. Amanda prayed without her feather, missing it. She fell asleep listening to the rain as it steadily pounded the roof.

*She was lost in a tunnel that ran under the houses in the city. She looked around, unsure which direction she wanted. Just then, several children, chatting excitedly, emerged from the tunnel behind her.*

*"Come with us," they yelled.*

*"But where does this go?" Amanda asked them.*

*"Under the houses," one girl explained patiently. "Come on! We'll come out right by the school." She reached out and took Amanda's hand. "Don't worry, we do this all the time. I know where we're going." The girl looked at Amanda from under her long dark bangs. "We know where you want to go. Come on!" She glanced ahead where the boys were already disappearing around the next corner. "Wait!" she yelled to them. "We're coming." She tugged on Amanda's hand again. This time, Amanda moved.*

The tunnels were apparently used for storage. Boxes and other objects were stacked along the walls. The kids ignored the mess, except to jump over anything that lay directly in their path. Finally they came to a room with dark wood paneling on the walls, a dirt ceiling, and a steep stairway that led up to a closed door. The kids didn't hesitate but took the stairs two at a time.

The door opened into a foyer that Amanda sensed was in a church or maybe a school. The front door was open, and distant whirling sounds entered the small area from the outside.

"The eagles!" the kids clamored. "They're here. Let's go see them!" Outside, the night was lit by a slice of pale moon and street lamps. It appeared to be autumn. Colored leaves decorated the trees along the sidewalk. The kids ran down the steps and into the street. "There they are," several of the children screamed. "Look!"

The girl still held Amanda's hand. "Come on," she said. With no other choice, Amanda followed. She squinted into the dark sky, unable to see anything. There," the girl pointed upward. "See them?" She jumped excitedly from foot to foot.

Amanda saw. At least twenty eagles whirled in a large circle near the moon. They dipped and dove, the moon's light glistening off their white heads and fantails. The eagles came closer. One daring bird hovered about ten feet above them, her wings beating the night air like a helicopter and swirling dry leaves around the feet of Amanda and the children. Suddenly she dove close to them. As she pulled up from her fast dive, several feathers dropped from her tail: long ones, short ones, and a few fluffs. The kids ran for the feathers.

"Stop!" Amanda yelled. "Don't touch them! No! Stop!" The kids stopped and waited. A couple of the boys, with feathers already in their hands, looked at her, then looked at the feathers, confused.

Amanda gathered the feathers from the ground and took the others from the boys. One brown, spotted fluff remained on the roadway. It was torn. "We'll burn that one," Amanda said. "We can't leave it there, and it isn't strong enough to be used for anything." The girl who had taken Amanda's hand picked up the damaged feather and handed it to her reverently.

Amanda woke. She turned toward the table at the end of her bed expecting Migizi to be there. But it was empty. The feather was still with Ben. Tomorrow she would call to see how he was coming with the beadwork. Amanda pulled the quilts up toher chin and went back to sleep, trying unsuccessfully to recapture the dream. In the morning she didn't even remember it.

Friday was dark and rainy again. Amanda decided to write to the office and let them know she would be back in a week. Triste-feliz entered her mind. To go back or not to go back, that was the burning question. She carefully worded two notes, then threw them both into the garbage.

Amanda spent the day watching TV without seeing it. This was the first time she'd turned on the tube since her first few days at the cabin. She didn't call Ben.

# Chapter 22

The sun greeted Amanda when she lifted the blinds in her bedroom on Saturday. "It's about time," she grumbled. Still groggy, she made her way to the kitchen: coffee first, then a shower and a walk. As she shuffled past the phone, it rang, making her jump.

"*Boozhoo,* Niijiikwe," Noah's voice said in her ear. "What a great day to be alive. What say we go visitin'?"

She smiled into the phone. "Good morning. How can you be so cheerful? It's barely daybreak." Her voice was thick and foggy.

Noah laughed. "That's what I like, a woman who's up with the dawn! Really, it's almost nine o'clock."

Amanda squinted at the wall clock. He was right. "Umm. What can I say?"

"I thought I'd like to take a ride out to see Ben and Yemmy. How'd ya like to go along?"

"Eventually," she said. "I need a cold shower and hot coffee first. Or rather, the other way around." She tucked the phone under her chin and rinsed out the coffee pot. "When were you thinking about going?"

"Oh, in about an hour or so," he laughed. "When can you be ready?"

"In about an hour or so. Want to come get me or should I pick you up?" Amanda asked.

"I'll come your way. Or do you just want to meet over there?"

"Don't make me make decisions this early in the day. What works best for you?" She had filled the pot with cold water and was scooping coffee into the filter.

"I'll come get you," he told her. "See you soon."

"Right." Amanda hung up the phone, flipped the Mr. Coffee ON switch and shuffled off to the bathroom. The shower woke her. She towel dried her hair, slipped into jeans and a sweatshirt, and, with her second cup of coffee in hand, went into the yard to see if the bear had done any damage the other night. The sun felt good, and she stayed warm as long as she remained out of the shadows. She checked the doorframe, but couldn't find any marks left by her visitor. She was taking the last swallow of her lukewarm coffee when she heard Noah's Bronco. She walked around to the front of the cabin and waited for him on the porch.

Noah was all smiles as he climbed out of the vehicle. Niijii jumped gingerly out of the door behind him. They walked toward her.

"Here they come, man and beast," she laughed.

"Don't insult Niijii by calling him a man," Noah said. "Happy spring." He presented Amanda with a small bundle of Arbutus that he had been holding behind his back.

"Oh, how wonderful!" she cried. She held them to her nose. "Um. This is a smell you never forget. They bring back so many memories. Thank you."

"Thank Niijii, he found them," Noah blushed.

"Thank you Niijii, my friend," Amanda patted the dog's head. Niijii smiled up at her.

"This is the damnedest dog," she laughed. Noah joined her laughter and Niijii barked once as if agreeing.

"I hope I didn't spoil any plans for today," Noah said.

"No, in fact, I was thinking about going to the Vincents' myself. Ben has my feather. He's beading it for me so I can put it on the wall of my apartment like you said."

"So, you're going back," Noah said. He followed her back into the kitchen and had to force himself not to say any more.

"Yeah. I have to. I always said I did. I have a job and a lease on an apartment there. I'll be back soon though. I thought maybe in a month or so. Maybe in time for the spring Pow Wow." She avoided Noah's eyes as she put the flowers into a shallow cereal bowl. "There, aren't they pretty?" She set the bowl in the middle of the table. "Ready?"

"We ain't left yet?" he asked.

Ben was standing on the stoop when they pulled into the yard. He waved and put out his cigarette.

"Yemmy won't let me smoke in the house," he confessed, "so I do my dirty work out here." He hugged Amanda and slapped Noah's back. "Come in. Noah,

I was going to call you a little later. I need help getting out that old stump over there," he directed pursed lips toward the backyard.

"Guess, that's why I came by today, Nimishoomis." Noah put his arm around the Elder's shoulder.

"Mandy, reckon you're here for Miigwan. She's ready. Come see." Ben led the way into the house.

Yemmy was sitting in her rocker, in a sunspot streaming through the kitchen window. "Well, look who's here. Get these young-uns some coffee, Ben." Amanda hugged the old lady. Yemmy held onto her hand for a long time. "You're gonna like your feather, my girl. This here old man outdid himself for you. This might be his best work ever."

"I was guided," Ben said. "She's a special one." Amanda didn't know if he meant her or the feather, but she didn't ask. Ben came back from the living room with the wrapped feather. He laid it on the table and carefully pulled the red cloth back. Brown, turquoise, yellow, and white beads followed a pattern from dark to light and back again. The beadwork covered at least four inches of the quill.

"It is beautiful, Ben. More than I expected." Tears filled her eyes.

"Don't get weepy on me, missy," Ben said fighting back his own tears.

Noah grunted quietly. "Good one, Ben. Since when did you get so talented?" he teased.

"You really like it?" Ben asked Amanda.

"Beyond words," Amanda said. "What do I owe you for this?"

"Don't insult me," Ben said. "It's my gift to you."

"But we're supposed to exchange gifts," Amanda said. "I haven't anything for you. I mean to pay you. This took time and beads."

"You spent many days with us old folks this spring, that's gift enough. You gave yourself."

Both Yemmy and Noah nodded in agreement. Amanda picked the feather up and turned it around. The beads sparkled. The feather looked younger, healthier, if that was possible.

"I don't know what to say," she said. She hugged Ben again. "You're too good to me."

Ben cleared his throat. "Grab your cup there, Noah, and let's get outside," he said in a husky voice. "The ground is soft from all that rain. We should be able to get that stump out of the ground in an hour or so.

We'll be out back if you need us," he told Yemmy. "Mandy here can visit with ya while we men are busy."

Noah grinned at Amanda as he held the door open for Ben.

Yemmy smiled. "Sit, my girl. Tell me what you been up to these last rainy ole days?"

Noah was sweating. He chopped at the long roots that had grown deep into the earth to hold the ancient pine until it was recently felled by a strong winter wind.

Ben sat on his wooden stool, watching. "Sure workin' hard, ain't I?" he chuckled as Noah threw him a look. "Want to break and get some coffee?"

"Nah. I want to talk," Noah said. He wiped sweat off his face with the sleeve of his shirt, leaned against the axe, and took a deep breath. Ben waited. "Remember I told you about the sweat I went to in the cities last weekend?"

"Uh-huh."

"Well, Roger told us all something that has been eatin' at my mind since then. I need to tell someone other than Niijii." The dog raised his head at the mention of his name. When Noah didn't appear to be talking to him, he put his head back between his paws and closed his eyes again. "He said I'm gonna be married by the pipe in four years." Noah waited for a reaction from Ben.

Ben lit another cigarette before he answered. "Yemmy won't be too happy if'n you're talking about Jess," he said. "She ain't never liked that woman since she hurt you before."

"It's not Jessie," Noah said.

Ben raised his eyebrows and looked at Noah through smoke. "Not Jessie? Who then?"

Noah looked toward the house.

"No!" Ben said. "Really? I'll be goddamned! That's good, my boy. That's real good! Wait till Yemmy hears this. I s'pose Mandy's in there telling the old gal now, ain't she?"

"Don't hardly think so," Noah said. He wiped his brow again. "She don't know herself yet."

"*HoWa!*" Ben shouted. Niijii raised his head again and this time looked at the old man.

"When ya gonna tell her?" Ben asked.

"I ain't," Noah answered. "Grandfather will tell her when she's ready to hear it, I s'pect." Noah grinned at the Elder. "Never thought it would happen to me, but when the Grandfather decides something's to be, we got to go along with it. Glad he gave me four years to get ready!" Noah looked off into the woods and coughed.

Ben stamped out his cigarette. "By golly, wish we could celebrate! Yemmy's been wishin' for a wife for you for the longest time. And she loves that Mandy girl. Grandfather willing, we'll be here to throw a wing-ding after you tie the knot." He paused. "Well, guess that must mean she ain't goin' back to the city, ain't it?"

"Darned if I know, Ben. She says she's going back. Guess I'll have to trust Grandfather on this one too. If he lets her go back, there's got to be a reason. I keep askin' him to let me understand but seems like he's gonna leave me hangin' on this one."

Ben looked at the sky and chuckled. "Migizi," he said, pointing off to the east with his cigarette.

Noah looked in the direction Ben indicated. Migizi circled lazily, moving slowly off into the cloudless, morning sky. The two men grinned at each other. "A good sign. I'd sure like to see her face when she hears about her future husband an' all," Ben said.

"Me too," Noah added. "At least she's been married before and knows a little bit about it. Me," he paused, "me and Niijii have been bachin' it for so long, I don't know how I'll take to it."

"You'll learn quick enough," Ben assured him. "Women got a way of teachin' old dogs like us new tricks."

Two hours later the men walked into the house caked with dirt and mud from head to toe. Amanda started to laugh, but stopped herself when Yemmy began scolding. "Wipe them feet off. You two look like you was rollin' in a pig sty . . . What happened anyway? Looks to me like you was wrestlin' with that stump!"

"Well, it gave Noah a mighty battle, so I had to help him out. Shucks, woman, it's danged muddy out there." He looked at Noah and grumbled, "She acts like she don't know it rained for two days." Then he turned to the women, "What's for lunch?"

Amanda put aside the pile of rags that she was ripping apart and pulled a hot dish from the oven. "Rice with chicken. But you might want to wash up. I don't think I want to eat at the same table looking like you do."

Ben looked at Noah, "See what I mean?" he teased. "Chip women know how to lay down the rules."

Yemmy and Amanda looked at each other. Yemmy shook her gray head. "Men. They don't have the sense the Creator gave 'em . . . bless their souls. I'm telling you girl, you do good to stay single!"

Ben coughed and laughed at the same time. "That's what you know, old lady," he chuckled.

After lunch Amanda did dishes while the men went back outside. Then she gathered up the rags she'd laid aside and begin tearing again: Yemmy wanted to braid a rug. "Haven't done it for so long," she grumbled. "But I feel so useless jest sittin' around. It may take me a while with these crippled-up hands, but all's I got is time. So what if it takes two years?" She smiled at Amanda. "What do you suppose that old man was carrying on about when they came in?"

Amanda shook her head. "God knows. I don't know who has the worse influence on who, but it seems like when those two men get together, they act like they're cooking up something." She worked quickly, tearing the cloth into narrow strips. Yemmy hummed off key as she rocked and watched. "Yemmy, Winnie told me about Annie and the cancer." Amanda finally said.

The elder woman nodded. "I hear she ain't no better," she said. "It's a shame too. We all thought Ella's baby'd give her a reason to live, but she keeps going downhill." Yemmy shook her head sadly.

Amanda laid the cloth strips in her lap. "She's gotten worse even since I've been here. At first she looked tired, but on Wednesday it was like she was on her deathbed. Sure seems like there's gotta be something the doctors can do."

"I heard, according to the doc, they got all the cancer. He can't do no more than that. She's gotta do it for herself now."

"I don't get it," Amanda said. "Why would she just give up like that? I remember as kids, she was always a fighter. About the only thing that got her down was when her dad was drunk and pushed everyone around."

"Yep, that Lem was a mean one," Yemmy said. "No disrespect meant to your pa and Uncle Dan—they's good men, but that brother of theirs," she shook her head, "he weren't no good right from when he was a kid. Always into trouble, that one. I knew when he married Frannie Harris *that* would come to a bad end."

Amanda stared at the old lady. "Who's Frannie Harris?"

"That was your uncle's first wife. A little bit of a thing, she was. A tiny, gentle girl, she was: an Indian from town. Shortly after she had that baby, she and the wee one disappeared. No one heard from her or saw her again. Some say Lem got rid of them by buying her a one-way ticket out of town on the bus, but others say he did it more permanent-like. Anyway, weren't but a year later he married Annie's ma. We worried about her too, but she managed to outlive him, thank the Creator." Yemmy clucked her tongue.

Amanda wondered if Annie knew about her father's first wife and child. She didn't think so. As close as the girls had been, they wouldn't have let such a secret sit untold between them. This was the first time Amanda had heard of such a thing. Ma and Dad never even once mentioned it.

"Uncle Lem was killed in a hunting accident, wasn't he?"

"Uh-huh. There's been different stories 'bout that too. They *say* it was an accident, but who knows? Lem cheated and lied to so many, someone might have decided to do the whole town a favor. He was jest born nasty, I guess."

Amanda picked up the rags and started tearing again. She hadn't really liked Uncle Lem, had been afraid of him in fact, but never realized he was disliked by so many. "Poor Annie," she sighed.

"I was wonderin' why Noah hasn't thought to help her. Maybe he has, but I guess we'd of heard if'n he had. Why don't you ask him?" Yemmy wasn't known for her subtlety.

As if on cue, the men came into the house. Ben went to the fridge and pulled out two diet root beers.

"Either of you good-lookin' gals want a beer?" he teased.

Yemmy shook her head no but Amanda said yes.

Noah opened a can and brought it to her. "Looks like you're doing a good job there, Mandy. You got a real talent for that. Tearing rags might just be your calling," he teased.

"Say, I got me an idee," Ben chimed in. "Why don't you give up them *compooters* and take up rag-tearing. Bet ya could have yerself a good business here—could work right out of yer cabin." Ben winked at Noah. "I could make you a big sign for the road by the cabin, "Strippin' done here, cheap."

Amanda ignored him. "Noah, we were just talking about Annie and how she doesn't seem to be getting any better. Doesn't even seem to want to for that matter. Have you thought about doing a ceremony for her?"

Noah shook his head. "Can't unless I'm asked. It might not be right for her."

"Her ma used to believe in the Indian religion; Catholic too. But Lem," Ben muttered quickly looking at Amanda, "Lem didn't want her practicing *any* way although me and Ma used to see her and the kids at church ever Sunday. Guess she'd slip out when he was home sleepin' off a hangover. He went off on a toot ever' weekend."

"What about J.R. and Winnie?" Amanda persisted. "Can't they ask you?"

"Sure if they want to, but they never have."

Amanda swallowed hard before she asked, "Can I ask you?"

"Course. But we need permission for us to go into her house. That's where the prayers work best."

Amanda sat quietly for a moment, then began tearing strips again. "If I can get her to agree, would do you do a ceremony before I have to leave for Milwaukee?"

"Course I would."

Amanda set her mouth in a determined line. "I'll talk to Winnie tomorrow," she said. "I'm supposed to spend the day with Dan, but I'll find some time during the day to talk to her."

"If'n it works, we'll help with tobacco ties," Ben offered. "I used to be pretty good at making 'em. While you're tearing away there, my girl, tear about two dozen blue and yellow, three-by-three inch squares. Ain't that about right, Noah? You'd want what? Maybe about a dozen blue and a dozen yellow ties?"

"Sounds about right," Noah agreed.

"I figure you'll get your way," Ben said to Amanda, "So we'll start making 'em first thing in the morning—what do you say, old girl?" He pointed his chin at Yemmy.

Yemmy smiled. "Been a long time since we was called on to help with a ceremony," she said. "Sounds like something I could be doin'. With these hands, I can at least put tobacco on the cloth, if you tie them, Ben."

Amanda glanced at Noah trying to gauge his reaction. He was sipping his soft drink, watching Amanda's hands tear the cloth. He wasn't smiling, but he didn't seem upset either.

Two hours later Noah and Amanda left the Vincents'. "I hope it was okay to ask for a ceremony for Annie," she said. "I've been so worried about her. Something's not right if the doctor got all the cancer and she's getting worse. A few weeks ago she talked about going to Duluth to take care of Ella's baby. Now she's the one who needs the care." She looked at Noah anxiously.

He smiled at her. "It's fine. There's something happening that I don't understand either. If we can have the ceremony at her house, we can find out. I'm glad you asked," he assured her. "But ya see, I couldn't have done it without an invite."

"Thanks," she smiled. "You've turned out to be a good friend. I'm glad we met again."

Noah reached over and covered her cold hands with a warm one. "No pro-blema," he said in his best Schwarzenegger voice.

When they reached her cabin he surprised her again. "Let's do something fun before you go."

"Like what?" she asked.

"Like go to a movie. You like movies, don't you?"

"Sure. Do you?" She sounded leery.

"Of course! I'm 'normal' most of the time," he laughed. "It's just *some* spiritual folks who lead super-normal lives. I'm still a novice, so I'm still kinda your basic normal novice."

She blushed. "I didn't mean to imply you weren't. It's just that, ah, just that you always seem so busy."

He chuckled as he walked her to the door. "I'll call you after you've had a chance to talk to Winnie. Then we'll pick a day for the healing and a night for a movie, okay?"

"Okay." She watched him climb back into the Bronco and drive away. She waved when he reached the end of the driveway, knowing he couldn't see her.

# Chapter 23

Amanda had time for one quick cup of coffee before Dan rushed her out of the house and into the car. He needed to greet his friends and neighbors in St. Mary's foyer as he did every Sunday. She cringed as she pulled up in front of the church. "Oh no," Amanda moaned. "I don't want to finagle another escape from Punky."

"Well, guess you'll just have to go out with him then," Dan teased. "Maybe I'll invite him to breakfast with us. What do you think?"

Amanda made a face at him. "I think you'll walk home if you do," she threatened.

Punky had just reached the top step and turned around. He waved when he saw them. Amanda waved back and looked quickly at her uncle. Dan laughed again and took her arm. He was walking better today she noticed. He introduced her to the same folks he had a few weeks ago. They smiled and nodded in recognition.

All had been polite except Mrs. Willems who was all decked out in her Sunday hat—an outdated blue pillbox with a dotted veil. "You gonna stay and take care of your uncle like a good niece should?" the old lady asked as she studied Amanda over the top of her bifocals. "Once family is all gone, you'll be sorry!" she admonished.

Amanda looked for her uncle who had wandered off. He was talking to a young priest off to the side. "I'm not sure, yet." Why did she feel she was apologizing?

"Well, think about it hard. You *look* like a good girl. I'm sure you'll do the right thing." Mrs. Willems patted Amanda's arm with a blue-gloved hand.

Uncle Dan came over with the young priest in tow. "Father, this is my brother's daughter, Amanda. Mandy, this is Father Jerome. He's gonna say Mass today."

"Hello Father," Amanda said as she took his strong, firm hand.

"Amanda," the priest replied, "how good to meet you. Dan tells me you're trying to decide whether to stay on here or go back to Milwaukee. I used to live there myself. Believe me, this is a much better place for a young woman," he said. He smiled at her uncle who looked around at the crowd of friends, ignoring the priest.

Before Amanda could think of an answer, someone called to Father Jerome. He excused himself with a slight wave of his hand and left. Uncle Dan cleared his throat and put on his best apologetic look.

Amanda smiled. "Trying to manipulate me again, Uncle? You're getting to be pretty good at it, ya know?"

Dan squirmed. "Well, it's just that—" he stopped mid-sentence, his attention caught by something over her shoulder. Amanda turned. Paula and her kids were coming up the steps. She looked beautiful today. A pale pink sweater showed under a black leather coat. A pink ribbon held her shining black hair in a ponytail at the back of her neck. Ashley smiled shyly at Amanda, but Paula frowned. The boys looked at their shoes.

"Good morning Paula," Amanda said. Paula nodded but continued by, saying nothing.

"There's one person who wouldn't mind seeing you go back," Dan teased. He grunted when Amanda jabbed him with her elbow. "Shhhhh!"

After Mass people greeted one another like they hadn't just passed each other on the way in.

Punky called out, "There's my girl! Hi Manda. What cha got planned for today?" Answering his own question he said, "I s'pose yer gonna tell me yer busy again, huh?"

"I'm going to spend the day with my uncle, then stop over and see Annie," she was happy not to be lying this time.

"Well damn it all. Looks like I ain't gonna see you before you leave, huh?"

"I'll be back, Punky. It's just that today has been promised."

"Yeah, yeah. That's okay. Say hi to Annie for me. How's she doin' anyhow?"

"Not too good, I'm afraid."

"I heard that. I saw that jerk husband of hers over at the Hi-Way 2 Inn the other night, drunker than a skunk. He had a good thing goin' once; too bad he messed it up," he said sadly.

Amanda wasn't sure if he was talking about Neil or himself.

"Well, catch ya on the next trip, Mandy. Take care of yerself now," he smiled at her and nodded at Dan.

"Yeah, you too, Punky." He walked away. "Such a sad-looking man. He used to be so happy," she said.

"Funny how things change, isn't it? Well, enough gloomy talk. Let's go eat," her uncle said.

"You're on!" Amanda said, and she took his arm. "You promised me a *downtown* breakfast brunch, and I won't settle for anything less!"

Shortly after four, Amanda left her uncle's and drove over to Annie's. The house was dark. She wondered if she could find Winnie and J.R.'s place on River Road by herself. Amanda drove around the winding streets trying to read mailboxes in the growing dusk. She was about to give up when she saw J.R. and Winnie pull into a driveway just ahead. She honked and waved. Winnie waited for her in the driveway. J.R. waved and went into the house carrying a Wal-Mart shopping bag.

"Hi Winnie," Amanda said. "I've got a favor to ask you and J.R. if you don't mind."

"Won't know that until you do, I reckon," Winnie said. "Come on in. J.R.'s gonna make some popcorn; we got enough to share."

"Thanks Winnie, I'd like that."

"Hi, Auntie!" J.R. smiled. "Do you like butter-flavored or nacho-cheese-flavored Redenbacher?"

"Butter, I guess. J.R., Winnie, I have something to talk to you about."

J.R. put a bag into the microwave and set it for four minutes. "It's about Ma, isn't it?"

Amanda nodded.

"Geez, did I get bawled out for tellin' ya about the cancer the other night," Winnie interrupted. "Made me feel bad cuz Ma's so good to me. I felt like a Judas. She ain't gonna like us talkin' about her now, neither."

"It's okay, Win." J.R. said. "I need to talk about it. It kills me to see her like that. Even worse, her not *trying* to get better. It's like she gave up hope. Used to be she was so full of life, so much fun." He shrugged. "What's on your mind, Auntie?"

She took a deep breath and plunged in, "Would you let Noah do a ceremony for her in the house?"

"*I* would!" J.R. said. "But Ma, she's another matter."

Winnie's eyes brightened, "You can talk her into it, J.R. She always listens to you, you know she does. Come on, what could it hurt?" she begged. She turned to Amanda. "She won't say no to him," she said.

J.R. took the popcorn out of the microwave and handed it to Winnie. She opened the bag and poured the popcorn into a blue plastic bowl. "Ow, it's hot," she said. She shook salt over it and put it on the table. J.R. nodded to Amanda. "Sit down, Auntie. Let's talk about how we can get Ma to agree to this."

Winnie beamed at him and grabbed a handful of the hot popcorn. So did Amanda.

It was set. Amanda called Noah from their house before she headed for the cabin. She was too excited to wait. She hadn't expected them to agree so readily, but then she hadn't considered how affected they were by Annie's failure to get better. When she left the house, Winnie hugged her tightly.

"I knew it would be good when you got here," she told Amanda. "I could feel it when you two was together in the same room. I knew you'd bring us luck."

"I haven't done anything, Winnie. Let's just wait and see what Noah can do."

"I know she's gonna be all right now," Annie's daughter-in-law insisted. "I can feel it."

J.R. walked her to the car. "Thanks, Auntie. I'm glad you're here. Mom used to tell us stories about you two when you was kids. That's how she entertained us when we was little. I know all about the bubble gum in the hair and the strawberry ice cream trick," he laughed. "Same as Winnie, we're glad you're back."

He kissed her forehead. "I'll go over and talk to Ma in the morning. Let's plan for Tuesday. Tomorrow's too soon, and she might change her mind by Wednesday. Just let me and Win know what we can do to get ready."

"I don't know myself what has to be done. I'll call after I talk to Noah again. I feel like we've taken a giant step forward by you and Winnie agreeing to talk to her. Do you think she'll be hard to persuade?"

"I don't know; maybe. She can be stubborn, but when she knows you want this too, who knows. She's always liked and trusted Noah," he paused and drew a deep breath. "I'll call you right after I talk to Ma," He slammed Amanda's car door. "Drive careful now, and watch out for the bears," he laughed.

Amanda prayed hard with her feather that night. She thanked the Creator for bringing her to this place at this time. "I guess there really is a reason for everything," she told Miigwan. "It just takes a while for some of us to get the picture." After her prayers, she drank a glass of warm milk—the Teena Greengrass trick.

*Amanda and Annie were romping in the lake, teasing one another; chasing, dunking each other's head under the incoming waves, then swimming away. It was probably the best day of the summer. Both families were together, picnicking. Uncle Lem was sober for a change. Gramma and Hobo were there too. And they were going to have ice cream sundaes later: a real treat, one seldom gotten.*

*Suddenly Annie screamed and went under the shallow water. "Stop playing around," Amanda said. "You're scaring me."*

*Annie came up. "Help! Please help me, Mandy!" She screamed and disappeared again. The water was turning red where she went under.*

*Amanda's heart pumped faster. "Oh God. Annie! Annie!" she cried. She turned toward shore. No one heard her. "Daddy! Help us!" Dad and Uncle Lem's laughter drowned out her screams. Mom and her aunt were hunting for round rocks several yards away. The little kids were building sand castles. It was up to her.*

*Amanda searched the water for any sign of Annie. "Annie, Annie!" she screamed again. Her legs pumped hard against the waves as she ran toward the ever-growing pool of red water. Something brushed her leg. She reached down. Annie's hand! She held on and pulled, inching backward, closer to help.*

*"Mandy, help me," Annie's voice rang clear although her head was still under water. A large green ball of light moved quickly toward them, swirling, growing larger. It started from somewhere near the center of the lake and moved with lighting speed directly at Amanda, skimming two or three feet above the choppy water—closer and closer. Amanda lost her grip on Annie's hand.*

*"Help! Help me. Please, Manda, don't let go!" Annie's voice started strong but quickly fell off. Amanda looked again at the green swirling ball. It got to within six feet before it exploded, showering sparks in every direction. Annie's hand came out of the lake, flailing blindly, reaching. Amanda grabbed it.*

*"Help her, Aman-jii," Hobo said from somewhere behind her. Amanda looked over her shoulder. Hobo was standing at the edge of the water, smiling and nodding "Help her, Aman-jii, you can do it. I'll help you."*

Several miles away, Noah tossed and turned in his sleep. A green swirling ball flew at him. He seemed to be standing on a plain unable to move; the grass around him, dead, brown. He'd seen this before, he knew. At a ceremony—a medicine ball. It came closer, within six feet of him, before exploding as he knew it would. Hobo's voice echoed in the night when he woke. "Help her," he said. The first time he'd had this vision Noah thought Hobo meant Amanda. Now he realized it was Annie who needed his help.

Amanda woke in a sweat; the smell of fear and death was heavy in the room. A greenish-white light sat at the foot of her bed. It moved slowly towards the door, fading as it went, leaving a smoky, veiled trail. She threw off her covers and followed it on bare feet through the dark cabin. She checked the doors and windows as she passed. The light got smaller. Only a wisp now, it slipped into the kitchen. She followed. Hobo stood near the rear door, his back to her. He was transparent. "Aman-jii." His voice familiar, loved. He turned, smiled, and disappeared.

Amanda woke the next morning, eager for the daylight—the dream barely a memory. She opened the bedroom window for fresh air. Migizi sat in a tall pine looking toward the pond. When she heard the window open, she turned and looked directly at Amanda. In a heartbeat, she slowly spread her beautiful spotted wings and pushed herself out of the tree.

"Thank you, Sister." Amanda watched the great bird fly away. She no longer felt, nor feared, the death she'd smelled the night before. After her walk to the pond, she called Ben.

"We're workin' on them ties right this minute," Ben told her. "Yemmy's filling the squares, and I'm tying them . . . to the best of my recollection, that is. Keep your fingers crossed that they hold together through the ceremony," he laughed. "Noah's got some strong prayers. Might bust these little ties to smithereens."

"I wouldn't be surprised," Amanda said. "I'll get back to you when everything is all set, but we're looking at Tuesday night. J.R. thinks Annie will agree." She paused. "Ben, do you believe that dreams tell us things?"

"Of course, young-un. Dreams give us all kind of answers. Lots of times they're about things we don't want to think about during the day. Sometimes they heal us or warn us, or sometimes they're a rehearsal for the future. But dreams are wonderful things. We should pay attention to them. Did you have a good one?"

"Yeah. It's like one I've had before. I'll tell you about it later. Give Yemmy my love."

"Ma," Ben said to Yemmy when he hung up. "I think our girl's comin' round." The couple had been married so long, she didn't even need to ask what he meant. Yemmy just nodded and continued to put small piles of tobacco in the center of each yellow and blue cloth square laid out on the table in front of her.

At noon Amanda got J.R.'s call. "Ma says she will do it, but she wants to see you first. Can you come by?"

"Absolutely! That's great, J.R. I'm gonna call Noah if that's okay with you. I think if he isn't tied up with something else, he should come too. Do you want me to call you back or should we just come over?"

"Just come when you can. Aunt Mandy," he paused, "I think she's real scared. I know I am."

"Me too," Amanda said.

Noah answered on the first ring. "I've been waiting to hear from you. What time should we go over?"

She didn't ask how he knew what she was going to say. "I'll meet you there in about two hours," she told him. "Annie always takes a nap after lunch, so let's give her time to do that. Anything I should be doing before I get there?"

"Not yet. After we talk to her and I check out the house we'll know better what we're dealing with. Amanda," he added, "bring Miigwan; you'll need protection."

"Okay. I'll see you there." She hung up; butterflies played tag in her stomach.

Two hours later she pulled up in front of Annie's. J.R. was standing on the porch smoking. From the pile of butts at his feet, one didn't need to guess that he'd been there awhile. He waved at Amanda with his left hand.

"Hey there, Auntie. Ma just got up from her nap. Winnie's inside with her."

They both turned as Noah's Bronco came around the corner of the red clay road. Amanda waited by her car, holding her feather, wrapped in its red cloth, in her hand. J.R. came and stood beside her.

"Let's go see what we're dealing with," Noah said when he got out of the car. Amanda walked into the house between the two men.

Annie was sitting at the kitchen table wearing the gold bathrobe Amanda had given her, trying on a brave smile. Winnie was leaning against the sink, her arms folded tightly over her ample chest. Her heavy-lidded eyes studied the braided rug under her feet. She didn't look up when Annie spoke.

"My son talked me into this," Annie whispered hoarsely. "Don't know if it will do any good, but I'm sick an' tired of being sick an' tired, ya know?" She sighed deeply. "I want to live to see my grandbaby, and how I'm goin' now, I won't make it." She ignored the tears that ran down her cheeks. Her eyes begged Noah. Winnie sniffled loudly. Amanda fought back her own tears.

With Annie's permission, Noah and Amanda walked from room to room. J.R. and Winnie waited in the kitchen with Annie. In the back of the house, Annie's bedroom, Noah stopped. "There's something in this room. Can you feel it? I felt something when we first came into the house, but it's definitely strongest right here."

Amanda's underarms itched. The air was stale; it hinted of something bitter. "I felt this before," she said. "But I thought it was Annie's sickness I was feeling."

"In a way it is. But it's sure more than that. It's a spirit of some kind. Not a healthy one either."

"A spirit?" Amanda whispered. "Can it hurt us?" When Noah didn't answer, she grabbed his shirtsleeve and tugged. "Can it hurt us?" she demanded.

"It's not a chain-rattling *ghost,* but it ain't Casper the Friendly either," he chuckled. "But it's living; a spirit that didn't move on when it was supposed to." He looked at her and grinned. "Let's get back to the kitchen." She trailed behind him wondering how he could be so casual.

Winnie had joined the other two at the table. All three looked up when Amanda and Noah came in. J.R. jumped up and handed Noah a cup of coffee. Too wound up for caffeine, Amanda declined.

Noah sat next to Annie. He sipped his coffee and weighed his words before he spoke. "There's a spirit in your house that needs to be sent home, Annie. I don't know if that's what's making you sick, but it doesn't belong here. We can start by sending it away, then we'll go from there."

"Can you do it right now?" J.R. asked.

"I could, but with fasting and offerings, we'd have a more powerful ceremony. I'll smudge the house for you now, and that will help a little, but it would be better to come back tomorrow evening. And I need to prepare so I don't get hurt. Amanda too, if she's gonna help me. She'll need to be prepped."

Annie looked at her son and daughter-in-law. "Let's wait then," she suggested.

"One more day ain't gonna hurt that much." J.R. nodded. Winnie looked at her feet; a whimpering sound came from her throat.

"What should *we* do to get ready?" J.R. asked.

"Fast from midnight on," Noah told him. "You can have water, juice, coffee, pop, whatever, but no food. Also, you'll need to pray at sun-up. Even if you go back to bed, you need to pray then." All three nodded that they understood. Amanda waited impatiently for Noah to give her some instruction, but he continued to ignore her. "After the ceremony we'll need a small feast," he continued. "Me an' Amanda will ask a few more folks to help. The more loving hearts we have here tomorrow night, the better." No one asked any questions, so Noah put his cup down. "I'll go get the stuff to smudge. That's a good start."

"This house ain't been smudged in a coon's age," Annie told him. "It's overdue, don't ya think?"

Noah smiled at her. He nodded to Amanda and pointed his lips toward the door. She followed him outside. At the Bronco he turned to her. "I want you to walk through the house with me now. Watch careful because I want you to do this tomorrow night while I set my altar, okay?"

When she agreed, he continued, "And I want you at my place tomorrow at sun-up. I'll cleanse myself and you so you can help me. In fact," he said after a short pause, "I got a better idea. When you leave here, go home and get some clothes, and stay with me so you're there on time. Yeah, that's what you should do." Without waiting for her answer he turned and dug into the back of his Bronco and pulled out his bag. "Ready?"

"I guess so," she said.

Back inside the house, Noah smudged himself first, then Amanda and Annie, then the other two. He walked through the house with Amanda close to his side. Without realizing it, she repeatedly wiped perspiration from her upper lip. "We'll be back about four tomorrow," Noah told the others when he had finished. "Don't forget sunrise prayers."

# Chapter 24

At the Escort, Noah said, "Get to my place around seven tonight." His voice was tense and strangely loud in the quiet of the afternoon. "I got lots to tell you before tomorrow. Call Dan and Winky and see if they want to help. Tell Dan don't fast. He needs to eat for his diabetes. We don't want him getting sick, do we? I'll go see how Ben and Yemmy are doing with the ties. Looks like there'll be seven not countin' me, and you—that's a good number. Oh! Bring some red and white cloth for ties. We'll need a dozen of those too." He shut her car door and slapped the roof. "Later," he said, then he climbed into his Bronco without a backward look. Amanda glanced at her watch. Dan would be at Winky's now.

A black pickup driven by a young man in a red beaded cap was pulling away from the reservation mini mart as Amanda pulled in. She recognized the rude guy at the pop machine and, remembering their last meeting, she glared at him. Undaunted, he smiled and waved.

The bell over the door clunked her arrival. The store was empty except for the two old cribbage buddies huddled over the card table at the back of the room. Amanda's uncle glanced at her and waved. It was so dark she barely made out his hand.

"Saving on electricity?" she asked Winky. "Or is that game so exciting you hadn't noticed it was getting dark?" She found the light switch. The florescent bulb hummed and blinked a few time before catching. Amanda walked over to the pop machine and selected a diet cola. From the far end of the counter she grabbed a chair that had seen better days, and she carried it to where the old men concentrated on their game. She tested the chair gingerly before sitting down.

"Turn them on," Winky grumbled pointing with his chin toward the lights, "and folks'll think I'm open. Can't ya see we're two busy men?" He scratched the stubble on his cheeks and studied his cards.

"Howdy gal," Dan said. "Whatcha been up to? I called earlier, but you weren't home. Been out with your new admirer?" He looked at her over his glasses. *"Mandy, it's been a coooooon's age since I seen you,"* he mimicked Punky.

"Oh, stop it!" she scolded. "I've been at Annie's, and you know it. With the rez hotline you guys haven't missed a thing, so don't pretend different. Noah's having a healing ceremony at her place tomorrow night—but I s'pose you knew that too." The men stopped playing and looked at her. "He wants me to ask if you two want to be part of it."

"Lord, help me," Winky wheezed and slapped his knee. "Been a long time since I was to one of them. Course we'll go. If Noah needs us, we'll be there, right?" He raised his bushy eyebrows at Dan.

Dan grunted with surprise. "How'd that happen?" he asked Amanda. "Can't imagine Annie okaying to anythin' like that. She ain't never been one for Indian ways."

"J.R. talked her into it. I saw him and Winnie last night. They're both worried sick. Me too. I can't believe how she's gone downhill just since I've been here. I'm scared for her." Amanda took a long sip of her cold soda.

"Good for J.R.," her uncle said. "Shoulda known. Annie never could say no to him, him being the man of the family since he was just a pup. His pa was always *damn* worthless if you know what I mean." Amanda winced. Dan didn't talk about people like that even if they were as worthless as Neil Butler. "That man could make babies, but not take care of 'em. I always did pity that Annie girl."

Amanda waited, but Dan didn't continue. She changed the subject back to the ceremony, telling the men about the spirit and how they planned to send it away. "Noah said you shouldn't fast because of your diabetes," she told her uncle.

"I know, I know." Dan had long since folded his cards, his interest in the game gone for the evening. His eyes now twinkled with excitement. "Winky, you donate some canned corn, and I'll make menomin for the feast. I still got enough to feed some Ghostbusters."

"I got fruit too," Winky said. "Dang, if this ain't the most excitin' thing that's happened around here fer a long, long time." He smiled a lopsided jack-o-lantern smile and leaned back in his chair. When he lit one of his smelly cigarettes Amanda decided it was time to leave. She left the men trying to out-do one another with stories of ceremonies they'd been to in the past. She doubted they even knew she was gone.

Amanda pulled into Noah's driveway at 7:30. Miss-never-late had spent more time looking for cloth than she should have and finally ran into Wal-Mart to pick up remnants for the ties.

In an uncommonly serious mood, Noah smudged each of them, the cloth, and the tobacco before they began making the ties. Amanda learned how to twist her wrist just so, in order to tie the tobacco solidly into the cloth, but only after she'd tied her fingers together a few times. While they worked, Noah told her what she needed to do both at sunrise and in the afternoon at Annie's. When they finished, they were both exhausted. Noah insisted she sleep in his bed, and he took the sofa. "I'll wake you just before sun-up," he told her.

Amanda tossed and turned, her body wanting sleep but her mind racing with thoughts of the ceremony and how she fit into the reservation after so long in Milwaukee. When she'd roll over she could smell sage smoke in her hair, reminding her of Hobo and Gram, and of the first time had Noah walked her to her car and his braids had slipped into the open window—was it really just a few short weeks ago?

She could hear Niijii snoring softly outside the bedroom door. He had adopted her this evening after Noah had locked him outside while they worked with the sacred items. He'd sidled up to Amanda when he'd been let back in, knowing it was Noah who had kept him out. *Friend by default,* Amanda thought as she drifted into a dreamless sleep.

Amanda woke to rapping on the door. "Amanda? Time to get up." She struggled to respond. Noah knocked again and waited until she grunted before he said, "Dress warm, it's chilly out there." He paused, "Are you up?"

"Yeah, coming," she mumbled. Sleep left her as soon as she remembered where she was and why. She threw on jeans and a sweatshirt. As she ran her fingers through her hair, the screen door slammed. Noah was already outside.

She rubbed her teeth with her finger, gulped down a glass of orange juice, then grabbed her jacket and followed Noah. In the middle of the yard a fire jumped and flickered in a pit Noah had dug. The pit was six inches deep and four feet across. Noah was squatting next to the fire and warming his hands over the flames. Amanda tripped as she crossed the yard and nearly fell over pieces of sod lying on the ground.

"Careful," he said not even looking at her. "I'll put that back when we're finished here. You'll never know a pit was dug. If we take care of mother earth, she'll take care of us." He looked at the still-dark sky in the east. "The sun will be up soon. Come pray with me."

As Amanda sat next to Noah, he pulled a pipe from his bag. "My tools," he grinned at her. "This bag holds everything I need." He handed her the pipe and then he dug in the bag again. "Special tools for special jobs," he grunted squinting into the bag. "Can't always find what I need right away . . . but . . . everything's here . . . someplace." He sat back on his heels. "Ah . . . *asema*. This stuff's special made for ceremonies. Hobo taught me how to make it from red willow. Someday I'll teach you." He tucked the other things back into the bag and retrieved the pipe. He held it skyward and prayed in Ojibwe.

To her surprise he handed it back to her. "I want you to fill it," he told her.

"I don't know how," her voice shook with excitement. Sweat peppered her forehead despite the cold.

"Then it's time you learn," he said in that old-time voice that went with all-important instruction.

The sky began to lighten behind the pines as he led her through each step. She repeated what he told her to say in English while he prayed in Ojibwe; their breath pierced the cool predawn air with ghostly puffs of punctuation.

They prayed for clear minds and good thoughts to face the duties ahead. They asked their spirit helpers to come and assist them. They explained, each in their own language, what was happening at Annie's and what they wanted to do. They prayed for help to send the lost spirit home. Noah again pulled all his other tools out of his bag and asked blessings for each. By the time they finished their prayers, red streams of morning sun filtered through the heavy pines.

"Can you feel the spirits?" He asked. "They're all around us."

"I felt the air pressure change," she whispered. "Did the spirits do that?"

An eagle screeched. Noah smiled. "Migizi just answered you," he said. They watched the Grandfather's messenger circle overhead four times before she moved out of sight behind the trees. Amanda saluted the Grandfather's sign.

"You're gonna do okay," Noah told Amanda. She added a silent prayer for courage and hoped she looked more sure of herself than she felt.

Noah added wood to the fire. "We'll keep the spirit fire going all day. When we leave this evening, we'll take some coals with us. Fire's an important part of the ceremony."

Amanda looked around. "I don't think I was ever up this early," she laughed. "We almost beat the birds up." She nodded toward a red-winged blackbird sitting on a thin reed near the edge of the trees; its whistle musically filled the otherwise quiet air.

"You'll be happy to know I saw a couple of robins in the backyard last week," Noah said. "Looked like a couple of scouts to me." Amanda returned his grin. His humor was returning. This was the Noah she knew.

By noon Amanda was exhausted. She sat by the fire resting, with her arms wrapped around her updrawn knees.

"Go take a nap," Noah said. "I'll get you up in an hour or so. You'll need your strength for tonight."

Too tired to argue with him she went inside, kicked off her shoes, and threw herself across the unmade bed. Niijii stood next to her, his head on the covers, eyes begging for attention. She fell asleep before she could put her hand out to pet him.

Amanda woke three hours later and looked outside. Noah still squatted near the pit. The fire was almost out. He looked up when she pushed open the screen door. "Go get that bucket out near the back door," he directed. "Bring it here. We'll use it to carry the fire to Annie's."

She did as she was told, ignoring the concern that was nagging at her. Noah should know what he was doing, she hoped as she watched him shovel the coals into the bucket. "Here," he said giving her the keys to the Bronco. "Go open up the back for me."

"Won't that start a fire?" she asked.

"I hope so, that's why we're taking it," he said. "Or did you think my old Bronc needs a heater?"

"No! I mean in the car. The bucket's hot, can't it set the carpet on fire?"

"Run and grab that piece of plastic from under the stoop. That should take care of any problem."

Amanda dug under the small porch and quickly found a piece of broken carpet protector. She put it on the floor in the back of the Bronco and eyed it warily as Noah put the bucket on it. Even with its wide bottom she was sure the bucket would tip when they went around corners. Noah shook his head at her concern, but he grinned. "Don't worry," he said. "The spirits are with us."

"Maybe so, but . . . do they want us taking foolish chances?" she asked.

He laughed at her but went to the unused garage out back and returned with an old washtub. "This won't tip," he said. Carefully, he poured the coals from the bucket into the tub. She tested the edge of the tub by shaking it. It sat solidly in place. "Satisfied?" he asked.

"Satisfied." she told him.

They arrived at Annie's just as Dan and Winky were walking up the shaky steps, each loaded down by a large box. The Vincents' and J.R.'s cars were already there. Dan waited by the door to give Amanda a hug.

"I'm proud of you," he said. "And Hobo would be too," he added, as though reading her concerns about her place in the ceremony.

She blushed and hugged him back. "And I'm proud of you."

"Hey, what about me?" Winky cried.

"I'm proud of you too," she said and smiled at him.

"No, I don't care about that," he groused. "Where's my hug, gal?"

She hugged the old man, noticing that the tic in his eye was worse tonight than it had been. It was almost one, long continuous wink.

J.R. met them at the door. The kitchen smelled of meat, pies, and fry bread. Annie was sitting at the table staring through a grease-stained window into the growing dark. She was dressed today; no worn chenille robe and plastic beach thongs. Her hair had been brushed, but it was still dull and stringy as it framed her thin face. Dark half-moons underlined her eyes. An ashtray full of butts sat in front of her. The fingers of her right hand worried the top button on the oversized denim shirt she wore.

"Might as well get started," Noah said. "Sundown in about twenty minutes, and we better be ready. I'll go grab my things out of the Bronco. J.R.?" J.R. nodded. "We'll meet you out back," Noah said.

When Amanda came around the corner of the house, she stopped up short. Amazing! A replica of Noah's pit had been dug in Annie's back yard. J.R. waited next to it. "How did he know to do that?" she asked Noah. "Did you call him?"

Noah shook his head. "Didn't have to. He was told what he needed to do this morning when he prayed. Our spirit helpers tell us everything we ever need to know if we just listen and believe. J.R.'s a listener and a believer."

In a few minutes Noah and J.R. had the fire going; everyone went back into the house, ready for the next step. "Amanda will smudge everybody out here and then do the house while I set up my altar in Annie's bedroom," Noah said. "Amanda," he turned to her. "Do that room first," he pointed with his lips to the bedroom, "Then come back and do them," he tipped his head toward those in the kitchen. "After you've done the house, join me."

She nodded and took the shell he handed her with one hand; she put a rolled ball of sage that her uncle handed her into the shell with the other. She lit the sage with a wooden match and blew lightly to help it catch. Noah took the shell and smudged her. Following his example, she smudged him. He pointed with his chin to the other room. Nervous and more than a little scared, she went to Annie's bedroom alone.

She directed the sage smoke into each corner, around all the windows and doors, under the bed (which had been made today), and into the closet, leaving the sliding door open. The presence hung heavily in the room and stirred the air as she smudged. The hair raised on Amanda's arms and the back of her neck. She was glad to get back with the others. Without a word, Noah took his bag and went back to the bedroom.

The four elders, Annie, J.R., and Winnie stood in a circle around Amanda. She smudged them one by one, starting with Annie. "I'm so glad you're here, my friend. I've missed you so," Annie hugged her. Amanda put her arms around her frail cousin. She prayed as she brushed smoke over Annie's head and up and down her body with Miigwan.

Done, Amanda walked through the house smudging every nook and corner, going back to the kitchen once to add sage to the shell. Then she went to the back room, where Noah had already begun to address the spirit. The room was filled with the good smell of cedar and bear medicine. As she entered the bedroom, unseen hands slipped an invisible shawl of protection around her shoulders. Noah ignored her, so she quietly knelt behind him on the worn linoleum, resting her weight on her heels, and waited for a word or a sign.

White and blue spirit lights zipped around Noah's head. She was watching them when he whispered, "There's more than one in here. Can you feel them?"

Amanda nodded. A male presence was strong, and there was at least one softer, female presence. Amanda's eyes were drawn up and to the left, into the farthest corner near the ceiling. She frowned.

"Yep, that's where he is. The others are afraid of that one. I think they'd be willing to go, but he won't let them." Noah continued to pray, first in Ojibwe, then in English. Using Annie's Indian name, he told the spirits to leave her house, told them they didn't belong there, that they couldn't stay. He repeated this four times.

Slowly the air around them began to move—so slowly at first that Amanda hardly noticed it—but it soon got stronger, moved faster. It was then that she felt, rather than heard, a high-pitched buzzing coming from somewhere inside the house.

Noah finally turned to her. "Go open the back door," he said. "But stand aside. Keep the others back too."

Amanda moved to do as she was told. Halfway to her feet, she heard Noah laugh. "No, she can't go with you. She has to stay here. *You* go!"

Amanda stopped and looked at him, confused. She was still half-standing.

"A male spirit insists you go with him," Noah told her and laughed again. "He's insisting. Wanna go?"

"You're kidding, right?" she whispered.

He turned from her and spoke to the spirit in the corner. This time the laughter had left his voice. *"Because she's alive,"* he said. "She still has many things to do here. She must stay. You're not alive, you *can't* stay. She belongs here; *you* don't. *You* go! *She* stays!"

Amanda's cramping legs began to shake. She knelt again. "What's happening?" Her constricted windpipe allowed only a whisper to squeak out. She wasn't sure he'd heard. She cleared her throat and tried again. "Noah, what the *hell* is going on?"

Noah didn't answer. More harshly this time, he repeated himself. Then he spoke in Ojibwe. After what felt like an hour, he spoke to Amanda. "Okay," he said, "Do as I told you. Go open the door and stand back—way back. I'm ready to send this guy out, but he still wants to take you with him. Make sure everyone stays back."

She did what she was told, glancing back as she limped from the bedroom, babying muscles that had been strained by her crouching. Noah followed, urging something forward, something invisible; guiding it toward the door with his eagle fan. He was praying in Ojibwe. A gust of wind ruffled Amanda's pant legs as he passed. He indicated to the others that he wanted help. The elders joined him in his repetitious, hypnotic prayers.

On the back porch, Noah motioned to Amanda to stand beside him. They watched J.R. step back from the fire as a cold wind whirled past him and over the pit, pushing tongues of flames out in several directions.

"That should do it," Noah said. His voice was tired but his eyes twinkled when he glanced at Amanda. J.R. looked at them for a second before raising his fist in a silent gesture of triumph.

Together the three went inside, where everybody was hugging everybody else, laughing, and wiping away tears. "Can't ya feel the difference already, Ma?" Winnie asked. "I sure can! What a relief. Thank you Noah; thank you, Amanda. You don't know what Annie means to me." Suddenly the big woman's shoulders shook. She turned her back and sobbed into the crook of her elbow.

Yemmy put her arthritic arms around her. "We all feel it, Winnie. Annie will get better now. You're gonna have your ma for a while yet." J.R. came and got his wife and led her to the table. He sat her next to his mother. Both of Annie's hands reached across the table and clamped on to her son's good one; unshed tears shone in her eyes. Winky slapped Dan on the back. "When we gonna eat?" he asked. Amanda noticed that his tic had slowed considerably.

"Right now!" Dan answered. The two old men began setting the table with the paper plates Winky had brought. Still sniffling, Winnie left the table and pulled a venison roast out of the oven. J.R. grabbed a brown, grease-stained bag of fry bread off the top of the refrigerator. With Winky's vegetables and fruit, and Dan's wild rice, the feast was ready.

Noah asked Annie to fill a dish for the spirits who'd come to help. "I think I'll put this offering in the other room. If it's outside, that stubborn spirit might see it as an invite and come back," he said. Amanda threw him a look he ignored while the others looked at him in confusion.

After Ben gave the prayer of thanks, the celebrants ate as if they'd been fasting forever. Even Annie. Noah livened up the already jubilant atmosphere in the kitchen with his story about Amanda's spirit admirer. As much as Amanda wanted to enjoy the story along with the others, she was too busy watching the door, unaware that she was chewing her thumbnail.

The meal was finished by 9:30, but it felt like midnight. Amanda's whole body screamed for sleep. The elders took turns yawning loudly. No one minded when Noah said, "Time to rest. We earned it."

Noah and Amanda waved at Dan and Winky as the three Elders drove off in Winky's noisy pickup. Amanda noticed that Winky hadn't fixed his taillight and smiled to herself. Noah turned to Amanda. "I'll call you Thursday morning, and we'll talk about a movie. Right now, I'm too tired to even think," he told her at her car. "We'll both sleep tomorrow."

"I won't sleep all day!" she said.

"Sure you will," he laughed. "But it's okay." He hugged her quickly. "Sweet dreams."

"You too," Amanda said. She yawned, then smiled at him. "Well, maybe you're right."

Amanda couldn't help herself. As he walked toward his Bronco she called, "Noah." He turned. "You were kidding about the spirit weren't you? I mean, that really couldn't happen, could it?"

"Yeah, it did. Probably, I shouldn't have said anything. I didn't think it would scare you so bad." He tried a smile. "You *are* scared, ain't ya?"

"No . . . I mean, yes!" She hadn't meant to sound so nasty. "What if he hasn't really left? Am I safe?"

Noah walked back to her. "Look, he's gone." He put his hand on her trembling shoulder. "I'm sorry I told ya. It's just that when you came into the room, he wanted to negotiate, to delay. He liked you. But a spirit can't take a living being any place that the human doesn't want to go. So stop worrying." He watched her face. "You gonna be okay?"

"Yeah, I guess. It was just a shock, that's all." The night eagle, an owl, hooted—a sound that used to scare a young Amanda until Hobo assured her that owls were the Creator's night messengers. An unseen hand tugged at the shawl of protection still around her. She felt Hobo nearby. "Yeah," she said again. "I'm alright!" She knew she was. "Thanks."

# Chapter 25

Noah was right. Amanda slept all night and most of the next day, completely unbothered by noises or dreams. She woke the first time around 5:30 in the morning, dragged herself to the kitchen, inhaled two glasses of orange juice, cut a chunk of cheese from a cheddar block in the fridge, and went back to bed. She woke again at noon, desperately needing fresh air. She carried her coffee mug to the pond. Small animal tracks that led to and from the water's edge indicated that winter hibernators had finally emerged. Bird songs filled the air, she noticed. Without fanfare, the north woods had come alive. Bright, pale green plants peeked through the ground so recently frozen. It was clear why spring was celebrated by Indian people: that so much could exist under the ice and snow that covered this part of the earth for up to six months a year and return to such vibrant life was reason to celebrate.

Back at the cabin she called Dan. "Hi there," she said. "Just wondering how you are."

"Fine-n-dandy," he answered. "The question is, how are *you?*"

"I'm still tired, but fine. I thought I'd come by early tomorrow morning and bring some hot biscuits, if you'll make the coffee. Then I'm going to see Annie, and I wondered if you'd like to come with."

"Grand idea, Sis." They chatted a few more minutes. After she hung up Amanda headed for the sofa and a no-thought-required TV program: some game show that she couldn't keep track of. She hadn't been this tired since she'd copped out of life after the accident. After dragging herself through the rest of the day, she gave up and went to bed at eight that evening. It was too much work to try to stay awake any longer.

Quarreling birds woke Amanda early Thursday. She said her morning prayers with Miigwan, then headed for the kitchen to make the biscuits she had promised her uncle. He was up by now, she knew. Although he didn't work anymore, old habits die hard. He'd been an early riser since his days on the railroad—even before that. Like most others on the reservation, his family had farmed, and farm life begins at sunrise each day—seven days a week, even for the kids. Amanda was sure her dislike of mornings had started in childhood. Not that she had farm chores, but the activity of others in the house would wake her and she'd get up and join the family at the breakfast table, tired and cranky.

Lights blazing in Dan's kitchen in the morning dark gave the weathered house a homey look. He was waiting for her, her coffee cup at the spot at the table she'd claimed as hers since that first visit weeks ago. Dan took the still-warm biscuits from her.

"Ummm. They smell delicious," he said. "We're gonna try some new margarine today; hope it doesn't spoil the taste." He set a tub of Promise on the table. "A big ole white nurse from the social offices come by the store last week to lecture me an' Winky 'bout our diets—like either one of us is interested in another sixty years!" he snorted. "But we promised her we'd take better care of ourselves. Had to. T'was the only way she'd leave us be. Ain't it amazing? When we was kids, we ate bacon and eggs every day, now they's supposed to cause cancer or clog up our arteries or some such thing. We drank fresh milk with yellow cream on the top. And bacon-grease *sang*-witches. Do you remember them?" When Amanda nodded he said, "Then we'd slick our hair back like this," he ran his hands over both sides of his head with a smirk on his face.

She laughed. "And that's why Indians have such shiny hair, right?"

"You got it, gal," her uncle agreed. "Now let me see how good you bake." He tore a biscuit open and smeared Promise all over it. "You made these from scratch, I reckon." He eyed the biscuit like it was an antique he was thinking of buying, margarine dripping down his fingers.

"Of course! I want you to know I got up with the birds this morning, so these are special, *early* morning ones!"

He munched the biscuit noisily. "J.R. came by last night," he told Amanda. "Had just come from his ma's. He was all cheered up. Said Annie was better already."

"Could the ceremony work that fast?"

"Oh, I s'pect so. If it's gonna work at all, seems like it should better work from the first minute them spirits left out the house."

"That reminds me," she said, "I didn't know you and Winky could pray in

Indian. I was impressed!"

"Were you now? Long ago we talked Indian all the time, but got away from it in them gover-ment schools. Those teachers forced us to talk white, but some things you don't forget. Prayers is one. Sounded pretty good, didn't we?" he asked smugly. She smiled and nodded. "Winky was real proud of himself," her uncle continued. "Says to me later, he says, 'Dan, I forgot how much I like Indian ways.' That man! I didn't have much time for him when we was kids, but he sure turned out to be a good friend in these here last few years." Dan shook his head and helped himself to another biscuit.

"Personally, I think you're *both* characters," Amanda teased. "Like something out of a book."

"A mystery book or a love novel?" he interrupted.

"More like a sci-fi," she said. "I wish I'd known you both when you were younger."

"You did!" Dan told her. "Ceptin' you don't remember cuz you was too busy *calf-eye-ing* that Brown boy. Except for your birthday and Christmas, you didn't spend much time with us *old* fogies." He laughed with her. "Not that we blamed ya. I guess ever' generation's the same. I didn't know my uncles or aunties much either til I was growed up. Well," he paused and grabbed his third biscuit. "Say, these are good!" He plastered it with Promise. Amanda stared at the gob of margarine and wondered if she should say something. "What time should we go to Annie's?" he asked, stopping her before she could say anything. "I expect she's up by now"

"Ummm, let's give her another hour. I want to make sure she's up; she's been real tired the last few times I've seen her. I hope J.R. is right and she's getting better. What a tribute to Noah."

"You best not let Noah hear you say that. He's like Hobo. Hobo always said *he* didn't help people, the Creator got the credit. He said he was a pipeline for the Grandfather to work through."

"I know," she nodded. "What I meant was, looks like he has a *good* pipeline to the Creator."

Dan patted her hand in a fatherly way. "You'd see *lots* of interestin' things if you'd stick around." His voice tempted. "Old-way Indian things that'd really surprise you and make you proud to be Indian."

"I am proud!" Amanda said defensively.

"Well, you'd be prouder then." Dan held up his hands to calm her. He wrapped two leftover biscuits and left them in the middle of the table. "They'll go great with my supper," he said.

Amanda washed their few dishes while her uncle shaved.

In spite of the fifty-degree weather, all the doors and windows were open in Annie's house. Winnie and an older woman, both wearing old jeans and shirts, were scrubbing the walls. The house smelled like Pine-Sol. Annie was sitting at the kitchen table in a heavy sweater, a quilt thrown over her lap, sipping coffee. Her hair was still dull, but the blackish-blue half-moons under her eyes had faded.

"Ain't ya a little early for spring cleanin', my girl?" Dan asked hugging her.

"Maybe. But I got to thinking that what with my uninvited guests having cleared out, the whole place should have a good scrubbin'," Annie answered. "Lucky for me, Winnie and her ma offered to help. Mandy, did ya ever meet Selma? She's Winnie's mother."

Amanda could see where Winnie had inherited her heavy-lidded eyes—except they gave Selma a sensual air, rather than the sullen look they gave Winnie. Selma was a small woman. She smiled shyly and nodded at the introduction. Amanda thought she saw a curious glance passed between Selma and Dan when he said hello. The woman actually blushed. Amanda wondered if anything had ever occurred between her uncle and Winnie's mother. The women picked up their pails, scrub brushes, and rags and moved off into the next room when Annie poured coffee for Dan and Amanda. "I'm grateful for the help," Annie said. "I couldn't do it myself."

When lunchtime rolled around, Dan offered to buy pizza from Emma's, a local parlor in town, if Amanda would go get them. "The best damn pizza this side of Italy," he told her. To everyone's surprise, Annie asked if she could ride along. "Seems like I ain't been to town 'cept to go to the doctor for most of a year," she said. "And I need a break from this piney smell. It's pluggin' up my nose somethin' awful!" She sneezed as if to prove it.

Amanda hugged her. "I'd love the company."

"So, how soon ya leaving out?" Annie asked as soon as they were in the car.

"In two days," Amanda said. "I'm leaving Saturday, so I have a day to dust the apartment. It's gonna need it. Have to get my clothes ready, stock my cupboards. You know, all the stuff I should do before I go back to work." She paused and looked at Annie. "I can't believe I've been here eight weeks already! The first two weeks felt long, but now I wonder where in hell the time went!"

"Seems like that should be tellin' you something," Annie suggested. Amanda didn't answer. They rode in silence for a while. "You ever coming back to the rez to live?" Annie finally broke the quiet.

"I don't know. Strange, but I don't know if I even want to go back to Milwaukee. It's peaceful here. And I've gotten reacquainted with you and Dan, and Winky, the Vincents. That's more friends than I've had *ever* in Milwaukee, and I kinda feel like I'm getting reacquainted with myself. But on the other hand, I don't know what I could do here. Uncle Dan can't continue to feed me. Course I wouldn't need a place to live. The cabin could use some fixing, but basically, it's fine—keeps out the snow and cold anyway. I found that out when I first arrived." She laughed. "I had almost forgotten how much snow you guys get up here."

"Couldn't ya teach some computer classes at the tribal school or someplace in town, a business or maybe the tech school? There's always secretary or office positions with the Tribe, if you'd want to do that. Have you checked out the papers or anything?"

"Huh-uh. Guess I didn't think too much about it cuz I didn't see it happening. I'm still not sure it could, but you know what?" she glanced at Annie, "I can tell you I'm not excited about driving in the city's bumper-to-bumper traffic for forty minutes every morning, and sitting across from *Ted* for eight hours a day, then fighting that miserable traffic again at night, and *then,* doing it again the next day! There's something to be said about no traffic jams, no foghorns, no horns blowing, people swearin' and yellin' out the windows!"

"Who's Ted?"

"Ted? He's an obnoxious S.O.B. You know his type. Can't say anything good about anything or anyone who doesn't fit his idea of normal. He hates Indians, Hispanics, Asians, Blacks, Jews, you name it; a first-class pain in the you-know-what." She glanced at Annie who nodded. "And he has the most disgusting breath you've ever smelled in your life," she finished.

"Worse than *Halitosis Heenan?*" Annie faked a gag. "Remember how we'd have to hold our breath when he'd explain our Algebra? I think I'd rather have flunked than have him leanin' over me."

"Ugh! Choke me, and send me to hell, but don't breathe on me," Amanda said, and the women laughed. Annie blinked back tears. "Please stay, Mandy. I'd love to have you back in my life and in my grandbaby's life. Everyone needs a good auntie, you know. I've missed you terribly."

Amanda swiped at a stray tear that started rolling down her face.

# Chapter 26

Winnie and Selma joined them for lunch. While they ate they took turns retelling old stories. Selma was as funny as Winnie. Amanda watched for more curious glances between Dan and Selma, but to her disappointment she didn't see any. Afterward, Annie lay down to rest, so Amanda and Dan went to Winky's. Luke, Noah's nephew, was just finishing a hunting tale when they walked in. Winky wheezed and coughed with laughter. Luke nodded when Winky introduced him.

"Luke here was askin' about a summer job," Winky told them. "Says he's got a head for retail business. Says he ain't gonna go to school no more."

"I ain't never gonna' get off the rez no-how, unless it's to go to jail like everyone else around here," Luke said in his own defense. "I read, I write, and I can do math. What else do I need to know?"

The three men looked at Amanda like they expected her to come up with an answer for them all.

She shrugged. "Well, education gives us access to more things." She saw Luke stiffen and realized she was talking down to him. She didn't want another confrontation with the young man in the red beaded cap. "But we all have to make our own choices," she added. Luke relaxed.

"I gotta shove off," he said. "Ma want me to do some errands for her." He smiled, tipped his cap to Amanda, slipped on his reflector sunglasses, and sauntered out to his truck. The young man looked like he hadn't a care in the world until Noah pulled up just as he reached for the truck's door. Noah made it clear he wanted to talk to his nephew. The boy took a defensive posture.

"Sure is hard being a kid, ain't it?" Dan asked. Winky and Amanda nodded agreement. "Especially with an uncle like Noah," he added.

"The boy's had a tough time lately. His ma was complaining the other day that he hangs out with a couple of toughies. Well," Winky changed the subject, "so, did ya recover from the other night? Sure was *sump-thin'* wasn't it?" He asked Amanda.

"The ceremony was great; scary though. Can't remember the last time I slept so hard or so long," she answered. "I'll probably stay awake for three days with all the rest I got."

"Well, I'll tell ya. I don't blame that spirit a bit for wantin' to take ya with him," Winky teased. "You're pretty an' you can cook, not that I reckon spirits eat too much." Winky laughed at his own joke.

"What with all those compliments, I hate to be pushy," Amanda told him, "but I think you ought to do something to take care of that cough. Like maybe smoke a little less. You trying to kill yourself?"

"Now, Mandy-girl—" he started.

"Just came from Annie's," Dan interrupted. "She looks better already, don'tcha think Mandy?"

The tinkling bell announced Noah and kept her from answering. "There you are," he said. The two old men nodded at him. He smiled at Amanda. "How are you today? Must say I'm glad you didn't get kidnapped by that spirit. Kinda got used to having you around; we'd all miss ya."

Amanda threw him a look, but when he didn't respond she said, "I can't believe anyone can sleep as much as I just did. I lost a whole day!"

The others had stories too. "I had a no-work day," Winky told them. "Nora Dustan held down the fort so I could stay home. Can you beat that? I ain't missed a day outta here in maybe ten, fifteen years!"

"That's the truth," Dan cut in. "I called to tell him I was gonna pass our cribbage game cuz I was too drug out to walk this far and almost fell over when Nora answered. Thought the excitement had sent him out to the hereafter!"

"You guys went a *whole* day without a game of cribbage?" Amanda asked laughing. "Geez!" *Geez?* She was sounding more rez everyday, she thought.

"Yeah, almost believe it myself," Winky said. Dan grunted an agreement.

Throughout the afternoon the teasing continued, as customers—the entire rez in fact—had heard that Winky missed. The rumor mill was working overtime, and folks came to see if he was still alive.

By three that afternoon, the rez knew that Winky was alive and business slowed enough to allow the two old friends to move from behind the counter to the beat-up table at the back of the store where the cribbage board was perpetually set up.

"What happens when someone comes in and wants to buy something?" Amanda asked. "Do you stop the game, or do they help themselves?"

"No one 'cept strangers come in while we're playin', girl. Ever' one else knows better!" Winky said.

"They wouldn't dare interrupt our game," Dan added. "Indians are *ritual* people; we respect rituals. You two can stay and watch," he told Amanda and Noah. "Pull up them stools and be comfortable. We got some serious game-playin' to do to make up for yesterday."

Winky started wheezing. He lit up one of his smelly cigarettes and snuck a guilty look at Amanda. She shook her head and grinned at him.

"We're gonna go grab a bite to eat, then go to a movie," Noah told them. "Otherwise we'd stay and cheer ya on." He took Amanda's arm.

"Enjoy," Dan said. "Sis, you'll be comin' by tomorrow before ya go, won't ya? Ya wouldn't go without saying good-bye to your old uncle, would ya?" His voice cracked.

"Course not. I'll come by. In fact," she added. "What say we go out for lunch? I'm treating!"

"Pick a fancy place," Winky told Dan. "Make her take you to that *Roy-L* Carriage House cafe, or that one in the *Holli-dome*. You might not get another chance like this."

Dan patted his buddy on the back and waved at Amanda and Noah. He didn't trust his voice. He blinked rapidly and studied the game board without speaking.

Noah noticed. "You're making a lot of folks sad, ya know," he said to Amanda. She didn't answer. He opened the store door and stood back. "Let's take the Bronco. Do you want to leave your car here, or should we drop it off at the cabin?" The door slammed behind them.

"Maybe I should drop it off at Dan's, then you won't have to backtrack. Just a minute." She ducked her head back inside the store. "I'll leave my car in your driveway, Uncle. I'll pick it up later."

"Sure thing, my girl. If I'm not already snoozin' when you come by, stop in," Dan called out.

"If your lights are on, I'll come in. Otherwise I'll pick you up around eleven tomorrow. Don't wait up for me, okay? Bye!" She waved at the two old men who ignored her.

"Thought we might go by Emma's. They got the best pizza for miles around. I seen folks there who come from as far away as Wyoming and North Dakota just to have a Emma's Special," Noah said when she climbed into the Bronco at Dan's.

"You're not gonna believe this, but that's what I had for lunch. Hadn't heard of it until today, and then I got two, mind you *two,* offers to try it," Amanda laughed. "It was good but I don't know that I'd drive all the way from North Dakota for it, so if you don't mind, I'd just as soon pass on more pizza tonight."

"Well, let's see, what's a good second choice? Hmm, okay then, how about the state's *best* hamburger? Half-pounder, cooked to order, lots of onions, sauerkraut, homemade bun?"

"Sauerkraut? I'll pass that, but the rest sounds like a winner."

"Ain't much for culture," he warned, "but I bet you'd never find anything like it in Milwaukee. In fact," he paused and grinned, "it's what some might call a dive. Used to be a bar, but the owner got caught sellin' to kids and lost his license, so he turned it into a cafe. But what it lacks in style it makes up for it in good food and better company." He backed the Bronco onto the road. "Jerry Slone runs it. Do you know him?" She shook her head. "He's *Chimook,* but he likes Indians. I'm guessin' he's in his late sixties or early seventies. He's chock-full of BS and tells stories while he's cookin'. Don't think I ever heard the same one twice neither. So we get free entertainment with our burgers," Noah paused. "You game?" he asked.

Amanda nodded. "Don't know how I could pass up a sales job like that!" They shared a laugh.

Frying onion odor hit them when they opened the door to Jerry's. It was full of Indian families. Kids were playing video games in the back room, and Jerry was entertaining their parents with one of his wild tales. A young couple was half–playing pool and half–listening to the stories. Jerry himself was a big man, tall with a wide girth. His red face held twinkling blue eyes, and his long white hair was tied in a ponytail. His apron was so badly stained with catsup, mustard, pickle juice, grease, and who knows what else, that there wasn't any distinct color. As he talked, he swirled onions around on the grill and pressed several hamburgers down with a spatula, making them sizzle. He nodded to Noah and Amanda and continued his story. His gum-snapping waitress shook her head each time he told a whopper and punctuated it by asking, "Ain't that right, Priscilla?"

"Don't ask me, Jerry," she'd answer. "It's *your* story."

Priscilla smiled at Amanda and Noah when they sat down at the counter. "What can I do for you folks this afternoon?" She reminded Amanda of Flo from the old sitcom set at Mel's Diner. Her dyed red hair was piled high into an outdated beehive with a pencil stuck in it, and she cocked her hip to the side when she spoke to them.

Noah and Amanda ordered cokes and listened to Jerry's tall tales along with the other patrons. They turned towards the door like everyone else did when a white couple stuck their heads in, looked around, saw all the Indians, and left.

"Tourists," Jerry said. Everyone laughed.

Later Amanda and Noah moved to a window booth and ordered burgers. Amanda couldn't wait any longer to talk about the ceremony. "So, were those spirits in Annie's house making her sick?"

Noah shrugged. "They could have been. We need to wait and see. That male spirit had lots of bad energy, and it was aimed at Annie, probably because she's alive and he isn't. He was angry."

"Is negative energy like, say, negative karma?"

"Some might call it that. Some would call it *bad medicine*. But whatever it's called, it hurts people, and that's what's important for us to know."

"How can that be?" Amanda shook her head. "It's just so hard to believe that *spirits* could actually hurt living people, or would even want to. How does it work?"

"To tell you the God's honest truth, I don't know how. It just does."

"But *how* do you know? How can you tell if it's spirits or just plain old sickness?"

Noah stared out the window, seeming to search for the right words. He shrugged and gave up. "Mandy, look. Haven't you ever just *known* something. Something hits you from out of the blue, like, suddenly you *know* something just *is?*"

"Yeah, I guess so."

"That's how I know things too. It's not like a voice exactly, not like the spirits really talk to me; it's more like a light going on and I *know* what I'm suppose to."

Amanda laughed, "Kinda like that old Ford commercial . . . 'Ford has a better idea'—bing!"

"I guess. You must be a lot older than me, cuz I don't remember that myself." He laughed and signaled Priscilla. "Can we have an order of onion rings?" he called. The red beehive bounced as she nodded.

"So . . . okay. How does the ceremony work? I mean, I know we asked for help to send the spirits home, but look at Annie. She looks better already. Almost like magic," she added.

"Maybe like magic, but *not* magic. That's a white man's concept. Indians call it medicine. Earlier you said something about the doctor working on Annie, remember?" He continued when Amanda agreed. "Well, Indian ceremonies work with the whole person not part-by-part like doctors do. You know, a doctor for the heart, one for the eyes, a specialist for the legs . . . that kind of thing. Indian medicine works with the body, the mind, and spirit too—all at the same time. That's a big difference. That's what makes it work."

"So that means that when you're doing a ceremony, you're like a doctor, a psychologist, and a priest all rolled into one?" she asked.

"Well, not that I like to brag, but yeah, kinda."

They stopped talking while Priscilla set a basket of onion rings in front of Noah. He poured catsup over them then pushed the plate to the center of the table and indicated that Amanda should help herself.

She took a large onion ring and shook off some catsup. "So when the doctor treated Annie's cancer, it was just the cancer; her mind and spirit weren't involved in the healing process . . . which, I'm guessing, had something to do with blocking total healing."

"My, such big words; your education is showing," Noah teased. "But yeah, white doctors treat each separate part of a person but they leave out the family."

"Is that why you wanted Uncle Dan, and me, and J.R. and Winnie there? We're her family, and you wanted us there to help, right?" Amanda took another onion ring, shook off the excess catsup, and popped it into her mouth.

"Uh-huh. Support's important, especially in healing ceremonies. The more voices praying and the more energy, the better it all works. Annie's lucky. A lot of people care and were willing to help her."

"So, the energy made by us praying was more powerful than the stuff the spirit sent off?"

"Yep, you catch on fast," Noah said.

"Hmmm, I like that," Amanda said. "I've always thought good was better than bad. Now I know it!" She laughed. "I'm not done asking questions yet. So, when the doctor took out the cancer from her body, Annie's spirit or soul or whatever, needed help to assist in recovery?"

Noah, chewing on an onion ring, nodded encouragingly.

Amanda continued. "At the ceremony, her mind, spirit, and her friends and family, her home . . . where her body and spirit lives together were all treated too!"

Noah grinned at her. "Very good!" He took the last onion ring and tore it. "Split this with ya."

Amanda took half and chewed on it thoughtfully. Before she could say anything, Priscilla sauntered over to their table. "Last call." She snapped her gum and tucked in a loose curl.

Amanda looked at her watch. "My God! It's after nine o'clock! Where did the time go?"

Noah grabbed her arm and looked at her watch. "Too late for the movie—must be half over," he said. "What do you want to do?"

"Go home, I guess. I can't believe this!" She glanced at the waitress.

"Time sure flies when you're havin' fun, huh, hon?" Priscilla said. She sounded tired.

"We've had enough," Noah said and then looked for Amanda's affirming nod. "Just give us the check."

"Sure nuff. Have yourselves a good one." Priscilla laid the check upside down in front of Noah. She had her apron off before she stepped behind the counter to hang it up. "Night Jerry," she said. "See ya tomorrow."

Jerry was scraping the grill and didn't even look at her. "Okay *Prissy*." Priscilla gave him a look that was deadly, picked up her purse, and huffed out the door. "Lock it behind ya, luv," he called. "She's a good girl," Jerry said to Noah and Amanda. "A hard worker that one; wish I had more like her." He smiled at them when Noah paid the bill. "I thank ye both. Come again!"

The two were quiet on the short ride back to the reservation. Amanda was thankful the lights were off when they arrived at Dan's. She had lots to think about, and she would see him at lunch tomorrow anyway.

"What time ya leavin' out on Saturday?" Noah asked as she reached for the door handle.

"About noon I guess. That'll get me into the city early evening, but late enough to miss the rush hour." She paused and looked at him unsure of what else she wanted to say.

"What?" he asked addressing the thought that hung in the air between them.

Amanda shook her head. "I'll see you before then?"

"Probably. I'll try to come by some time in the morning for coffee. Might even help you load up if you don't have too much."

She smiled. "I might even let you. Thanks for the nice evening. I had a great time."

"Hey," Noah called as Amanda reached the Escort. "Was I *normal* enough for you?"

"Yeah. What a surprise," she teased.

Noah waited until the Escort sputtered to life, waved at Amanda, and backed out of the driveway. She watched the Bronco's red taillights to the highway; Noah turned left and she went right.

# Chapter 27

Noah watched his rearview mirror until the taillights of Amanda's car were lost as she rounded a curve; his feelings rode a roller coaster. He understood the message he'd gotten from the Grandfather in the sweat lodge, and accepted it as he had to, but something inside resisted. Still, his heart sank when her car disappeared from his sight. He had a premonition that she, herself, was disappearing.

He was torn: he had decided to walk his path alone like Hobo, but now the Grandfather sent word of a helpmate, and worse, *He* doesn't tell *her*. Even though Noah trusted the Creator in everything He did, her leaving the reservation sent a shiver of fear down into his lower gut. Frank Walking Good Heart had called her Ogichidaakwe, *Warrior Woman*. She had a battle to fight all right: the worst kind—with herself.

As he'd done before, Noah wondered why he'd been called to serve the Earth Maker. Surely there were more deserving men. More than once Noah questioned if he could do it. Why wasn't the path easy if you were doing what you were supposed to be doing?

Noah's thoughts went back to the ceremony at Annie's, and he caught himself grinning. The male spirit who wanted Amanda to go with him when he left Annie's house had been strong. How could he know this, Amanda had asked. *How had he always known?* Just as he had told Amanda, simple thoughts came to him that were as clear and understandable as a voice speaking in his ear.

He felt good about the ceremony, both during and after. The bad medicine in Annie's house almost overwhelmed him the first time he'd entered. No wonder she'd been sick. Luckily, the good spirit helpers he'd called on were eager to assist him. Annie was loved in the spirit world. She'd endured much in her thirty-odd years on Earth, still she remained a solid believer in the Grandfather's—her God's—love. She followed the good path, continuing to be gracious, regardless of the abuses inflicted by an alcoholic father and an alcoholic husband—a rock for her children. Another Ogichidaakwe. Noah had known her by reputation. Little, if anything that happened on any rez went unnoticed, and Annie's burdens and the dignity she bore them with were well-known in this community.

That angry male spirit knew this too, and he wanted Annie with him, wanted her life's energy—he almost had her too. Then when Amanda came in, he recognized her potential, and wanted that more than he wanted Annie's life. He tried to bargain with Noah for her. Noah didn't know who the male spirit had been in life but, whoever he was, he would bet he'd been bad news for sure. Noah had never had to bargain with a spirit before—an experience he didn't want again soon.

Noah thought that if Amanda had lived in the house instead of Annie, she probably wouldn't have fallen under the spirit's intentions. Maybe before she'd met Migizi she couldn't have resisted either, but her gift of perception would have kicked in and she never would have stayed in that house. He remembered the first time Amanda stood on his tiny front porch with Ben and Yemmy—the white mantilla of light around her head. Noah knew then that she was special, that she had good gifts. But he never guessed how special she would be. Apparently the Grandfather liked practical jokes.

Ben had grinned like a country boy discovering city girls when he had heard the news of Noah's wedding—four years off, but pending just the same. Although he was dying to tell Yemmy, he would keep the secret for Noah no matter how tempted he might be to spill the beans.

"It sure would be a lot easier if Amanda knew the Grandfather's plans too," Noah had told Niijii later that same day. Noah could have sworn the dog smiled. He glanced in the mirror knowing he wouldn't see Amanda's car but imagining it behind him. He turned into his driveway. For a moment the light of the full moon played a trick on his eyes and he saw Hobo waiting on the porch like in the old days. He shook his head and the image disappeared. Noah missed his old teacher and friend. "I wish you were here my grandfather," he whispered to the dark that surrounded his tiny cabin. Hobo's laughter mingled with the wind whispering in the pines, then slowly faded.

Amanda's last day at the cabin began with the kind of spring day the north country had been waiting for. The smells of damp earth and musty pines competed for her nose. New plants were barely peeking out of the recently frozen ground. Amanda lingered at the pond, not a bit anxious to start the day. She drank in the feeling of connection she felt here. She searched the sky for Migizi but didn't see her. A vague sense of desertion fell over her.

Back at the cabin she gathered her belongings and put them in a box near the front door. She could load up the Escort tomorrow, or let Noah do it. By eleven Amanda was ready for lunch.

Dan was waiting. He'd shaved and put on a new shirt, the packing creases still visible. Smiling at his niece's jeans and sweater, he pulled on a dark blue sports coat. Amanda suddenly felt underdressed. She watched her uncle move carefully down the steps, holding the crudely made handrail. He smelled of Old Spice, same as her dad used to use.

"Where we going? Have you got us a plan?" she asked him.

"Sure do! Let's try the Holiday Inn. I hear they got a restaurant that advertises *ho-made* bread in baskets and wild rice soup. Umm, umm, good!" He grinned at her.

"You'd think you'd get sick of wild rice. You eat it almost every day, don't you?"

"It's the stuff of life, young woman. The Creator gave it to us Indians to eat ever' day. You'd best not forget it!"

"Just teasing," she said in self-defense. "What I'm interested in is dessert. What they got?"

"Cherry Cheesecake—*the finest New York has to offer.*" He surprised her by pulling a crumpled advertisement out of his pocket. "Says so right here." He held the tattered paper up in front of her.

Amanda's throat tightened, and she blinked rapidly against tears as she backed out his driveway. She already was missing her uncle. "I hope they're ready for the two of us," she said. "I'm really hungry."

The Holiday Inn stood on the lake. The wind was coming from the north, and the hotel, unprotected by pines and birches, caught the brunt of it. Amanda hugged her arms around her as they walked through the parking lot. "This almost feels like a different day than we were having on the rez," she told her uncle. He agreed.

Inside, Dan flirted shamelessly with the twenty-year-old waitress as he ordered. To her credit, Mona, as she was identified by red stitching across the left shoulder of her uniform, flirted with the old man in return. Amanda's mood lifted just watching her uncle enjoy the attention.

"I don't know when was the last time I ate at such a fancy place," he told Amanda when Mona left.

"Me neither," she admitted. "When I eat out in Milwaukee it's either Wendy's or Micky D's. Once in a while we go to Denny's or Perkins. That's about as fancy as we get." She stopped, remembering she went to Denny's or Perkins with Becca or Ken. "Such a long time ago," she said to herself.

"What's that?" Dan was sipping the hot coffee the young waitress had just brought.

"Oh nothing. I mean," she said when she saw Dan's hurt, "I just remembered my friends who were killed at Christmas, and I'm embarrassed to say it feels like a lifetime ago." She grimaced, then laughed. "I feel like I've been caught up in a time warp. I can't believe I've almost forgotten . . . I've almost forgotten their faces. Time has stood still or shot ahead, or . . . I don't know. Goofy, huh?"

"You got a right, my girl. You been through a lot in a short time." He patted her hand. "But I'm real glad you came home to heal. That's what we're all about. It's been good to be here, hasn't it?"

She smiled through the tears that were flowing freely down her cheeks. "Wonderful," she said. "I thought I was all over this crying," she sniffled.

"Can I help?" Mona inquired, her voice filled with concern. She stood with a carafe of coffee in each hand. The sight made Amanda laugh. *What would she do if I answered yes,* she wondered.

"No thanks. I'm just feeling sentimental, is all," Amanda managed to answer. She glanced at Dan, hoping she hadn't embarrassed him, but he sat there beaming at her.

Between bites, Amanda shared yesterday with him. He nodded occasionally, saying nothing. The two took their time, enjoying their meal together. Both avoided the subject of her leaving.

After a bit of haggling with his niece, Dan asked Mona to bring one *big* piece of cherry cheesecake from New York, but insisted she bring two spoons.

"One or *two* bites won't hurt my sugar dia-bee-tees," he assured Amanda for the fourth time.

"Well, it won't do my figure any good," she said. "This thing probably has at least 2,000 calories in each bite." She put a forkful of New York's finest in her mouth. "Ummmmm . . ."

"You look in good shape, Sis. What ya been doin'?"

"Just walking, like I told you before, but I've been eating better too." She laughed, "What else can I do with all those *commods* in the cupboard and no McDonalds a block away."

"Are you gonna behave better when you get back to that city?" He said the last word like it left a dirty taste in his mouth. "Maybe you should take some commods to keep you healthy?"

"I go with good intentions, and I made a promise to myself, cuz I feel better when I'm not so heavy, but the proof will be in the pudding, so to speak. We'll see when I come back next month."

Dan's face brightened. "Ya'll comin' back that soon?"

"I'm planning on it. I promised Ben and Yemmy that I'd be here for the Mother's Day Pow Wow."

"Well honey, that's great!" Dan's voice boomed, causing diners to scowl at them. He hunched his shoulders and chuckled. "Guess my excitement showed. I didn't know you'd be back so soon." He patted her hand; his voice tightened. "But I'd really like to convince ya to stay. I'm an old man and you're the only family I have around, ya know."

"Uncle, don't do that to me," she scolded. Amanda swallowed the last of her coffee. "I've about had it. Couldn't eat another bite. I want to go say good-bye to Annie and the Vincents. Want to come with?"

"Love to, Sis. Let me hit the Chief's room on the way out. I gotta pee real bad. My bladder's old too; won't hold as much coffee as it used to," he whispered. Dan pushed away from the table, grabbing his jacket from the back of the chair. "I'll meet ya by the door, and, oh," he leaned close, "see that you leave Mona there a good tip," he whispered, pointing with his chin at the young waitress.

Annie was rocking on the porch, soaking in the warmth of the sun. She was dressed in baggy wool slacks and a heavy sweater. Much improved from the usual housecoat and flip-flops, Amanda thought. Annie's hair was pulled back from her thin face, and there was a pink blush on her cheeks. Amanda hoped it wasn't just a reflection of her pink sweater. Annie waved enthusiastically when they got out of the Escort.

"*Boozhoo!* Hello, Cousin! *Boozhoo,* Uncle! I been waitin' for you two."

Winnie came out of the house with a pot of coffee and cups, smiling a smile that hid her eyes.

Dan reluctantly held on to Amanda as they made their way up the wooden steps. He trusted them less than he trusted his legs. "You look better, Sis," he said to Annie. He kissed her cheek.

"She's bloomin' again," Winnie said. "Thanks to Noah and Mandy."

"I s'pose ya come to say good-bye." Annie ignored any side talk and went straight to the heart of what was on her mind. "You're runnin' your butt off to the city again, ain't ya?" She frowned at her cousin.

"At least for now," Amanda started to explain. "I've got a job—"

"Oh, I know all about that *job*," Annie interrupted. "What makes ya think they can't get along without you? What do ya think they been doing for the past month? Why can't you find a job here and stay where you belong?"

*This from someone who couldn't wait to leave the reservation,* Amanda thought.

"The reason is," Amanda responded in a testy voice, "I have a job there, one I trained for, and one I'm good at, and there are people there who are depending on me to show up Monday."

"What about those here on the rez who depend on you?"

"No one here depends on me," Amanda retorted in an angry voice that she immediately regretted. "What are you on about anyway?" she asked more calmly.

"Now girls," Uncle Dan interrupted, "no bad feelin's over this. Annie," he said turning to her, "if Mandy feels she needs to go, we can't fault that. Mandy," he looked at Amanda with sad eyes, "you know how we all feel. We want ya to stay— can't help feelin' you belong with us. That city ain't for you, girl." He turned back to Annie. "So, we need to be patient until *she* understands that the way *we* do."

Winnie handed Amanda her cup of coffee and winked. Amanda sipped her hot drink, then took a deep breath. "Well this sure isn't going the way I wanted it to." She hated the pout she heard in her voice.

Annie grabbed her cousin's hand. "It's just that I'll miss you. When you'll be back?"

"For the Mother's Day Pow Wow," Amanda answered. She fought against the constriction in her throat. Annie smiled her appreciation. After an hour of visiting and avoiding mention of Amanda's leaving, Dan announced a need to move on. There were more places they wanted to stop today. Amanda hugged her cousin and childhood friend. Annie's thin shoulders quivered, but already Amanda thought she could feel a new strength in them. "I'll see you soon," Annie whispered in her ear.

"Uh-huh. Almost before you know it, Annie," Amanda answered.

Ben and Yemmy were arguing. Dan and Amanda heard loud angry voices as they stepped into the small enclosed back porch. Amanda looked at her uncle and raised her eyebrows. "Should we stay?"

Dan grinned at her and rapped hard against the door. Instantly the voices fell silent and they heard footsteps approaching. Ben looked out the tiny grease-stained window and unlocked the door.

"Come on in," he boomed. "We need a break. This old woman got out on the wrong side of the bed again this mornin'. She's crabbier than a fat duck looking into the wrong end of a shotgun!"

"*Bizindawaa!* Listen to him!" Yemmy waved a hand in his direction. "*Gigiianim!* You're the crabby one, Old Man!" she said to her husband. "Hello Child, Dan," she smiled at her guests. "Come on in. Been waitin' on ya. Hoped we'd see ya before you left. About to head out, my girl?"

Amanda nodded. She couldn't speak as she hugged the elder couple. "You're comin' back for the Pow Wow, ain't ya?" Ben asked. "It's a special one for us, ya 'member." Amanda nodded again.

"Dan, can't you say anythin' to make this girl stay?" Yemmy asked. Before he could answer she shook her head. "*Makade-mashkiki-waboo?*" She pointed her lips at Dan.

"Ye gods, no!" Dan said. "I've had more than enough coffee for one day. How 'bout plain water?"

"Got some O.J.," Ben said. "Florida special . . . hand squeezed by Juan Valdez!"

"I think he squeezes coffee beans, Ben," Amanda laughed.

Ben chuckled. "Well, Mister Dan?"

"Sounds like a *wiener* to me, no matter *who* squeezed it." Dan pulled a chair from the back of the table and sat beside Yemmy next to the stove. "Told ya long ago," he said to her, "ya shoulda married me. I wouldn't *never* yell at a lady like you." He grinned at Amanda.

"Shush you," Yemmy said. "Yer ever' bit as ornery as this old man here," she pointed her chin at her husband. "You just *pretend* better than him." They all laughed.

Time went too quickly. It felt like they'd just arrived when they were saying good-bye. "I got to get to Winky's," Dan told them. "Got me a game to win. Gotta keep that old bachelor in his place, or he gets too uppity. And there ain't nothin' worse than a uppity Indian spinster man, ya know."

Amanda hugged the elder couple again, remembering her visit here several weeks ago. "You're family you know," Ben had told her then. "Come back often." She wished now that she'd had.

"I'll be back real soon," she whispered to Yemmy. "You won't even have time to miss me."

Yemmy patted Amanda's cheek.

Ben walked them to the car. He gave Amanda a small, battered jackknife. "It's for luck," he said. "I been carryin' it for years." He coughed and cleared his throat. "We'll see ya soon." He shifted back and forth on his legs. "Well, I gotta get back inside and finish the argument with that old woman in there."

"What ya arguing about this time?" Dan asked.

"Hell, I don't 'member," the Elder scoffed. "What's it about ain't what's important. Winnin' is." He grinned at them and touched Amanda's shoulder. "So, I gotta go win me a argument. Drive careful."

Amanda smiled through tears and hugged him again, the old jackknife firmly clenched in one hand. She went into Winky's with Dan. "I want to tell that old codger good-bye too," she told Dan. Winky was packing an order into three large brown bags. "Right with yous," he yelled. He put the last item into one of the bags, then pushed them toward Luke. "We're getting' to be like up-town, got me a delivery boy," he grinned. "Don't that beat all?"

Luke doffed his red beaded cap in a mock salute, picked up all three bags, and whistled his way out the door. "Be back quicker than you can blink," he laughed.

"That'd be pretty hard," Winky grumbled. "Been thinkin' 'bout slowin' down some," Winky said in way of an explanation. "Could use a little help, and Luke still wants a job. Thought I'd give it a try."

Dan grunted his approval.

"Told the boy that if he'd stay away from that riffraff he's been hangin' with, he'd do okay. Couple a friends of his ain't worth the powder to blow 'em up with—drinkers, ya know?" They's gonna end up in jail sure as bears shit in the woods, and I tol' 'em so, too! Luke, now, he's got a chance. He's got a good head on them shoulders if'n he'd use it." He smiled his almost toothless smile at Amanda. "So, my girl, ya gettin ready to leave us?" he asked.

"Yep. Heading out in the morning. Thought I'd drop uncle off, and stop to give you a hug before I go."

"Damn! Whad I'd do to deserve that?" Winky leaned over the counter and put his arms around her. He smelled of stale cigarette smoke and old perspiration. "Comin' back, ain't ya?"

"Course. I'll be back next month for the Pow Wow. You won't even know I'm gone."

He patted her shoulder. "If'n you decide to come back for keeps, Dan would be a happy man."

Amanda swallowed hard. "Gotta run," she croaked. She turned to her uncle. A large silent tear ran down his cheek and dropped on to his creased shirt. She laughed in spite of her tears. A sudden fear grabbed her insides as she realized how old he was getting. He opened his arms and she snuggled into them. Neither spoke. They nodded at each other, and she turned and walked to the door.

"I *still* liked your old Coke machine better, Winky," she managed to get out. She heard Dan blow his nose. She couldn't turn around; the door slammed shut behind her.

Amanda had intended to go to Gichi Gumii, but when she got to the lake road, three saw horses with *Road Closed—Do Not Pass* signs, blocked it. The melting snow and spring rain made the clay road impassable. That clay could stop any kind of vehicle; it could stop anything. She remembered when, almost thirty years ago it stole one of her new Easter shoes.

*Amanda and Buddy were running behind his parents' house near the pines. They'd just come from Mass and were hoping to find a few colored eggs, and maybe some coins, hidden in the yard. They both knew they should have taken the time to change from their church clothes and shoes; it was very muddy outside. But the thought of chocolates waiting to be discovered was too much this morning.*

*Suddenly, with a loud sucking noise, one of her new Mary Jane patent leather slippers came off in the mud. "Buddy, help!" she yelled. "My shoe came off." She giggled, hopping around on one foot.*

*Buddy joined her where she was digging in the muddy red clay while trying to keep her balance. Here," he said, "I'll do that." He dug around for a*

*few minutes then looked at her, his eyes large. "I can't find it. Sure this is where*
*you lost it?"*

*"I didn't lose it," she started to cry. "The* mud *took it." She imagined all sorts*
*of punishment in store for her. Her new shoes! How could she be so careless?*

*"Mandy!" her dad called from across the road. "Dinner's ready."*

*"Oh no!" she looked at Buddy who was made blurry by her tears. She blinked*
*and they spilled over and ran down her cheeks "Buddy, what can I do? They'll*
*kill me!"*

*"Nah. They won't. They'd go to jail if'n they did. Besides, I'll tell them it was a*
*accident." Buddy pulled his stout body into a macho stance. Amanda loved her*
*friend dearly at that moment.*

*Of course they didn't kill her. In fact, when Hobo and Gram heard the*
*story, they started laughing. Soon Mom and Dad joined them. Amanda wanted*
*to laugh, too, but was afraid. Buddy, however, laughed with them, and for years*
*he teased her with stories about the Red Clay Gnomes who live in the mud and*
*collect shiny new patent leather shoes with bows and a strap.*

She'd have to wait until next month to go to the lake. Amanda made a U-turn back
onto the highway and headed back toward the Point. Rose was working in her yard
when Amanda got to the road leading to the cabin. Amanda honked, and Rose
turned and smiled; she waved Amanda in.

"I'm so glad you came by, honey." Rose pulled off green flowered
gardening gloves and dropped them on the plastic pad she'd been kneeling on.
She held her hands out and took both of Amanda's in her own. "I hoped you'd
come by, and here you are! I know it's too early to plant, but I got the spring bug
and been trying to get this front yard ready for my flowers." She pointed to a
newly cleared spot near her front door. "Look over there! I put some of your mom's
giant Peonies over there. Remember how big hers got? Mine get almost as big,
but transplanting takes something outta them, I think. But they do real good. My,
yes! Your ma loved her flowers, didn't she?" Rose smiled. "Come on inside. I got
fresh tea."

Rose's house looked like many others on the reservation from the outside—in
need of paint. But inside it reminded Amanda of a storybook house. It was small,
like Uncle Dan's but, unlike his plain home, the kitchen was painted a bright sunshine yellow. Green and white gingham curtains and matching chair cushions

and tablecloth brightened the room. The living room had pale pink walls with pink and blue ruffled pillows and a large mirror trimmed with plastic pink flowers hung on one wall. Plants sat in imitation stone jars on wooden stands throughout the whole house and hung from macramé cords at each window. Colorful braided rugs lay scattered across the floors.

A small white Persian cat, curled up in one of the kitchen chairs, looked up at Amanda with one blue eye and one brown eye. A furry Himalayan-type cat sat on top of the refrigerator, ignoring the women. "That's Jackpot," Rose said as she nodded to the feline. A third, Morris-type cat, lay on a rug in the middle of the kitchen floor, catching the last of the afternoon sun.

"These cats and my plants are all I have," Rose explained. "It gets pretty lonely around here sometimes, especially in the winter, when others my age stay home. Course, I go to Bingo twice a week, even when it snows, but it ain't the same as having visitors. So these cats are my family." The Morris-cat meowed a welcome and rubbed his head against Rose's legs, arching its back.

"Stop that J.D.; you're gonna trip me," Rose scolded playfully. "Sit there," she told Amanda pointing to the chair the Persian was claiming. "Shoo, Shaheenie!" Rose tipped the chair forward, and the cat jumped off and scowled at them and snapped her tail back and forth a few times before walking slowly out of the room. "Oh you!" Rose said to the cat. "She'll get over it," she told Amanda smiling. "Sit, sit. I'll get us some lemonade and cookies. I made gingersnaps yesterday."

"How did I know that?" Amanda wondered.

"When I saw you at Wal-Mart, you said you might be comin' home to stay," Rose said. She put a plate of cookies in front of Amanda. "Your folks would like that."

"Think so?" Amanda asked. "I got the feeling that they wanted me away from here, didn't you?"

"Oh no, child! Your ma only wanted you to have a chance to meet new people and get a better job than you could get round here. She was afraid you would marry that Brown boy and cut off any other chances."

"She didn't like Brownie?" Amanda was surprised. "She always seemed to."

"Oh, she liked him fine. She just didn't like it that you weren't interested in no one but him." Rose smiled. "I remember how that boy'd ride his bicycle all the way from town just to see you for twenty minutes. Took him longer than that to ride this far." She laughed. "He sure was a shy one, wasn't he? He'd wave when he saw me in the yard, but I don't remember him ever saying a word. You couldn't have sworn by me that that boy could talk at all, though I guess he could."

Amanda smiled at the memory. "He could, he just didn't want to. 'Not one to waste his words,' Dad used to say about him."

"It was just that your ma didn't want you missin' out on anything," Rose continued. "But deep down inside, she wanted you home. If she had broke down and called you back when your pa died, I don't think she woulda. I told her to, but she was stubborn; said you had your own life by then." Rose shook her head. "I spent almost every day with her from when your dad walked on until she went. She had a broken heart, you know. With him gone, she gave up on life too. They were so close." Rose's voice drifted off as she thought about her friend.

She shook her head, "But, course, you knew that. Your dad was quite a bit older'n her, and she depended on him for everything! Guess another reason she wanted you to have choices is that she felt she never had any. She came here from Red Cliff as a new bride and lived with his folks and uncle at your cabin. Never had a home of her own. Not that she didn't like them folks, but they weren't hers. And I know she didn't trust Hobo," Rose paused long enough to add more lemonade to Amanda's empty glass. "He wanted to teach you Indian ways, said you had 'gifts.' Cuz of your odd eyes, I guess." Amanda blinked, suddenly self-conscious. Rose continued. "Your ma didn't want none of that for you. Nope!" Rose shook her head. "Her daddy was spiritual, and it took him away from his family. Any time he was needed elsewhere, he left out; didn't matter what was happening at his own home. Your ma grew up lonely; guess she felt she never had a dad, really. Everyone else always came before his family, she said to me once. Think maybe she stayed a little angry about that."

"Rose, I didn't know you knew so much about my mom and her family," Amanda said. "You know more than I ever did. She never talked much about herself or her life. How come you know so much?"

"Oh, honey. Me and your ma knew each other from the time she got to the reservation. Back then, I was a newlywed too, and I lived right here in this very place, my Charlie and me. Yep, your ma and I got to be good friends. Before you came along she didn't have anyone but your pa, so when he was at work, and my own husband was away workin' on the railroad, we spent lots of time together. Got to be closer than sisters."

"I didn't realize that. I don't remember your husband, Rose, what was he like?"

"Course you don't remember him, child. He's been gone more'n forty years already. Ain't that somethin'? I been a widow most of my life." She smiled sadly. "Something just snapped in Charlie's head, one day—that's what the doctor told me—and he fell over dead. Real quick. Probably didn't even realize what was happenin' to him. I couldn't believe it. So young; can you imagine?" Rose looked at her guest with far-away eyes. "I was a widow when I was only twenty-six. Had been married just three years. When he married me, I was considered an old maid around here," Rose chuckled. "In those days, girls on the rez married at sixteen, sometimes fifteen. He was four years younger than me—only nineteen; we caused a real scandal back in them days," she snickered. "We ignored it, and it went away in time. He treated me real good."

"I can't imagine being alone for so long. Didn't you ever think about getting re-married?"

"No one around *here* to do that with," Rose answered. "But don't feel sorry for me. I had a few flings in my younger years." Amanda smiled as Rose actually blushed. "So don't feel sorry for me."

Amanda shook her head, "I don't—" she started.

Rose interrupted her. "That was when most of our young men were *relocatin'* to the city by the government," she laughed. "Know what happened to them? They didn't know if they was white or Indian. We lost so much then. Ain't never recovered all the way, I guess." She paused. "Have more cookies, child. You're too thin." Rose pushed the plate at her again.

Amanda laughed. Thin wasn't how she'd describe herself, but she took a cookie just the same.

"I had a couple of chances to remarry," Rose continued, "but I didn't want to leave here and start over again in a city. So I had a fling or two." Rose giggled. "I was good-looking back then. But I'd had a good man; Charlie couldn't be beat. I didn't need another one or maybe someone who wasn't as good." She smiled a Mona Lisa smile.

Amanda chewed on her ice waiting for her hostess to continue.

"So, what are your plans, my girl?" Rose abruptly changed the subject.

"Well, I'm going back to Milwaukee tomorrow. Pick up my job where I left off, and see if I can start over again without my friends." She told Rose about the accident.

"What a shame," Rose said. "We never know, do we? We just gotta trust." She fell silent again.

"Sometimes I think about coming back here," Amanda stated. "But I don't know if I've been gone too long; you know what they say about not being able to go home again."

"Oh heavens, child, those are just words! We can do anything we want. Would you like to stay for supper?" she asked suddenly. "I didn't realize it was getting so late."

Amanda looked at her watch in amazement; she'd been here almost two hours. She shook her head. "I need to pack and get ready to leave in the morning," she said. "But, thank you for the invitation and your hospitality, Rose. And I thank you for being my mother's friend. I know you were good for her."

Rose hugged Amanda. "It was my pleasure, believe me. Your folks were *real* good people."

# Chapter 28

The cabin felt empty, much like it did during Amanda's first few days there. She couldn't say how or when, but the cabin had taken on a feeling of being hers. Now it seemed to have returned to its former state—as if she were already gone. Amanda spent the evening cleaning out the refrigerator and cupboards, taking stock of what she had, and making a list of what she wanted to bring with her next month.

*If I come back here to live, I'll get a dog and cat,* she told herself. There hadn't been any pets at the cabin for years. After Jimbo died, her dad had got a part-wolf, part-shepard, and named him Maen'gun—*Wolf.* Uncle Dan teased him unmercifully for being so *original.* Maen'gun never was a real pet, and he ran off after a year or so. "Looking for a wife," Dad told her. Buddy told her he got shot because he was a chicken-killer, but Amanda didn't believe it; Dad wouldn't lie.

Then a stray cat, she named Smoky Russell, took up residence for a while one summer, but it got sick and Dad had to kill it. Amanda cried for days. Dad helped her bury it under the lilac bushes out back. She'd created a coffin out of an old shoebox and begged Hobo to come out and say a few words. By then Hobo didn't get out of the cabin much, but he was thrilled to be a part of the funeral service. Amanda cared for the grave carefully that first summer, but by the next year, went unattended; weeds grew over it undisturbed.

A shuffling noise from the backyard startled her out of the past. She tossed the scarf she'd been folding into her bag and looked out the bedroom window. It was too dark to see anything. Probably a raccoon she decided, and she went back to her packing.

She listened to the radio and played several games of solitaire before giving in and crawling into bed shortly after midnight. Still, she tossed and turned into the morning hours, thinking about all that had happened to her in the last two months and what it all meant, before she finally fell into a dreamless sleep.

Noah arrived at 8:30, just as Amanda was getting out of the shower. Niijii was with him. She answered the door in her bathrobe with her hair wrapped in a towel.

"I always seem to catch you in the middle of something," he said holding up a white bakery sack. He and Niijii walked past Amanda and went straight to the kitchen. "We brought something to go with that coffee I'm smellin'."

"You're pretty early, aren't you?"

"Too early?" He stopped and looked over his shoulder at her.

"No, it's alright. Help yourself," she told him. "I'll just be a minute." She ducked into her room.

"Looks like you been busy," Noah said when she joined him, fully dressed, hair combed, at the kitchen table. "No one can accuse you of wasting time." He smiled. "Looks like you're ready."

"These are nice and fresh," she said taking a custard filled donut from the bag.

"Right out of the oven," he told her. "If I remember right, you weren't too crazy about those sugar donuts I gave ya a few weeks ago. I admit they could have been a little stale, so Niijii and me thought we'd do it right this time. We was waitin' by the door when the bakery opened this morning." Both he and Niijii grinned, proud of themselves.

Niijii lay next to Noah's chair watching Amanda while they carried on a light conversation. He looked uncomfortable, Amanda thought. Sometimes it was hard to remember that Niijii was just a dog.

Finally, they had to quit stalling. "Well," Noah stood and stretched. "I guess I'll help put your stuff in your car." He followed her into the living room and looked at her few boxes, her one suitcase.

"You travel light, don't you?"

She nodded without speaking. When the car was packed, the cabin doors were locked—tested and retested—Amanda turned towards Noah without knowing exactly what to say except, "Thanks!"

"Drive safely, Niijiikwe. Keep Miigwan with you," Noah said. He paused slightly. "And don't let the city get you down." She took his outstretched hand; he squeezed it gently.

"I'll be back soon . . . almost before you know it," she told him.

"Oh, watch out for street people."

"Where did that come from?" she asked.

He shrugged. "Don't know. Just something to say." He started to say more but stopped. She had to resist the urge to press him. Noah shifted his weight and turned toward the Bronco and the moment was lost.

Amanda tested the cabin door for a third time, then turned back towards her car, unsure of what was important to say right now. Noah stood by his Bronco, arms folded over his chest, a faint smile on his lips. Niijii sat by his side looking like *he* wanted to say something.

"What is it, Niijii," she asked. She felt foolish talking to the dog, but couldn't help herself. "You know, I'm gonna miss you two."

Niijii woofed twice then tilted his head at Noah. Amanda thought he was saying, "Okay, that's over, let's go." Noah's shaggy friend jumped into the Bronco and sat on the passenger's side looking out at her.

Noah waved and climbed into the driver's seat. Amanda got into her Escort. She turned the key: the car sputtered, stopped, sputtered, stopped, then sparked to life. "Don't tell me you don't want to leave either," she scolded the Escort.

Noah followed Amanda to the end of the long drive, where he turned one way and she turned the other. He watched her car grow smaller as she headed away from him. He reached over and stroked the black shaggy dog sitting next to him. Niijii looked at him with understanding eyes.

"What do think, Niijii?" he asked. "We in for a long summer?"

Niijii barked once and kept watching the two-legged beside him.

Noah's thoughts slid back to his teacher and friend. "My left side will be empty for a while," he told Niijii. "How I wish Hobo was here to help me figure things out!" Niijii curled himself into a comfortable position on the seat and closed his eyes; this human would have to think through this one by himself.

*Noah laid the cardboard box containing his clothing and few personal items near the worn green couch and looked around at his new home. He was almost sixteen and had refused to return to school.*

*Only two weeks ago Hobo's sister had died, and the old man decided it was time for the young family who'd inherited the cabin to be on their own. He'd heard that Junior Brown, a young man with good gifts according to reservation gossip, was drifting.*

*"We'll help each other," he told Noah. "You hunt and fish and trap our food. Once you get warmed up, you can chop wood and shovel snow." He waited but*

*Noah just grinned. "Okay then," he continued, "I will cook and pray for us—that is a pretty important job too. And when you are ready to learn, I will help teach you how to carry on the Grandfather's ways!"*

*Noah eagerly accepted his responsibilities; he assured Hobo he was ready for adulthood. He never tired of learning. Hobo had told him many times how well he was doing with the gifts the Creator had given him. The only thing that troubled Noah through the months and years they were together was how fragile Hobo became with each passing day. Every winter sent fear into Noah that his teacher wouldn't see another spring, but the old man hung on until he was comfortable that Noah was ready to carry on in the right way. Hobo knew when it was okay to walk on to meet his Creator.*

*"The Grandfather gifted me with a long life to walk this world," Hobo said one evening. "I go back to the spirit world this night. It is normal to feel sad now," he added quickly when he saw the fear and sadness in his pupil's eyes. "That's good, but remember my son, your heart will be full again some day. When the time is right, and I know you are ready, you will get a message from me in a sweat lodge ceremony."*

*"I will miss you my grandfather," Noah's voice cracked, and tears clouded his vision. Unashamed, Noah let them fall. "You have taught me many things—for this I am grateful. I will always do my best for you—to make you proud of me in the spirit world."*

*Hobo's trembling hand patted Noah's cheek. "I have saved you a helping song. Whenever you need me and my spirit helpers, sing it, and we will come. This song is the last of the gifts I can give you in this life, but the first of many gifts that I have for you when you are ready. Wait and watch for them. Be vigilant—a spirit can sneak up on you if you're not careful." His laugh ended in a cough. "I won't send them Western Union either, 'cause they charge too damn much. Migizi carries messages for free!" Hobo smiled a tired smile and started his traveling song.*

*The next morning Noah found Hobo in bed, already cool to the touch.*

Noah hadn't been sure of his own knowledge at first, but he soon realized that he did get excellent training. He knew Hobo hadn't really left, and he would always be there when Noah needed him—and he always had been, until now.

"Sometimes," Noah remembered Hobo telling him time after time, "we can't have things our own way. We must trust that the Grandfather looks out for us and gives us what is best for us. We can't do nothing but *trust!*"

"I guess this is such a time," Noah said to Niijii as they pulled into their driveway. But the old dog was snoring and didn't hear him.

Shortly before noon Amanda topped the hill that marked the boundary of the reservation and pulled over onto a wide spot on the shoulder of the highway. Leaving the car door open and the car running, she got out and looked back. As far as she could see the snow was gone, but she knew that in the thick under-brush of the woods white cold snow lingered. She smiled remembering that just eight short weeks ago she had been confined to the cabin, first by a blizzard, then by bitter cold.

She could barely see the horizon curve over Gichi Gumii at the far end of the reservation. The lake was dark gray today, blending into the overcast sky. She jumped, lost in thoughts of the past two months, when a noisy Buick zoomed past her and the horn blew. Halfway down the hill, a hand came out of its open window and waved; she waved back knowing the driver couldn't see her any-more.

Voices seemed to speak to her on the wind. The words were indistinct, dis-torted, but they demanded her attention. She tipped her head to the side and heard Hobo's strange Ojibwe-English mix and Noah's deep-chested laughter; then her uncle's soft, sad voice, maybe asking her to stay. She imagined girlish giggles carried on wind-wings from the past—hers and Annie's, no doubt. Then she heard just the wind again.

Amanda slowly rubbed her closed eyes with her fingertips. "Help me Migizi. I don't know what to do." Instead of answers, questions came. Had she stayed away from the reservation too long? Was it too late to come back? The answers eluded her for now.

She thought about Brownie, and again wondered about the life she might have had. She cringed inside when she remembered the anger, the hurt in his voice during their last conversation.

*"I knew you wouldn't come back," he said. "The white world was too much for you. You were weak. I thought you were Indian, but you're not. You think you're too good for us now," he spit out the words knowing he was hurting her. "And*

*where is the necklace you said you'd wear forever?" His angry eyes blazed in a
face twisted in an effort to maintain control. "Go, then! Stay away you damned
half-breed!" He turned on his heel and stormed away. Amanda's hand went to
her throat. Where was it? Somewhere along the line, she'd removed it, not thinking what it meant to Brownie. Panic rose in her chest.*

*"Brownie, wait!" she called after him. But he didn't hesitate, didn't slow down,
not even the slightest pause was visible in his long, angry strides to let her know
he'd even heard her.*

The breeze picked up again and blew Amanda's hair across her face. She tucked
it behind her ears where it didn't want to stay. This time she heard Winky's
voice in the wind: Them cities ain't for Indians. Once it kilt the spirit, it kilt the
Indian.

Did she want to go back to Milwaukee? Could she? Did she want to put Dan
and Annie out of her life again? Migizi's screech jolted her. She searched the
sky, her sight blurred from the pressure of her fingers on her eyes. Migizi called
again, and Amanda finally found her perched in a large pine across the road.
The eagle's head jutted out from her body as she looked directly at Amanda. Her
beak was closed; no indication she would speak today. Her wings were slightly
opened, but not enough to show the spotted undersides. She looked upset.

"Help me, Sister," Amanda whispered. As if to answer, the eagle suddenly
pushed herself off the branch and dipped slightly as she passed directly over
Amanda. As she lifted off, Amanda saw a feather fall, and after Migizi swung
herself into the blue-gray sky, Amanda crossed the road. She stepped into a
small patch of snow protected by the shade of the giant pine and spotted the
feather stuck in the branches of a small scrub. Amanda reached into her jacket
pocket and pulled out the *asema* she always carried now. She sprinkled it on the
ground around the feather and prayed as first Hobo, then Noah, had taught her
to. She picked up the mate to the feather, wrapped it in a red scrap of fabric and
tucked it safely under the sun visor of the Escort.

*It's good to bless a feather in four days,* Noah said in the wind.

Then all Amanda heard was a semi-truck downshifting as it started down the
long hill. Back across the road her car door was still open; the buzzer protesting.
She looked for Migizi. The Grandfather's messenger had reached a great height
and was circling off towards the lake.

"Thank you, sister. Miigwich!" Amanda held the feather up over her head in salute. She climbed into the Escort and put on her turning signal even though hers was the only car around now. She made a U-turn onto the highway. "I'll call the office tomorrow," she told herself. "A few more days won't hurt me or them."

Michigan State University Press is committed to preserving ancient forests and natural resources. We have elected to print this title on Thor Offset, which is 30% recycled (30% post-consumer waste). As a result of our paper choice, Michigan State University Press has saved the following natural resources*:

| | |
|---:|---|
| 3.96 | Trees (40 feet in height) |
| 1,155 | Gallons of Water |
| 676.5 | Kilowatt-hours of Electricity |
| 9.9 | Pounds of Air Pollution |

We are a member of Green Press Initiative—a nonprofit program dedicated to supporting book publishers in maximizing their use of fiber that is not sourced from ancient or endangered forests. For more information about Green Press Initiative and the use of recycled paper in book publishing, please visit *www.greenpressinitiative.org.*

*Environmental benefits were calculated based on research provided by Conservatree and Californians Against Waste.